ADVANCE PRAISE FOR

The LOST MEMOIRS OF

Jane Austen

"Utterly charming and remarkably authentic in creating Jane Austen's voice, Syrie James's *Memoir* made me want to pull out all my Jane Austen novels and read them again."

— DEBORAH CROMBIE, author of *Water Like a Stone*

"Remarkable. Delicious. Syrie James is a literary genii who fulfilled one of my most cherished fantasies. I felt as if she'd cozied me up to a tea table with the real Jane Austen for a heart-felt chat."

— KIMBERLY CATES, author of *The Gazebo*

"This is an amazing book. Jane Austen lives again in the pages of Ms. James's novel. She . . . captures the heart and mind of Jane Austen . . ."

—SUSAN CARROLL, author of *The Huntress*

"This fascinating novel will make readers swear there was such a man as Mr. Ashford, and that there is such a memoir. Tantalizing, tender, and true to the Austen mythos . . ."

—BETTE-LEE FOX, *Library Journal*

The Lost Memoirs
of
Jane Austen

By Syrie James

THE LOST MEMOIRS OF JANE AUSTEN

The Lost Memoirs of Jane Austen

SYRIE JAMES

AVON

An Imprint of HarperCollinsPublishers

THE LOST MEMOIRS OF JANE AUSTEN. Copyright © 2008 by Syrie James. All rights reserved. Printed in the United States of America. No part of this book may be used or reproduced in any manner whatsoever without written permission except in the case of brief quotations embodied in critical articles and reviews. For information, address HarperCollins Publishers, 10 East 53rd Street, New York, NY 10022.

HarperCollins books may be purchased for educational, business, or sales promotional use. For information, please write: Special Markets Department, HarperCollins Publishers, 10 East 53rd Street, New York, NY 10022.

FIRST EDITION

Interior text designed by Diahann Sturge

Library of Congress Cataloging-in-Publication Data

James, Syrie.
    The lost memoirs of Jane Austen / Syrie James.—1st ed.
        p. cm.
    ISBN: 978-0-06-134142-7
    1. Austen, Jane, 1775–1817—Fiction. 2. Women novelists—Fiction. 3. Diary fiction. I. Title.

PS3610.A457L67 2008
813'.6—dc22   2007014802

07 08 09 10 11 WBC/RRD 10 9 8 7 6 5 4 3 2 1

To my husband Bill, my own Mr. Ashford, whose love makes me complete, and whose support and encouragement have made it possible for me to enjoy this wonderful life as a writer . . .

To my sons Ryan and Jeff, my finest creations, whose insightful input and animated conversations keep me on my creative and intellectual toes. I could not be prouder . . .

To Jane Austen, with the greatest admiration, appreciation, and respect . . .

To my agent Tamar Rydzinski, and my editor, Lucia Macro, whose dedication to and enthusiasm for this project cannot be measured . . .

Thank you with all my heart. You prove to me, on a daily basis, that all things are possible.

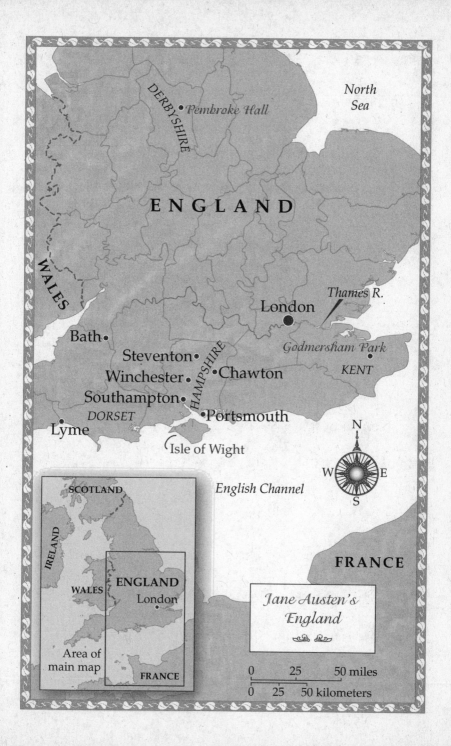

North
Sea

DERBYSHIRE
• Pembroke Hall

ENGLAND

WALES

Thames R.

London •

Godmersham Park

Bath •

Steventon •
Winchester •   • Chawton
Southampton •   HAMPSHIRE
                  • Portsmouth
DORSET
Lyme •

KENT

Isle of Wight

N
W   E
S

English Channel

SCOTLAND

IRELAND

WALES   ENGLAND
               London •

Area of
main map   FRANCE

FRANCE

Jane Austen's
England

0   25   50 miles
0   25   50 kilometers

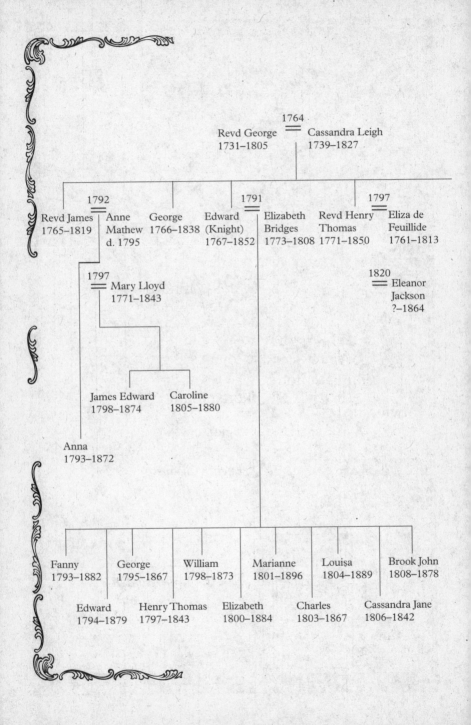

Jane Austen's Family Tree

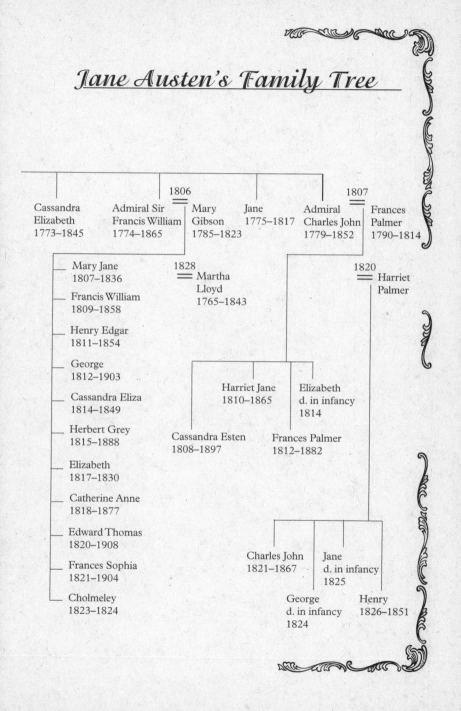

Cassandra
Elizabeth
1773–1845

Admiral Sir
Francis William
1774–1865

1806

Mary
Gibson
1785–1823

Jane
1775–1817

Admiral
Charles John
1779–1852

1807

Frances
Palmer
1790–1814

Mary Jane
1807–1836

1828
Martha
Lloyd
1765–1843

1820
Harriet
Palmer

Francis William
1809–1858

Henry Edgar
1811–1854

George
1812–1903

Cassandra Eliza
1814–1849

Herbert Grey
1815–1888

Elizabeth
1817–1830

Catherine Anne
1818–1877

Edward Thomas
1820–1908

Frances Sophia
1821–1904

Cholmeley
1823–1824

Harriet Jane
1810–1865

Elizabeth
d. in infancy
1814

Cassandra Esten
1808–1897

Frances Palmer
1812–1882

Charles John
1821–1867

Jane
d. in infancy
1825

George
d. in infancy
1824

Henry
1826–1851

Editor's Foreword

⁓⊷ ⊶⁓

Jane Austen, who gave the world six beloved novels, was a self-avowed, addicted letter-writer; many of her letters have been preserved and provide valuable insight into the author's mind, character, and private life. Although biographers have often pondered the question as to whether or not the author kept a memoir or a journal, no sign of any such documents had ever been found. Until now.

Chawton Manor House—one of the many homes owned by Jane Austen's brother, Edward Austen Knight (who was adopted by his father's cousins, and inherited many valuable properties)—has been in the Knight family since the late sixteenth century. Jane Austen lived for many years in a cottage in the village nearby and was a frequent visitor.

A workman recently employed to repair the roof of the manor house, in an attempt to trap an errant family of mice, discovered an old seaman's chest bricked up behind a wall in a far corner of the immense, rambling attic. The chest, to the befuddlement of the entire work crew, was filled with what appeared to be old manuscripts. Incongruously, at the bottom of the chest, in a tiny velvet box, lay a delicate gold-and-ruby ring.

The current owner of the residence, Chawton House Library—a charitable organization that has restored and refurbished the manor house, gardens and park to operate as a centre for the study of early English women's writing— brought in experts to appraise the ruby ring (of fine workmanship, dating from the late eighteenth century), and scholars to review the documents. Upon even cursory review, the scholars immediately sensed the enormous historical value of this discovery.

The chest, which is the type a seaman might have used to store his gear during the Napoleonic wars, may have belonged to one of Jane Austen's other brothers, Frank or Charles, both of whom were in the Royal Navy. To the astonishment and exhilaration of the scholars who were first privileged to review its contents (myself included), the numerous documents stored inside appear to have been written during the late eighteenth and early nineteenth centuries, and have been formally authenticated as being the work of Jane Austen herself.

Although only one of the manuscripts has as yet been fully reviewed, they appear to be none other than Jane Austen's long-lost memoirs, relating stories and events that occurred either to the author herself or to her family members, friends, and acquaintances.

Desiring no remunerary compensation for their find, the Chawton House Library graciously donated the chest and all its contents to the Jane Austen Literary Foundation for authentication and preservation.

The physical aspect of the memoirs is interesting; they were composed and assembled in a similar manner to the manuscript of Jane Austen's last, uncompleted work, *Sanditon*; that is, they were all written on ordinary sheets of writing-paper which had been folded in half, then assembled into small booklets ranging in size from forty-eight to eighty pages, and neatly hand-stitched along the spine. They appear to have been written in a variety of formats; some are day-to-day entries, as in a diary; most are divided into chapters, resembling her novels. A few have been damaged by mould and decay, but most (thanks to the air-tight nature of the chest, and inherently dry conditions of the attic in which they were stored) have survived in a nearly pristine state.

These manuscripts are now being painstakingly preserved by a team of experts; they will each, in turn, be reviewed and edited for a modern audience. Although there are undoubtedly a great many other Jane Austen scholars equal to or more worthy of the occupation than I, the enviable task of editing these precious works has fallen to me.

The memoir you have before you, although it covers an earlier period in Jane Austen's life, was apparently written sometime between 1815 and 1817, when the author began to suffer from the illness that resulted in her death. Although it seems to be the final volume of her memoirs, it was selected for publication first, partly because of the immaculate physical state of the document itself and partly because of its surprising and revealing subject matter.

Several theories have been put forward as to how the manuscripts came to be bricked up and forgotten behind an attic wall at Chawton Manor House. Many of the bricks used were fired in 1816, but the dates of the remaining bricks are more difficult to determine. It is possible that Jane Austen herself, ill and knowing that she might die, arranged for some trusted family member or hired hand (with or without her brother

Edward's knowledge) to hide these documents in his attic, feeling that they were of too personal a nature to be read by others at the time but unwilling to destroy them.

It is also quite possible that the chest was placed there, years later, by Jane's sister Cassandra. It is well-known that the sisters were very close, shared every thought and confidence, and exchanged frequent, lengthy letters when they were apart. Cassandra, who lived to be seventy-two, kept all the letters Jane had written her, and she may have been the keeper of Jane's memoirs as well. However, a few years before Cassandra died, she admitted to her niece, Caroline Austen, that she burnt the greater part of Jane's letters (thought to be many hundreds in all), and cut out or otherwise expunged parts of those remaining. This loss to history is incalculable.

The reason for Cassandra's censorship was, no doubt, a desire to preserve her sister's privacy, as well as an act of diplomacy. It is unlikely that Cassandra could have foreseen a time when her sister's work would be so popular, and public interest in her so great, that her letters would be published; it is more likely that she feared Jane's letters might have contained criticisms of people and descriptions of persons and events of a very personal nature, which Cassandra did not wish the younger generations of her family to read.

Jane does say, in the first pages of this memoir, that she is writing to ". . . make some record of what happened, to prevent that memory from vanishing into the recesses of my mind, and from there to disappear for ever from history . . ."

Perhaps Cassandra, after burning the letters, could not bring herself to destroy her sister's memoirs as well, (resembling, as they did, the manuscripts of her revered novels) and so decided to "entomb" them instead. The plan was quite successful; if not for an extensive roof renovation, an inquisitive workman, and a wayward mouse, the manuscripts might have remained undiscovered for many more centuries to come.

This memoir is of remarkable interest, not only because it offers a new, particularly intimate window into the workings of Jane Austen's mind and heart, but in that it reveals, for the first time, the existence of a love affair that she was apparently determined, during her lifetime, at least, to keep secret. It may also shed light on one of the most infamous stories in Jane Austen lore—a subject that has been endlessly discussed and debated amongst historians, concerning a "seaside gentleman" with whom Jane reputedly fell in love.

As the story goes, Cassandra told her niece Carolyn (many years after Jane's death) that Jane met a curate in the early 1800s while on holiday at a seaside resort, and that they became attached and agreed to meet again; she later learned that he had died. Cassandra never named the man, the place, or the date of the meeting, but insisted that this mysterious gentleman was the "only man Jane ever truly loved."

Considering that Cassandra was so particular about the type of information she allowed to be disseminated about her sister, it is possible that the "mysterious, nameless, dateless romance" that she described was only a partial truth, intentionally vague and misleading—a theory that is backed up in this memoir by Jane Austen herself. Apparently, Jane did meet a man at a seaside resort; they did indeed fall deeply in love; but, according to Jane, he was not a clergyman—and he did not die.

To conjecture further would be to give too much away; the reader is left to draw his or her own conclusions from Jane's romantic and poignant tale.

One final note, regarding the editing of this text:

There were many idiosyncrasies in Jane Austen's manuscript, including abbreviations, misspellings, alternative spellings such as "chuse" and "choose," the use of capitals where they would not be expected by rule, and the use or disuse of paragraphs and quotation marks, which would no doubt have been changed, had the work been made ready for publication during her lifetime. I have made such corrections as I thought necessary (while maintaining most period and alternative spellings), to ensure a smooth and fluent reading experience by a modern audience; but for the most part, this is the memoir exactly as Jane Austen wrote it.

All editorial comments are my own.

Dr. Mary I. Jesse
Ph.D. English Literature, Oxford University
President, Jane Austen Literary Foundation

Chapter One

_____ ✦ ✦ _____

Why I feel the sudden urge to relate, in pen and ink, a relationship of the most personal nature, which I have never before acknowledged, I cannot say. Perhaps it is this maddening illness which has been troubling me now and again of late—this cunning reminder of my own mortality—that compels me to make some record of what happened, to prevent that memory from vanishing into the recesses of my mind, and from there to disappear for ever from history, as fleeting as a ghost in the mist.

Whatever the reason, I find that I must write it all down; for there may, I think, be speculation when I am gone. People may read what I have written, and wonder: how could this _spinster,_ this woman who, to all appearances, never even _courted_—who never felt that wondrous connection of mind and spirit between a man and woman, which, inspired by friendship and affection, blooms into something deeper—how could _she_ have had the temerity to write about the revered institutions of love and courtship, having never experienced them herself?

To those few friends and relations who, upon learning of my authorship, have dared to pose a similar question (although, I must admit, in a rather more genteel turn of phrase), I have given the self-same reply: "Is it not conceivable that an active mind and an observant eye and ear, combined with a vivid imagination, might produce a literary work of some merit and amusement, which may, in turn, evoke sentiments and feelings which resemble life itself?"

There is much truth in this observation.

But there are many levels of veracity, are there not, between that truth which we reveal publicly and that which we silently acknowledge, in the privacy of our own thoughts, and perhaps to one or two of our most intimate acquaintances?

I did *attempt* to write of love—first, in jest, as a girl; then in a more serious vein, in my early twenties, though I had known only young love then;[1] in consequence, those early works were of only passing merit. It was only years later that I met the man who would come to inspire the true depth of that emotion, and who would reawaken my voice, which had long lain dormant.

Of this gentleman—the one, true, great love in my life—I have, for good reason, vowed never to speak; indeed, it was agreed amongst the few close members of my family who knew him, that it was best for all concerned to keep the facts of that affair strictly to ourselves. In consequence, I have rel-

---

[1] Jane Austen may be referring here to her relationship with Tom Lefroy, her "Irish friend" with whom she shared at brief flirtation at age twenty.

egated my thoughts of him to the farthest reaches of my heart; banished for ever—but *not* forgotten.

No, never forgotten. For how can one forget that which has become a part of one's very soul? Every word, every thought, every look and feeling that passed between us, is as fresh in my mind now, years later, as if it had occurred only yesterday.

The tale must be told; a tale which will explain all the others.

But I get ahead of myself.

It is a truth (I believe, universally acknowledged) that, with few exceptions, the introduction of the hero in a love-story should never take place in the first chapter, but should, ideally, be deferred to the third; that a brief foundation should initially be laid, acquainting the reader with the principal persons, places, circumstances and emotional content of the story, so as to allow a greater appreciation for the proceedings as they unfold.

Therefore, before we meet the gentleman in question, I must go further back to relate two events which occurred some years earlier—both of which altered my life, suddenly and irrevocably, in a most dreadful and painful way.

In December 1800, shortly before the twenty-fifth anniversary of my birth, I had been away, visiting my dear friend Martha Lloyd. Upon returning home, my mother startled me by announcing, "Well, Jane, it is all settled! We have decided to leave Steventon behind us for good, and go to Bath."

"Leave Steventon?" I stared at her in disbelief. "You cannot mean it."

"Oh, but I do," said my mother as she bustled happily about the small parlour, pausing to study the pictures on the wall with a look of fond farewell, as if making peace with the thought of leaving them all behind. "Your father and I talked it over while you were gone. He will be seventy in May. It is high time he retired, after nearly forty years as the rector of this parish, not to mention Deane.[2] Giving up the post, you know, means giving up the house, but your brother James will benefit by it, as it will go to him; and as your father has always longed to travel, we thought, what better time than the present? Let us go, while we still have our health! But *where* we should go, that was a matter of great debate, and we have at last come to conclusion that it should be Bath!"

My head began to swim; my legs crumpled under me, and I sank heavily into the nearest chair, wishing that my beloved sister was there to share the burden of this distressing news. Cassandra, who is three years older than I, and far more beautiful, is possessed of a calm and gentle disposition; I can always depend on her to rally my spirits in even the worst of situations. But she was away at the time, visiting our brother Edward and his family in Kent.

"Jane!" I heard my mother cry. "Why, I believe the poor girl has fainted. Mr. Austen! Do come help! Where are the smelling-salts?"

I had been born at Steventon, and had passed all the happy days of my life there. I could no more imagine leaving that

---

[2] George Austen served a long and distinguished career in the clergy, first as a curate at Tonbridge School, then as rector of Steventon, in Hampshire County (often abbreviated as Hants), from 1761, adding the living of Deane (a neighbouring parish) to his duties in 1773. A "living" as a clergyman generally included a house or parsonage and a modest stipend, both of which had to be relinquished upon retirement.

beloved place than I could sprout wings and fly. I loved the trellised front porch of the parsonage house, the perfectly balanced arrangement of sash windows in its flat front façade, and the unadorned, white-washed walls and open-beam ceilings within. I had grown to cherish every elm, chestnut and fir which towered above its roof, and every plant and shrub in the back garden, where I strolled almost daily along the turf walk, bordered by strawberry beds.

The rectory had been considerably enlarged and improved over the years to meet the needs of my father and mother's growing family, which included my sister Cassandra, myself and six sons, as well as a parade of young boys who came for long months at a time to be schooled by my father. The seven bed-rooms up stairs and three attic rooms had always been full during the days of my childhood, and the halls had resounded incessantly with the sounds of boyish laughter and the stomping of boots.

To be so suddenly uprooted, and parted for ever from my home—to never more stroll the lanes of the neighbourhood, where each thatched cottage nestled amongst the trees was familiar, and each face was known; to never again visit a dear friend, enjoy a dinner-party or attend a ball at one of the imposing brick manor houses; to never more walk up the hill to Cheesedown Farm, beyond the village, with its cows and pigs, and fields of wheat and barley; to never again walk to church of a Sunday, through woodlands of sycamores and elms, to hear my father's weekly sermons. How was it to be borne?

At Steventon, I had enjoyed the perfect blend of loving family and pleasant society, which only a small country village can afford; in later years, as each of my brothers moved away, I had found refuge in my own little study up stairs, which had provided me with the blessed solitude I required to write.

How could I leave all that behind, I wondered in alarm—to remove to a tall, narrow rented house on a stone-paved street, in the white glare of dreaded Bath? My spirits sank at the very thought. I had enjoyed Bath as a visitor several times but had no desire to live there.

I understood the reasoning behind my parents' choice; to *them,* after a lifetime of living and working in the country, they must have looked forward to the cheerfulness and society of city life; at their age, to take advantage of its healthful waters and excellent doctors could only be an added compensation. But to me, Bath was a city of vapour, noise, shadow and smoke, populated by the itinerant and the insincere; its celebrated concerts and balls could never substitute for close friends, a home, and the beauty of natural surroundings.

I suspected that there was another reason for our removal to Bath, although it remained unspoken, and it was this thought that was particularly mortifying. In addition to its status as a fashionable resort, Bath was known as a reputable place for securing a husband for unattached young ladies. My own mother's parents, on retirement, had moved to Bath in precisely the same manner, taking their two unmarried daughters with them, and both my mother and her sister had, indeed, found husbands there.[3]

Undoubtedly my parents thought they were doing Cassandra and me a service by bringing us to Bath, to parade us in

---

[3] Jane Austen's mother and father, Cassandra Leigh and George Austen, met in Bath, and were married there several years later, on 26 April 1764.

the Assembly Rooms or at the Pump Room before a succession of single gentlemen; what worked for one generation, they must have hoped, might work for another. If that was their aim, however, they could only have been severely disappointed; for the next four years did not produce a suitable marriage prospect for either of us.

Of the painful circumstances of our removal from Steventon, and my anguished feelings connected with the sale—or should I say the *giving away*—of my father's library of five hundred volumes, as well as my own much-loved books, the piano on which I had learnt, my large collection of music, and all the furniture and family pictures which had become so dear to me, I will not breathe a word. Of the years we spent in exile (of which I have previously written elsewhere)[4], I will say only that, in spite of my dislike of Bath itself, I *did* have several interesting adventures, made some memorable acquaintances, and very much enjoyed the daily company of my father, my mother and my sister. I found particular pleasure in our travels to the resort towns of the Devon and Dorset coast, which my father was keen on seeing at the time.

Which brings me to the second, even more heart-breaking event which irrevocably altered my life, as well as the fortunes of my mother and my sister: the day my beloved father died.

At four-and-seventy years of age, George Austen was still quite spry, with a shock of fine white hair, bright, intelligent eyes, a sweet, benevolent smile, and a grand sense of humour

---

[4] I assume she refers to one of her other memoirs, recently discovered, which I have not yet read.

that inspired the admiration of all who knew him. Although he had suffered from a fever and forgetfulness on several occasions, he had always rallied and recovered, and his enjoyment of retirement and our itinerant years had been considerable.

On Saturday, the 19th of January, 1805, my father again took ill, suffering a renewal of his feverish complaint. The next morning, he was so much recovered, that he was up and walking about our Bath apartments at Green Park Buildings East with only the help of a stick; but by evening, the fever grew stronger, and he lay in bed with violent tremulousness and the greatest degree of feebleness. My mother, Cassandra and I took turns ministering to him throughout the night, greatly alarmed by his condition, and making every possible provision to assure his comfort.

I shall never forget the last words he spoke to me.

"Jane," said he that night, as I sat at his bedside, gently wiping his feverish brow, "I am sorry. So very sorry." His voice was but a hoarse whisper, his breathing short and very laboured.

"Do not be sorry, papa," said I, believing, nay *insisting* that he would improve, and if not, hoping that he would not concern himself, in his final hours, with what might become of those he left behind; for he must have been aware, that when he did in fact depart this earth, his wife and daughters would be left in the most dire of financial circumstances. But thankfully, his mind was not occupied with such lowly matters; he did not even seem aware of the severity of his condition, or that he might, at any moment, be about to quit the objects so beloved, so fondly cherished, as his wife and children ever were.

"I am sorry, Jane," said he again, "that I have not been of more help to you, as yet, with your books."

"My books?" said I in great surprise. He referred to the three manuscripts I had written years earlier, manuscripts which were but early efforts, and, I knew, unworthy of publication. I had proof of that; my father had submitted one, *First Impressions,* to a publisher some years past, but it had been rapidly declined by return of post; my brother Henry had managed to sell another (*Susan*) for £10, but their promise of publication had never materialized. They all now resided (very much in need of alteration), along with a collection of other youthful works, in a sturdy box which traveled with me everywhere I went. "Please, papa, do not think of my books."

"I cannot help but think of them," said he with effort. "You have a gift, Jane. Do not forget it."

I knew he meant well; but in truth, it was a father's pride and love speaking. My brothers were all excellent writers; my work was not that special. "Nothing I have so far written, papa, seems to me of any worth, except perhaps as a diversion for my family. I have given it up. Hereafter, I have vowed to restrict my efforts with a pen solely to correspondence."

My father closed his eyes briefly and shook his head. "That would be very wrong. Your work, it should be published. When I am better, I will take it upon myself to see that it is done."

By morning he was gone.

My father's passing, in addition to being the cause of much sorrow to his entire family, had a most disastrous effect on the financial situation of the three women in his household. His living at Steventon, upon retirement, had gone to his successor, my oldest brother James; and his small annuity died with him.

"For forty years, he was the light of my life; my love, my anchor!" sobbed my mother, dabbing at her red, swollen eyes with a handkerchief, as we sat in the parlour of our rented rooms with my brothers James and Henry, after the funeral at Bath's Walcot Church. "To be taken from me, and so suddenly! How am I to go on without him?"

"It is a very heavy blow; he was a most excellent father," said James, as he set down his cup of tea. A solemn, serious, dependable curate of forty, James had rushed from his wife and children at Steventon to share in our hour of grief.

"But we must find comfort in the suddenness of the event," said Henry. At three-and-thirty, he had always been the most witty, ambitious, charming and optimistic of my brothers, and I thought him the most handsome. "It means his suffering was brief."

"Indeed," said I, struggling to contain my tears. "I think he was quite insensible of his own state."

"As such, he was spared all the pain of separation," said Cassandra stoically. "For that I am grateful."

"To have seen him languishing long, struggling for hours— it would have been dreadful!" I agreed.

"Oh! But what are we to do?" wailed my mother. "I am so ill, I can hardly speak. You know the church does nothing for widows and children of clergymen! To think, that in the midst of my despair, I must be weighed down by such matters, but we are homeless and nearly penniless, girls. With the ending of your father's stipends, my income will fall to less than £200. Jane has nothing. Even with the interest on Cassandra's legacy, there is not enough to support the three of us. How ever shall we survive?"

I felt my cheeks go crimson at this declaration. The fact

that I had no money of any kind was a source of great mortification to me.

Cassandra had a legacy, from a tragic source; she had been engaged, at two-and-twenty, to the young Reverend Thomas Fowle; since Tom's income was small, they had waited to marry. Two years later, Tom agreed to act as chaplain to a regiment bound for the West Indies, with the promise of a good living upon his return; but a year after setting sail, he caught yellow fever off St. Domingo and died. He left a legacy of £1000 to my grieving sister, the interest of which, invested in Government stocks, brought in £35 a year; a tiny sum, but it gave her some sense of consequence. I, on the other hand, was completely dependent on others for my support.

My mother was right; we were in dire circumstances, and should be subject to a life of the most miserable, abject poverty if we did not receive help.

"Do not despair, mother," said James. "My brothers and I will not let you starve. I myself will be glad to pledge you £50 per annum from my own earnings."

"Spoken like a man of feeling, and a true son," said Henry, rising from his chair and clapping James on the back. "I will match that pledge."

This, I thought, was a kind offer; Henry and his wife Eliza lived in London in good style, but he had a habit of changing occupations rather frequently, and had made it known that his income, at the time, was precarious.

"Oh! You are both goodness itself!" cried my mother.

We knew that Charles, my youngest brother and a Commander in the Royal Navy, who was away patrolling the Atlantic, could do nothing for us. But my brother Frank, a naval Captain on blockade, had written to Henry from Spit-head with an offer of £100 a year, insisting that it be kept a secret. Henry, in his enthusiasm, could not hide the news from my mother, who was moved to tears.

"Never were there children as good as mine!" cried my mother rapturously. "Write and tell Frank that I feel the magnificence of his offer, but I will accept only half."

We had yet to hear from my brother Edward, who was, by a fortunate twist of fate, far wealthier than all my other brothers combined. At age sixteen, my parents had agreed to let Edward be adopted by my father's childless, distant cousin, Thomas Knight II; from him, Edward had inherited a fortune and three large and prosperous estates: Steventon Manor and Chawton in Hampshire, and Godmersham Park in Kent. At Chawton alone, Edward owned a manor house and a village of some thirty homes.

"Let us hope that Edward offers us the use of one of his houses," said my mother. "Even a small cottage would do."

To our disappointment, when we heard from Edward the next morning, he did not make such an offer; instead, he agreed to contribute a yearly stipend of £100 towards our support.

"What can he be thinking?" cried my mother, waving Edward's newly arrived letter in dismay, as she joined me and Cassandra at the breakfast-table. Henry and James were upstairs, packing to depart. "I am his mother; you are his sisters! He is so very rich, and they live in such wealth and splendour at Godmersham. With so many houses at his disposal, surely he could spare the income from one tenant!"

"Still, his offer of £100 a year is very generous, mamma," said I.

"Not generous enough by half, to my way of thinking." My

mother seized a large slice of toast from the toast rack and spread a great dab of butter upon it. "It is a drop in the bucket for Edward. I cannot believe this is his doing. It must be that wife of his! Elizabeth wants to keep all their income for herself and her children. She would not think of sparing a penny for her husband's poor mother and sisters!"

"It is Edward's property to do with as he wishes," I reminded her, as I poured her a dish of cocoa. "Elizabeth can have no say over it."

"Indeed she can!" cried my mother, biting into her toast and chewing furiously. "*You* do not know the sway that a wife may have over her husband, Jane, particularly when they are as close as *those* two. Edward is so yielding, so opposed to contention of any kind, if Elizabeth raised even the slightest objection to any thing, he would go out of his way to appease her."

"Mamma, I am certain Elizabeth would never be so unfeeling," said Cassandra. "She is a sweet and lovely woman."

"A sweet and lovely woman with airs," replied my mother with a sniff, "proud of her high upbringing and education, but without many natural abilities, and no regard for those of us who are blessed to possess them. Oh yes, a little talent goes a long way with the Goodnestone Bridgeses, but too much goes a long way too far."

I could not agree with my mother's assessment of the situation. Edward had married eighteen-year-old Elizabeth Bridges of Goodnestone Park in Kent in 1791, a union based on love, and blessed with many children. An elegant and pretty woman, Elizabeth had been educated at the most prestigious girls' boarding school in London, where the curriculum included French, music, dancing and social etiquette, but very minimal academic content. Elizabeth was a woman of solid principles, a devoted wife and mother who adored her husband, and always treated us with great affection. I thought my mother's sentiments had more to do with her own discomfort at the vast difference in material wealth between herself and Elizabeth than any thing Elizabeth had ever said or done.

"Even if Elizabeth *has* influenced our brother in this matter, mamma," said I, "and we cannot be certain that she has, we must still be grateful for Edward's offer."

"You are right," said my mother with a sigh, just as James and Henry entered the room, setting their valises by the door. I quickly acquainted them with the contents of Edward's letter, which seemed to please them both immensely.

My mother rose and kissed my brothers on the cheek with a grateful look. "Thank you, boys. You have saved us from the poorhouse. If we observe strict economies, I am certain we shall be able to get by. But where we shall live, I am sure I do not know, for even with £450 pounds a year, we cannot afford our own house."

"I believe you and the girls will do quite well and be very happy, mother," said Henry.

"Yes, we have talked it over," added James as he glanced out the window, scanning the traffic in the foggy streets below, no doubt hoping for a glimpse of his expected carriage. "You may pass your winters in comfortable rented lodgings here in Bath, and the remainder of the year, you may spend in the country, amongst your relations."

Cassandra and I exchanged a dismayed glance; from the discomfited expression on my mother's countenance, I knew they both felt the humiliation of our circumstances as keenly as did I. To be parceled out amongst our relations! Without a permanent home, we would be wholly dependent on my brothers' kindness, obliged to accept whatever living arrangements they chose to make for us—and dependent on them for transportation to and fro as well.

We would never again, I feared, be able to call our lives our own.

Chapter Two

At first we divided our time, as James suggested, between temporary lodgings in Bath and extended visits to friends and relations, including stays with James and his wife and children at Steventon, and with Edward and Elizabeth and their brood at Godmersham Park.

I always enjoyed my visits to Godmersham; one could not help but feel pampered there. Edward lived in elegance, ease, and luxury, as befitted his income and the upbringing of his wife. The large, handsome, red-brick mansion was situated in splendid isolation, set in a landscaped park with wooded downland rising behind it. The house, which was maintained by dozens of servants, contained an excellent library and a beautifully appointed hall and drawing-room, decorated with superb plasterwork and carving, and marble chimneypieces; the rest of the rooms, though numerous, were rather simply furnished. It was pleasant to stroll through the manicured gardens and orchard, or to the Greek garden temple set on a knoll across the grounds. There was always activity and entertainment and fine dining; while at Godmersham, I ate ice, drank fine wine, and enjoyed being above vulgar economy.

I particularly enjoyed playing with the children, who numbered nine or ten at the time. We went boating on the river; I made paper ships with the boys, which we bombarded with chestnuts; I played school with the girls, as well as cards and spillikins and charades, and we made up riddles. On several occasions, I sequestered myself in one of the up-stairs bedrooms and read aloud from one of my old manuscripts for the amusement of their eldest daughters, Fanny and Lizzie.

Cassandra was especially welcome at Godmersham, and was invited to help with the children during Elizabeth's many confinements. But although Elizabeth was very sweet to all of us, my mother and I were always keenly aware of our status there as the poor, widowed and spinster relations, and of the burden that we had become.

Our itinerant, dependent life mercifully came to an end some two years later, when my brother Frank made an unexpected proposition. Frank had recently fallen in love with a Ramsgate girl, Mary Gibson, whom he'd met while commanding the Sea Fencibles on the North Foreland. At two-and-thirty, Frank was eager to be married, and with prize money in hand and a good income, he could at last afford to do so. It was his suggestion that we should live with him and his new bride at Southampton.

Although Cassandra and I protested that we did not wish to intrude on the new couple's happiness, Frank insisted it was the ideal arrangement; he would be away for many months at a time at sea, and we could keep his Mary company. The sharing of living expenses would greatly ease both his burden and ours. When I requested that our dear friend Martha

Lloyd should also join us, as she had been rendered homeless since the death of her mother, Frank was most agreeable. Such a merry, receptive, sympathetic presence as Martha would be most welcome in any household. A pleasant-looking woman ten years my senior, Martha had been my most intimate friend since girlhood; she was also family, as her sister Mary was married to my brother James.

We were all delighted at the thought of a home of our own, and we left Bath with happy feelings of escape. I was not so keen, at first, on removing to Southampton; Cassandra and I had been sent away to school there when I was just seven years of age, and there we had both nearly died of an infectious fever.

I soon discovered, however, that Southampton, with its castellated folly in the square, and its old houses newly equipped with fashionable bow-windows, was a very picturesque and pleasant town indeed. The location, situated as it was at the mouth of the River Itchen, on the confluence of two large waters, and surrounded by mediaeval walls and open walks beside the sea, was ideal for Frank's purposes, as he might often put into port at Portsmouth; and there was the added benefit of its being in Hampshire, only twenty-three miles from Steventon.

Arrangements were soon made. After temporary lodgings, we moved in March of 1807 into a rented house on a corner of Castle Square, and engaged the services of two maids and a cook. The house was old and not in the best repair, but it had a pleasant garden, and was bounded on one side by the old city wall; the top of the wall, reached by steps, was wide enough to walk upon, and offered a delightful view of the river and its wooded banks.

No sooner had we moved in, than Frank received his next appointment, to command HMS *St. Albans*. I believe it was a great comfort to him that while he was away, fitting out the ship for a long voyage, we were there to attend the birth of his daughter; for Mary had quite a difficult time of it.

As grateful as I was to be settled for a time, and as much as I enjoyed the society of my family, I soon found that the company of so many people, confined to one city household, left little room to breathe—particularly when we had visitors, as we did one memorable day in late June, when my brother Henry came to town.

Imagine the scene, if you will: eight of us gathered in the parlour, perched on the sofa and an assortment of chairs. Henry, looking smart in his light brown full-dress coat, sat reading the newspaper. My mother, Cassandra, Martha and Frank (home for his daughter's christening, and his last month of home life before setting sail) were occupied by knotting fringe onto some curtains. Mary held her baby, Mary Jane, then two months old. I sat at my little mahogany writing desk, a gift from my father on my nineteenth birthday and my most prized possession, composing a letter.

"You are looking well, Frank," said Henry, "for a weather-beaten old sea Captain."

"Weather-beaten, indeed," said Cassandra with a wry smile. "Our Frank is as young and handsome as ever."

"If any one is weather-beaten, it is I," exclaimed my mother. "I declare, I have never seen a June so hot. It makes one feel very ill. I cannot sleep, I have a heat in my throat and my chest, and my appetite is never what it used to be."

Since my mother had consumed nearly half a boiled chicken and a large slice of apple pie at dinner, I found her pronouncement rather startling. "I am sorry you are not well, mamma," said I, looking up from my letter and stifling a yawn, for I had not slept well, either; the little infant's cries had kept me up half the night. "Perhaps you would feel better if you were to lie down."

"It is too hot to lie down," replied my mother crossly, as she continued with her knotting, "and I could not get a moment's rest, knowing there is all this work to be done."

My mother was of middling height, spare and thin, with handsome grey eyes, dark hair that still retained its colour, and an aristocratic nose (of which she was quite proud, and which she had had the pleasure of transmitting to a great many of her children). Although a quick-witted woman of sparkle and spirit, she suffered from a variety of maladies which could not always be diagnosed by a physician.[5]

"Frank, tell us: how does Her Majesty's Ship, the *St. Albans*?" enquired Henry, by way of changing the subject.

"She is fit as a fiddle, and ready to set sail for the Cape next week, and from there, on to China."

"China! Are we at war with China?" enquired Mary in some alarm.

"No, my dear. Our duty is to convoy and protect a shipping fleet."[6]

"Thank goodness. I hope you will not be near any fighting. Do take more care with your knots, dear. You want knots to be of equal size, and fringe of equal length."

"There is nothing wrong with my knots, Mary," rejoined Frank calmly. "I have heard it said, in certain circles, that my knotting ability is unparalleled, and among the best in the Royal Navy."

---

[5] Mrs. Austen outlived her daughter Jane by ten years, attaining the ripe old age of eighty-seven.

[6] In 1807, England was still embroiled in the long, drawn-out struggle against Napoleon.

"No one would say such a thing, unless it were your own mother," replied Mary.

"And so I would," said my mother proudly. "My Frank has always been clever with his hands, and his time at sea has certainly prepared him well for *this* occupation."

"It would *knot* be a lie," said I, "to say that Frank *knots* fringe on curtains better than any man I ever saw."

The others laughed. "A fine honour, is it *knot?*" said Martha, giggling.

"Indeed," added my mother, "for I have *knot,* in all my days, seen any other man with such a talent."

More merry laughter ensued, and the conversation continued on in this vein for some time longer, as I struggled to put words on paper.

"What are you so busy writing, Jane?" asked Henry of a sudden. "Is it a new novel, I hope?"

"No. Only a letter to Fanny."

"You are for ever writing letters," said Mary as she gently rocked her sleeping infant in her arms. "I think you write more letters than any body I ever met."

"Letter-writing is a worthy occupation," I replied, as I dipped my pen in the inkpot. "I think there is nothing quite so satisfying as the receipt of an excellent letter, full of interesting news."

Cassandra glanced up from her fringe-knotting with an avid nod. "When Jane and I are parted, I know not what I should do, without her regular communications."

"I enjoy writing a letter now and then myself," said my mother, "but I prefer, on the whole, to put my efforts into poetry, when I find the time."

"We have all enjoyed your verses since childhood, mamma," I replied sincerely.

"You *are* a talent, mother," said Henry. "The poem you wrote when you recovered from your illness at Bath, under Bowen's care—that was particularly good."

"Oh! It was!" cried Martha. At which point—on catching Cassandra's eye—she put down her needlework, and the two both proceeded to recite in merry unison:

> "Says Death: I've been trying these three week or more
> To seize an old Madam here at Number Four,
> Yet I still try in vain, tho she's turned of three score;
> To what is my ill-success owing?
>
> I'll tell you, old Fellow, if you cannot guess,
> To what you're indebted for your ill success—
> To the prayers of my husband, whose love I possess,
> To the care of my daughters, whom Heaven will bless,
> To the skill and attention of Bowen."

Laughter followed, along with a succession of very pretty and well-deserved compliments on behalf of my mother's wit, which thrilled her no end.

"Your brother James is also an excellent poet,"[7] said my mother modestly.

"Jane's poetry does credit to the Austen name, as well," said Henry, "but *she*, I think, has an even greater talent for prose. It irritates me no end that Crosby has never published her book *Susan,* after all their promises."

---

[7] James Austen was at one time considered to be *the* writer of the family, with both serious and amusing poetry to his credit. In 1789 he began producing his own professional weekly magazine, *The Loiterer,* which was widely distributed and greatly admired, but lasted only fourteen months.

"I cannot understand why a publisher would pay good money for a manuscript, and then not print it," said my mother.

"Clearly, it was not good enough," said I.[8]

"I cannot agree," said Martha. "*Susan* is great fun! Although *First Impressions*[9] is my favourite. I adore Mr. Darcy and Elizabeth—and I think it most unfair that you only allowed me to read it three times, and that a great many years ago."

"I could not risk a fourth reading," said I with a smile. "With one more perusal, I fear you would have stolen away *First Impressions* and published it from memory."

Martha laughed. "As if I would do such a thing."

"That book *should* be published," said Henry.

"Papa tried," I reminded him. "It was refused."

"Refused *unread*," insisted Henry. "That is no reflection on the book's merit; only that one publisher could not be bothered to read something sent in by an unknown clergyman. I wish you would allow me to submit it for you now. We might have better luck than we did with *Susan*."

"I doubt it. Ten years have passed since I wrote *First Impressions*. The world has changed, so have its tastes in literature, and so have I. It would require a great deal of alteration, I am certain, before I would deem it ready."

"What about that other book you wrote about the two sisters, Elinor and Marianne?" enquired Henry. "What was it called?"

---

[8] *Susan* was published after Jane Austen's death under the title *Northanger Abbey*. Because it was a satire by an unknown writer ridiculing the popular "Gothic romances" of the time, the publisher may have had second thoughts after purchasing it, concerned about offending his established authors, and/or losing money if the new book failed to sell.

[9] Years later, Jane Austen revised *First Impressions* and sold it under the title *Pride and Prejudice*. It is considered by many to be her masterpiece.

"*Sense and Sensibility*. That was a revised version of an epistolary novel. I am not at all satisfied with the attempt."

"I remember it as a nice little story," said Cassandra.

"A nice little story," I agreed, "which is enjoying a nice, quiet little life at the bottom of my writing-box, where I am convinced that it belongs."

"How you have managed to keep track of that writing-box all these years, Jane, is beyond me," said my mother. "I believe that trunk has travelled with us every single place we have gone, ever since you were a child. Do you recall the time we stopped at Dartford, on our return from Godmersham, and it was accidentally packed into a chaise that drove off with it? Where was it headed again?"

"To Gravesend, on their way to the West Indies," I replied, with a shudder. That box, which held all my manuscripts, seemed at the time to contain all my worldly wealth; no part of my property was ever so dear to me.

"Thank the good Lord they were able to stop the chaise before it had got more than a few miles off," said my mother, "or we should never have set eyes on those manuscripts again in *this* lifetime."

"Indeed," said I, as I returned my attention once again to my letter; but I had written no more than two words, when Mary Jane awoke and began to cry.

"There, there," exclaimed her mother, as she stood and paced about the room, bouncing the infant against her chest. "Don't fret, now. Don't fret."

"I think she is tired," said my mother.

"She just awoke from her nap," replied Mary, greatly vexed.

"Perhaps she is wet," said Martha.

"She is dry as a bone. Oh dear, dear; whatever is the matter?"

"She might stop crying if you did not jostle her about so," admonished Frank.

"Are you the expert on caring for babies now?" replied Mary with some annoyance. "I have been with her every moment since her birth, while you have been here but three weeks."

"A naval officer need never apologize for his time at sea," answered Frank. "May I remind you that it is that very living which buys your gowns and bonnets, and feeds our family. Furthermore, and a hundred *years* at home could not convince me otherwise, a child can derive no comfort from being shaken about like a butter churn."

"She might be hungry," remarked Cassandra.

"You might give her some molasses," suggested Martha.

"She is too young. Molasses will only cloy her stomach," said my mother. "Oh! Dear! All this heat and noise has given me a headache."

The ladies immediately proceeded to debate all known cures for a headache, as well as every possible cause of the infant's misery. The baby let out an ear-piercing shriek; I started, and the nib of my pen broke, splashing ink across the page. Mary, beside herself, burst into tears.

"I know what I need," said my mother. "There is a nice ale in the larder. Jane, you are not doing any thing. Be a dear and fetch me some."

I put my pen down and wiped ink from my fingers. "Yes, mamma. Right away."

"Mamma," said I that evening, as I sat upon my mother's bed and brushed her hair, "how long do you think we shall live here, with Frank and Mary?"

"A very long time, I hope," replied my mother. "For I have

done with moving about. There is great comfort in waking up every morning in the same bed, in the same room."

"I could not agree more. But does it seem right to you, for us to trespass on Frank's generosity?"

"What do you mean, trespass? We contribute our share to household expenses. We were here for that child's birth, and we shall be here for Mary during Frank's long absences. It is quite an equitable arrangement for all concerned."

"I understand. But Frank is paying the larger share. And he and Mary are sure to have more children. One day they will have done with putting up with us."

"I pray that will not be so. For then, what is to become of us? We cannot afford separate accommodation. Are we to go back to long visits to friends, and shifting between your brothers? I could not bear it."

"Neither could I." I sighed. "Oh! Mamma! I do not wish to sound ungrateful; Frank and Mary have been so welcoming, and we *do* have our amusing moments. But there is so little quiet here, and no privacy. Do you never dream of a home of our own?"

"Every night and every day," said my mother, in a wistful tone. "But I try not to think of such things. It is not profitable. Mary is not a bad sort, and that baby is as pretty as a picture. We are fortunate to have a roof above our heads, and that is that."

"If only there was some way I could earn my own money. It is so unfair. Men may chuse a profession, and with hard work, acquire wealth and respect, while we are forced to sit home, completely dependent. It is a great indignity."

"It is the way of the world, Jane. Better to accept it and live within it, for nothing can be done to change it." My mother met my gaze in the looking-glass above her dressing-table. "Of course, things might be different for us, if only—"

"If only what?" said I quietly, knowing only too well what she was about to say.

"If only you or Cassandra were to marry."

I lay down my mother's hairbrush and stood. This was a well-worn topic, and it never ceased to vex me. "Please, mamma."

"Your poor sister, of course, had it very hard. But she was still young and beautiful when Tom died."

Cassandra was indeed the beauty of the family; with her pale complexion, lovely dark eyes, high-arched nose, and sweet smile, she continued to be admired by many of the gentlemen of our acquaintance, yet she turned her head away. "She has professed that she could only love but once," said I.

"What a lot of nonsense *that* is. With the world full of so many fine men! Well, if she chuses to spend her life mourning her one true love, I suppose no one will think the worse of her, for at least she *had* a prospect, and her happiness was snatched away by forces not within her control. But you, Jane, *you* remain single, and you have nothing like her excuse."

I knew she referred to an offer of marriage which had been made to me some years previously by a young man of wealth and property, an offer which I had declined.[10] "Surely you would not have liked me to marry for convenience, mamma, when there was no love in the connection?"

"A mother always hopes her daughters will marry men they love, *or come to love* the men they marry. As you may recall, *I*

---

[10] Jane refers here to a proposal made by a family friend in December 1802, the details of which are recounted later in this journal.

was disinclined to marry; but I took your father, because I needed a home for my widowed mother. And all came out well, did it not?"

"Yes, mamma. But you chose well in my father. He was the very best of men. If I ever meet such a man, and if I love him, I shall happily accept him."

"You girls to-day, you are too romantic in your expectations; it is not always possible to find both love *and* a decent husband, Jane. Let us speak in truth, my dear: you are not getting any younger."

She spoke in such a serious tone, and seemed so full of genuine concern, I could not take offence at the remark. "Indeed, I am one-and-thirty," I agreed, "well beyond all hope."

"All is not yet lost," said my mother consolingly, not sensing the irony in my voice. "You still have your beauty, and lovely hazel eyes, and a very fine complexion."

"*And* all my teeth. And do not you think my hair, which curls so naturally, is quite a lovely shade of brown? I have heard it, more than once, called auburn. Why, at market I might fetch as high a price as one of Edward's best horses."

"You always jest, Jane. This is a serious matter. Plenty of women past the age of thirty have found happiness with a nice, eligible widower. What about Mr. Lutterell? He has a fine house, a good income, and he is very kind."

"He is an imbecile, and fat, and twice my age."

"Poor women do not have the luxury of choice, my dear."

"Choice is all we *do* have, mamma," said I emphatically. "If I ever marry, it will be for love. Deep, true, passionate *love*, built on respect, esteem, friendship, and a meeting of the minds. Never, *never* for economic security." I then made my way from my mother's chambers, my emotions battling between righteous indignation and despondency.

The next morning, I was walking out in the garden, delighting in the fresh air and the warmth of the sun which dared to peek at intervals from behind the clouds, when I caught sight of Henry hurrying down the gravel walk to join me.

"Good morning!" cried Henry. "Is not it a beautiful day?"

"It is indeed. Look at our roses blooming so nicely. And do you see what we have planted there, under the terrace wall?"

"Some sort of shrubs?"

"Currants! And gooseberry bushes and raspberries. And what do you think of our new syringas?" I pointed out the two small, newly planted trees. "I had our man put these in by special request. I could not *do* without a syringa, you know, for the sake of Cowper's line."

"Ah! Yes. *The Winter Walk at Noon. Laburnum rich—*" he began, and I finished with him:

"*—in streaming gold; syringa, iv'ry pure.*"

"You are such a romantic, Jane."

"And you are not? You, who married for deepest love, and are always gallivanting about the countryside, looking for adventure?"

Henry had married Eliza de Feuillide, our beautiful, stylish, widowed cousin, whose first husband, a French count, had been guillotined during the French Revolution. Although ten years his senior, Eliza was Henry's match in lively temperament and disposition.

Henry stopped and turned to me. "Do I detect a melancholy note in that remark?"

"Do not be silly. Who can be melancholy, on a morning as glorious as this?"

"*You* can, I think." Henry frowned and studied me a long moment with his bright hazel eyes, eyes that reminded me of our father, and matched my own. "Jane, you have been cooped up in this house too long. You require a change. What do you say? Would you like to come away with me tomorrow?"

"Thank you, Henry. But I am in no mood for the noise and confusion of London at present."

"I was not thinking of London," said Henry. "I was thinking of Lyme."

Chapter Three

⁓⁓⁓⁓⁓

I had visited many seaside towns of the southern and westerly coasts with my mother and father during our years at Bath; Lyme, with its mild climate, delightful walks and beautiful scenery, had remained my favourite. We had returned there, with great pleasure, several times—but it had been a refuge then, from a city which I despised.

"Henry, I have no need to travel all the way to Lyme," said I as I admired the gracefully waving branches of the trees in our back garden. "I have all the seaside walks and breezes I could want here."

"Yes, but they are *Southampton* breezes. The sea-bathing here is nowhere near as good as at Lyme—I would not put my foot in Southampton water—and this is a town of some 8,000 people. Lyme is but a village."

"You are forgetting the summer crowds."

"Even so. I would suggest Brighton, but it is not within my budget at present, and I know how you love Lyme, Jane. It has been three years since our last visit; I have never seen you so happy any where else. I want to take you there and help you find your smile again, for it has been a great while since it has gone missing."

I *did* love Lyme; all at once I could envision myself strolling beside its pretty little bay and out onto the Cobb, marvelling at the view of its bright, pebbly beaches, sparkling waves and majestic surrounding cliffs. Still, I shook my head. "Mary needs us now. Frank sets sail in a se'en night. We cannot leave her."

"She will have mother and Cassandra and Martha."

She would indeed, I thought. It was a highly tempting offer, and I realised, of a sudden, that I would dearly love to get away. "But how can I leave them all behind, for a holiday at Lyme? And what of Eliza? And your business? Can you be gone so long?"

"I was not thinking of a lengthy stay; a week perhaps, a fortnight at most. Eliza will applaud my mission. Just think of it! We shall take long walks. We shall bathe every other day. We shall make new acquaintances, and provide fascinating company for others at the Assembly Room balls. Here, you are forced to keep the same society, day in and day out. You have no time for yourself, no respite from a wailing baby."

"Mary Jane is a delightful infant. I believe there was an entire hour Tuesday last when she did not cry at all."

Henry laughed. From my expression, he knew that I required no more convincing.

Some days later, after an uneventful journey, I gazed out the window of Henry's carriage with happy anticipation as we passed through the cheerful village of Uplyme, and then descended the long, craggy, precipitous downward slope towards

Lyme, finally entering upon the still steeper street of the town itself.

I have written of Lyme in earlier journals, and may feature it again in the book on which I am now working,[11] but I shall risk repetition for the sake of the pleasure that the town has afforded me, on each and every visit.

Lyme may not be as fashionable as Brighton or Weymouth, but for those who seek to replenish their exhausted or wounded spirits in lodgings not calculated to ruin their fortunes, the sea-air, the pleasant society and delightful scenery of this humble town will surely mend many a constitution. The little town's charm is not attributable in any way to the buildings themselves, but to its remarkable situation along the sea. Lyme's charming harbour is formed by a kind of rude pier, called the Cobb, behind which ships may lie in safety, and upon which it is pleasant to walk in fine weather.

On previous visits of a month or more, my mother and father had always rented a cottage; since there were only the two of us this time, and our stay would be of much shorter duration, we secured lodgings in a quaint little boarding-house in the upper part of town with a large, red-faced, cheerful woman who was rather appropriately named Mrs. Stout.

"I trust you'll find everything to yer liking," said Mrs. Stout, as she threw open the window in my room, letting in a cool, fresh breeze. I stood transfixed for a long moment, gazing out with pleasure over the fine view before me, of the town's roof-tops, and lines of waving linen, in a gradual descent towards the harbour and the sea, which danced and sparkled in the summer sunshine of late afternoon.

---

[11] A reference to *Persuasion*, which Jane Austen wrote from August 1815 to August 1816. This crucial comment helps to fix the time period during which this journal was composed.

"You can take yer meals here, as you like, or you can find a decent dinner at the Royal Lion, although they do get a bit crowded this time of year."

We happily accepted Mrs. Stout's offer to dine in, as we had arrived so late in the day, and retired for an early night.

Next morning, we awoke to find the July sun shining in a bright blue sky filled with puffy clouds. I felt such a surge of excitement in expectation of the day's excursions, that I fear I took very little time to consider my appearance. Women of greater fortune might have shuddered to be seen in any thing less than the new, short-hemmed seaside bathing dresses which revealed the ankle, and had become fashionable of late; but I thought them quite ugly, and would not have been caught dead in one, had they been distributed at the beach free of charge.

My interest in fashion had always been curtailed by a frugal allowance, and my choices were limited. I had with me three gowns, all still respectable, but none of them very new. I pulled on one of my favourites, a simple, white sprigged muslin with three-quarter-length sleeves, a small tail at the back, and a front that was drawn in and sloped round to the bosom. My belt was of dark blue satin, which, I may reflect without embarrassment, matched the trimmings and flowers of my straw bonnet, to a very good effect. I styled my long brown tresses as quickly as I could (in actuality, plaiting and shoving them up under my hat) and pulled a few loose curls free about my face. Grabbing my reticule[12] and parasol, I pronounced myself ready, and dashed off to breakfast with Henry.

Following our morning repast, Henry and I strode down-hill along the busy principal street which seemed to hurry to-

------

[12] A small drawstring purse.

wards the water, just as the River Lyme flowed on a bed of rocks and emptied itself into the sea. When we reached the Walk, which skirts the pleasant little bay of Lyme from the town to the harbour along the foot of a green hill, we paused to admire the scene before us.

Several ships were anchored in the harbour, and a very beautiful line of high cliffs stretched to the east. The seaside path bustled with fashionably attired men and women taking their morning stroll. The bay itself was animated with company and bathing machines, the rows of little horse-drawn wooden chambers on wheels backed up into the sea. The horses stood patiently by, waves lapping at their flanks, as bathers in their flannel gowns eagerly or timidly plunged into the water from the rear of their machines[1], with the help of their stalwart guides. The sun shone brightly, although a few threatening grey clouds had gathered.

"I do not think Lyme belongs on the Dorset coast at all," said I, delighting in the fresh-feeling breeze which cooled my cheeks.

"Where, pray tell, does it belong?" asked Henry.

"It seems to me a very outpost of heaven."

Henry agreed.

Deciding to leave the shore for later, we proceeded directly to the Cobb, the long, semicircular stone jetty on the far side of the harbour which projects out into the sea, and upon which stretch two broad causeways on different levels. We had walked part of the way along the Lower Cobb when we reached a flight of stairs leading to the Upper causeway. The Upper Cobb is very breezy and has a sloping surface, which makes it difficult to

---

[1] Bathing machines were portable dressing rooms that allowed occupants to undress without being seen by passerby.

walk upon for some; but I had always found it a stroll of delight, affording a magnificent view of the coast, the sea and the surrounding cliffs.

"Let us go up," said I eagerly.

"Are you certain?" said Henry, with a glance at the rough blocks of stone which projected, like the teeth of a rake, from the wall behind, and offered no handholds or railings. "The stairs are very steep."

"I can manage the stairs, I assure you."

"I should go behind, in case you need a supporting hand."

"Please go ahead," I insisted. "With my skirts, I am too slow; I shall only frustrate you."

With a doubtful look, Henry proceeded up the stairs first, and I followed carefully, keeping hold of my gown and parasol with one hand, and the stone wall to the side with the other. There were a great many other people about; I was aware of a small party approaching behind us, but although my climbing efforts prevented me from looking back, I was concerned that my halting progress would impede them. I increased my pace, and had nearly attained the topmost step, when a gust of wind caught me by surprise; I inadvertently trod upon my skirt and lost my footing and, with sudden terror, felt myself wavering backwards above a treacherous drop.[13]

I would have surely fallen to the hard pavement below, resulting in my death, or at the very least, considerable physical harm, had not two strong arms, of a sudden, caught hold of me.

"Steady," said a deep voice into my ear, as I felt those strong

---

[13] Jane's near tumble from these steps, now called Granny's Teeth, may have inspired Louisa Musgrove's treacherous fall from the Cobb in Jane Austen's *Persuasion*, one of the most famous events in the history of Lyme. Indeed, when the poet Tennyson visited Lyme, he exclaimed: "Don't talk to me of the Duke of Monmouth. Show me the exact spot where Louisa Musgrove fell!"

arms gently and firmly propel me up the final step to the safety of the Upper causeway, where Henry waited and watched in great alarm. Once there, the man released me from his grasp and stepped back. My mind still reeling from my misadventure, I turned to face my rescuer and found myself looking up into the liveliest, most intelligent pair of deep blue eyes I had ever seen.

"Forgive me. Are you hurt?" enquired the gentleman, doffing his hat. He was a tall, dark-haired, vital-looking man of perhaps three-and-thirty years of age, dressed in a perfectly tailored dark blue coat and cream-coloured breeches, which did nothing to disguise his fine figure.

"No, no. I am perfectly fine." My heart beat rapidly and I struggled to catch my breath, a result, I convinced myself, of the danger of my interrupted fall, and not by the proximity of the very handsome man before me.

"Jane! Thank God, for a moment I thought you would surely fall," cried Henry in concern while hurrying to my side. "Pray tell me, sir, to whom we are so much obliged?"

The man bowed graciously. "Frederick Ashford, sir, at your service."

"A pleasure to meet you, sir. I am Henry Austen. And may I—"

Before Henry could complete his introductions, a well-dressed couple appeared at the top of the steps, and the newly arrived gentleman cried: "Good work, Ashford. I always say there is no quicker way to win a lady's admiration than to save her in distress."

I felt myself blush deeply at this remark. Thankfully, no one seemed to notice; they were occupied by a far more startling circumstance. Henry, it seems, was acquainted with the newcomer in question.

"Charles Churchill?" said Henry, gazing at the gentleman in some astonishment. "Is it really you?"

The man, who was of middling height, good-looking, and sported a head of curly light brown hair, stared back at him. "Henry Austen? What an unexpected delight! It has been an age!"

The two men embraced heartily. "Churchill and I were at Oxford together," said Henry, beaming. "We got into all manner of scrapes."

"All his fault, of course," rejoined Mr. Churchill with a laugh.

Mr. Ashford's gaze turned to mine, and he smiled. "Do introduce me to your lovely companion, Mr. Austen."

"With pleasure. Mr. Ashford, Mr. Churchill, may I present my sister Miss Jane Austen."

"Miss Austen: a pleasure," said Mr. Ashford with a bow.

"May I introduce my wife, Maria," said Mr. Churchill, bringing forward his female companion.

"How do you do," said Maria, as bows and courtesies were exchanged. A slight, fair-haired woman of my approximate age, I thought her face might have been pretty had she not looked as though she had just bitten into something very sour. "It is too windy up here. And I do not like the look of those clouds, Charles. It is going to rain. We should go back."

"We cannot go back now," declared Mr. Churchill. "I have only just met up with my old friend."

"It *will* rain, I shall catch my death, and it will ruin my shoes."

"If you die, my dear, it will not matter if your shoes are ruined," said Mr. Churchill unsympathetically. "And if you survive, I shall gladly buy you another pair."

"Oh! You are insufferable," replied Maria with an irritated snort. Henry and Mr. Ashford laughed out loud.

As I struggled, out of respect to the lady, to hold back my own mirth, Henry clapped his friend on the back. "Be nice to Churchill, Jane. He has a great big estate up in Derbyshire and is worth a fortune."

"I am nothing to my good friend and neighbor Ashford, here," replied Mr. Churchill. "He is heir to Pembroke Hall and a baronetcy, and worth three of me."

"*Three* of you? And a future baronet?" Henry bowed to Mr. Ashford with a respectful flourish. "I am duly impressed and honoured, sir."

"Please, think nothing of it," said Mr. Ashford with a good-natured smile. "It is barely a title, and an honour hardly worth coveting, I assure you."[14]

"Ask his *father* how he feels about that," observed Mr. Churchill, laughing. "*He,* no doubt, would convince you otherwise."

"What brings you good people to Lyme?" asked Henry. "I would have thought you to be more the Brighton type."

"I have never liked Brighton. It is too large and overgrown," said Mr. Ashford. "I had some business in Bath, after London, when my companions and I felt the sudden need for a few days of fresh sea-air, before returning home. Lyme seemed the logical conclusion."

"A highly pleasing conclusion, as well," declared Henry,

---

[14] A baronet, although a highly desirable title, is the lowest hereditary title of honour, ranking immediately below the barons, and above all orders of knighthood except the Garter; it is not a peerage. Baronets did not sit in the House of Lords; they might be elected to the House of Commons, but were more often preoccupied with local, county affairs.

"for I believe you may have saved my sister's life, and allowed me to run into an old friend at the same time." Turning to Mr. Churchill, he said with a smile: "So what have you been up to, you old goat?"

"No good, if I could help it."

The two men walked on, chatting amiably, with Maria on her husband's arm, leaving Mr. Ashford and myself alone behind. We fell in step together. It was some moments before either of us spoke; when we did, our first attempts overlapped in a confusing manner.

"I am sorry," I began again, to which he replied,

"Pray, continue."

"I have not properly thanked you, Mr. Ashford, for preventing my fall."

"No thanks are necessary."

"Indeed they are. Reaching out as you did, you might have lost your footing and come to harm yourself."

"Had that been the case, I would have given my life—or limb—in a worthy cause."

"Do you mean to imply that it was worth risking your own life, to save mine?"

"I do."

"A bold statement, on such a short acquaintance."

"In what way bold?"

"You are a gentleman and the heir to a title and, apparently, a vast estate. Whereas I am a woman with no fortune, and of very little consequence."

"If first impressions are to be believed, Miss Austen—" he began.

"Never trust your first impressions, Mr. Ashford. They are invariably wrong."

"Mine are invariably right. And they lead me to this conclusion: that you, Miss Austen, are a woman of greater fortune and consequence than I."

"On what grounds do you base this claim?"

"On these grounds: if you were to have perished just now, how many people would have missed you?"

"How many people?"

"Yes."

"I would like to think my mother, my sister, my friend Martha, and my six brothers would miss me. My brothers' wives, my nieces and nephews, who number more than a dozen, and perhaps several dear old friends."

"Whereas I have only my father and one younger sister to regret my passing."

"No wife, then?"

"No. So you see, although I may be rich in property, you are rich in family, and therefore the far more wealthy and important of us two."

I laughed. "If wealth were based on your principle, Mr. Ashford, the entire class system of England would fall apart at the seams."

Chapter Four

─────────────── ❧ ❧ ───────────────

Our walk had brought us down from the Cobb to the sea-shore, when the clouds, as Maria had predicted, gathered and darkened, and a light rain began to fall. A shout came up from the bathers, who escaped into the safety of their machines. The profusion of visitors strolling the pebbly beach began to run, as one, back in the direction from which they had come; our party followed. Unfortunately, my parasol, designed to shield the sun, provided little protection from the rain; but only a minute or two later, before we reached the steps leading up to the Walk, the rain stopped as quickly as it had begun, and the sun reappeared.

"I adore a little summer shower," said I, with a deep, appreciative intake of the damp, salty air. "It makes the world smell fresh and new."

"That was hardly a *little* shower," cried Maria petulantly. "I am soaked through, and half dead with walking. Charles, you *must* take me back to the inn at once."

"Yes, my dear. You will all come with us, I hope? We are staying at the Royal Lion."

"I would prefer to continue walking a bit longer," I admitted. "The sun will dry me. Would any one care to join me?"

"I would be delighted to accompany you," said Mr. Ashford with a smile. Henry decided to go back with the others, and we agreed to meet later at the inn.

Mr. Ashford and I strolled on down the beach, which was far less crowded now, and continued our conversation to the accompanying sounds of crashing waves and sea-gull cries.

"We moved to Southampton after my father passed away," I explained, when he enquired into my place of residence. I told him where I had grown up, and of our removal to Bath. "The country life has always been my ideal."

"And mine. Your heart, I take it, belongs to Hampshire?"

"Yes. Although I have heard the beauty of Derbyshire is unparalleled," I added diplomatically.

Mr. Ashford stopped, observing the spectacular line of distant cliffs and the surging movement of the tides. "On any other day I might agree with you. But is there a felicity in the world superior to this? Lyme seems to me a very outpost of heaven."

I stared at him in wonder at hearing my own sentiment on his lips, and followed his gaze. In the distant sky, the clouds had parted, and the sun was shining above a shimmering, perfectly formed rainbow.

"My heart leaps up when I behold a rainbow in the sky," I quoted.

Mr. Ashford glanced at me in surprise, and said, *"So was it when my life began. So is it now I am a man—"*

"So be it when I shall grow old," I continued, *"or let me die!"*

"You read Wordsworth," said he with delight.

"I prefer Cowper and Scott."

"Have you read Walter Scott's *The Lay of the Last Minstrel*?"

"It is a favourite of mine. Are you familiar with Dr. Samuel Johnson?"

"His *Rambler* essays? They are among his best."

"I do not suppose you read novels?" said he with some hesitation.

"My family and I are unabashedly enthusiastic novel readers."

A wide smile lit his countenance. "And you are not ashamed of being so?"

"Pray do not tell me, sir, that you hold the conservative view, that novels are the basest form of literature?"

"On the contrary. I am a passionate novel reader myself. But there are few women of my acquaintance who share my interest."

Our eyes met and we smiled. I was entirely captivated, and sensed that he felt the same. I could not help myself; I felt compelled to ask the question that had been on my mind since the moment we first met.

"Tell me, Mr. Ashford, since you mention the women of your acquaintance. A man like yourself, of considerable property and heir to a title, with all the manners and good-breeding required of a gentleman"—(and, I added privately, a man so amiable and handsome, with a quick imagination and such lively spirits)—"you must have been the object of the greatest interest to every family in Derbyshire County for the past decade, and considered the rightful property of any one or other of their daughters. How is it that you have never married?"

His cheeks reddened, and he went silent for a moment; I felt that I had embarrassed him, and regretted my bold remark. But at length, he brought his gaze up to mine with a direct and earnest look. "Perhaps," said he softly, "I prefer to be particular in my choice."

"Harriet in *Sir Charles Grandison,*" I said.

We were at dinner at the Royal Lion. After a long and delightful walk, Mr. Ashford and I had met the rest of the party at the inn, where we found Maria in dry clothes, very much alive, and sipping tea, while Charles and Henry traded reminiscences about their school-days. Their lively conversation continued over roast fish and fowl at one end of the table, while Mr. Ashford and I spoke amongst ourselves at the other. The past few hours had passed as in the blink of an eye, and I felt a sense of magic in the air; I could not think when I had ever found the company of a gentleman so thoroughly engaging.

"Of all the heroines in literature, Harriet is the one you most admire?" enquired Mr. Ashford.

"One of the most."

"Why?"

"For her intelligence and strength of character."

"Because she refused to marry a man she did not like?"

"Because she refused to marry a wealthy man, despite her lack of fortune."

"Ah," said he. "And in the same vein, do you find much to admire in its hero, Sir Charles?"

"I find him as perfect as a man in fiction can be. Although he is, in my opinion, more virtuous than romantic."

"I do not find him quite so virtuous," declared Mr. Ashford with a frown. "He is inconstant. He is divided for the entire length of the novel between Harriet and the Italian Lady Clementina."

"Only because he has given Lady Clementina his word,

and honour prevents him from breaking that vow. But he *is* constant; he saves Harriet from abduction and ruination, and remains in love with her throughout seven volumes."

"A true measure of his character, indeed," said he with a laugh.

"I have never seen you so engrossed, Mr. Ashford," cried Maria of a sudden, her face appearing somewhat contorted in the flickering candlelight across the great table. "What ever are you two talking about?"

"Heroes and heroines. Virtue and devotion. And the courage to follow your own convictions."

"That sounds more like a sermon than evening conversation," said Mr. Churchill with a laugh as he finished his coffee and set down the cup with a clatter.

"Not if you know our Jane," said Henry, smiling.

Mr. Churchill went quiet, staring briefly at Mr. Ashford and myself; then he emitted a small cough, followed by a sudden, loud yawn. "Ashford, it is getting late. Are you not tired, Maria?

"I am quite exhausted," admitted she. "That long walk and the damp air nearly did me in."

"We had best be getting on," said Mr. Churchill, pushing his chair back and rising to his feet. "Are you coming, Ashford?"

A regretful look crossed Mr. Ashford's face as he turned to me. "Perhaps we could continue our discussion tomorrow? If you and your party are not otherwise engaged?"

We all stood. "I believe we are quite at liberty tomorrow, are we not, Henry?"

"No plans whatsoever," replied Henry.

"Let us make a day of it, then," said Mr. Ashford. "A ride to the countryside, and a picnic. I understand there is a lovely valley nearby, between the hills."

"Yes, Charmouth," said I. "It has a delightful view."

"Charmouth it is. What say you, Charles, Maria? Are you in?"

Mr. Churchill and Maria exchanged what I thought was a rather odd look, which I could not account for at the time. At last, Maria said, "We are always in for a picnic."

"Shall I send my carriage to your cottage at eleven o'clock?" asked Mr. Ashford.

"We shall be ready and waiting," replied Henry.

Mr. Ashford turned, and—how shall I describe the look he gave me? It was so warm, so filled with feeling, it seemed to me the same look that Romeo must have given Juliet the night they parted on the balcony.

"Until tomorrow, then," said he.

"Until tomorrow," was my reply.

We never picnicked at Charmouth.

I was dressed, ready, and flushed with anticipation the next morning, as Henry and I waited in Mrs. Stout's tiny parlour for Mr. Ashford's carriage to arrive. I eagerly looked forward to spending the day together, and to becoming better acquainted with him.

"I wish I had brought my blue gown," said I, attempting fruitlessly to smooth out the wrinkles in my pale green muslin, which, although presentable, had seen better days.

"Mr. Ashford will not care if you wear blue, pink or puce," said Henry. "It is your company he seeks."

"Surely he hopes to enjoy both our company," I replied quickly. "And I did not dress hoping to please him specifically."

Henry laughed, a twinkle in his eyes. "And I am not sitting here, and I am not your favourite brother."

A knock sounded at the door. Henry and I started in surprise. "Who can that be?" said he, glancing out the window. "I see no carriage."

Mrs. Stout answered the door; as the room was no more than four yards across, and the open doorway in our direct view, we could perfectly see and hear the caller; he asked for Mr. Henry Austen. Henry darted up; the man handed him a letter, which he said he had been asked to deliver from a guest at the Royal Lion. Henry tried to pay him, but the man insisted that the matter had been taken care of, and quickly departed.

"Who is it from?" I asked, as Mrs. Stout vanished back into the kitchen, and Henry unfolded the letter.

"Mr. Ashford," said Henry, surprised, as he proceeded to read the letter aloud.

Royal Lion, Lyme—5 July, 1807

Dear friends—

It is with deepest regret that I send this letter, but a family matter calls me back to Derbyshire at once. As my friends travelled with me, we must all leave post-haste. Please accept our deepest apologies for cancelling to-day's engagement, and for any inconvenience it might cause you. I hope and trust that we may have the opportunity to renew our acquaintance at some time in the near future.

I am, most sincerely yours and etc.,
Frederick Ashford

"A family matter?" said I, as Henry gave me the letter, and I read it through myself. "I wonder what happened? I hope it is nothing serious."

"As do I," said Henry. "Well, Jane, this is most disappointing."

He could not have felt the disappointment half as keenly as did I.

I returned to Southampton ten days later in a disquieted state of mind. The balls at the Lyme Assembly Hall had held no attraction for me; and even the sea-bathing, which I had so enjoyed in the past, had lost its appeal, so distressed was I by the sudden departure of my new friend, and the attending uncertainty as to whether or not I would ever see or hear from him again.

"Why has he not written?" I enquired of my sister as we prepared for bed one evening, some weeks after Henry had made his departure for London.

"Do you expect him to write?" replied Cassandra in surprise.

I had related to her all the particulars of my meeting with Mr. Ashford, both in my letters from Lyme, and in several conversations since; but I had made her promise to say nothing of it to Martha or my mother, knowing that if either of *them* gained the slightest suspicion that I had met a gentleman of even the remotest interest, they would not let another subject pass their lips for months.

"I thought he might," said I, as we sat, side by side, at our looking-glass, taking the pins from our hair and vigorously brushing our long brown tresses. "I did like him a great deal, and I think that—I *felt* that he liked me."

"I thought you said that you had no chance to give him our direction."[15]

"True. But he could have learned it from Henry, had he written to *him*. Henry said he exchanged directions with Mr. Churchill."

"Even if he had written to you, Jane, you could not have replied. It would hardly be proper."

"I realise that. But just to have heard from him, even a line or two. His leaving was so abrupt, and the nature of it so unclear. A *family matter*, is all he said. I would like to know if he—if all is well with him. And to know if there might be the possibility that—that we should meet again one day." We climbed into our beds, and I settled back against the pillow with a frown. "Could it be that his friends disapproved of me? I noticed an odd look pass between them at the dinner-table. Perhaps they consider me unworthy of his acquaintance."

"Perhaps," said Cassandra gently, as she gazed at me with compassion from the bed next to mine, adding, "Jane. You passed a few pleasant hours with Mr. Ashford at Lyme, nothing more. I fear you must not expect to hear from him again."

"I expect you are right." I felt the sharp sting of tears in my eyes as my sister blew out the candle, enveloping us in darkness.

My earlier fears concerning the stability of our shared residence at Castle Square proved only too prescient. A twelvemonth later (during which time, I heard not a word from Mr. Ashford) my brother Frank wrote to his wife Mary, asking her to join him in September in Great Yarmouth when the

---

[15] Address.

St. Albans returned from its latest sea voyage and was being serviced, and from there to move to a place of their own.

"I should like to find a snug little cottage, just big enough for three," said Mary brightly, unmindful of the anxiety her announcement had engendered in the other four women of the household. "Fish will be almost for nothing in Yarmouth, and I have always longed to live on the Isle of Wight."

I was relieved to hear of Frank's safe return, and delighted that he and Mary should be together at last, after such a long separation. I did not begrudge them their desire to live alone; in addition to the favourable price of fish, they would have plenty of engagements and plenty of each other while he was in port, and I knew they would be very happy.

My mother was inconsolable.

"We are tossed to the winds *again,*" cried she as she paced between window and fire-place in the drawing-room, wringing her hands, after Mary went out for a walk with Mary Jane and Martha. "We shall be forced to pull up roots and leave this delightful town, to remove to God knows where! For with rents increasing, we surely cannot stay at Castle Square, once Frank and Mary leave."

"We can stay on for quite some time, mamma," Cassandra reassured her. "Frank has agreed to continue paying his share of the rent, until we can find another place."

"How can I accept more money from Frank, now that he has his own family to support, and another household to pay for?" My mother burst into tears and sank down heavily on the sofa.

"Do not distress yourself, mamma," said I, handing her my handkerchief. "Frank would not have made the offer if he could not afford it. In the mean time, we can make his burden lighter by practising greater economy. We shall get by."

"But where shall we go in the end?" sobbed my mother. "All this moving about, it is so unsettling. I am sorry to complain. I do not mean to be weak and unfeeling. But oh! Jane! If only you had married! If you had accepted Harris's proposal all those years ago, as you ought, we would have all been living in a great country house these past six years, without a care in the world!"

I sighed. My decision not to marry the man in question was a subject that had passed many times between us, and never failed to vex me. Indeed, it is still a painful memory.

Chapter Five

⚜

*I*n the waning weeks of 1802, when my father was still very much alive, and he and my mother were enjoying their second year of city life at Bath, my sister and I escaped back to Steventon, to stay with my brother James and his family. While there, we received an invitation from our friends the Bigg sisters, for a visit of several weeks at Manydown Park, their stately ancestral home that lay four miles distant.

I had been particular friends with the Bigg sisters since I was fourteen years of age, when their father, Lovelace Bigg, a wealthy widower with seven children, inherited Manydown from his cousins, the Withers, and moved into our neighbourhood. The squire later extended Manydown Park by adding more than a thousand additional acres of farms and country land. In keeping with their inheritance, the men of the family chose to add "Wither" to their surnames, while the girls chose to simply keep the surname "Bigg."

The two eldest daughters soon married and departed, and

the elder son died young, leaving a shy little brother, Harris, and three sisters, Elizabeth, Catherine and Alethea, who were close in age to Cassandra and myself, and became our dearest friends during those years of parties, balls, over-night visits, all-night conversations and shared intimacies, as we grew and matured from girlhood to womanhood.

As Cassandra and I gazed out the carriage window on that brisk afternoon of the 25th November in 1802 on our approach to Manydown, we could not help but admire the home's splendid surroundings. Although it was late autumn, and many of the trees were leafless and bare, the ride through the green park, forested with oaks, beeches and lush, verdant cedars was a delight to the eye, culminating in the regal presentation of the large, square, stone Tudor manor house itself, with its spacious brick-walled garden.

As we stepped down eagerly from the coach, the three Bigg sisters greeted us with animation and affectionate embraces.

"Here you are at last!" cried Elizabeth Heathcote, as she kissed our cheeks. The eldest of the three, Elizabeth had returned home a widow to her father's house earlier that year with her young son William, following the tragic death of her husband. We reiterated our deepest sympathies, but she insisted that there was no need to speak further of that event, which had been covered many times over in correspondence; she would rather be merry during our time together, and let nothing mar our congenial mood.

"I cannot tell you how excited I am to see you!" exclaimed Alethea, the youngest sister at five-and-twenty. "I have been counting the days until your arrival!" A vibrant, pleasant, cheerful person, Alethea took interest in every one and every thing about her. She and I shared many similar tastes, and (quite naturally) I thought her extremely clever.

Catherine, at seven-and-twenty, was but a few months older than myself. She possessed a calm, serene nature, much like Cassandra, and her long, thin face, although not considered beautiful, was enhanced by intelligent eyes, engaging manners and a warm smile. "We look forward to many long morning visits," said she, "and as many evening fireside chats as you can stand. Promise me you will stay three weeks at least."

"We shall be glad to," I replied, "provided we spend those weeks engaged in the most wicked, malicious gossip ever heard in the county of Hampshire; interrupted, of course, for our own edification, by one or two brief poetry readings."

As the servants brought our luggage up to our rooms, we hurried up the front steps to the inner courtyard, and from there climbed the grand iron-work staircase up to the spacious, handsome drawing-room.

"How are your mother and father?" asked Catherine, as we settled by the fire to warm our hands and sip refreshments. "Is Mr. Austen still engaged in collecting books?"

"In a rather modest fashion now," replied Cassandra. "We travel and move about so much, he has nearly had to give up the pleasure. But he is hale and hearty, and quite spry for his age."

"My mother professed herself to be quite well on *three* separate occasions in the past *week*," said I, "which, I believe, is three times more than any se'en night in history, and a tribute to the pleasure she finds in living at Bath and taking its waters."

"She deserves to delight in her surroundings," said Alethea. "I am glad for her. I only wish, since you *must* live at Bath, that *you* could find something to be happy about."

"I am happy," I replied with a smile. "Happy to be here, and not *there*." Every one laughed.

We had been chatting amiably for nearly an hour, apprising each other of the details of our lives, and all the news regarding our brothers and their families, when Lovelace Bigg-Wither entered the room, demanding, in a booming voice, to know what all the frivolity was about. A genial widower of one-and-sixty, the squire was a large, broad-shouldered man with a fringe of downy white hair that framed a red, jowled face, and a squat, stubby nose, giving him, I thought, a rather aristocratic look, as if a horse had sat upon a very fine face.

"Why, look who is here!" exclaimed he, crossing the room to greet my sister and myself with a broad smile and a warm embrace. "What a delight, to see two beautiful new faces in a room full of such lovely ladies. It has been far too long since we were graced with the presence of a Miss Austen, I can tell you. When I think of all the years that you girls practically lived in this house, and all the laughter going on up stairs at all hours of the night in those bed-chambers after a ball, why, at times I quite forgot which one of you was mine, and thought of you all as my own daughters. I do hope you will stay on with us for a long while, now."

We promised him we would. The squire was a man of great character, respectability and worth who had served as an able and charitable county magistrate; and he was, in my opinion, one of the best and most generous men I had ever met. His only faults, if one could call them that, lay in a tendency towards verbosity when discussing a favourite subject, and a rather strict attitude towards his son.

"You know Harris is home from Oxford," said he. "Hard to believe it, but the boy managed to finish his education."

"Do not sound so surprised that Harris completed his studies, papa," said Alethea reproachfully. "Harris is more clever than you think."

"A more clever boy might do more with his time than lounge about all day in expensive Hessian boots, and ride and hunt," said the squire.

"Harris is hardly a *boy* any longer, papa," observed Catherine. "He reached his majority in May."

"Harris is one-and-twenty?" said I in surprise, wondering where the years had gone. I had not seen Harris in some time, as he had been away at school, but I remembered him as a shy, awkward and sometimes rude young man, who had often been ill, and suffered from a pronounced speech impediment. His father, concerned about his son's health, and worried that he would be teased by other boys for his stammer, had educated him at home in his youth by a private tutor.

"He has grown so, I daresay you will hardly recognise him," said Elizabeth.

"The one who takes the prize for growing is my grandson," declared the squire, to which Elizabeth beamed with maternal pride. "Have you met our William?" When we admitted that we had not, he called for the boy to be brought down from the nursery straight away. William proved to be a lively, good-tempered boy of nineteen months, with a captivating smile that went straight to my heart. "*There* is a lad who is going places," said the squire. "One day, he will be the 5th Baronet of Hursley Park, hold any number of public offices, and prove himself a credit to the family, mark my words."

After young William returned to the nursery, and the squire quitted the room, Cassandra and I convinced our friends to take a turn in the garden. Despite the crisp chill of the November afternoon, the sky was bright and clear. We bundled up in our cloaks, bonnets and gloves, and strolled along the winding paths and manicured hedgerows.

"How beautiful are the evergreens!" I cried, deeply inhaling the heady aroma of a copse of nearby cedars. "Some may prefer the tree that sheds its leaves, but on the eve of winter, when all the other groves stand so stark and grim, the evergreens are for ever regal, delighting the eye in all their splendour. Is it not wonderful that the same soil and the same sun should nurture plants differing in the first rule and law of their existence?"[16]

"Only Jane would think to rhapsodize about the nature of a tree," remarked my sister with a smile.

"I cannot help it. Every day that we are forced to live at Bath makes me appreciate the sight and smell of the natural world all the more. I am sure there can be no scent more delicious in a garden than that of a cedar."

"Are you forgetting the rose?" enquired Catherine.

"And the lilac?" said Elizabeth.

"And a syringa in full bloom?" added Cassandra.

As every one began, at once, to call out their favourite aromatic trees and flowers, I laughed and raised my hands in surrender. "I withdraw my statement, with particular regard to the syringa. I see there can be no competition between plants and trees; they are all my favourites."

"Oh!" cried Alethea, stopping of a sudden. "Do you remember the summer that we all attempted to draw Catherine's portrait, here in the garden?"

"I do," replied Cassandra. "I believe we set up our easels on this very spot."

"Your drawings were rather good," said I. "Mine, as I recall, so mortified me, that I threw it into the fire before any one could inspect it."

---

[16] Jane Austen's character Fanny Price rhapsodizes about evergreens in a similar manner in *Mansfield Park,* clearly echoing the author's sentiments on the subject.

"You are too hard on your self," remarked Cassandra. "You always were. You are quite as skilled at drawing and painting, as you are at needlework and dancing."

"I beg you, do not insult my skills at dancing and needle-work, of which I am quite proud," I cried in mock alarm, "by mentioning them in the same breath as drawing and painting."

"I do admire your satin stitch, and you were always very light on your feet at our balls," declared Alethea.

"I remember one ball, in particular, at which I danced every one of the twenty dances," I said nostalgically.

"Do you recall the time, Jane, that you danced with Harris?" enquired Alethea.

"I do. I was, I think, fully seventeen at the time, and considered myself quite a grown-up lady."

"And our Harris was but a shy little boy of twelve," said Catherine, smiling. "You took pity on him, seeing him alone and miserable in a corner, admiring all the dancers."

"It was a very sweet thing to do," said Elizabeth. "I daresay he has not forgotten it."

"*I* shall never forget the time Jane posted her own ficti-tious marriage banns in her father's parish register!" cried Alethea.

"That was so delightfully wicked," agreed Catherine. "Who was the groom to be, again?"

"There were *three* grooms," said Alethea. "Jane was not content to marry just one."

"I never heard that story," said Elizabeth. "Do tell us, Jane; what did you inscribe in the church registry?"

"I think the first was *Henry* something," said I, smiling at the memory of that silly, youthful impulse, which was now recorded for all posterity to see. "*Henry Howard*, was it? Oh, yes! I recall it now. I wrote: *Henry Howard Edmund Mortimer Fitzwilliam of London, to be married to Jane Austen.*"

"Shortly thereafter," said Alethea, when the laughter died down, "I believe she registered to marry an *Edmund Arthur William Mortimer, of Liverpool.*"

"And finally," I added, "I was betrothed to a rather common fellow called *Jack Smith.*" My companions found that entry the most comical of all.

As we left the walled garden, and strolled along the main path through the park, Alethea said, "Did you hear? Emma Smith gave birth last week to her sixth child, a girl."

"Six children!" I cried teasingly. "Poor animal. She will be worn out before she is thirty."

"Jane!" exclaimed Cassandra, with reproach.

"You know I adore children as much as you do, dearest. But *six*?" I spoke lightly, but there was truth behind it; I had observed the bloom fade from the cheek of too many women at too young an age, the result of endless years of child-bearing. Yet my companions, it seemed, did not see any humour in the subject, and even less an evil; the ladies' smiles vanished; they all gazed into the distance with identical expressions of the utmost wistfulness.

"I have seen many a happy household with seven or eight children," said Cassandra, referring, no doubt, to our own family, and to my brother Edward and his wife Elizabeth's brood.

"Yet perhaps four or five is more practical," said Catherine.

"Yes. Four, I think, would be ideal," agreed Alethea with a sigh.

I found, of a sudden, that I could not debate the point. In a few short weeks, I realised, I would turn seven-and-twenty. I had always hoped that I might, one day, marry and have children. "Four," I heard myself say, in a voice so soft I did not recognise it, "would be a very handsome number."

We walked on in silence for some minutes, each lost in our own thoughts; when, across the way, I caught sight of a large man on horseback heading our way, returning from the hunt with a pair of hounds. I thought him a new neighbour or hired hand, or perhaps a visitor, when Catherine cried out, "Look! Harris approaches. You will see now, how tall and handsome he has become."

I stared as Harris drew up and reined in his steed, his dogs dropping good-naturedly to the grass beside him. The small, ungainly boy that I remembered had indeed matured, at one-and-twenty, into a big, broad-shouldered man; but there the change had ended. He was still very plain of face, and the angle of his body, as he regarded us from astride his horse, could only be called self-conscious and withdrawn. I found myself wondering, as I had so many times in the past, how a family with so many composed and disarming daughters, could have produced so awkward and unappealing a son.

"How was the hunting?" enquired Elizabeth. "It looks as if you bagged a few."

Harris darted a brief glance at Cassandra and myself, but did not answer.

"What a beautiful mare," said I, in an attempt to help him overcome his shyness. "I do not recognise her. Is she new?"

Still Harris said nothing, his furrowed brow indicating, presumably, an aspect of deep thought.

"Harris purchased her a fortnight ago," answered Alethea.

"What do you call her?" asked Cassandra.

Harris opened his mouth, shut it, and then opened it again. "F-f-f-felicity," said he at last.

"A lovely name," said I. Hoping to put an end to Harris's

suffering, I smiled, and said, "We all look forward to seeing you at dinner, Harris."

He frowned. "Le-le-le-le-let us hope that cook prepares something fi-fi-fi-fit to eat for a ch-ch-ch-change." He nodded, but did not tip his hat as he rode away.

Our party assembled that evening in the large, lavishly appointed dining-room, where a delicious dinner had been prepared in honour of our visit. The cook acquitted herself marvelously well, proving Harris's critique unfounded.

"The wine is excellent, squire," said I. "I do not know when I have tasted a more full-bodied red. Is it, by any chance, of Spanish vintage?"

"Right you are, Miss Austen," replied the Squire. "It is from Seville, a brand-new vintage, and very hard to come by."

"Father is very proud of his wines," said Catherine.

"Harris, once again, you have barely touched yours," admonished the Squire.

"You know that I ca-ca-ca-cannot abide Spanish w-w-w-wine, sir." Harris sat beside his father near the head of the table, his body slumped in his chair, appearing rather ill at ease. "I have ordered a little s-s-s-s-something that I think our guests may pref-fe-fe-fer."

"Young man, may I remind you that one day my entire wine-cellar will be yours," replied the squire in some annoyance. "You *shall* learn to appreciate it all. I insist that you drink up."

"I w-w-w-will not, sir. It is vi-vi-vi-vile."

The squire's face grew red. I sensed that this sort of altercation had occurred on more than one previous occasion. Fearing that he was about to force the young man to drink something he so despised, I interjected, "Pray give it me, Harris. If a lady may be indulged with a second glass."

Harris quickly slid his glass of wine down the table in my direction, with a brief, silent look that bespoke his surprise.

"To your health, squire," said I, raising my new glass.

"To your health," repeated the company. Everyone (except Harris) drank.

"What are you writing now, Jane?" enquired Alethea, as the next course, a filet of sole and a very nice fricando of veal, arrived. "Have you begun a new book?"

The Bigg-Wither family were the only people, other than Martha, a few close relatives, and the members of my immediate household, with whom I had shared my desire to write, and had allowed to read my novels. "Not at present," said I regretfully.

"We are kept so busy at Bath, and have travelled about so much," said my sister, "I fear Jane has not been settled enough to write anything except her journal."

"That is a shame," cried Elizabeth. "I enjoyed your books so much. I would love to read another."

"As would I," said Cassandra.

"How many long, happy hours did we pass merrily ensconced in one bed-chamber or another," said Alethea fondly, with a sigh, "reading aloud from your pages?"

"I loved that story where the heroine finds herself at an abbey, and terrifies herself with all sorts of imaginary horrors," said Catherine. "*Susan* I think it was called?"

"Yes, yes! That book was quite wonderful!" exclaimed Alethea.

"Did you really think so?" I enquired, pleased that they remembered it, since it had been at least three years since we had read it.

"It was very entertaining, and made excellent fun of Mrs. Radcliffe's *The Mysteries of Udolpho*," replied Alethea.

"I finished *Udolpho* in two days," I cried, "my hair standing on end the whole time."

"You must try to get *Susan* published, Jane," said Alethea. "Get Henry to help you. He has many contacts."

"But none in the publishing world, I am afraid."

"He must know some one who does. Promise me you will ask him."

"If you insist," said I, smiling.

"May I make one small but crucial suggestion," said Catherine, "which I think might improve that book, or am I being too bold?"

"Not at all," said I. "I fear my work is rudimentary, at best, and I welcome all critiques."

"It is the heroine's name," observed Catherine with mock solemnity. "There is nothing romantic about a girl called Susan. If she had any other name, *Catherine,* perhaps, I am certain the book would be a great success."

The ladies laughed. "I shall keep that in mind, Catherine dearest, should I ever determine to revise it."[17]

Harris, who had remained silent during this discourse, dropped his fork to his plate with a sudden clatter. "Is th-th-th-that all you ladies can ta-ta-ta-talk about? S-s-s-silly n-n-n-novels?"

"Novels are far from silly," insisted Alethea.

"Indeed, Harris," said the squire. "My taste in reading, I admit, tends to the more serious subjects, such as law, history, architecture, current events and, of course, on a Sunday, ecclesiastical matters. But the novel, the very name of which, as

---

[17] Years later, Jane Austen did revise the book, changing the heroine's name from Susan to Catherine. It was published after the author's death under the title *Northanger Abbey.*

you may know, is founded on the newness of the genre, continues to gain increasing respect in many circles."

"The novel is a most estimable work," I agreed, "in which the greatest powers of the mind are displayed."

"What po-po-po-po-powers of the mind?" enquired Harris with a snort of disgust.

"Why, only the most thorough knowledge of human nature," I replied, "the happiest delineation of its varieties, and the liveliest effusions of wit and humour, which are conveyed to the world in the best chosen language."

"Hear, hear!" exclaimed Alethea, as the ladies all broke out into applause.

"In my op-p-p-pinion," said Harris, "novels are read by the w-w-w-weak of mind, and are nothing but a great w-w-w-waste of time."

"That is a most ungentlemanly comment, Harris," said the squire with stern disapproval, "when you know full well how much your sisters enjoy reading these novels, and that Jane here has admitted she made several attempts in the writing of them. I feel a new-found tolerance of late towards the person, be it gentleman or lady, who can find pleasure in a good novel, and so should you."

Harris appeared more annoyed than embarrassed by this chastisement, but before he could reply, the butler appeared with a tureen.

"Here is the p-p-p-p-punch I ordered, in y-y-y-y-your honour, fa-fa-fa-fa-father." Harris stood up with a sardonic smile, as the butler dished out and served a red wine punch to the entire party. "*D-d-d-d-drink up*, father."

We all tried the brew, with wry faces; it had a dreadful taste, as if made from a combination of ill-assorted wines.

The squire spit his out into his glass in revulsion. "What in God's name is this, son?"

"L-l-l-l-ladies—and gentleman," said Harris, with a particular nod to his father, "my p-p-p-p-punch is like you. In your individual ca-ca-ca-ca-capacity, you are all very g-g-g-g-good sorts, but in your co-co-co-co-corporate capacity, you are very d-d-d-d-disagreeable."

A stultifying silence followed this pronouncement, as Harris sat down. Catherine, Elizabeth and Alethea looked mortified. The squire's brows bristled with fury. Although the remark was insufferably rude, when I considered the trouble Harris must have taken in designing the retaliatory scheme, I could not help but see the comedy in it; my lips began to twitch with amusement. I caught my sister's eye, and found an answering look there; we could no longer hold back our mirth, and we burst out laughing.

The Bigg sisters, sensing the absurdity of the event, were soon infected by our hilarity, and joined in the laughter; even the squire at last let out a loud guffaw. Harris sat back in his chair, looking very pleased with himself.

A week passed most agreeably, giving me no preparation for the debacle which was shortly to occur. Harris ordered no more wine punches, and for the most part, kept to himself, although on several occasions, I noticed him engaged in whispered conversations with one sister or another, exchanges which abruptly ended whenever Cassandra and I entered the room.

On Thursday, the 2nd of December, 1802, we were passing a quiet morning in the parlour with the Bigg sisters, when Harris strode, of a sudden, into the room, in an aspect of nervous anticipation. In perfect unison the sisters rose, each proclaiming that they had something to do which they had nearly forgotten; and, with the pretext of needing Cassandra's particular advice, they spirited her away (to her great surprise) *ensemble*. Before I knew what had happened, I found myself alone with Harris.

Neither of us spoke. Harris stood before the fire, resting one big hand uncomfortably upon the mantel, the other hanging limply at his side, staring down at the hearth with such a fixed and serious expression that I wondered if he had found some defect there. He wore pale yellow breeches and, as his father had noted, a pair of the new, black, tasselled Hessian boots which came up to just below the knee, an attempt at style which was entirely defeated by his overgrown, ungainly stature, the sheen of perspiration on his brow, and the flat look of his countenance.

I sat upon the sofa in quiet surprise and the dawning realisation that this meeting might have been orchestrated. Perhaps Harris had something he wished to tell me, although I could not begin to guess what it could be.

"Good morning, Harris," said I politely, after a lengthy silence, knowing that he often required assistance to begin a conversation.

Harris nodded in my general direction, and then returned his gaze to the fire.

"It is a fine morning, is it not? Your sisters thought it might rain, but I proved them wrong."

Still he said nothing, but stood in discomfited silence. I cast about for a new topic, and had just decided to ask how he had enjoyed school, when he turned with sudden resolve and approached me, stopping several feet away, and said in a determined voice, "Mi-mi-mi-miss Jane."

"Yes?" I was relieved to find that he actually *did* intend to speak, and I would not be required to converse for two.

"Y-y-y-y-you know that I am the heir to Ma-ma-ma-manydown Park."

"Yes."

"As su-su-su-su-such, I have a great de-de-de-deal to offer the w-w-w-woman who consents to be my w-w-w-wife."

"Indeed you do, Harris."

"W-w-w-would you do me that honour, Mi-mi-mi-miss Ja-ja-ja-ja-jane?"

Chapter Six

"He asked you to *marry* him?" cried Cassandra in astonishment.

Her stunned expression was a perfect reflection of my own; I had been in a state of the utmost shock and confusion ever since Harris made his startling declaration, at which time I had immediately quit the room. I had found Cassandra up stairs in the company of the Bigg sisters, whose averted eyes, hidden smiles, and eager, anticipatory air communicated their secret knowledge of Harris's intended proposal.

My sister and I were now locked behind closed doors in the guest bed-room we shared, and I had only just related the events which had transpired.

"He made an actual *proposal of marriage*?" repeated Cassandra. "*Harris?*"

"He did." I paced the room, my stomach clenched, my mind all in a whirl, uncertain what to think or feel.

"What did you say?"

"I said—I hardly know what I said. I said I needed time to think."

"This is most unexpected. I confess, I am all astonishment."

"As am I."

"I had no idea he thought of you that way. As, as—"

"As a wife?"

"More than that," replied Cassandra. "As a lover."

"Neither did I. Truth be told, I am not certain he does."

"What do you mean?"

"He made no exclamation of love. Nor did he make a pretence at any sentiment of affection."

"None?"

"None whatsoever. The great emphasis was on the honour, as heir to Manydown Park, that he was bestowing." I sighed. "Let us be frank. Harris is one-and-twenty years of age, with few social skills, and very little to occupy his time. I think he may just want a wife—*any* wife. His sisters, I am certain, had a hand in it. He had their urging and approval; I am well-known to him and the family; and I was here, and convenient."

"Surely you are more than that. To ask you to marry him, he must admire you."

"If he does, he has never said so."

"He is not a man of many words."

"No. He is not." Wickedly, I added, "When he proposed, I think it took him a full three minutes to utter the simple proclamation." We burst out laughing; then, feeling remorseful, we struggled to compose ourselves. "Forgive me. We should not laugh. His affliction has caused him and his family a great deal of distress. It is not funny."

"No. It is not. And his proposal, it is a very serious matter, Jane."

"I understand. To receive an offer at my advanced age, of nearly seven-and-twenty! A woman with no home, no money, no property; it is flattering, and rather reassuring."

Cassandra did not smile, apparently seeing no humour in the remark. "It is a *most desirable* match, Jane."

"Is it? *Is it?*"

"You *know* it is. Harris is the heir to Manydown Park and all its holdings."

"I am fully aware of how rich he is—or will be. But he is five years younger than I."

"What of it? Five years is nothing. Henry is a full ten years younger than his wife, and they are very happy. And women often do outlive their husbands."

"But he is so plain, so awkward and so uncouth in manner. There is no connection or feeling between us. Our minds are so dissimilar. Harris rarely speaks. And when he *does* speak, he is often rude, or he says nothing of interest."

"Silence, in a case like this, might be considered a blessing."

I saw, to my dismay, that Cassandra was completely serious. "How can you say that? You *cannot* believe it. Good, healthy communication is the foundation, the very touchstone of any close relationship."

"He is still young, Jane. Remember, he was schooled at home as a boy, and he never really knew his mother. Marriage is a great improver. With you at his side to instruct and guide him, his conversational skills may increase."

"They may. But what if they do not? You know I do not love him. In truth, I do not even *like* him very much. And he cannot possibly love me."

"There are many tracts of feeling between esteem, fondness, amiability and love."

"But I have *none* of those feelings where Harris is concerned.

Oh, I suppose I might have a sort of fondness for him, or for the boy that he once was. But do I esteem him? *No.*"

"Not now, but you will learn to care for him, perhaps, in time, just as he will come to care for you."

"*Perhaps? In time?* That seems a rather great risk to take, do not you think? To spend a lifetime tied to some one you do not love—how trapped we should both feel. I cannot imagine it!"

"I have come to believe," said Cassandra, "that romantic love among the gentry is preached far more often than it is practised."

I stared at her composed face a long moment, then shook my head. "You would not say that, had your Tom lived."

"But he did not live. Not every one has a chance at true love, Jane."

"But every body has the right to *seek* it, to *believe* that she can and should marry for love, at least once in her life, does she not? Must I sacrifice all my hopes?"

"You must be practical, Jane. At your age, you may never receive another offer of marriage, and certainly not one so advantageous. Consider your future. As mistress of Manydown Park, you will oversee a grand estate and much property. You will enjoy every comfort and advantage in life. Your children will grow up in wealth and splendour, and attend the finest schools."

I nodded, troubled, and spoke the thought that had been weighing heavily on my mind, "And you and mother and father can live here, if you wish."

"Do not think of us."

"But I must." I sighed. "As long as father lives, we have security of a sort, however rootless we have become. But if father should die, our income will be so reduced that you and mother and I might face penury, and we shall surely become a burden to our brothers." I thought of my friend Martha, ten years my senior, who lived at the time with her old, infirm, widowed mother and her mother's friend, poor Mrs. Stent. "One day, we might become Mrs. Stents ourselves, unequal to any thing, and unwelcome to every body. Marrying Harris would prevent that."

"Yes," admitted Cassandra quietly. "But apart from the money. No family could be more beloved to us than the Bigg-Withers. Catherine, Alethea and Elizabeth are like our own dear sisters. Harris may be young and yet unformed, but you could be the making of him. The match could be advantageous on both sides. And—" She paused, as if carefully selecting her next words. "Since Tom died, I have often thought that perhaps you and I were meant to spend our lives together. I cannot help but think, if you married Harris—"

"We could remain together."

Cassandra nodded, her eyes alight with excitement. "And escape from dreaded Bath."

"To a real home, at last."

"A home in the country!"

"In our beloved Hampshire!"

Our eyes met. We clasped hands, enthralled.

On entering the parlour that evening, I found Harris conspicuously alone, busily cleaning his gun, while the family was gathered in the adjoining drawing-room. My heart pounded as I crossed to where he sat, and declared, "I have considered your proposal. I wish to accept."

Harris quickly stood and faced me in awkward silence. Our gazes met in mute acknowledgment of my consent, and he briefly smiled.

I wondered, did he intend to speak? Did he mean to kiss me? I felt some apprehension at this last prospect, and realised I did not welcome it. To my relief, he only took my right hand in his, and squeezed it gently. I realised it was the first time we had touched in any way since I had danced with him at a ball in that very house, when he was a boy of twelve.

He seemed to be devising some kind of verbal response when Alethea appeared at the open door, and on seeing us standing so together, cried, "Did you say yes? Did you, Jane?"

Harris dropped my hand, his face flushing as he quickly stepped aside.

I nodded, glancing at Alethea.

She squealed with delight, then turned back into the drawing-room, and cried, "Jane said yes! She is to be our sister!"

A noisy burst of activity followed. The Bigg sisters and Cassandra all made their entrances, exclaiming with happy laughter and excitement as they embraced me and Harris in turn.

"My dearest wish has come true," said Catherine, taking my hands into her own with an affectionate smile. "You are truly my own sister now."

The squire, alone, seemed taken aback by the proceedings, but soon recovering from his surprise, his booming voice added to the air of celebration in the room. "I had no idea this was brewing right under my own nose," said he, shaking Harris's hand and smiling heartily. "Son, you shew a greater understanding than I gave you credit for. I hope you will be very happy."

"Th-th-th-thank you, sir," said Harris.

Giving me a warm hug, the squire said, "My heartiest congratulations, my dear Jane. Welcome to the family."

I smiled, carried away by the sense of joy that pervaded the room. I was to marry Harris Bigg-Wither. I would have a home. I would have the children I dreamt of. I would be part of a family I loved. My parents and sister and I would never want for any thing.

As Cassandra said, it was a most desirable match.

I did not sleep that night. I lay awake in the darkness, hour after hour, reflecting on the new life which lay before me. I sat up. I stood. I lit a candle and paced the room, filled with increasing horror and revulsion at what I had done.

The first rays of dawn were peeking from beneath the curtains when Cassandra stirred and looked up at me in drowsy puzzlement. "Jane? What is the matter? Why are you not in bed?"

"For six days," said I in profound anguish, "I have been surrounded by our dearest friends. I have enjoyed the delights of Manydown's lovely grounds and beautiful, spacious, wainscoted chambers, and Harris's proposal bewitched me. But my acceptance was based too much on pecuniary reasons. I do not love him! I do not even have the potential to love him! I feel as if I have just made a bargain with the devil; a life of ease and comfort in exchange for one of misery and loneliness!"

"Jane. Be calm. Come to bed, and sleep. All will be well in the morning."

"It *is* morning!" I cried. "I cannot rest until I have undone what I did so rashly. Oh, Cassandra! When I think of the pain that I shall cause, the rash of bad feelings that will ensue, I am vexed and mortified and full of grief. But I cannot marry Harris. I *cannot*."

I believe that nothing I have ever said or done, before or since, has upset so many people as my retraction of my word that day.

I found Harris in the breakfast parlour. Through a blur of tears, I spoke the words that needed to be spoken: I was sorry, I had been too hasty, I had made a mistake and I was to blame. His response was entirely within his nature. His face darkened, he stared at me in consternation, then he turned and fled the room without a word.

The outpouring of grief expressed by his sisters was more than I could bear. I insisted that I could not stay in that house, nay in that neighbourhood, another minute longer. A carriage was called, servants rushed to and fro with our belongings, and amidst much sobbing and many tremulous embraces, Cassandra and I left Manydown and were expeditiously returned to Steventon, from whence I pressed my brother James into giving up the writing of his weekly sermon to deliver us straight away to Bath.

Once returned to the safety of our parents' shelter, I broke the news as gently as I could. My mother and father were aghast.

"You accepted him and then *denied* him?" cried my mother.

"I was wrong to say yes. It was a momentary fit of self-delusion."

"What delusion? It was an offer of marriage, and a *most* desirable one. What can you be thinking?"

"I am thinking of his welfare, mamma, as well as my own. I am convinced I could never make him happy, and he would be not be happy with me. We are not suited to one another."

"I always thought him a decent young man," said my father. "He is not an acquaintance of to-day; you practically grew up together. He is like your own brother."

"That is the point, papa. I do not love him as a wife should love a husband, and he does not love me."

"*Take him* and trust to love *after* marriage," insisted my mother.

"No, mamma."

"But to live at Manydown!" cried she. "Such a renowned family!"

My father sighed, and said, "Jane, I know that you have always said, since you were a girl, that you would never marry for any thing less than love. But do you realise what you do? You may live another eighteen years in the world, without being addressed by a man of half of Harris's estate. You are throwing away from you an opportunity of being settled in life, eligibly, honourably, nobly settled, as will probably never occur to you again."[18]

"Perhaps not, papa. But I have done the right thing. I am only sorry that the way I did it has caused so much grief."

---

[18] Interestingly, Jane Austen included an almost identical speech in *Mansfield Park* when Sir Thomas reprimands Fanny Price for her refusal to marry Henry Crawford.

Chapter Seven

⎯⎯⎯⎯⎯⎯⎯⎯⎯ ❧ ❧ ⎯⎯⎯⎯⎯⎯⎯⎯⎯

*A*s my mother agitatedly paced the room beside us on that hot August morning of 1808 in Southampton, she bemoaned my single state as grievously as if the news of my aborted acceptance of Harris's proposal had only just occurred, instead of six years before.

"I think you must have lost your senses that day, Jane," said she. "I do not understand it, and I declare I never shall."

"Mamma," scolded Cassandra, "it is high time that you stopped grieving over that affair. It happened so long ago."

"*I* have long since regarded my refusal of Harris's proposal as a lucky escape," said I. Privately, I added, particularly *now*, when I could reflect how differently I would have responded had a man like Mr. Ashford offered me his hand. Even if Mr. Ashford had not had a penny to his name, I believe I would have accepted him on the spot and been happy to be his wife, for we had shared, in only a matter of hours, a connection which I knew I could never have achieved in a lifetime with Harris Bigg-Wither.

Thankfully, our friendship with the Bigg sisters had not been altered by the incident, a tribute to the depth of our understanding and affection for one another. Two years after he proposed to me, Harris married Anne Howe Frith, an Isle of Wight heiress, and the union was apparently a most congenial one; to escape his father, Harris had moved away to a house of his own, and so we were able to stay at Manydown whenever we liked. "Be happy for Harris, mamma," I said. "He found a wife who suits him perfectly. They are very happily settled at Wymering, and she is bearing him all the babies he could ever want."

"Babies that should have been yours!" cried my mother. "You could have had five children by now!"

"Five little Bigg-Withers in six years, who all resemble Harris," I replied, suppressing a shudder. "*There* is a frightening thought."

"And now Catherine is betrothed," continued my mother with a sigh, as if I had not spoken.

I had recently hem-stitched some cambrick pocket handkerchiefs as a wedding gift for Catherine Bigg, who was engaged to marry the Reverend Herbert Hill, a man some seven-and-twenty years her senior. She had confided to me that she did not love him, but as Manydown would one day pass to her brother and his wife, she was forced to think of material comforts.

"Mamma, what do you think of the verse I just wrote to accompany my gift of handkerchiefs for Catherine?" I enquired, reading aloud:

> "Cambrick! Thou'st been to me a Good,
> And I would bless thee if I could.

> Go, serve my Mistress with delight,
> Be small in compass, soft & white;
> Enjoy thy fortune, honour'd much
> To bear her name & feel her touch;
> And that thy worth may last for years,
> Slight be her Colds & few her Tears."

"It is charming enough," said my mother, "but too long. And if it were *my* poem, I should never make reference to *illness* in a wedding present.[19] Oh!" added she, as tears started in her eyes. "To think of Catherine at the altar! *She* was not so fastidious in her choice!"

"If only I had met Mr. Hill, instead of Catherine," said I, putting down my pen with a feigned sigh, "*I* could have set my cap at him. But Catherine has all the luck."

"Oh! You are impossible," cried my mother. "With Frank and Mary leaving, we face removal from our home yet *again,* every one we know is getting married, and all *you* can do is make jokes."

The dilemma of how and where we should live weighed heavily on us; but this worry was soon eclipsed—and, ironically, at the same time resolved—upon facing a much larger grief. My brother Edward's wife, Elizabeth, died that October, a fortnight after giving birth to their eleventh child.

We were stunned and distraught by the news. Elizabeth was a beautiful, wealthy, well-born, well-looked-after woman, who had married for love at eighteen and been with child nearly every day since. She had often looked and felt ill during

---

[19] Jane Austen did, in fact, revise her verse, and sent a shorter poem to Catherine (with no mention of Colds). She must have also liked the original, though, since she retained copies of both.

her last pregnancy, but had appeared to be making a full recovery following her delivery. Then one night, shortly after consuming a hearty dinner, to the horror of her family and the complete bafflement of her doctors, she collapsed and died. Edward had loved Elizabeth, I believe, more than life itself. To lose her so suddenly and inexplicably was a dreadful tragedy. I grieved for him; for Lizzy, who had, at far too young an age, left the life she adored; and for the eleven motherless children she left behind.

Cassandra, who was already at Godmersham, stayed on to assist and comfort Edward and the children, while I received two of my young nephews for a few days at Southampton and did my best to console and distract them before sending them off to school at Winchester.

In the midst of this terrible grief, came a letter from Cassandra with additional news of a most startling nature. After the first few paragraphs, which dealt primarily with the daily sufferings of the mournful party at Godmersham, she wrote:

> *I have news to impart from Edward which may appear most unexpected, coming, as it does, at such a melancholy hour, but which, at the same time, may help revive your spirits—and which I believe you, my mother and Martha will find extremely gratifying. Edward is making us the offer of a house. He acquainted me with the particulars this morning, and requested that I deliver the intelligence myself, since he, at present, is not equal to the task. It is his wish that we should have the use of one of the cottages on his estates as a freehold, and he offers two for us to chuse from: a house not far from Godmersham at Wye, which as you know, is a very pretty village; or his bailiff's cottage at Chawton,*

close to the Great House (his bailiff having recently died).—Edward says that Chawton Cottage, which is a good size, has a nice garden, six bed-rooms and gar-rets above for storage, and could be put in order for us without much expense.

My sister then went into a few further details about the houses themselves, as much as she could recall from her discussion with Edward. This report, which Cassandra (in keeping with her calm, composed nature) delivered in such a matter-of-fact manner, was met with great rejoicing at Castle Square.

"A house of our very own!" cried my mother, clapping her hand to her chest in astonishment when I had imparted the news, upon her return from an expedition to Miss Baker, the dress-maker, to have her black bombazine gown made over in a newer style. "Free of charge! To live in as long as we like! Oh! It is too good to be true!"

"We have only to chuse which location we prefer," said I, referring again to the letter in my hand, which I had already perused in wonderment a dozen times at least.

"Oh! I am overcome! I am flushed, I cannot think!" exclaimed my mother, as she sat down in her favourite spot on the sofa with a dazed expression, fanning her face with her hand. "I feel as if I might faint with joy. But I suppose I like the idea of Wye. I do love Kent, and I should like to be near Edward and the children."

"There are many advantages to the cottage at Chawton, as well," I observed. We had all visited Edward's property at Chawton the previous summer. Although I did not remember the bailiff's cottage specifically, we had admired the ancient, rambling Great House, which had been between tenants at the time, and the village, which comprised some thirty houses. "We know the village. It is charming. Steventon is only some twelve miles distant. And Chawton is within walking distance of Alton, a very good town. Remember, Henry's bank is there."

"That is true," mused my mother. "Henry would have reason to visit there quite often, I imagine."

"And it is in *Hampshire,* mamma," said I. "To live at Chawton would be akin to moving *home*."

"Does she say how large these cottages are?" asked Martha, in some trepidation.

"Do not fear, Martha," I replied with a reassuring smile. "They are both, apparently, large enough to house all four of us, in addition to several servants."

"That is good news, indeed," said Martha with relief. "Although if it should prove otherwise, I can surely find lodgings elsewhere. I would not wish to be a burden."

"You could never be a burden, Martha dear," said I. "You are one of the family, and always will be."

Martha beamed at this, her eyes filling with tears, and she appeared incapable of speech.

The sight of her dear, tremulous face prompted answering moisture in my own eyes, as I smoothed out my new gown of black silk, covered with crape. "Oh dear. To feel joy at such a moment, does not seem right. To think that Edward considers us, and our needs, at a time when he must be plunged into the greatest depths of despair of his life. He is too good."

"It is a generous offer," agreed my mother, "and I could not be more grateful to that dear boy. But in truth, it is no more than he should have done three years past, when your father, God rest his soul, left this earth. And it only goes to prove what I said at that time: it was that wife of his who kept Edward from acting on his better judgment."

"Mamma!" I cried, aghast. "You cannot still believe that!"

"I do, indeed! Why else would Edward be making us this belated offer, on the very heels of his wife's demise?"

"Surely it is because Edward's great loss has engendered in him the desire to keep his family closer to him," I replied.

"I am certain that is part of it," said my mother, "and *equally* certain that he would have given us a house years ago, and an income, as well, had Elizabeth not voiced her objection."

My mother's words inspired, of a sudden, a kind of reverie, in which I imagined what *might* have occurred, had Lizzy indeed attempted, through subtle verbal manoeuvring, to convince Edward to substantially alter the amount of assistance that he intended to offer his mother and sisters.[20] The little scene that ensued in my mind, I fear, caused me to laugh out loud.

"I see no humour in the situation, Jane," said my mother, frowning fiercely.

"Jane meant no disrespect, depend on it," cut in Martha diplomatically, with an understanding glance at me. She had long ago learnt to recognise and tolerate those moments when my mind drifted unexpectedly. "I think she was writing in her head again."

"Who can think of writing at a time like this?" cried my mother. "We have a decision to make! Chawton, or Wye!"

After much discussion, we chose Chawton Cottage, based on its proximity to our family and friends in Hampshire, and Henry's enthusiastic report upon viewing the accommodation. However, the bailiff's wife could not leave until late spring, at

---

[20] Jane Austen brilliantly wrote just such a scene in Chapter 2 of *Sense and Sensibility,* in which the despicable Fanny Dashwood cunningly convinces her husband to disinherit his widowed mother and sisters; presumably, this is the conversation which inspired it.

which point Edward had several improvements he wanted to make, and so the move would not take place until July.

The winter passed quickly. While Cassandra remained at Godmersham, my mother, Martha and I spent many cozy evenings by the fire, reading aloud from the newest works, our unanimous favourites being *Margiana* and *Marmion*.[21]

When weather permitted, Martha and I went out, determined, in our remaining months at Southampton, to crowd in as many engagements, and go to as many balls as possible, before our removal to the country. I was, to my surprise, asked to dance on several occasions, and enjoyed myself well enough, although the dearth of wit, sense or good conversation in every gentleman I met always propelled my thoughts back to Mr. Ashford. I frequently and wistfully wondered what might have been, had we been blessed with more time to become better acquainted.

Little did I know that I *was* to meet Mr. Ashford again, and soon, in the most unexpected of circumstances.

---

[21] *Margiana, or Widdrington Tower,* by Mrs. S. Sykes, 5 vols. (1808); *Marmion: A Tale of Flodden Field,* a poem by Walter Scott (1808).

Chapter Eight

"How very wet the weather is!" said my mother as she paused in her needlework with a sigh, watching the rain-drops of a late February storm beat a steady rhythm against the window panes.

"Yet you must admit, it is delightfully mild," I replied. "After so many weeks of snow, I am thrilled to see rain. Even the store closet is behaving charmingly. It is very nearly dried out from last month's flood."

"The rain in the closet nearly drowned us," said my mother. "This entire house is falling to pieces. I shall be very glad to leave it."

Once the idea of Chawton Cottage had become fixed in my mother's mind, she had been anxious to get the move underway, and began to find fault with the very situation she had once been so loathe to leave. Martha had already left to spend the spring with a friend in town; Cassandra had just returned from Godmersham, and we were making plans to close up the Castle Square house for an April departure.

"There is nothing the matter with the house, mamma," said I. "The evil proceeded from the gutter being choked up, and we have had it cleared."

"A new evil will follow soon enough," declared my mother. "It always does in a house of this age. There will be a leak in this very drawing-room next, you wait and see. All this damp is very, very bad for one's health, particularly for the lungs." She put a hand to her chest and drew in a long slow breath, then whimpered, "I am quite certain I feel the onset of a congestion. The last time I felt this poorly, I became very seriously ill, and was thought to never recover."

"You always feel better in the country, mamma," said Cassandra. "Perhaps you should get away now, and not wait until April."

"The country air *would* do me good, after all this damp sea-air," agreed my mother. "The place I should most like to be is at Steventon. But I could never leave now. There is so much packing to do before our removal."

"Do not trouble yourself about the packing," replied Cassandra. "Jane and I will take care of it."

"I would not think to leave all the work to you girls!" cried my mother. "I will shoulder my part of the burden."

"Please, mamma, it is no burden," said I. "If you are ill, you know we would never let you lift a finger. Let us see to our belongings. Eliza can help us.[22] I am certain James and Mary will welcome your visit. We can join you later at Steventon, and then travel on to Godmersham together, as we first intended, until Chawton Cottage is ready."

---

[22] Their maidservant.

This plan was determined agreeable to all, and my mother soon made her departure with tearful hugs of gratitude. Cassandra and I, left on our own, determined to put off the process of packing as long as possible, and to enjoy what little time we had remaining in Southampton.

The next afternoon being very fine, we ventured out for a walk along the High Street, admiring the displays in the shop-windows. I enjoyed the bite of the brisk, salty air which brought the roses to our cheeks; with the sea surrounding the town on three sides, a fresh breeze was always sure to find us from one direction or another.

"Is not that a pretty bonnet?" said I, all at one transfixed by a charming hat in a milliner's shop-window. Made of white straw with a smartly swept-up brim, it was trimmed with white lace and scarlet ribbons, and crowned with the *sweetest*-looking bunch of cherries. We had only just dispensed with wearing mourning for poor Lizzy, and after months of black, the sight of any thing brightly coloured and cheerful was like a panacea to the senses.

Before I knew what I was about, I found myself inside the shop, with the smiling clerk taking the hat from its stand and giving it me. "Fruit is very much the thing again this year," said she. "We have a looking-glass in back, if you would care to try it on."

"Pray, what is the price?" I asked.

The lady named the sum. "The colour suits you; it will go nicely with your complexion."

"So it may," said I with a sigh, "but not with our pocket-book." As I had no real money to call my own—every penny I *did* have was due to the generosity of my mother and brothers—I could hardly afford to purchase bonnets solely for their beauty. I thanked her for her time, and Cassandra and I moved on along the busy street.

"Our old hats are still quite serviceable, and will dress up nicely with some new ornaments," said Cassandra, by way of comforting me. "We could get four or five very pretty sprigs of flowers from the cheap shop for the same money as *one* of those clusters of cherries."

"I am sure you are right," said I, still lamenting the loss of the pretty red and white bonnet, until, of a sudden, my eyes were drawn to another hat of much larger and more costly proportions, which rested upon the head of a formidable-looking woman who was marching in our direction. Her gown was attractively styled in the newest fashion, and her hat so covered in every imaginable type of fruit, that it resembled more a salad than a head adornment.

"I suppose it *is* more natural to have flowers grow out of the head than fruit," said I, as Cassandra and I both struggled to suppress a laugh.

At the same moment, we both let out a little gasp, realizing that we knew the woman who was approaching.

"Mrs. Jenkins!" I cried. An acquaintance (although not particularly close) of our mother's since our move to Southampton, Mrs. Jenkins was a widow of sixty years of age with no children, whose husband had earned his living in trade and left her very comfortably well off, with two houses, one in London and one in Southampton. Although we did not generally travel in the same circles, we had been invited to a party at her home on one occasion, and it had been an elegant affair. Mrs. Jenkins was not, I thought, possessed of a particularly keen wit, but she was kind and well-meaning, with a warm and ready smile for every one she met. Her features brightened as she hurried to greet us.

"Miss Austen! Miss Jane![23] What a fortunate meeting! It has been far too long. I am only just this week returned from town, where I passed the greater part of the winter. How does your dear mother?"

"She was feeling rather poorly of late, which she attributed to the rain and the damp sea-air," said I. "She left only yesterday to take refuge with our brother James at Steventon."

"Oh! I am sorry to hear she is ill. Do you expect her return at any time in the near future?"

"I think not," answered Cassandra. "My sister and I have just six weeks to pack, before joining her."

"That is right! I had nearly forgotten. So, it is all fixed, then? You are all to go gallivanting off to the countryside, and quit our fair city altogether?"

"We are," I replied.

"Well! You will be missed around here, that is a fact. I would have dearly liked to say good-bye to your mother. I will have to write and scold her for not even *attempting* to pay me a visit before her removal! You girls must promise to visit me some time, and not bury yourselves for ever in the country. But oh! How relieved you must all be feeling, to have a home of your own at last, and a freehold at that! There is nothing quite so comforting in life as the knowledge that your house is your very own, and cannot be taken from you. I should know, for I have been blessed with two very nice houses, and had a good husband, God rest his soul. I have every thing a woman could wish for, excepting, of course, the company of children. But I

---

[23] It was the custom at the time, when sisters were together, to single out the eldest daughter in a family by addressing her as Miss, followed by her surname; younger siblings were called Miss, followed by their Christian name, or both names.

cannot complain; I have never suffered from want of money, although I am not insensitive to the difficulties of those who do. You ladies, for example. I have long marvelled that you manage on so little, yet somehow your home is always present-able, you do not seem to lack vital comforts or necessities, and you are always in good looks, with cheerful smiles upon your faces. I wonder, how ever do you do it?"

"We survive, Mrs. Jenkins, by eating only once every third day," I replied.

Mrs. Jenkins clapped her hands together and laughed mer-rily for what seemed a full two minutes. "A very pretty little joke, Miss Jane," said she, when she had at last caught her breath. "You always did have a way with words. Oh! What is the time? I daresay I must go, I am late for the dress-maker's—but first: tell me, are you free on Thursday?"

"Thursday? I expect so," said I.

"Excellent! I am having a small dinner-party in honour of my dear niece and nephew and his wife, who are coming to visit from up north with a friend. They are such fine young people, interesting and accomplished; I know that you will find them most agreeable. You two ladies will round out my party quite nicely. The invitations go out tomorrow. I would so love for you to join us."

"We would be honoured," said Cassandra.

"Good. Then it is settled. Thursday! Do not disappoint me!" cried Mrs. Jenkins in parting, as she moved off down the street, her fruit hat bobbing in the wind.

On the appointed Thursday evening, Cassandra and I, attired in our best white muslin gowns, walked the two short blocks to Mrs. Jenkins's house, escorted by our man-servant Sam and a lanthorn.[24] In honour of the occasion, I paid more than usual attention to my hair; instead of covering it with a cap, as was often my custom, I wore it plaited up in what I hoped was an attractive style, with a band of bugle beads that matched the border on the hem of my gown. Cassandra wore her best velvet cap.

Upon arrival (precisely at seven), we doffed our cloaks in the vestibule with another newly arrived couple in formal dress, who were a great deal older than ourselves, and whom we did not recognise.

"I wonder if we shall have any acquaintance here," whispered Cassandra in concern, as we were led up the stairs.

"We could live a full year for the price of that gown," I whispered in return, taking care not to tread on the train of the stunning, beaded evening dress enveloping the elderly lady preceding us. As Cassandra pressed her lips to hold back a smile, we emerged into the beautifully appointed drawing-room, where Mrs. Jenkins, a vision in cream-coloured silk and ostrich plumes, greeted us with enthusiasm.

"Ladies! I am so delighted that you were able to come!" cried she, adding privately, "Among such an elderly crowd, we desperately required a few more young faces." Taking us each by an arm, she drew us towards the fire-place, where a small group was chatting, several with their backs to us. "My niece Isabella fell ill and was unable to travel after all, it is such a pity, I know you would have got on famously. But do allow me to introduce you to my nephew and his wife. Charles! Maria! Come here and meet the daughters of a dear friend of mine!"

The couple in question turned to face us, and I gasped in

---

[24] A lantern whose opaque side panels were made of animal horn rather than glass.

surprise. It was Charles and Maria Churchill, the couple I had met with Mr. Ashford at Lyme.

"Mr. Churchill! Mrs. Churchill!" I cried. "What an unexpected pleasure."

"Is it possible that you know each other?" said Mrs. Jenkins, all astonishment.

Mr. Churchill looked puzzled, but Maria said, "We do," and produced a smile that (I thought I might be imagining it) did not quite reach her eyes. "We met at Lyme, the summer before last, I believe. Miss Austen, is it not?"

At my nod, Mr. Churchill cried with sudden recognition, "So we did! Well I'll be dashed! How extraordinary!"

The gentleman who had been standing behind him suddenly whirled to face us; my breath caught in my throat.

It was Mr. Ashford.

"Miss Austen! How wonderful to see you!" exclaimed Mr. Ashford, his handsome features lighting up with what appeared to be equal parts pleasure and surprise.

"And you, Mr. Ashford," was all that I could manage. Many months had passed since I had seen him, and I had begun to wonder, should I ever be so fortunate as to meet him again, if I would even recognise him; but standing before him now, it was as if time had melted away. His hunter green full-dress coat and snowy white cravat were a pleasing contrast to the deep blue of his eyes and the natural wave of his dark hair, and his smile was warm and genuine.

"My, my, is it not a small world!" cried Mrs. Jenkins, as I stood mute and tongue-tied.

The gentleman turned to my sister. "We have not met. I am Frederick Ashford."

"I beg your pardon," said I, my cheeks reddening. "May I present my sister, Miss Cassandra Austen?"

"A pleasure to meet you, Miss Austen," said Mr. Ashford with a bow, as the Churchills echoed the sentiment.

"The pleasure is mine, I assure you," replied Cassandra, giving me a private, meaningful look which conveyed at once her understanding of the gentleman's identity, and her thrilled awareness of its importance.

Turning to me behind her fan, Mrs. Jenkins said in a lowered tone, "To think, of all people you should know Mr. Ashford, a most distinguished man from a very great family, the son of a baronet, and one of Charles's intimate friends. They travelled down together, you know, and I am honoured that he chose to stay with me, and to join us at our little *soirée*." Closing her fan with a flick of her wrist, she put her hand upon Mr. Ashford's arm and gave him her brightest smile. "I *do* hope you will do me the honour of escorting me in to dinner, Mr. Ashford, at the head of the line."

"It would be my privilege, madam," said he with a bow, although, as he straightened, his eyes met mine, and I felt certain I detected there a look of frustration and regret.

"You must forgive me, Jane," said Mrs. Jenkins, as, to my consternation and dismay, she quickly drew me and my sister away towards the other end of the room, "for depriving you of your acquaintance, but these little things are, as you know, so difficult to manage."[25]

In a matter of moments, she quickly and discreetly paired us off with the other single gentlemen in the room, who were of appropriate status—in my case, the fat and perspiring

---

[25] It was the custom at the time to pair off and arrange guests at a dinner party in order of precedence for the formal promenade in to dinner, a very tricky process which involved questions of status and rank, and was no doubt the most nerve-wracking moment of a hostess's evening. Mr. Ashford, as the son of a baronet, must have been the man of highest rank at the party, since he was chosen to escort the hostess.

widower Mr. Lutterell, a man who had long since passed the age of sixty, and who my mother had once suggested as my ideal mate in life; for Cassandra, a bald-headed banker named Woodhole, with thick spectacles and a jutting tooth.

A servant rang a bell and announced that dinner was served.

We all proceeded down to the dining-room, where a fire blazed in the hearth and an elegantly laid table awaited us, with Dresden baskets of preserved fruits as décor and a bill of fare placed next to every setting. Mr. Ashford was, of course, seated beside Mrs. Jenkins at the head of the table, in the company of Mr. and Mrs. Churchill; my sister and I were relegated to the lower end with our solicitous but rather witless escorts, with whom, for the next two hours, we engaged in conversation of little sense and no real content.

The dinner was excellent, and exactly as it should be on such occasions, with a succession of far too many courses, and more food than any one could possibly consume in a single sitting. As the evening progressed, I found my eyes drifting frequently to the other end of the table, as if to reassure myself that I was not dreaming, that it was truly *Mr. Ashford* sitting in the very same room, chatting amiably with our hostess and his friends. Several times, as I glanced in his direction, I found him looking at me. When our eyes met, he did not glance away, but rewarded me with a smile, and later with a slight apologetic shrug, as if to acknowledge his own frustration with the seating arrangements.

When the desserts and wine had finally been served, Cassandra and I made our way with the ladies back to the drawing-room for coffee and tea, where I waited for half an hour in anxious expectation for the men to finish their port and join us. They made their arrival *ensemble* just as the clock chimed ten. Mr. Ashford's eyes sought and found mine the moment he entered the room, and he quickly crossed to the sofa where I sat alone, finishing my tea.

"Miss Austen," said he with a relieved and rueful smile, as I stood to greet him, "at last, we have a chance to speak."

My heart began to pound; there was so much I wanted to ask him, I hardly knew where to begin. "You are looking well, Mr. Ashford."

"As are you, Miss Austen. I cannot tell you how delighted I am to find you here."

"It has been a long time since our meeting at Lyme."

"Indeed it has. Too long. And I believe I owe you an apology."

"An apology? Whatever for?"

"For my hasty departure. My friends and I left Lyme that day with barely a word. I worried that you might think us rude, and I regretted, most sincerely, that we had not exchanged information, so that I might have written. I felt I owed you an explanation."

Unwilling to betray the intensity of my feelings on the subject, I said lightly: "You owed me nothing, I assure you, Mr. Ashford. Although it could be argued that you saved my life at Lyme, in truth, our acquaintanceship there was very brief and incidental."

He looked taken aback and fell silent for a moment, as if a little hurt by my reply. "I see. I am relieved to hear that in communicating no further, I have done you no harm. But for *my* part, I must admit"—(here he shrugged with a charming, unpretending smile)—"I have often reflected with great pleasure on the afternoon we shared at Lyme, brief and incidental though you may have found it."

My cheeks flamed, even as an unexpected surge of happiness rushed through me. He had reflected on our meeting of long ago! He had not forgotten me! "Forgive me; I meant no offence," I said quickly. "I only wished to relieve you of any feelings of obligation on the matter. I, too, have often found myself reflecting on our meeting that day, and the interesting discussion which followed."

Before I could say more, Mrs. Jenkins tapped me on the shoulder with her fan. "Miss Jane! We could do with a little music. May I entreat you to play for us?"

"Surely some one else should have the honour," I replied, forcing a smile at this unwelcome interruption. I had loved the pianoforte since I was a girl, and had hired one for the past two years, so that I might stay in practice; but I much preferred playing for myself or for my family, than a public show. "I assure you, I have little talent for it."

"That is not how I remember it! You entertained us all most beautifully the last time you were here. Come, do play for us."

"If you would be so kind as to indulge us with a few airs, Miss Austen," said Mr. Ashford, "I would be honoured to turn the pages for you, if it would be of any help."

"It would be. Thank you." I was immensely pleased by his offer, which (as we both acknowledged, with a smile) would allow me not only to appease our hostess, but afford us the opportunity to continue our conversation, as well.

I took my seat at the instrument, found a sheet of music I recognised, and began to play.

"I see you are too modest, Miss Austen," said Mr. Ashford as he sat down beside me. "You play very well."

"You are too kind." His nearness, I confess, sent my heart skittering into a little dance; it required my most concerted efforts to concentrate and follow the music. "I would be most grateful, sir, to hear your account of the reason behind your sudden departure from Lyme, if you still wish to share it."

"I would," replied he. "Early that morning, before we were all to meet, the innkeeper roused me from my sleep. A letter of some urgency had arrived for me, for which the messenger had been travelling for several days, and ridden through the night. The missive brought word that my father had been taken ill. I made a hasty departure as there was no time to lose. There was some question as to whether he would live or die."

"I am so sorry. I hope he has recovered?"

"He has, completely, thank you. But while he was indisposed, he insisted that I stay by his bedside at every waking moment. Fearing for his life, he said he wanted to acquaint me, for the first time, with certain affairs of our family estate, which he had always kept closely guarded. To my dismay, when I began to look into the matters he described, I encountered numerous problems. It took a great deal of time to try to set things right."

"And were you successful?"

"I hope so. I tell you all this, by way of explaining my preoccupation in the weeks and months following my departure from Lyme. When, at last, I had the leisure and presence of mind to think of writing to you, so much time had passed, that even if I *could* have learnt your direction, I felt foolish at making the attempt."

"I understand completely, and am flattered that you feel you can confide in me."

"I have long hoped for an opportunity to share that confidence," said he, as he turned a page of my music. "It is indeed wonderful that we should meet again."

"Your timing could not have been more opportune, for we are soon to quit Southampton, permanently."

"Indeed? To go where?"

I told him of our impending move to Chawton Cottage, and answered his many enquiries on the subject.

"Well then," said he, "I consider myself most fortunate that my business in Portsmouth brought me here when it did. I had planned to travel on my own, when Charles announced his intention to visit his aunt nearby for a fortnight. I recalled you mentioning that you lived at Southampton, and had found it charming. I was, of a sudden, consumed by an intense desire to see the place for myself."

"And what do you think of our town, Mr. Ashford? I hope you are enjoying your visit, and that I did not mislead you in my description."

"I hardly know. I am only just arrived this afternoon, and have seen very little. But as of this evening, I believe my chances of enjoying Southampton are greatly improving."

The lively sparkle in his eyes and tone, as he glanced at me, made me smile. "Do you, indeed? This presumption, I assume, can only be based on your appreciation of my remarkable skill at the pianoforte."

"That, and the fact that I intend to take advantage of my time here, by making good on a promise I made to you all those months ago, at Lyme."

"Pray tell, what promise was that?" I enquired.

"To take you, and my friends, on a picnic."

Chapter Nine

❧ ❦

I told Mr. Ashford that a picnic in early March was an undertaking bordering on madness, particularly since it had rained nearly every day for the last fortnight; but nothing could dissuade him. The weather in the south, he insisted, was much milder than in the north, and he was determined to enjoy the countryside while in the area. He predicted that the day would be lastingly fair.

He enquired if I could suggest any place in the vicinity that might offer a restful respite from the city, and would provide that pleasing atmosphere of natural beauty which was so necessary to a picnic; if the location could include a view of the sea, so much the better. I told him that I knew of the ideal place, Netley Abbey.

An extensive, picturesque Gothic ruin, Netley Abbey lay only a few miles to the south-east across Southampton Water, in the tranquillity of a wooded valley, not far from shore. The visitants of Southampton, I explained, seldom made any considerable stay without surveying the abbey's ancient ruins. Cassandra and I had made several excursions there, both alone and in each other's company, and I thought it would make for a most agreeable day, if we had good weather.

There was no good road leading directly to the abbey. The ruins could be reached by water or on foot. The three-mile walk began by crossing at the Itchen Ferry, followed by a delightful wander through varied fields and woods, embellished with water-views. "The recent rains, however, will have turned the lanes and fields to mud, making for a very dirty walk. It would be best, at this time of year, to take a boat thither. It is the more direct route, and the tide should be right, I think, for our going immediately after noonshine."

Mr. Ashford expressed his enthusiasm for the prospect, seeming particularly pleased by the notion of going by sea. A plan was immediately made for a little water-party the next morning which would include Cassandra, myself, and Mr. and Mrs. Churchill. Mr. Ashford promised to make arrangements to bring along a supply of cold provisions, and any thing else that might be required.

Having long since resigned myself to the fact that I would never see Mr. Ashford again, the sudden expectation of spending a day with him was so thrilling that I spent the better part of the night listening anxiously to the incessant drum of a heavy rain, lapsing into a brief sleep only a few hours before dawn. To my relief, when I awoke early the next morning, the clouds were dispersing across the sky, and the sun was making a frequent appearance.

Cassandra, who had admitted the night before that she approved of the gentleman, at least in looks and general manner, did not appear surprised to find me up long before breakfast and dressed in my blue sprigged muslin gown, with my hair tidily arranged. "I always liked that colour on you," said she with a knowing smile. "I only hope you will be warm enough for a water crossing."

"Our wool cloaks will protect us from any sea-breeze, no matter how frigid," I insisted, eager to enjoy every aspect of the experience before us.

When Maria first learned of the proposed journey, she had insisted that she would not go, so certain was she that the weather would be miserable. But when Mr. Ashford arrived in happy spirits at Castle Square at ten o'clock the next morning on horseback, alongside his carriage—a sleek, black equipage painted on both sides with the family's coat of arms in gold—we were pleased to find both Mr. Churchill and Maria on board.

"I am prepared to be wet through, fatigued, and frightened," said Maria as we sat down opposite the couple in the coach for the short ride to the quay, "but I am determined to submit to the greatest inconveniences and hardships, if it will make you all happy."

The city of Southampton lies along a very pretty bay called Southampton Water, which is fed by the waters of the rivers Test and Itchen and resembles an arm of the sea, as it joins with the tide some miles distant at Portsmouth. The Southampton quay, as we arrived, was a bustle of activity, lined with barges, boats and ships of every size and description, countless crates of oysters, and nets bursting with fish. Upon leaving the carriage and horses with Mr. Ashford's coachman and post-boy, we made our way to the docks. My nostrils were at once overcome by the pleasing tang of the salty air, overladen with the scents of fish, tar and hemp, while my ears rang from the raucous cries of gulls overhead, and the thud and clatter of the sturdy seamen moving to and fro as they loaded and unloaded great drums and chests and barrels from the vessels docked nearby. Adding to the clamour was the banter of the seamen's wives, who sat in huddled groups making nets and shouting at the loiterers hanging about, the farmers' wives and kitchen maids come to buy their fish, and the cries of the fishmongers, vying for attention to sell their wares.

Mr. Ashford had hired a skiff, which was to be guided by a gruff-looking sailor who introduced himself as Mr. Grady. In a merry mood, Mr. Ashford hopped down into the boat, stowed the picnic baskets he had brought, then turned and held out his hand to help us each climb aboard. As I raised my skirts with one hand and took his hand with the other, I felt great pleasure in the strength of his grip and the warmth of his touch, which I could feel through the soft leather of my glove.

I took the bench beside my sister, and when all were situated, with Mr. Ashford to the aft, the Churchills to the fore, and Mr. Grady at the oars, the seaman propelled us away from the crowds and noise of the docks, onto the dark, gently undulating sea.

"I could not imagine a more perfect day, or more perfect weather for our excursion," I said, breathing deeply of the fresh sea-air and turning my face to the breeze, which was far milder than expected. Behind us was a fine view of Southampton, beneath a blue sky replete with puffy white clouds.

"It is lovely," agreed Cassandra.

"The breeze is too strong," said Maria, with a shiver, "and the air too chill. I shall most certainly catch my death of cold. I fear you will all be bringing hot soup to my sick-bed at this same time tomorrow."

"If you die of the cold, my dear," Mr. Churchill calmly told his wife, "we shall have no need to bring you soup."

"Do not be so tiresome, Charles," said Maria, vexed. "You know full well what I mean."

"I believe that fresh sea-air always does one good," observed Mr. Ashford. "What say you, Mr. Grady? Is the saline air not beneficial to the health?"

"Aye, but it is," said Mr. Grady, as he guided the small boat past the mouth of the River Itchen, and out into Southampton Water. "A month at the seaside will cure more ills than any amount of medicine, and that's a fact."

"Say all you like about the saline air," said Maria, "but if I lived here for a month, I would surely be ill the whole time from the stink of fish."

"I am quite fond of fish, myself," remarked Mr. Churchill.

"Then this be the place for you, sir," said Mr. Grady, "for these rivers abound with fine salmons and wholesome oysters. Although, truth be told, not so many be sold in this neighbourhood any more."

"So I hear," said Mr. Ashford. "Apparently they are sending all the best fish by land carriage now to the London Markets."

"Indeed they are, sir. But day was, not so long past, that Southampton was so fully supplied with these delicious fish, it was laid down in the indentures of apprentices that their masters should not oblige them to eat salmons oftener than thrice a week."

"Thrice a week!" cried Maria, aghast. "No one should be required to eat salmon three times in the same week."

"There are many, I am sure, who would not see it as a penance, and be grateful for the provision," said Mr. Churchill.

"Look! Porpoises!" cried Cassandra of a sudden, pointing

out a pair of the elegant creatures darting through the waves not twenty yards distant.

"That's fortune smiling on us," said Mr. Grady. "This'll indeed be a lucky day."

"How so?" asked Mr. Ashford.

"Porpoises be common along the coasts of the Isle of Wight, but only on occasion do they come thus far into the estuary, in pursuit of their prey. Locals say as how it be a good sign to catch sight of one in Southampton Water."

This proclamation only served to increase the festive mood of our party, with the exception of Maria, who did not believe in good luck signs, and spent the next five minutes insisting, despite all our protestations to the contrary, that a porpoise was a fish.

As we passed the village of Hythe and the woody district in its neighbourhood, Mr. Ashford enquired, "What is that castle there?"

"That be Calshot Castle," answered Mr. Grady. "And there, beyond the woods of Woolston House, that manor which edges the river, be Netley Fort. Both built by Henry VIII, for the defence of the harbour. They are nothing remarkable to look at, not compared to our great abbey, that is, even if it be a ruin, and none so interesting neither, as they be not haunted."

"Haunted?" I enquired, with great interest. "Is the abbey said to be haunted?"

"Aye, to be sure. Folks foolish enough to go there at night have reported seeing many an apparition floating over the sacristy and elsewheres. The ghosts, they say, be protecting some treasure belonging to the abbey that has been long hidden there within the grounds."

I was delighted by this story, and even Maria began to shew

a dubious interest when, some minutes later, we landed at the shore.

"Yer likely to find the place empty of folk, this time of year," said Mr. Grady.

His prediction proved to be true, when, leaving the able seaman to wait with the boat, we followed the path which rose up from the grassy banks, and arrived after a few minutes' walk in sight of the deserted abbey. Our companions, on seeing the ruins for the first time, gave a little gasp of pleasure. Its appearance was, as always, very striking.

An immense, ivy-covered ruin of fine white stone, surrounded by bright green lawns and thickly intertwined with trees, Netley Abbey encompassed a variety of large, interconnected buildings. Only the high walls were still standing, roofless and open to the sky, but enough remained of the numerous graceful, curving arches and delicate rib-vaulting to display the structure's former beauty and elegant design.

As we strolled through the ruin from one spacious open room to another, I gave a little history of the place, as it had been explained to me. The abbey, I knew, had been built by the Cistercian monks in 1239 at the order of King Henry III, and had remained in use until the Dissolution by Henry VIII in 1536. The abbey was then granted to a man who was in favour with the king, who converted the nave and some of the domestic buildings into a luxurious private Tudor residence, which entailed the destruction of many of the abbey buildings in the process, but left the walls of the church and some of the windows still standing. Evidence of the abbey's incarnation as a dwelling-house could be observed among the ruins in the front, where various traces of brick construction and the remains of fire-places still stood.

"Is not that a Westminster Abbey chapter-house motif?"

asked Mr. Ashford, as we stood before the east window in the church, which was fairly well preserved and beautifully proportioned.

"It is," I replied. "Netley, they believe, was built by the same mason who constructed Westminster Abbey."

"It is truly magnificent," declared Mr. Ashford. "The whole place has a most romantic aspect."

"In my opinion, it is quite hideous," said Maria.

We all turned to her in unison, startled. "You cannot mean it," cried Mr. Churchill. "Maria, look about you. This place is like a Roman temple, a thing of beauty."

"It is nothing but a sprawling old ruin," insisted Maria. "Just a lot of roofless stone walls and windows embedded in the trees, with ivy all grown over."

"Maria has never had any respect for antiquity," said Mr. Ashford, laughing.

"That is not true," said she. "I admire an old building as much as the next person, when it is in fine shape and suitable to live in. But when the roof goes and the walls begin to crumble, some one ought to tear it down."

"Actually, some one tried to," said I, "and died horribly in the attempt."

"Did they?" said Mr. Ashford, intrigued. "How so?"

"In the last century," I explained, "the abbey passed to a builder who intended to demolish it entirely and to sell off all the building material. One night, he had a dream that the arch keystone of the east window fell from its situation, crushing his skull. His friends warned him not to proceed with his plan, deeming it sacrilegious to destroy the abbey, but he paid them no heed. In his exertion to tear down a board, he loosed the fatal stone, which fell upon his head, and produced a fracture. The injury was not at first deemed mortal, but it seemed that the decree had gone forth—the spoiler of the holy edifice was doomed—for he died shortly thereafter under the operation of extracting a splinter."

The men laughed. Maria gave a little gasp of astonishment. "Is that true?"

"Upon my honour," said I. "His death was interpreted as a sign not to proceed with the abbey's destruction, and so the site was left as it is."

"Well then," said Maria, "since every body seems so very fond of the place, I suppose his death must be seen an act of providence."

We retreated to the spacious lawn outside the east end of the abbey, where we found a spot that was not too damp at the base of a great tree. Spreading our blankets, we enjoyed the picnic of cold meats, bread and cheese which Mr. Ashford had brought.

"I love this place," said I, staring at the roofless abbey with its endless display of open windows. "I love to think of the people who lived there, what their lives must have been like."

"Cold, I expect," observed Mr. Ashford.

Every one laughed.

"I mean, before it was a ruin," said I, smiling.

"When it was a working monastery, you mean?" enquired Cassandra.

"No," said I, "for the monks must have led a very rigid and circumspect life, if they strictly conformed to the injunctions of the Cistercian order. I am thinking more of the period when the great Tudor mansion was still standing, when some earl or other lived here with his lady."

A brief silence fell, as we all took in the beauty and romantic atmospheric of the ruin. My mind began to drift. I had, in the past, invented tales quite frequently for my young nieces and nephews, but I had not been inspired to tell a story, aloud or on paper, in quite some time. All at once, however, sights and sounds began to form in my mind; my imagination caught and sprouted wings.

"The year was 1637," I heard myself say, in a hushed, dramatic tone, "when the abbey was not as you see it now." The eyes of my companions turned as one to me with interest.

"The Fountain Court had all the aspect, then, of a small Tudor castle, with red-brick fascia, a turret, and a tower to the north. It belonged to a man who had lived here for many years since the death of his young wife, with only his servants and hounds to keep him company; a man whose name was Phillip Worthington, the Earl of Monstro."

"The Earl of Monstro?" Mr. Ashford laughed.

"There never was such a place!" said Maria indignantly.

"Oh, but there is," I insisted.

"It exists, with absolute certainty," agreed Cassandra, "in Jane's imagination."

"Oh!" cried Maria, her countenance brightening for the first time since I had met her. "I see! It is a *story*! I do *love* stories!" With that, she turned her attention fully to me.

"On the occasion of his fortieth birthday," I went on, "Lord Monstro decided to take a bride. Her name was"—(since Cassandra never liked her name in a story)—"her name was Maria."

Maria clapped her hands with delight. "An excellent name."

"Maria, the beautiful daughter of a wealthy country squire, was fifteen years younger than Lord Monstro. She could have had any eligible young man in the county, but Lord Monstro wooed and won her in just a few short weeks. They shared many similarities in tastes, interests and values, and fell very much in love. In the first months of their marriage, Lord Monstro shewed his wife the same tenderness and generosity of spirit which had won her heart during their courtship, reading aloud to her from her favourite books, showering her with gifts, and ensuring that all her favourite foods were at her disposal, no matter what the season. In return, Maria was a most devoted wife, hoping to match that perfection which she saw in her mate."

"It sounds as if it were the ideal marriage," said Mr. Ashford.

"So it would seem," said I. "But all was not well for long."

Chapter Ten

"What happened?" cried Maria anxiously, as I paused in my story.

"Yes, do go on," prodded Mr. Churchill.

My companions were all listening with rapt attention, which was a thrilling sight to behold.

"As Lord Monstro's love for his wife grew stronger each day, so did his fear that she might one day find him too old for her, and leave him. Although Maria did nothing to inspire this fear, Lord Monstro's worries increased until one day, when she spoke to the man-servant in a kindly tone, Lord Monstro flew into a jealous rage, leapt upon his horse and disappeared."

"Disappeared!" cried Cassandra. "Where did he go?"

"*That* was the great mystery. Days went by, and Maria heard nothing from her husband. She was greatly concerned. Where was her lord? Had something happened to him? Was he even still alive? Then one night, she was awakened from a deep slumber by a terrible new sound: a violent pounding from the top of the north tower."

"Oh! My!" cried Maria.

"Maria drew on a dressing-gown, lit a candle, and made her way to the great oak door leading to the north tower. The door was locked. She knocked loudly, and called out: 'Who goes there?' No one answered, but the terrible pounding from above increased in intensity, so violent now that the very walls and floor of the house trembled."

"Was this sound all in her mind? Or did the servants hear it, too?" enquired Mr. Ashford.

"Every one heard it, from the footman to the stable boy. They all appeared in a frenzy and tried, in turn, every means at their disposal to open the door, but it was firmly bolted from within. There was nothing to be done, so the servants retired. The pounding continued all week long with very little respite. On the seventh day, the sound changed. It became lighter, like the chinking of a hammer upon chains. This continued for a fortnight. Maria could not sleep, she could not eat, she could not think, so filled was she with terror. Who or what was locked up in the tower? Was it human or spirit? If indeed her husband was dead, had his ghost come back to haunt her? Then a new fear struck. Perhaps it was not her husband's ghost at all. Perhaps it was the ghost of his first departed wife, who, displeased by her husband's new marriage, had come back to haunt his new wife, and drive her mad."

I paused, feeling the eyes of all the party on me. It was then that I caught sight of something new in Mr. Ashford's gaze, a look of deep pleasure and admiration, directed at myself, such as I had never witnessed in another person before; and a hint of something else, something very like wonder. As our gazes met and held, my heart began to skip about, and all at once I found my thoughts scattering to the winds.

"What happened next?" asked Mr. Churchill eagerly.

"Yes, what did Maria do?" enquired Cassandra.

I tore my gaze from Mr. Ashford's and cleared my throat, struggling to collect myself. "At last, when she could bear it no longer, afraid she might go mad, she—she—" For the first time that I could recall in the telling of a story, words failed me.

Mr. Ashford, apparently sensing my distress, interjected: "Did she fetch an axe?"

"Yes!" I cried in relief. "Exactly so. She fetched an axe."

"And then what?" enquired Mr. Churchill.

"And then what?" I repeated, turning to Mr. Ashford with a smile.

"And then," replied Mr. Ashford in a lively voice, "with great effort, and a strength borne of desperation, Maria took the axe and smashed through the wood of the tower door."

"After which," I continued, "she reached in and threw the bolt—"

"—whereupon she swung open the door—"

"—and raced up the stairs—"

"—to the turret room atop the tower—"

"—where she burst through the open doorway—"

"—only to find—" Here Mr. Ashford paused, waiting for me to finish.

"Lord Monstro himself," said I.

"You mean his ghost?" cried Maria in horror.

"No, he was very much alive and well. Maria's relief was great, as you might imagine; but even more wondrous than his miraculous reappearance was the sight of the object which stood beside him."

"What was it?" breathed Cassandra.

"In the center of the room was a magnificent marble statue of Maria herself, that Lord Monstro had been carving to shew his love for her."

Every one gasped with surprised delight, the ladies sighed appreciatively, and there was a general burst of applause.

"Bravo!" cried Mr. Churchill.

"Marvelous," said Cassandra.

"I was on the edge of my seat the whole time," exclaimed Maria.

"Thank you—" I laughed—"but I must share the honours with Mr. Ashford."

"Hardly," said he. "The genius is all of your doing. I could no more make up a story than I could single-handedly sail a frigate."

"Now *there* is a frightening image," said Mr. Churchill with a laugh. "A land-locked country gentleman, who has never so much as gotten his hands dirty in his life, at the helm of a ship in Her Majesty's Royal Navy."

The smile briefly left Mr. Ashford's face, the remark seeming to cause him pain; but he quickly recovered and stood up. "I feel like a stroll. Who would care to join me?"

The party all protested that they were too tired, and too full, to do any more walking than was necessary to reach the boat that was to carry us home.

"I would love to take one last stroll about the place," said I, rising to my feet.

"Charles, be a sport and keep the other ladies company," said Mr. Ashford, offering his arm to me.

Together we moved off across the lawn. Glancing back, I noticed a happy smile on Cassandra's face, but a look passed between Maria and her husband which I could not identify; it puzzled me, and I felt a stab of guilt. "Perhaps it is rude for us to abandon the others," I said hesitantly.

"Nonsense," declared Mr. Ashford, as he drew me on towards the abbey. "If they want to lie about all afternoon, then let them. I want to take a look at that east window up close again."

"There was an old ruin not far from Steventon Rectory, where I grew up," I said, as we wandered through the abbey ruins. "It was nothing like this—just the remnants of a stone foundation with a few crumbling walls—but when I was very young, my brothers, Cassandra and I pretended it was a castle and played there for hours. We were knights of the Round Table and their ladies, or Robin Hood and his merry men."

"And you were Maid Marian, I presume?"

"Oh no, that was Cassandra's part. She was three years older and always the good and virtuous one, in play, as well as in real life. I was generally cast as the handmaiden, or the serving wench with a limp. Although on several occasions I remember playing Little John, which I was told I carried off with great distinction by adopting a booming voice and displaying a keen aptitude for archery."

Mr. Ashford laughed. "Archery? I see you are a woman of many hidden talents."

"I doubt I could hit the side of a barn with an arrow to-day. It was purely a childhood pursuit. Along with home theatricals, cricket, tree-climbing and sliding down stairs."

"Sliding down stairs?"

"Did you never practise it yourself?" At the puzzled shake of his head, I explained, "It was one of our favourite games. My sister and I would sit upon a sturdy tablecloth at the top of the stairs, as if it were a magic carpet, and our brothers and my father's pupils—my mother and father ran a boys' school, you see, so there was always a houseful of noisy young men, clomping up and down the halls—they took hold of the corners of the cloth and pulled it down to the bottom. We always shrieked with laughter and every one ended in a heap."

"It sounds as if you had a most agreeable childhood," he said, with a wistful look.

"I did. And you? It must have been pleasant, growing up on a vast estate."

Mr. Ashford hesitated before answering. "In truth, it was lonely. You were fortunate, to grow up in a happy household of noisy, active boys. I was an only child for many years. Charles was my only companion, and he lived many miles distant. When I look back on my childhood, it seems as if I spent all my time at lessons, studying Greek and Latin—or thinking of running away."

"Running away?"

"I had this plan, you see. When I was fourteen I would steal away and join the navy."

"I have two brothers, Frank and Charles, who are both commanders in the Royal Navy."

"How proud you must be of them! That was my boyhood dream—to sail away on a great ship and see the world." He shrugged ruefully. "But that was not to be. The heir to Pembroke Hall will never go to sea."

"Surely, Mr. Ashford, you cannot regret the life you lead; you are destined for greater things."

"Greater things? I do not look at it that way. I consider the navy a most noble profession." He paused. "Please do not misunderstand me; I cherish my family's land. I love my father and my sister dearly. The work of managing an estate is interesting and fulfilling, and I am most grateful for all I have. But at the same time, it is a duty, rather than a choice. I was born into a life that was prescribed for me since I first drew breath."

"And you wish that you had been given more choices in life?"

"Does not every one? It is human nature, I believe, to want something different from that which we have, no matter how fortunate we are." We had left the far end of the abbey now, and emerged into a grassy field leading to some woods. "Tell me, what did you dream of, as a girl?"

"A girl cannot dream of much beyond marriage and children."

"A typical girl, yes. But you, I think, are far from typical."

I smiled at that. "I did have a dream once, but—"

"But?"

I caught myself, stopped and shook my head. "It was nothing, it is too ridiculous."

"No dream is too ridiculous."

"This one is. I gave it up long ago. Please. Let us talk of something else."

"After I have bared my soul to you? Admitted that I wanted to give up my inheritance, and run away and join the navy? Surely nothing you would say could be more ridiculous than that." When I did not respond, he said, "Let me guess: you wanted to be—a strong man in a circus?"

"There! You have guessed it," I replied, laughing.

"A commissioned officer in Her Majesty's Royal Dragoons?"

I laughed again. "Without my uttering a word, you know my deepest, darkest secrets."

"Seriously now. All your life, you dreamed of becoming—let me see—a magistrate?"

"Impossible."

"A physician?"

"A female physician? Are you mad?"

"You could be the first."

"I have not the aptitude, nor the patience."

"An actress upon the stage?"

"Never."

"A renowned novelist?"

His guess caught me unprepared; my smile froze on my face, and I looked away, lapsing into awkward silence.

"Is that it?" I felt his eyes on me, searching my face. "A novelist?" To my mortification, a laugh escaped his lips. I felt my cheeks grow hot. I turned, gathered up my skirts and darted away.

"Miss Austen! Wait!" I heard his chagrined voice and quick steps behind me as I hurried across the field, into the woods.

"Stop," cried he. "Please. Forgive me! I did not mean—"

He was fleet of foot, but so was I; although my stays prevented me from achieving the full potential of my exertion, I managed to elude him as I darted into the cover of the trees; but after a short distance, upon reaching a large pond edged with undergrowth and overhung by leafless, flourishing oaks, I had to pause to catch my breath. Mr. Ashford darted around and in front of me and stopped.

"My word, you can run!" said he, struggling between every word to breathe. "Please hear me out. I think you misunderstood me. I meant no disrespect."

"Is that so?" I replied, in a heated tone. "Your laugh implies otherwise. It was that *laugh,* that *very reaction,* that I have, all my life, sought to avoid."

"I am sorry. But I assure you it was not a derisive laugh. It was a laugh of *recognition,* and of unqualified delight. Surely you agree with Dr. Johnson, that to write, 'To be able to furnish pleasure that is harmless pleasure, pure and unalloyed, is as great a power as man can possess."[26]

I knew the quotation; it was one I had often cited myself. The sincerity and admiration in his voice was unmistakeable, and the mortification in my breast began to dissipate.

"Having heard your talent from your own lips not half an hour past, it should have been my first guess," said he. "Tell me, what do you write?"

"Nothing of importance."

"And how long have you been writing nothing of importance?"

I hesitated. He had a way about him—the kindness in his eyes, the directness of his gaze, the deep tone of his voice, which harboured both sensitivity and gentle amusement at the same time—that made me feel as if I could tell him any thing. But very few people knew that my efforts with a pen had been directed at any thing but the writing of letters. "I would rather not discuss it."

"Why ever not?"

"Because writing is not considered a respectable female occupation. Because I do not welcome ridicule, or censure, or the scorn that accompanies failure."

"What about the admiration that accompanies success?"

"I have the approval of my family. It is enough."

He sat down upon a large fallen log not far from the pond's edge. "I do not believe you. If you write, you must crave to share the fruits of your creation with the world."

[26] Dr. Samuel Johnson, (1709–1784) was one of England's greatest literary figures: a poet, essayist, biographer, lexicographer and often considered the finest critic of English literature. He was also a great wit and prose stylist whose *bon mots* are still frequently quoted in print today. Jane Austen greatly admired his work.

Once more, I felt heat rise to my cheeks and looked away. I felt as if he could see through my countenance, to glimpse those thoughts and feelings which lay buried in the private depths of my very soul. I had, indeed, always written for the pure enjoyment of the endeavour, and for a love of language; I had never sought nor expected fame. But as a woman without income, dependent on the support of others, I also had to be practical. *Some* kind of financial remuneration for my efforts would be most welcome; and to be published—to see my work in print, for others to read—that would indeed be a dream come true!

"I would venture to guess," said he, "that you have been writing ever since you played that serving wench with a limp, with her brothers in the wood—and it is *that* occupation which gives you more joy than any other thing."

I could not lie to him, or to myself, any longer. "*Yes*. I have." I sat beside him with a sigh. "But it has all come to naught. I am too unworldly, too ignorant."

"Nonsense. You are the most well read person of my acquaintance, man or woman. And you have the most vivid imagination of any one I have ever met. Tell me," he prodded gently. "What have you written? Stories? Plays? Essays?"

"Some of each, in my youth. And since then—"

"And since then, what?"

"My journals. The occasional poem. Several short works. And—three novels."

"Three novels!" He could not have looked more astonished, had I told him that I had swum the Channel to France and back. "Three novels!" he repeated. "I would think it a great triumph to have written *one* book, but *three*! You leave me speechless. What are they about?"

"The subjects I know best: the trivialities and domestic

lives of families in small country villages; kindled romances, hearts joined or broken, love and friendship, follies exposed, lessons learned."

"They sound charming. What has become of them?"

"Not a thing. They are youthful efforts, wanting, in need of alteration."

"Then alter them. What are you waiting for?"

"My life has not been my own since I left Steventon, Mr. Ashford," I said indignantly. "Writing is not an occupation which is easily picked up and accomplished on a whim."

He went quiet for a moment, and then said, "I am not a writer, I admit. But in my experience, I have found that there is never a perfect time or place for any thing. We can always find a reason to put off that which we aspire to do, or fear to do, until tomorrow, next week, next month, next year—until, in the end, we never accomplish any thing at all."

His words shocked me. I stood and walked some little distance away, feeling all at once a little ashamed. Had it indeed been *fear* that had prevented me from indulging in my most beloved pursuit for so many years, and that was holding me back from it even now?

"I am sorry," said he, crossing to where I stood, "if I have spoken too openly or harshly; I only wished to share my own observations on the matter."

"I appreciate your honesty," said I at last. "Perhaps you are right. Perhaps I have been finding excuses not to write. And I do not wish to make further excuse now, but—even if I *were* to write my books afresh, and address all those faults which concern me, where would I send them? I know not a single person in the literary world. No one."

"What does that matter? In the end, talent will win out. Do you want to be a published novelist?"

"It is all I have ever wanted."

His eyes locked with mine, as a sudden breeze stirred the branches of the trees above us.

"Then a published novelist is what you shall be, Miss Jane Austen."

Chapter Eleven

⇛ ⇚

That night, when I was certain that Cassandra was asleep, I lit a candle, drew a shawl about my shoulders, and, as silently as I could, pulled out my writing-box from beneath my bed and rummaged quietly through the precious manuscripts within, regarding each one with affection.

Some, I believed, were superior in content; one or two were no good at all; others (the three volumes of my juvenilia, painstakingly reproduced into copy-books, complete with title-pages, to appear like a published work) were merely silly, girlish efforts; and my journals had no value other than the nostalgic pleasure they afforded me. Yet they all felt like my children in one way or another, for I had given birth to them, and spent a significant portion of my life with them.

"A published novelist is what you shall be, Miss Jane Austen," Mr. Ashford had said. I was filled with both excitement and trepidation at the thought. For many long years, I had abandoned my dearest pursuit, convinced that my circumstances

were not amenable to writing, and that the work was, after all, to no purpose. All at once I understood that this very attitude had been at the root of my misery, and I knew, without question, that I could not waste another moment.

I must write again, no matter what the consequences.

Which book to work on? That was the question. I set aside *The Watsons*, a novel I had begun while living at Bath, and had no wish to return to, and *Lady Susan*, a brief epistolary novel from my youth, which I had recopied. I barely glanced at *Susan*, which Crosby & Co. still possessed.

I considered, for a moment, *First Impressions*, the novel which was perhaps dearest to my heart. I knew it was desperately in need of contraction. It suffered from a rather stagnant segment at the end of the second volume, in which Lizzy (some months after receiving Mr. Darcy's letter) returned to Kent, to visit her aunt and uncle, Mr. and Mrs. Gardiner; and I was particularly troubled by a sequence in which Mr. Darcy invited Lizzy to tea at his estate at Eastham Park, in Kent.

No, I was not ready, I felt, to tackle that tome just yet, not until I had arrived at a satisfactory conclusion as to how to remedy the evils.

I turned my eyes instead to the manuscript at the bottom of the trunk: a novel I had titled *Sense and Sensibility*. That endeavour—to adapt an earlier, epistolary work called *Elinor and Marianne*—had proved very problematical; but I liked the characters, and believed the concept of the book yet had merit. All at once, an idea sprang to mind, a way in which I might improve the book with a radically new beginning.

With a rapidly beating heart, I retrieved the first part of *Sense and Sensibility*, replaced the box beneath my bed, and stole from the room.

The first light of dawn had begun to make its presence

known beneath the fringe of the drawing-room drapes, when I heard the door creak open and my sister appeared, sleepy-eyed, carrying a candle. My own candle, I noticed, of a sudden, had burned down to its nub, and the fire in the grate was nearly out; how long I had been working in the frigid near darkness, I could not be certain.

"Jane? Are you all right?" said Cassandra softly. "What are you doing? It is freezing in here." She added more coal to the grate, then drew open the curtains, flooding the room with early-morning light. Taking sudden notice of the quill in my hand, my ink-stained fingers, and the stack of completed pages lying on my desk before me, she gasped with delight. "Oh! Jane! What are you writing?"

I quickly finished the sentence I was scribbling, and said, "A brand-new version of a very old book."

"Which book?"

"*Sense and Sensibility.* I have written a completely new beginning."

"What was wrong with the old beginning?"

"Everything." I set down my quill and dried my fingers on a scrap of cloth. "The Digweed sisters lived in ease and comfort with both their parents in a country village, and Elinor met Edward Ferrars at a ball."

"What is wrong with that? As I recall, your description of Edward at the ball was most amusing."

"Well, I have thrown all that out. It was too similar to the opening of *First Impressions,* and there was no immediacy to it. Elinor and Marianne were simply two sisters with dramatically opposing views, but they had no particular troubles or cares. Their lives were in good order, so we did not worry about them. My new beginning, I hope, is vastly superior, as it immediately throws them into drastic circumstances. Their father dies, you see, and they and their mother and younger sister are forced to leave the home they love to their older brother. They have nowhere to go, and very little income."

Cassandra stared at me. "How very familiar that sounds."

I felt a blush sweep over my countenance. "Yes. Well. It *is* a little based on what has happened to us. Since Marianne is such a feeling person, it seemed only right to tap the depth of pain I experienced when we left Steventon, and when papa passed away."

"What a good notion. To write of what you yourself have felt can only enhance your work, I should think."

"That is my hope." I gathered up my new pages and thrust them at her. "Here. Read it for yourself, while I continue to work. I have finished the first chapter, and am making excellent progress with the second."

"You must have been up all night!" she admonished.

"And I will not sleep a wink, until I hear your thoughts."

Cassandra sighed, smiling all the while, and took a seat beside me. "You know I have never been able to resist your writing, Jane. I will take a look."

Cassandra loved what I had written. Encouraged, I took a brief nap, awakening shortly before Mr. Ashford called, as promised, that afternoon.

I was very pleased to see him, and told him so. That I looked forward to continuing our acquaintance, was a fact; that I had felt happier, more engaged, and lighter of heart in his company than I had with any other man of my acquaintance, I could not deny; but at that moment, my head ached from two consecutive nights of little sleep, and it was only with the greatest degree of difficulty that I managed to stifle a continual urge to yawn.

We had not been seated in the drawing-room five minutes, engaged in conversation regarding the success of our outing the previous day, when I felt my eyelids droop and my head begin to sag and, to my horror, I began to plummet from my chair. I quickly caught myself and sat upright, but Mr. Ashford leapt to his feet and glanced at me with great concern.

"Are you quite well, Miss Austen?"

"Forgive me, I am not myself, I did not sleep all night," said I, adding with a smile: "And you, Mr. Ashford, are chiefly to blame." He looked dismayed, until I explained that his inspiration and encouragement had been so great, I had spent the entire night engaged in writing.

"I admit, I did not sleep well, myself," said he. "I was concerned that what I said might have offended you, but you have set my heart at ease about it. I am thrilled to hear that you are at work again."

I acquainted him with some particulars regarding the book itself, and agreed, at his request, to let him read it when I felt ready. Then, insisting that I should take my rest, and satisfying himself that he might call again the next day, he took his leave.

Mr. Ashford convinced the Churchills to extend their visit in Southampton to a stay of three weeks. During that time, Cassandra was adamant that I should devote myself to writing, and to spending time with my new friend, while she and our maid took it upon themselves to pack up our belongings, leaving only those basics required for our subsistence.

The next few weeks passed in a happy blur. In the morning, I wrote. In the afternoon, Mr. Ashford came to call.

Our impending removal precipitated invitations from several neighbours, which my sister and I declined. We attended no more dinner-parties, and no more balls at the Dolphin Inn, preferring to keep to ourselves. On warm afternoons, we sat in the garden, or took a stroll along the top of the old city wall which bounded our property on one side, and admired the view out over the river and the water of the West Bay, all the while talking and discovering that we shared similar views on many topics, and entering into lively debate on those topics on which we did not agree. One fine day, Mr. Ashford, Cassandra and I took a lovely drive to New Forest. When it rained, we sat in the drawing-room by the fire, and I read aloud to him and my sister from the new pages I had been writing, voicing the respective parts as best I could to comic effect.

Mr. Ashford professed himself to be an immediate fan of my story and my work. Both he and Cassandra seemed to look forward eagerly to hearing me read, even if I had only finished a new page or two.

"Your book is charming and witty and romantic," declared Mr. Ashford with enthusiasm one afternoon, as we took a walk beyond the city walls in a wooded area beside the sea. "And, if I may be so bold, it is in a style entirely new. Your writing possesses an almost lyric quality, something intangible, I cannot put it into words. I have never read or heard any thing quite like it before."

"Surely it is not so unique as all that," said I modestly. "It is only a story of two young sisters with differing views."

"It is more than a mere story," insisted he. "Although I have heard but a small part, it seems to me a *debate,* brilliantly conceived, regarding how much emotion it is right and proper to feel and shew."

"Yes!" I replied excitedly. "That was always my intent with this book; I fear I did not succeed in expressing it in my previous attempts. I am delighted that it should come across now."

"Your characters, I feel I know them as if I have lived with them all my life. Chapter two is exceptional; I believe it to be some of the most clever dialogue ever written."

"You are too kind," said I, blushing at his praise.

"I am not being kind. I speak the truth. You *shall* be published, you *must* be. You have only to finish this book and submit it. I feel certain of it." He turned to me with a hesitant glance. "Although—"

"Although?" I smiled. "Is there something you are not telling me, Mr. Ashford? Some imperfection in my work, perhaps, that you have perceived?"

"There *is* one small suggestion I would make, if I may?"

"Please."

"The family's name, Digweed."

"Yes?"

"It is a singularly unappealing name."

"But we have old friends called Digweed."

"Please. Do not make us suffer as they do." He glanced at the nearby woods, thick with undergrowth, and his expression brightened. "How about Wood? Digwood? Dogwood? Dashwood? There you have it, Dashwood. Now *there* is a name."

"Dashwood," I repeated, with a nod. It had a nice ring to it.

The next day, as I read aloud my newly completed pages, I noticed a change in Mr. Ashford. He seemed in low spirits, which was unlike him, and appeared lost in thought several times. When I asked if any thing was the matter, he apologized, said his mind had only wandered for a moment, and pressed me to read on.

I thought that perhaps Mr. Ashford's melancholy stemmed from the thought of the necessity of his returning to Derbyshire at the end of the week, and of our intended removal to Chawton. Indeed, I could not contemplate this impending separation without the lowest of feelings.

Although it had been only a few short weeks since Mr. Ashford and I had renewed our acquaintance, I could not be insensible of a sincere and mutual growing attachment between us. When we were parted, except for those hours spent in writing, I thought of little else but him. My heart quickened at the sound of his carriage drawing up outside, and his footstep approaching our door. In the hours we spent together, in our discourse, debate, and exchange of thoughts and feelings, I experienced a kind of complete happiness, which had, until that time, been foreign to me.

I had given up the idea of marriage long ago, and had found contentment in my single status; but I could not help but think of marriage now. In Mr. Ashford, I saw grace and spirit united to great worth; his manners were equal to his heart and understanding. He was, in every respect, a man with whom I believed I could share my life long and happily. I loved him. I loved him! How he felt about me, however, was a matter still in question.

He had, in our time together, shewn every proof of his pleasure in my acquaintance; I had little—scarcely any—doubt in my mind that his feelings matched my own. But of those feelings he had never spoken. I could hardly dare to raise the subject myself; he was, after all, a gentleman of great fortune and heir to a baronetcy, whereas I was a woman of three-and-thirty, with nothing to recommend me but a wit he seemed to admire. If indeed he thought of me in any way stronger than friendship, I could not be certain.

One afternoon, as we sat alone together on an old wooden bench in my back garden, with no thought but to enjoy each other's company and the beauty of the day, Mr. Ashford said, "What do you like most about writing, Miss Austen?"

"Creating my own world, I suppose, filled with people who must think and act and speak as I tell them to." His very proximity, as he sat beside me, made my heart beat more rapidly than usual and brought a thrilled flush to my countenance, which I hoped he would attribute to the sun's warmth.

"In other words, playing God."

"Mr. Ashford, please. I am a clergyman's daughter."

He laughed. "Which sister is based on you? Elinor or Marianne?"

"Neither one, I should think."

"Oh come now. Surely every author and authoress reveals a measure of their own thoughts and feelings through their characters."

"Perhaps I do, a bit. I think of Elinor as the model of goodness, discretion and self-control, the way every one *should* think and act, in any given circumstance. Many times since her creation, when I have faced an important decision, I have found myself asking: What would Elinor do?"

"And does Elinor answer?" enquired he, amused.

"She does. She is an infallible guide to correct and prudent behaviour."

"But surely you do not think of Elinor as perfect," said he. "She is practical, she is admirable, she governs her emotions beautifully. But can any one truly live their life that way? Do not you find something very appealing in Marianne's openness and enthusiasm for life?"

"Yes. Although at times, Marianne carries things too far."

"But she has such spirit and fire! If I were to fall in love, sense be damned! I—" Here he caught himself, paused, and glanced away, as if struggling to check his feelings.

He had opened the door. I saw no reason not to run through it. "If I were to fall in love," I replied, with rising emotion, "I would want to act as Marianne does."

He turned to face me with a fervent nod, sliding closer to me on the bench. "Yes. To speak spontaneously."

"From the heart."

"To feel love beyond reason."

"All wonder and amazement."

"An all-consuming passion!"

"Yes."

"Yes!"

Our gazes locked. I saw deep, ardent affection in his eyes. Was this the moment? I wondered, my heart beating so wildly, I thought surely he must be able to see and hear its pounding. Was he about to say that he loved me? Did he intend to kiss me? Would he ask me to marry him?

But all at once, to my dismay, his countenance clouded over, and he drew back, colouring slightly. A brief, awkward silence ensued in which he seemed distracted and agitated. At last, he said: "In your novel, you express those feelings very well."

My cheeks grew warm with disappointment. I hardly know what I said in reply. I was astonished at myself. For the first time in many years, I had desired—nay, I had longed for—a man to kiss me.

Chapter Twelve

ake care, Jane!" said Cassandra the next morning. "You must wrap each dish full round with the gauze, or it will never survive the journey."

"I thought I had," said I, quickly rewrapping the dish in question.

"To what do we owe this distracted air?" asked my sister. "Not to your book, I think."

I placed the wrapped dish in the crate and buried my face in my hands, struggling to contain the wealth of emotions coursing through me. "Oh, Cassandra!" I cried at length, throwing out my arms wide, "How can I tell you what I feel? I want to take the entire world in my arms and embrace it! I think—I think I am in love!"

I seized Cassandra by the hands and spun her in circles around the dining-room, laughing, until we careened into a chair and sent it crashing to the floor, which provoked further bursts of laughter.

"I have never known a man who is Mr. Ashford's equal!" said I, as I stopped to right the fallen chair, and to catch my breath. "In my eyes, he is perfection. From the first moment we met, I felt such a connection between us, I can scarcely describe it."

"I am so happy for you," cried Cassandra. "He is, indeed, a most *engaging* man." The words had no sooner left her lips than she let out another laugh. "Pray, do not keep me in suspense another moment. Tell me all, and quickly. Are you engaged?"

"Engaged? Do not be silly. Things have not progressed with *that* degree of rapidity. We have been together less than three weeks."

"Yes, but when feeling and inclination are in harmony, people have been known to reach an understanding in a shorter time than that. Has he said that he loves you?"

"He has not said the words. I believe he was on the point of it yesterday when we were in the garden, but he lost his nerve." My smile faded as a sudden, niggling voice of caution called from deep within me. I sank into a chair. "The truth is, as much as *I* feel for him, I am by no means assured of his regard for *me*."

"Oh, but Mr. Ashford loves you, of that I am certain."

"I cannot be so sure. In the last few days especially, there have been moments when he seemed distracted, and at times even melancholy."

"I have noticed that, as well. Perhaps he has been concerned with business matters, or received an unsettling letter from his father or sister."

"That is what I thought, but he does not seem to wish to speak of it, so I have not enquired further. His family, you know, may not approve of his forming an attachment with me," I added with a frown.

"There is that possibility. But he is a man of four-and-thirty who can surely make his own decisions. He has been here nearly every day, Jane, for more than a fortnight. That alone speaks highly of his regard for you. His manners, his attention and respect, his delight in every thing you think and say and do, all bespeak his interest and affection; and if that were not enough, I have witnessed what you could not. I have seen the look in his eyes as he listens to you read aloud. It is a glowing look, filled with such admiration and esteem, that I have felt certain for some days now that he is as much in love with you, as you are with him."

A burst of joy and hope coursed through me at her pronouncement. "I pray that you are right. But I am growing most anxious. We cannot correspond unless we are engaged."

"Let us pray, then, that he declares himself before he leaves Southampton."

I sighed. "That does not leave much time. He departs to-morrow."

At eleven o'clock the following morning, when Mr. Ashford called, he seemed distracted. He expressed his regret that he had only an hour remaining before his departure, and suggested that we take a walk. I quickly donned my pelisse.[27]

As we passed the castle in the tiny open square—a fantastic edifice built by the Marquis of Landsdowne, of a style and shape far too large for the contracted space in which it stood—we were treated to the sight of the Marchioness's phaeton[28] as it departed on an outing. The equipage was drawn by eight

---

[27] A coat worn by women over the thin frocks of the time, usually about three-quarter length and buttoning in front.

[28] A phaeton was a light-weight, four-wheeled open carriage; with four horses, it was the sports car of the time. Eight horses was unusual, and an affectation of the very wealthy.

little ponies, each matched pair decreasing in size and becoming lighter in colour, through all the shades of brown from dark to light, as it was placed farther away from the carriage.

"My nephew Edward loves to see these horses when he comes to visit," said I, as we watched the boyish postilions drive the phaeton away. "He says it is like something out of a fairy tale."

"It is indeed. Would that we could all drive ponies that are perfect, and live in a fairy tale." As we walked on, he added, with a brief glance at me, "I am sorry to leave this place. I shall miss our daily readings."

"As shall I."

"Every morning I shall awake and wonder: what has become of the Dashwood sisters? What new torments will Miss Austen put them through to-day?" His smile seemed forced, and his voice and eyes held a rather grim and subdued look, which caused me much alarm.

"We shall be moving, ourselves, soon," said I, hoping to prompt him into a discussion regarding a possible correspondence.

"But not straight to Chawton?"

"No, the cottage there will not be ready until July. We plan to first join my mother at Steventon for a few weeks, and from there to my brother Edward's estate at Godmersham."

He nodded. We walked on for some minutes in silence, as my anxiety grew. He seemed equally agitated, as if turning over a matter of some great importance in his mind. At last he said: "Miss Austen. There is something I must speak to you about."

My imagination leapt forward, anticipating his next words. "Yes?" said I, hoping not to appear too eager.

"These past few weeks have—we have only been acquainted a short time, and yet—"

"It is true that our acquaintance is not of long standing."

"There is something which I should have—you do know that my family estate is in Derbyshire?"

"You have mentioned it." My heart pounded. I knew little about his estate, only that it was large, and apparently very beautiful.

"And you know the Churchills. My friend, Charles Churchill."

"Charles Churchill?"

"Yes. My family, we have long been acquainted with—with that family. They reside some six miles to the west."

"To the west?" I repeated uncertainly.

"Our fathers have been the best of friends for years."

"Your fathers?" Why was I idiotically repeating every thing he said, like a parrot? Why was he talking about their fathers, instead of asking for my hand in marriage?

"Exactly," said he. "And you see—what I mean to say, is that—"

At that moment, a carriage turned into the narrow street, four horses trotting smartly in our direction. I recognised the black, gleaming equipage with its family crest immediately; it belonged to Mr. Ashford. We stopped in surprise as the driver pulled up beside us. Mr. Churchill, seated inside, called out from the open window:

"Ashford! There you are. We have been all over town look-ing for you."

"Why?" Mr. Ashford glanced at his pocket watch. "It is not half past eleven. I promised to meet you at noon."

"What? No! We said *nine*."

Maria Churchill poked her head out. "We have been packed and ready all morning. We could not imagine what had be-come of you!" Nodding in my direction, she added: "Good-bye, Miss Austen."

"Good-bye," I echoed softly, with mounting apprehension. Was this to be *our* good-bye? This enigmatic conversation, which had barely begun? Would I never see Mr. Ashford again?

"Forgive me," said Mr. Ashford in some confusion, a comment which seemed to be directed at both the Churchills and myself.

"No matter," replied Mr. Churchill, with a farewell wave in my direction, as the postilion opened the coach door and pulled down the steps, "but do come, Ashford. All your luggage is on board with ours, and we are most anxious to get underway."

"I so long to go home!" cried Maria. "We have a long journey ahead of us. Do not keep us waiting another instant!"

Mr. Ashford turned to me with a look of intense frustration. "Forgive me," said he again, with a formal bow. "I shall write to you." With reluctance, he climbed aboard, the door slammed shut, and I watched in speechless dismay as the carriage rumbled off down the street.

Chapter Thirteen

⁓⧂ ⧁⁓

"It is cruel to leave me in such suspense," said Cassandra unhappily, as we folded linens into a packing box. "If you will not give me new pages of your book to read, at least satisfy my curiosity, as it has been many years since I read that story, and this version is very different. Why did Edward not declare his love for Elinor before he left Norland? Why was he so reticent to speak?"

"I cannot tell you."

"Cannot? Or will not?"

"I cannot tell you," said I, "because I do not know."

In the four days since Mr. Ashford's departure from Southampton, I had found myself unable to write a word. I had made the attempt. I had read over my old copy of *Sense and Sensibility,* seeking sections which I might alter or copy out, but nothing pleased me, and page after page found their way into the fire. I pored over the new chapters I had recently written, which I *believed* to be an improvement over my earlier effort, but the characters and the story's plot had, of a sudden, become an enigma to me. I felt I did not know or understand Edward, in particular; and Willoughby, who was designed to be a charming rascal, had become so appealing to me of late, that I could not bear to let him break poor Marianne's heart.

"But you *must* know," cried Cassandra. "It is your story. They are your characters. You invented them."

"I did. I had *intended* for Edward's reticence to stem from the knowledge that his mother will disinherit him if he marries any one of whom she does not approve. But the more I have written of Elinor and Edward, the more I think that is not enough. A man of Edward's character and principles would not care about the money, and he would never allow his mother to dictate his choice in a wife. To keep *true* lovers apart, I believe the reason must go far deeper. But what it is—what it should be—" To my dismay, my voice broke, and I felt unexpected tears sting my eyes.

Cassandra turned to me with a look which bespoke her understanding of the pain that lay behind my words. She took me tenderly in her arms, and said, "Jane. Mr. Ashford would have declared himself the day he left, if he could have, I am sure of it. He was only prevented by the Churchills' inopportune arrival."

"I wish I could believe that."

She stepped back, took my hands in hers, and looked me calmly in the eye. "He seemed agitated, did he not? And distracted of mind, you said?"

"Yes."

"That was *exactly* Tom's behaviour when he proposed to me. Mr. Ashford meant to make an offer, I promise you."

"I do not think so. When I look back on our conversation, I cannot help but think that he did not have the aspect of a lover in his words or tone."

"Men are always nervous on such occasions, and find themselves robbed by the power of speech. Did you not find it so when Harris proposed to you?"

I nodded. "But that was typical behaviour for Harris. He was rather permanently robbed of the power of speech."

"It is *not* typical behaviour for Mr. Ashford, is it?"

"No."

"You see? Circumstances have only delayed events. You must be patient. He will write to you. He will come to visit us at Chawton, and every thing will be well in time." She sighed. "And then you will be engaged, and married, off to live on a grand estate in Derbyshire, and I—I shall lose my Jane, my dearest sister and companion, and I shall spend the rest of my days living with mamma and Martha, only to see you once or twice a year if I am very lucky."

She looked so forlorn, but said it with such a twinkle in her eyes, that I could not help but laugh. "Do not think so far ahead, dearest," said I, my spirits recovering. "It will be three long months before we are settled at Chawton, and we have only ten days left to enjoy our acquaintance here. So let us make the most of the bargain."

That very afternoon, we accepted an invitation from our neighbours, Mr. and Mrs. Smith, to a small musical party to be held the following evening, a party which proved to be unremarkable in and of itself, distinguished only by the shocking circumstances which followed.

As most of our clothes were already packed, Cassandra and

I were obliged to wear our second best gowns, a pretty pink muslin in my sister's case, the spotted blue in mine—the very same gown I had worn on our excursion to Netley Abbey, I reflected with a sad little twinge as I dressed.

We arrived, were pleasantly greeted, and shewn to the Smiths' drawing-room, where all the furniture had been removed and replaced with rows of chairs. At the appointed hour, when all the guests had been seated, an elegantly dressed woman made her way to the front, and, accompanied by a grand pianoforte, a harp, and a violoncello, sang very prettily for the better part of an hour.

Like many such parties, the company in attendance comprehended a great many people who had real taste for the performance, and a great many more who had none at all. I considered myself to be just musical enough to find true pleasure in the proceedings, although that enjoyment was somewhat diminished by an attitude on the part of the musicians themselves, who seemed to think that they were, in their own estimation, the first private performers in all of England.

"What a touching love song," whispered Cassandra, at the end of the first recital.

"It would have been more touching," I replied in a low voice, "had the performer not been so obviously singing to herself."

In one of my excursive glances about the room, I perceived a familiar face several rows to the fore: Mrs. Jenkins. I pointed her out to Cassandra, at which moment the lady herself turned and caught my eye, broke into an effusive smile, and began an urgent and quiet discourse with the attractive, finely dressed young woman seated next to her.

"Who is the girl she is talking to?" whispered Cassandra.

"I have no idea."

The mystery was solved when, at the concert's conclusion, Mrs. Jenkins marched through the crowd with the young woman in question upon her arm, and upon reaching us, called out, "Hallooo there, ladies! This is a piece of luck! I had no idea you were still in town, I thought you had long since left for the country, and I did so want you to meet my darling niece. Miss Austen, Miss Jane, may I present Miss Isabella Churchill."

"How do you do," said Isabella. A slender young woman of perhaps seventeen years of age, she was of middling height, with dark, stylishly arranged curls, a delicate porcelain complexion, and brown eyes which studied us with an air of self-importance. She appeared at first glance to be the epitome of a carefree young woman, untried by the stresses of life, accustomed to all the comforts and privileges that wealth, youth and beauty could provide.

We exchanged courtesies, but were prevented from further speech as Mrs. Jenkins went on, "Isabella was so disappointed that her recent illness caused her to miss out when her brother and his wife were in town, that I insisted she come down on her own as soon as her health improved. And what do you think, no sooner had we said good-bye to Charles and Maria, than a letter arrived from Isabella that she was right as rain again, and ready to take their place. And here she is! What do you think of her? Is she not the prettiest girl you have ever seen?"

Cassandra and I readily agreed that she was. I glanced at Isabella, expecting her to blush or protest, but she did neither; she only giggled and smiled demurely, as if accustomed to such praise.

"It is four years now since my dear, dear sister—Isabella and Charles's poor mother—passed on, leaving us all quite inconsolable, particularly Isabella," said Mrs. Jenkins.

At this, the smile left Isabella's face, and she endeavoured to appear inconsolable.

"It is a hard, hard thing to lose one's mother at such a young age," continued Mrs. Jenkins, "and having no children of my own, I was only too happy to provide solace where ever I could. Why, I do believe Isabella and I are as close to-day as any mother and daughter could be. Do not you agree, Isabella?"

"Indeed I do, Aunt Jenkins," said Isabella, with a polite smile.

"Ladies, you simply must join us for tea tomorrow," cried Mrs. Jenkins, "so you can get better acquainted. It may be the last time I see you for a great, great while! I will not take no for an answer."

Feeling that we had little choice in the matter, we graciously accepted her invitation.

The next afternoon, as promised, found us seated in Mrs. Jenkins's parlour around her tea service, awaiting a break in that lady's enthusiastic conversation, to utter a word.

"Did you enjoy the concert last night, Miss Isabella?" I asked, when Mrs. Jenkins briefly paused between soliloquies to sip her tea.

"Oh yes! Very much," replied Isabella.

"Isabella loves music," said Mrs. Jenkins. "She has just taken up the pianoforte again. I expect she will become a proficient in no time."

"I have always found the pianoforte a most enjoyable pursuit," said I.

"It might be more enjoyable," said Isabella in a petulant

tone, "if only it did not require so many *hours* and *hours* of practice."

"But the practice itself is a great part of the pleasure, is it not?" was my reply.

Isabella looked at me blankly. "Is it?"

"Isabella adores art as well," declared Mrs. Jenkins. "She had a private tutor for years, of course, and studied both drawing and painting. She has *dozens* of unfinished sketches with such promise, they would take your breath away."

"I would love to see them," said Cassandra courteously.

"You should have brought one or two of them with you, my dear," said Mrs. Jenkins. "You could have worked on them here."

"Oh! No! I have given up art, Aunt Jenkins. It was not for me. I am far too busy these days calling on friends, to bother with a pencil or water-colours. And are we not going to London again, soon? The season begins next month."

"So it does!" cried Mrs. Jenkins. "I have a house there, you know, in Berkeley Square. Isabella has stayed with me many times, and we always have such a grand time. Do you remember that wonderful play we saw last year, Isabella?"

"Which one, aunt? We saw so many."

"I was thinking of *King John*."

"Oh, yes! With Sarah Siddons playing Constance, the bereaved mother! Was she not to *die* for?"

"To die for?" repeated Mrs. Jenkins. "The *bereaved* mother!" Whereupon the two burst into laughter. "Isabella! I declare! Is she not the world's cleverest girl?"

Cassandra agreed that she was. I nodded and smiled, striving to appear sincere.

"I think London the most exciting place on earth," cried Isabella, her eyes shining. "I would live there if I could."

"Last year was particularly memorable, of course," added Mrs. Jenkins, wiping away happy tears, "since it followed Isabella's coming out."

"You came out in London, Miss Churchill?" I enquired. "How wonderful that must have been."

"Well, no. I wanted to, *desperately,* of course," said Isabella. "To be presented with the other debutantes to the sovereign at St. James, oh! It would have been the most thrilling moment of my life! But papa would not hear of it. He said there was no point in wasting money on a London season, when I was already engaged."

"Still, you had a very nice ball at home to mark the occasion," said Mrs. Jenkins consolingly. "I do hope you will not give up our trips to London once you are married, Isabella."

"Oh! I would not think of it, aunt."

"Are you to be married, Miss Churchill?" I enquired.

"Why, yes," answered Isabella, in a tone which implied that every one in the world should be well acquainted with the fact.

"We expect the date to be set within the year," said Mrs. Jenkins.

"I know that I am very fortunate," said Isabella, in a matter-of-fact tone. "He is a most honourable man."

"If you met a thousand men," said Mrs. Jenkins, "you could not find one more decent or more honourable than Mr. Ashford."

Cassandra and I both froze with surprise at the same moment. "Mr. Ashford?" repeated Cassandra.

"Yes," nodded Isabella, with a heavy sigh. "My friends *will* keep remarking that he is *very* old, and it is true, for he is *twice* my age, and old enough to be my father. But I remind myself that he has always treated me with the highest regard and affection."

"Some of the world's most successful marriages were founded on an age disparity far greater than yours, my dear," said Mrs. Jenkins.

"He *is* still in good looks," admitted Isabella, "for an *older* man. I can only hope that he will not grow infirm *too* soon."

My sister and I sat in stunned disbelief. My heart pounded; I saw that the colour had drained from Cassandra's face, and knew that I must look ghostly pale as well. At last I managed, in a halting voice: "Surely you are not speaking of Mr. Frederick Ashford? Of Pembroke Hall, in Derbyshire?"

"Why, indeed I am, Miss Jane," replied Isabella. "Do you know him?"

"I—we—we are a little acquainted with that gentleman," said I. "We had the pleasure of meeting him again at your aunt's house, just this past month."

"Why, that is so!" cried Mrs. Jenkins. "Dear me, I had quite forgotten! Then you know what a fine man Mr. Ashford is, and why her family is so *delighted* in the match, for he is so intelligent, so modest and unassuming, without a trace of arrogance, qualities not often found in a man of title, with so large a fortune. Think of it! When the title and property pass from father to son, our Isabella will be Lady Ashford, mistress of the largest estate in all of Derbyshire. Such a grand property, such an excellent house and such beautiful gardens, and his woods! In all my travels, I have not seen such timber any where!"

"No one really cares about *timber*, do they?" said Isabella. "And there are far too many gardens for my taste, although Mr. Ashford *does* seem to think so highly of them. Miss Jane, are you unwell?"

"I am fine, thank you," said I, although it had suddenly become difficult to breathe.

Cassandra, recovering her powers of speech, said, "My sister will not mention it, but in fact, she has not been well of late, and I see that she needs some air. If you will please excuse us, Mrs. Jenkins, Miss Churchill, we will take our leave. Thank you so much for the tea."

Chapter Fourteen

⁓⸱⸰⸱⁓

*M*r. Ashford *engaged?*" I cried with great emotion, when we were safely on the street and on our way home. "To *Isabella Churchill?* It cannot be true!"

"It must be true," said Cassandra gravely. "Mrs. Jenkins backed up every word."

"*How* could he do this? I do not understand! Not six days ago, he was here, calling on *me,* giving rise to *my* hopes that—" I was so stunned, I could not go on.

"Oh, Jane, Jane. I am so very sorry."

I burst into tears. For some moments, I was too consumed by shock and grief to speak. "*Why* did he not tell me?" I cried, at length, as I withdrew my handkerchief from my reticule and tried to stem my flow of tears. "There was, apparently, nothing secretive about their engagement. Isabella seemed to think that all the world knew."

"Perhaps that is what he was attempting, with such

difficulty, to explain on the morning of his departure from Southampton."

"If so, his admission came many months too late. He should have told me the truth of his circumstances the very first day we met, at Lyme."

"We cannot be certain, Jane, that he was engaged when you met at Lyme. Isabella said that she was engaged last year, at her coming out; his offer to her may have come shortly before. You went to Lyme nearly two years ago."

"That is true," said I, softening a bit. Perhaps Mr. Ashford *had* been unattached when we first met. But anger and mortification soon returned full force. "Still, it does not excuse his behaviour in the past few weeks!"

"No. In this, he has treated you very ill."

Pain seared through my chest, as I struggled to hold fresh tears at bay. "It seems too impossible to believe! Why would a man like Mr. Ashford choose a girl like Isabella? They are so unlike. Can he truly love her?"

"I do not see how. And it seems clear that she does not love him."

"She called him old. Old! Mr. Ashford, a man of four-and-thirty, and one of the most handsome, fit and virile men I have ever met!"

"I found that quite offensive," admitted Cassandra, "particularly since he is two years *younger* than myself."

"Perhaps he had reached an age when he was made to feel he must marry, to produce an heir."

"That is likely."

"But why, in that event, choose Isabella?"

"She is the sister of his best friend. The family is well-known to him. Perhaps he was infatuated by her youth and beauty."

"This must explain the strange look I saw pass between Charles and Maria on several occasions," I cried. "They knew of his engagement, and yet observed his attentions to me. Why did they not say any thing?"

"Mr. Ashford is the son of a baronet, and engaged to their sister. They would not dare say any thing which might offend him."

"Oh! It is too horrible! To think that I fell in love with him! To learn, in this manner, that he is not at all the man I thought he was!"

"I do not think we were completely deceived in him," said Cassandra softly. "Mr. Ashford seemed to me an honourable man. You said yourself that you could not be certain of his feelings for you. I am the one who insisted he was in love. Perhaps he *did* come to us only in friendship. I still believe his regard for you was sincere."

"Sincere? How can you call him sincere, or a man of honour?" I cried. "What man of honour would call on a woman day after day, affecting a deep interest in her, and cultivating an atmosphere in which she would come to feel affection for him, when he was already promised to another? No; I would not call Mr. Ashford sincere. Clearly, he is adept at presenting one face to the world, while all the time shielding his true nature from view. He is nothing but a blackguard and a villain. I was only a dalliance, an amusement to occupy his time while he was in town."

"I cannot imagine that is so," said Cassandra. "Still, I find this very difficult to understand. It does not seem in Mr. Ashford's character to behave in this manner."

"Oh how I wish I could hate him! But—"

"You do not?"

"To be tied for life to that self-important girl—who is so

young and unaccomplished, and has no feelings for him—it is a travesty! Can they possibly be happy together? I think not. No, I cannot hate him. I feel sorry for him."

"I feel sorry for them both," said Cassandra, "and my heart bleeds for *you,* Jane."

"How could I let this happen? *How* could I have allowed myself to feel so much, and to be so deceived?"

"Do not berate yourself. *You* have done nothing wrong. His every word, every action *seemed* to speak of his intentions to you."

"If any one should find out, I would die of shame."

Cassandra took my hand and squeezed it tightly. "We shall never mention his name again."

Misery, I discovered, is a great inducement to art.

Whereas my previous confusion and sadness had inhibited my creativity, now my ability to write returned with a vengeance. Never before had I felt such a burning desire, nay, a *requirement* to put pen to paper. For days, I wrote in a blind rage, pausing only when need overcame me to eat or drink or sleep.

No longer did I feel any compulsion to soften my character of Willoughby. The world, I had been reminded, was not fair where love was concerned, and never would be. No matter that Marianne loved her Willoughby deeply, no matter that her heart would be broken. I could paint him as a cad and rascal, bereft of conscience, ruled by selfish interests, and be justified. When he married another woman, Marianne could suffer all the pain of rejection and humiliation that I was now feeling.

Of Edward and Elinor's fate, I experienced a similar awakening. At last, I knew what terrible secret Edward harboured, which kept him from declaring his love to her.

"Good God!" cried Cassandra, when she had finished

reading the newest chapters of my book, in which I added two brand-new and quite unlikeable characters, the Steele sisters. "This secret engagement of four years standing, which you have introduced between Edward and Miss Lucy Steele—"

"Do not you think it a brilliant and inspired touch?"

"I do," agreed Cassandra, "but it is so—"

"Sad? Infuriating? Familiar? A case of life begetting art?"

"I was going to say dark. Your story is much darker than before."

"Darker fits my mood," I replied.

A few days before we removed from Southampton, a letter arrived for me. I recognised the handwriting at once as Mr. Ashford's, and, indeed, the direction indicated that it came from Pembroke Hall, Derbyshire. Whereas I might have once received such a missive with great joy, the sight of it now produced only pain and sickness of heart, followed by coolness and resolve.

"I beg your pardon," said I, as I turned to the postman and handed the letter back, "but there must be some mistake. This was not meant for me. Please return it to sender."

"Yes, Miss," replied the postman, as he took the offending letter and disappeared down the street.

"Whatever possessed you to send it back?" cried Cassandra, when she heard what I had done. "Perhaps he meant to offer an explanation for what has passed. Were you not interested in what he had to say?"

"Not at all," said I vehemently. "I know the truth already, and however prettily he chuses to word his explanation, it can make no difference. He is bound to another, that is a fact. He will marry her, of that we have no doubt. What can he offer me now, but apologies and a promise of friendship—which would, after the deep attachment I have felt, be quite impossible. No;

if my heart is ever to mend, if my mind is ever to be clear again, I must go back to what I was before I met Mr. Ashford, and banish him from my thoughts."

"I applaud your strength and resolve, dearest," said Cassandra, her expression replete with sympathy and kindness, "but not to *think* of some one for whom you have embraced such deep feelings, *that* is easier said than done."

She spoke the truth; but what other course was open to me? Indeed, not five minutes later, as I was engaged in assembling several dozen new manuscript pages into a sort of book, and sewing the seam to bind them, Mr. Ashford's voice, and his pretty words from the preceding weeks, kept repeating in my head: *"Your work is charming and witty and romantic—in a style entirely new—I have never read or heard any thing quite like it before—You shall be published; you must be."*

Was it all just idle flattery? I wondered. He had seemed so sincere in his praise. Well, I thought, in a sudden fit of temper, there is one way to find out. It would be a long while before *Sense and Sensibility* was finished, but I did have another book, complete, which *should* have been published years ago.

I picked up my pen, deciding, at that very instant, to address a subject which had been plaguing me for some time. Preserving my anonymity by adopting the name "Mrs. Ashton Dennis," I dashed off the following letter to the publisher, Crosby & Co., in London:

Wednesday 5 April 1809

Gentlemen

In the Spring of the year 1803 a MS. Novel in 2 vol. entitled Susan *was sold to you by a Gentleman of the name of Seymour, & the purchase money £10 rec'd at the same time. Six years have since passed, & this work of which I avow myself the Authoress, has never to the best of my knowledge, appeared in print, tho' an early publication was stipulated for at the time of Sale. I can only account for such an extraordinary circumstance by supposing the MS by some carelessness to have been lost; & if that was the case, am willing to supply you with another copy if you are disposed to avail yourselves of it, & will engage for no farther delay when it comes into your hands.—It will not be in my power from particular circumstances[29] to command this copy before the month of August, but then, if you accept my proposal, you may depend on receiving it. Be so good as to send me a line in answer, as soon as possible, as my stay in this place will not exceed a few days. Should no notice be taken of this address, I shall feel myself at liberty to secure the publication of my work, by applying elsewhere. I am*

Gentlemen &c &c

> *MAD—*

The initials of my fictitious signature formed a word which perfectly reflected my sentiments and state of mind of the day.

The reply, which arrived at the post office on the very morning of our departure, was as follows:

---

[29] Her copy of the manuscript was no doubt inaccessible, as the household was then packed up in expectation of their move from Southampton.

Saturday 8 April 1809

Madam

We have to acknowledge the receipt of your letter of the 5ᵗʰ inst. It is true that at the time mentioned we purchased of Mr. Seymour a MS. novel entitled Susan *and paid him for it the sum of 10£ for which we have his stamped receipt as a full consideration, but there was not any time stipulated for its publication, neither are we bound to publish it, Should you or anyone else, we shall take proceedings to stop the sale. The MS shall be yours for the same as we paid for it.*

For R. Crosby & Co
I am yours etc.
Richard Crosby

I was both saddened and infuriated by this correspondence. I could, in no way, produce the sum required to buy back my book. *Susan,* I realised, was dead to me; the sooner I finished *Sense and Sensibility,* the better.

But that task, I knew, could not be attended to for quite some time. All our furniture and possessions were now packed and boarded upon several wagons, which had, earlier that morning, embarked for Steventon, where they would be stored until the cottage at Chawton was ready. With a heavy heart, I knew that I must yet again say good-bye to independence, privacy, and writing, for a time.

Chapter Fifteen

ear, dear Steventon," I said, gazing out the window of my brother James's carriage, as we turned up the rutted drive towards the parsonage where I had passed all the happy days of my youth. Our drive through the familiar, rolling green hills and meadows, dotted with elms sprouting tiny new leaves of early spring, had inspired a much-needed sense of peace and quiet within me. "It will be good to be home again."

"Steventon is no longer *our* home," Cassandra reminded me. "It belongs to James now, and has for quite some time. *He* may be pleased to host us, but I am not so assured of a gracious welcome from Mary."

James's second wife, Mary (my brothers seemed to make a habit of marrying women named Mary), was sister to our dear friend Martha Lloyd, and had been a favourite of my mother's upon their marriage; but *this* Mary had proved herself to be a less than a congenial wife and stepmother. Mrs. James Austen seemed permanently scarred by her pock-marked face (ruined by smallpox) and by the knowledge that James had not only been married once before (his first wife had died, leaving a lovely daughter, Anna) but had also once had a passion for Eliza de Feuillide, now Henry's wife.

Although James seemed content enough in his marriage, I believe the rest of the family shared my opinion that Mary's jealous insecurities had rendered her irritatingly tactless, ill-tempered and overbearing, and she was less than kind to poor Anna. (Not to mention her greatest fault, in my eyes: she distrusted books, and read very few of them.) Still, despite complaints from my mother in her recent letters, I had *hoped* for a kind reception from Mary, considering that my mother had been ill, and had hoped to rest and recover in the home that had been *hers* for nearly four decades.

As we emerged from the coach, however, my mother swept through the front door and met us with open arms and a foreboding warning.

"How glad I am that you girls are here, at last! I have missed you so!" My mother embraced us in turn, wiping tears of joy from her eyes; then, glancing behind her to the open door, she added in a low voice, "Do not expect a hearty greeting from that Mary; she has been in a most foul temper all month."

At that moment my young nephew Edward burst through the door, with all the energy and enthusiasm that a youth of nine can possess. "Aunt Jane! Aunt Cassandra!" cried he, throwing himself into our arms. "Wait until you see the fort that I have built in the garden! It is a marvel, and a most wonderful place. You *shall* tell me stories while you are here, will you not, Aunt Jane? There is a bird in a tree outside my window, which I have never seen before. You must come, Aunt Jane, and tell me what kind of bird it is."[30]

I laughed, promising to tell him stories, and to look at the bird as soon as ever I could. My brother James welcomed us with his usual gravity, expressing concern that we had not been overtired by our journey. The other children soon appeared to greet us. Anna, at fifteen years of age, was a lovely, intelligent young woman of whom I was especially fond, and Caroline was a shy, darling little girl of four.

"La, and where are we to store all *this*," cried Mary disagreeably, as the wagons containing all our worldly possessions drew up behind us.

"It will only be for a few months, dear," said James. "I am certain we can find room in the shed and barn."

As my mother expressed her great appreciation for their help during this interim period in our lives, Mary turned to my sister and me with a frown, and said, "You shall have to share one of the attic rooms, as your mother has already taken over Anna's bed-room, and all the other rooms are spoken for."

"I am certain we shall be very comfortable," I replied. "We are indeed fortunate to have family to take us in so graciously."

"Look what Aunt Jane and I found in the meadow to-day," said Edward proudly at dinner that evening, as he opened his hand to reveal three tiny, empty robin eggshells for inspection.

"A fine addition to your collection, son," observed James.

"Put those filthy things away!" cried Mary, her nose

---

[30] James-Edward Austen-Leigh (called Edward by his family) was one of Jane Austen's favourite nephews. He inherited a great-aunt's estate in 1836, taking the name of "Leigh" in addition to Austen. He became a country clergyman, and later a vicar; in 1869 he wrote *A Memoir of Jane Austen*, the very first biography of the authoress.

wrinkling in disgust. "We are at table! Last week, it was a dead mouse. Before that, the most grotesque beetle. The things that little boys *will* play with, it is absolutely appalling."

Edward's face fell, and he quickly replaced the offending objects in his pocket. James fell silent and busied himself with the task of eating.

"The boy delights in nature," said I, with a reassuring smile to my nephew.

"He delights in *vexing* me," said Mary. (Turning now to her step-daughter) "Anna, stop frowning! And sit up straight when you eat."

"If she sits up any straighter," declared my mother, "she will be standing."

"I am only trying to make a lady of her, which is not easy, given her proclivity for indolence and self-indulgence."

Anna's face went scarlet with mortification at this statement; but before any of us could rush in to defend her (for Anna was, in fact, a very dutiful child, with a generous temper) Mary turned to Edward, who was just then serving himself from the dish of potatoes, and sternly cried, "*One* potato, Edward! There will not be enough to go around."

There seemed to be plenty of potatoes. Edward faltered, then dutifully put one of his potatoes back, as Mary turned to my mother, my sister and myself with a tight, sweet smile. "How long did you ladies think you might be staying?"

"I feel like an unwanted parcel," said I that evening, in the privacy of my mother's bed-room, as she sat softly weeping.

"We all do," replied Cassandra, unsmiling.

"Would it not be best if we went straight away to Godmersham, mamma?" I enquired. "Surely we would be more welcome there."

"If only we could," replied my mother, drying her eyes, "but I am not well enough to travel; my nerves would not be equal to the effort. I have been suffering from a fierce throbbing in my head of late, and six leeches a day for ten days together has done nothing to relieve me. I feel so languid, some mornings it is all I can do to climb out of bed; I fear for my liver. In my present state, even five minutes in a coach would probably be the death of me. So we must make the best of it, and remain here for another few weeks at least, I imagine. But a very, very hard thing it is, to stay where you are not wanted."

On Sunday morning, as Carolyn and Edward, attired in their best clothes, waited impatiently in the nursery for their mother to finish dressing in order to depart for church, I entertained their earnest request to tell them a story. Anna, on passing by the room and overhearing the other children's laughter, slipped in quietly to listen in the doorway. I quickly added a character of her name and description to the tale, which elicited from her a smile of quiet delight.

"When Anna opened her eyes, she thought herself in a great forest. But what seemed like trees were actually a bed of brilliant bellflowers. For the sorcerer's potion had worked its wonders, and Anna was now no bigger than a dragonfly."

Carolyn gasped. Edward laughed and shook his head. "Aunt Jane, that is impossible."

"All things are possible, Edward, if only you believe."

He fell silent for a moment, pondering that concept, and then enquired, "Do you mean to say, that if I believe in your story as you have told it, then it is as good as if it were true?"

"You understand my meaning precisely, Edward."

He smiled.

"When she saw that she was even smaller than a flower, was she frightened?" enquired Anna.

"She was too amazed to be frightened. Most amazing of all was the tiny fairy prince she saw reclining in the fold of a bright green leaf, as if it were a sofa. He was very handsome, with thick golden hair and dark blue eyes, precisely the colour of the bellflower which he wore as a cap. "*'Welcome to my kingdom,'* said he in a deep, soft voice. *'I am the Flower Prince. Will you join me in a cup of dandelion tea?' 'Join you in a cup of tea?'* enquired Anna in surprise. *'Would that be to drink it, or to swim in it?'*""

The children laughed. At that moment, their mother burst through the nursery door, dressed in her Sunday best, with a sour look on her face. "What is going on in here? What is all this laughter?"

"Aunt Jane is telling us a story," answered Edward, attempting, without success, to hide his smile.

"It is the Lord's day, not a day for stories and frivolity," declared Mary sternly. "Come now, children. Let us to church."

"But Aunt Jane has not finished," cried little Carolyn in dismay.

"I shall finish it at bed-time," I whispered solemnly, "I promise."

At church, I was delighted to see Alethea Bigg and her sister Elizabeth Heathcoate in attendance. After the service (at which my brother James delivered a very fine sermon), while Elizabeth dashed off after her son William, who was hurling stones over the rectory wall at the grazing cows, Cassandra and I chatted amiably with Alethea. She reassured us that Harris and his wife and children were doing well, and that her sister Catherine, who had been married the previous October, was quite content in her newly betrothed state.

"I am so pleased for them," said Cassandra.

"I cannot tell you how pleased *I* am that you two have returned to the neighbourhood," exclaimed Alethea, "even if it is only for a short time."

"The shorter the better," said I, "for Mary has made it plain that she does not wish us here."

"I always thought her a most disagreeable woman," replied Alethea. "I wish I could invite you to stay with us at Manydown, but Elizabeth leaves tomorrow to visit friends in Sussex, and my father and I depart not two days hence on a holiday of some weeks." All at once she let out a little gasp, and cried, "Oh! I have had the most inspired idea. You must both come away with papa and me!"

"Come away with you?" I replied in surprise. "Where are you going?"

"We are touring to the north; papa is resolved upon a sight-seeing party, while he is still well enough to make the journey. The furthest destination is to be a stay of a week's duration with my father's cousin, Mr. Lucian Morton, a clergyman who resides in Brimington, in Derbyshire. I have never met the man, nor has my father, since he lives such a great distance away, but papa is anxious to make the acquaintance. From all accounts, Mr. Morton is a very decent sort of person and lives in a beautiful part of the country. I am certain he would be delighted to have two more ladies among the party."

"Thank you for the kind offer, Alethea," said Cassandra, "but we have only just arrived at Steventon, and I would not like to leave my mother again. Jane, you go."

Although I was delighted by the idea of a sight-seeing journey to the north, a place I had never visited, the mention of

Derbyshire was all the provocation I needed to decline the invitation; it was impossible for me to hear the name of that county without thinking of Pembroke Hall, and its owner. I had no wish whatsoever to travel anywhere within proximity of that place.

"Alethea, this is a trip your father has planned, to be enjoyed with you alone. I would not think of imposing on your company."

"Imposing?" cried Alethea. "On the contrary; you would be doing me a favour if you come!" In a lowered voice, she added, "Try as my father might to call this journey a holiday, he cannot disguise his true intent. I know what he is about. He means to parade me in front of his eligible cousin, Mr. Morton. Having married off one spinster daughter to a respectable, older clergyman, he hopes to have a similar success with the other."

"I *am* sorry," said I with sympathy, well aware of the horrors of such a situation, recalling my parents' hopes for Cassandra and myself during our years at Bath. "But perhaps this Mr. Morton is a worthy gentleman, and you will like him, in which instance, you would surely not require *my* company."

"There is little chance of that, for he is forty years of age, has a good living, and yet has never married. There *must* be something wrong with a man, to remain so long unattached."

"Many good and amiable men chuse to marry later in life," said I, trying not to think of Mr. Ashford, who, until recently, I would have placed in that category, but now could only think of with disdain, "and you risk nothing by going, as you cannot be forced to marry him."

"No, but I shall be obliged to endure his company for several days at least. How much more pleasant it will be if you are there! The journey itself, just think of it, Jane!" Alethea clasped her hands rapturously, her eyes lighting up with excitement. "The places we shall see, the experiences we shall share! Oh, how I have dreaded this trip up until now—three weeks or more with my stodgy old father—but it need not be so. Please, Jane, save me from that fate, or I will surely go mad."

I could not say no to such a heartfelt plea. I was anxious to get away from Steventon, the idea of travelling with my dear friends was very appealing, and the stops along the way were of great interest to me. Although I would have preferred *any* final destination other than Derbyshire, I convinced myself that that county was large enough, that I would certainly be safe in making a brief visit to one of its smaller villages, without Mr. Ashford's perceiving me.

Our northward journey was perfectly free from accident or event. Our route lay through such charming places as Oxford, Blenheim, Warwick, Kenelworth and Birmingham, all of which we enjoyed exceedingly, taking in the main sights and enjoying generally good weather. The squire, although seven-and-sixty, and not as fit as my father had been at that age (and possessed of a rather loquacious and serious disposition), did have an enthusiasm for architecture and nature, and was most generous and solicitous of our comforts all the way. He insisted that we chuse our own dinners at the inns; as we traveled, he sat snoring in the opposite seat of the coach, while Alethea and I maintained a steady barrage of happy chatter.

Alethea was her energetic, amiable self, quick to find pleasure in every thing she saw and did, to praise that which she admired, and to poke fun at that which she found absurd. Our daily diversions worked wonders in improving my mental disposition; I soon banished all thoughts of my recent disappointment in a certain gentleman to the farthest corner of my mind, and enjoyed each new day with a purity of spirits and a willing laugh.

One sunny afternoon towards the end of the second week of our travels, as I gazed out the window with delight at the beautiful wooded land through which we were passing, the driver announced that we had just entered the county of Derbyshire. Alethea turned to me with quiet dread, and murmured, "Here we are at last. Soon I am to be thrown to the wolves."

As promised, the squire's cousin lived in a very pretty neighbourhood. We left the high road for the lane, and soon the parsonage came into view. The house itself was a modest edifice of brick, not overly large, surrounded by a green lawn and a laurel hedge. Our carriage stopped at the gate, and in a moment we were all out of the chaise and crossing the short gravel walk to the front door, where we were met by Mr. Morton.

A tall, heavy looking man of forty, Mr. Morton had beady, pale eyes in a round face, and an affected smile which revealed a row of very crooked teeth. He had become most dreadfully bald, and in compensation, he had combed forward several long, thin, curling clumps of brown and grey hair over his pate.

"Welcome, welcome, to my humble abode," said Mr. Morton, ushering us inside with an air of the utmost formal civility, as he directed our luggage to be sent up to particular apartments. "It is a great honour to make your acquaintance at last, squire," said he, shaking that man's hand effusively, "for I think that family connexions are the most important thing in the world. I am only too aware, squire, of your prominent position in Hampshire, of the size of your fortune, and the splendour of your estate, which fills me with silent awe. I have always thought it a great misfortune that we should have gone so many years without meeting, but as we are separated, in geographical location, by such a very great distance, it can certainly be understood. I trust your journey was not too unpleasant?"

All of this passed Mr. Morton's lips as we stood in the front hall, before introductions had yet been made. Alethea and I exchanged a private look of horror at the appearance and ostentatious manner of the man; it was all we could do not to laugh.

Chapter Sixteen

⁓❧ ❧⁓

The squire assured Mr. Morton that our journey had been most satisfactory, in a speech which would, I fear, have been as long-winded as that of his cousin, had not Mr. Morton interrupted him to introduce himself to Alethea and myself.

"Miss Alethea," said he, with an enthusiastic bow, "it is indeed a pleasure. I have heard much of your beauty from your father's letters, and I see that, in this instance, fame has not fallen short of the truth." Bowing to me next, he added, "And may I extend the same compliments to you, Miss Austen, for the squire was good enough to write and inform me of your coming, and I find his tributes to you were of equal merit. Be assured that any friend of my cousin's is a friend of mine, and I am delighted to make your acquaintance; if there is any thing, however small, which I can do to make your stay here more comfortable, please do not hesitate to mention it."

I thanked Mr. Morton most sincerely for his kindness, after

which he invited us to sit before the fire in his parlour and take some refreshment.

As the serving-maid brought in the tea-set, Mr. Morton gave us a detailed account of every article of furniture in the room, calling our particular attention to a mahogany sideboard, a piece of rather alarming size and no great beauty. "I purchased it myself at an auction, at far less expense than one might imagine," said he with great pride, "and believe it will be a very useful piece. Why, my neighbour, the Lady Cordelia Delacroix—a most affable and condescending woman of great means and property, who resides at Bretton Hall, not two miles from here, where I have been invited *twice* to tea—her ladyship, upon viewing the table, expressed her opinion of its fine workmanship and durability, and insisted that I had made a very good bargain."

I glanced at the squire, seeking to detect even the briefest smile on his countenance, to reflect his recognition of the absurdity of the man before us, but he seemed quite insensible of it; rather, he expressed his admiration for the good proportion of the room, its aspect and sturdiness of build, and asked several probing questions concerning the structure of the parsonage, a subject to which our host replied with the greatest enthusiasm. For the next three-quarters of an hour, Alethea and I sat in silent wonder as the two men avidly discussed the minute architectural details of the rectory and church, as well as every other building, barn and cottage in the parish, with the possible exception of a shed or two, and several privies.

Following this discourse, Mr. Morton led us on a very complete tour of the house, which, although an edifice of rather compact size, seemed very neat and comfortable, and held many delights for him.

"You have every thing here that one could want in a house," declared the squire, "although I believe it could be even further improved by the warmth that a *woman's* touch would provide."

"Yes, indeed, squire," said Mr. Morton, "I have given a great deal of thought to that very subject, and it is a matter of vital interest to me. I think it a right thing for every clergyman to set the example of matrimony in his parish, *if* he is in easy circumstances; which, until recently, was not the case in *my* instance, owing to the small living I had been afforded. But to my great good fortune, I have just been offered the living of the neighbouring parish of Oxcroth, as well, and with this additional income, I find I am now, at last, in a position to offer a wife a most desirable situation."

"That you are," agreed the squire. "I have only just had the pleasure of seeing my daughter Catherine married to a good clergyman like yourself, and I cannot begin to tell you what happiness *that* union has brought the family." Alethea turned to her father, secretly imploringly him, with the most desperate face, not to pursue the topic further; but the squire did not appear to notice. "Alethea quite runs the household now," he went on, "and she is such an excellent manager, I declare any man would be fortunate to have her."

Alethea's countenance flushed crimson, and she closed her eyes, as if willing herself to disappear on the spot.

I said quickly, "After the confinement of the carriage, I would welcome an opportunity to stretch my legs in the open air, Mr. Morton. Might I entreat you to take us for a turn in your garden?"

The idea was met with a most enthusiastic response. Alethea, with a glance that implored me to help her put as much space as possible between herself and Mr. Morton, firmly linked her arm through her father's, so that I was obliged to walk with our host.

"I tend to the cultivation of the garden myself," said Mr. Morton, as we strolled the many well-tended paths and cross walks, "which, I believe, is one of life's most respectable plea-sures, and a most healthful occupation." Without pausing to allow us to utter a syllable of the praise he seemed to be seek-ing, he pointed out each shrub and tree with great self-satisfaction. "I planted every one of these roses with my own hands, each selection made on the basis of its form, hardiness, colour and fragrance. I flatter myself to think that if you were to return in summer, you would, as my neighbours have re-marked on several occasions, be quite overwhelmed by the magnificence of the sight; the orderliness of the presentation, the multiple array of hues, the extensive number of blooms, and the delightful, sweet aromas which they engender, are enough to inspire awe in a person of even the most jaundiced disposition."

At the edge of the garden, Mr. Morton pointed out several fields dotted with distant trees. "That is the Camperdown elm, also known as *U. glabra camperdonii,* a variety of Wych elm. There are six elms in that clump alone," said he proudly (although I saw much to be pleased with, I could not be in such raptures as Mr. Morton expected the scene to inspire) "and there to the right, you will see three chestnuts and two oaks." He was keen to lead us around his meadow, but Ale-thea and the squire admitted that they were tired, and ex-pressed an interest in being shewn to their rooms, where they might rest before dinner.

Mr. Morton instantly and profusely apologized. "I alone must take the blame for your fatigue. I never should have taken you on such an extensive tour, at the very moment of your arrival, and the ladies wearing such delicate shoes! Watch your step, Miss Austen! There is a rather large pebble in your path."

Mr. Morton bent down and whisked away the offending stone, inadvertently, in the process, striking a squirrel squarely in the back. The creature froze in momentary astonishment, then scampered off. All the way back to the house, Mr. Morton could talk of nothing but his relief that he had not caused the poor animal's early demise.

"I pray that I will not be obliged to sit beside him at dinner," said Alethea, as we freshened up later, in the bed-chamber that we shared. "He is the most odious, tedious, ridiculous man that I have ever met."

"I think him quite amusing," I replied.

"Then *you* may sit beside him, and carry on the whole of the conversation. For my part, I intend to say nothing whatsoever, and appear as the most dull and uncaptivating female who ever lived."

"That may not work to your advantage," I teased, as I splashed water from the basin on my face. "He may prefer a woman who is the quiet type."

"Oh! I had not thought of that. But I cannot be rude, that would only upset papa."

"My dear Alethea, do not look so distressed. We are by no means assured that Mr. Morton is considering you as his future wife. Should he in fact make you an offer of marriage, you may simply refuse."

"But my *refusal,* I fear, would anger papa more than the *absence* of an offer. Oh! What am I to do?"

"You have only to be yourself, and leave the rest to providence."

"Providence can only take us so far. Sometimes we must help it along." Alethea was silent for some moments, and then said, "I have decided. I will endeavour to appear as politely *disagreeable* as possible, by making some counterpoint to every thing he says."

"You must do as you think best." Sitting down before the looking-glass, I settled my black velvet cap on my head, loosening a few short curls about my face. The effect was rather pleasing. I was no great beauty, I knew, but tonight, *some* might call me pretty. "As for me, I intend to study his every move and expression, and try to recall every word of his unique phraseology."

"Why ever would you wish to do that?"

"Because I delight in his absurdity. It has occurred to me that, one day, I might use Mr. Morton as a model for a character, in one of my books."

Alethea laughed. "That is so like you, Jane. Where the rest of us perceive only awkwardness in a person or circumstance, you see humour and possibility." She sat down on the chair beside me and clasped my hands in hers, regarding me with sincerity and affection. "Are you saying what I think—what I hope? After all these years of silence, have you taken up your pen again?"

I admitted that I had. "Please do not tell any one—I am certain nothing will come of it—but I have just begun revising *Sense and Sensibility*. When I met Mr. Morton, however, I could not help but think of *First Impressions*."

"Oh! Yes! I remember the clergyman in that book. He was most amusing."

"But he was never half so idiotic or insufferable as Mr. Morton."

"No, indeed, he was not!" We laughed for a long and merry

moment. "To see Mr. Morton on the page would be great fun," agreed Alethea. "But, Jane, you have not been honest with me, all these years, on a rather important point."

"What point is that?"

"You have always maintained that you did not copy the characters and places in your books from life, that they were all invented. I see, now, that the opposite is true."

"You could not be more wrong," I insisted. "Of the *places,* I admit, I have taken inspiration from homes I have seen. I patterned Mr. Darcy's estate at Eastham Park after a great house I saw at Kent, and I patterned Rosings and Hunsford after the manor house and parsonage at Chevening. But of the *people* in my books, my aim is to create, not to reproduce. Consider, if I did not, if the people I described should recognise themselves!"

"I do not think people would take so much offense as you seem to believe, Jane. They might, in fact, be flattered to find themselves in one of your books."

"Perhaps so, but I dread such an invasion of privacy. And there is more. Naturally, I have drawn fragments of personality and manner of speech from a variety of different people whom I have met, but I am far too *proud* of my creations to admit that they were only *Mrs. A,* or *Colonel B.*" With a wicked smile, I added, "However, in *this* instance, I may be forced to break my rule. For your Mr. Morton is simply *too* great a gem to use by halves."

"I must say, you keep a very fine carriage, squire," remarked Mr. Morton at dinner that evening, where we supped on pease-soup and roast fowl, and a wine of such indifferent quality and colour that I suspected it had been watered down by the cook. "I do not keep a carriage of my own, of course; I see not the necessity of such expense, every place in the village being so readily accessible on foot. When the need has arisen to attend an event at a greater distance than I can manage, I have had the good fortune to receive an offer of transport from Lady Cordelia Delacroix, who has condescended to allow me to join her in her carriage *three* times; I should say, *one* of her ladyship's carriages, rather, for she has several. Her equipages are among the most splendid of their kind in the county. Every Sunday, when I see her, I reaffirm my view, in perfect accordance with hers, that a chaise and four, elegantly liveried, is indeed *the* most comfortable and preferred mode of transport in the world."

"I myself have no affection for a chaise," said Alethea disagreeably, the twitch of a smile conveying, to me alone, the true intent behind her argument. "For extended travel, of course, we have no choice, but in truth, sir, they are so stuffy and confining. For shorter distances, I much prefer an open carriage."

"Oh, yes!" I cried. "A low phaeton with a nice little pair of ponies is always quaint, but I particularly adore a gig or curricle."

"A curricle is an entirely impracticable equipage," said Mr. Morton, "except for the very rich. Consider that, alone of the two-wheeled vehicles, it is built for *two* horses, instead of one, and its owner faces the difficulty and expense of finding a well-matched, high-quality pair of animals."

"Indeed," observed Squire Bigg-Wither, "riding about up high in the open air on two wheels has never seemed quite the thing to me."

"But I love sitting in the open," argued Alethea, "especially when riding in the country; and a curricle is so much more expedient than a coach."

"The chaise and four may wheel off with more grandeur," I agreed, "but it is a heavy and troublesome business. A curricle can pass a carriage with ease any day of the week."

"If speed were the only object, then you may have your curricle," said Mr. Morton. "But may I remind you that it holds no more than two occupants, who are both subjected to sun and wind and rain, not to mention a horrible dust. I can never keep a shirt clean when riding in an open carriage. All this cannot be pleasing to a lady."

"On the contrary, Mr. Morton," said Alethea, "every lady I have ever met finds the open carriage extremely pleasing."

"We would not think to go out in the rain," I added. "We are never out without a bonnet, sir, and we find the fresh air most exhilarating. As for the dirt and dust, its disadvantages are far outweighed by the attraction of the drive."

"I believe there are merits to both points of view," said Squire Bigg-Wither diplomatically, with a rather stern look at Alethea, "and may I suggest a vehicle that might be acceptable to all: the barouche."

"Ah yes," conceded Mr. Morton, "a barouche can make a fine compromise. For the power of two horses, you can accommodate a party of six; and with the top up, it affords a modicum of protection from the elements."

"I have nothing against a barouche," said Alethea sweetly, with an acquiescent smile for her father, "as long as I am allowed to sit on the box, for it is the only seat that affords a charming view."

With the arrival of dessert, in the form of a very decent apple pie, the discussion turned to Mr. Morton's library, a collection of some fifty or sixty volumes which, I had noticed earlier, were devoted to history and ecumenical studies, and were a source of some pride.

"Alethea fancies books, herself," said the squire. "Why, hardly a day goes by that I do not see her engaged in reading something or other."

"Oh, but I read only novels, papa," said Alethea quickly, "and have no taste or aptitude for the books which seem to interest Mr. Morton."

"It is true that I am devoted to the more serious works," agreed Mr. Morton, "but I admit, I have read one or two novels myself, and found them quite diverting. Have you read *Coelebs in Search of a Wife,* by Hannah More?"

"No," replied Alethea. "But I am sure Jane has; Jane has read every thing. She adores novels; why, she has even written several." No sooner had Alethea spoken the words than she gasped and covered her mouth, with a look of apology at me.

"Is that so, Miss Austen?" cried Mr. Morton, his pale eyes widening with interest as he turned to me. "Have you indeed written several novels?"

"Long ago," said I quickly. "It was a hobby of my youth. They remain unpublished. To-day I write only letters and the occasional poem."

"That is a great shame," said Mr. Morton. "I have always thought the story of my life would make a fascinating novel: the habits of life and character and enthusiasm of an English clergyman, beloved by his parish, renowned for his sensible views, and his sensitivity and expertise in the management of his duties. I would write the book myself—I flatter myself that I have some talent with the pen, for my parishioners tell me that my weekly sermons are exceedingly inspirational—but I feel a more objective view is preferred. Perhaps, Miss Austen, you could be convinced to take up the occupation again, and this could be your next work."

"I am flattered," I replied, trying to conceal my amusement

and dismay, "that you would consider trusting me with the story of your life, Mr. Morton. But I am afraid, sir, I must decline. I am certain I would not be equal to the task of portraying such a complex and interesting character as yourself."

For the next three days, Mr. Morton took us on a tour of every church and manor home and field and graveyard in his vicinity, with a long, slow drive past the celebrated Bretton Hall, home of Lady Delacroix. The area *was* lovely, and despite Mr. Morton's over-solicitous attention and ridiculous manner, I enjoyed myself. Events took a different turn, however, when, at breakfast on the morning of our fourth day, Mr. Morton suggested, to my great dismay, that we visit Pembroke Hall.

"Pembroke Hall is only a distance of some six miles," said he, "and if, during your visit to this county, I did not include it as a required point of destination, I would be remiss."

Alethea and the squire, who had heard of the place, expressed their wish to see it. I was distressed. I had no desire to go to Pembroke Hall; the possibility of meeting Mr. Ashford there filled me with alarm, and I could only imagine the discomfort and embarrassment it would cause *him*. I considered, for the briefest instant, telling Alethea about my relationship with Mr. Ashford; but I could not bear the thought. *No,* I decided, the less said about *that* affair, the better. As I could not speak openly of my objections, I was obliged to assume a disinclination to see the place.

"We have gone over so many great houses in the past fortnight," said I. "I would as well stay here, if you do not mind, and write a letter to my sister."

"Oh, but Pembroke Hall is one of the best houses in the

country!" cried Mr. Morton. "The grounds are splendid, and they have some excellent woods."

"You must come, Jane," insisted Alethea. "I have heard that Pembroke Hall is owned by a very great family, and is not be missed."

"To be sure," said Mr. Morton, "the family *is* very great; Sir Thomas Ashford is a baronet and a widower with two grown children, a son and daughter. Although I have not had the good fortune to become acquainted with them, I believe I am correct in saying that they are among the most gracious and condescending people of their class. Sir Thomas allows all persons whatsoever to see the mansion and the grounds every day in the year, Sundays not excepted, from ten in the morning until five in the afternoon. The humblest individual is not only shewn the whole, but the owner has expressly or- dered the waterworks to be played for every one without ex- ception. This generosity, I feel, is acting in the true spirit of great wealth and enlightened liberality."

"Do you happen to know," I enquired, striving to maintain a steadiness of voice, "if the family is currently in residence at this time?"

"No, I am sorry to say they are not," replied Mr. Morton with a sad shake of his head. "I have heard, on good authority, that they are all away in London."

Mr. Morton's reply filled me with relief. My fears being now removed, I was free to examine my others feelings in the matter. While it was true, I admitted, that any thing which served to remind me of Mr. Ashford (and a visit to the very place where he resided, must be placed at the top of the list of such evils) could only heighten that sense of mortification and outrage which I felt as a result of our association, at the same time, I could not deny that I felt a great deal of curiosity to see the house which he had spoken of several times, and which was of such interest to every body else.

Surely, I told myself, having travelled so far, it would be foolish not to see the place; for who knew when, or if, I would ever find myself in Derbyshire again? And surely, I insisted further, I was not so weak of spirit, that I should tremble at the idea of passing a few hours at the house and gardens of a family who would themselves be absent, no matter that I had been injured by a member of that family in the past.

I made no further objection. And so it was, that within the hour, our foursome boarded the squire's carriage and departed in the direction of Pembroke Hall.

Chapter Seventeen

H̲ere we are!" cried Mr. Morton, as we turned into a winding road on the outskirts of a very large, forested park. "You see before you only the farthest reaches of Pembroke woods, which, as you will discover, are trees so perfectly formed, and so beautifully situated, that human praise cannot do them justice."

I had told myself, en route, that Pembroke Hall and its woods could, in no way, be superior to my brother's estate at Godmersham, or any of the other great houses and groves of trees that I had seen. But as we drove on, I found, for the first time since meeting Mr. Morton, that his assessment did not exceed the truth. The woods through which we passed, which extended for more than a mile, projected an extremely regal and harmonious beauty which delighted the eye, and I could not help but admire every picturesque landscape and remarkable point of view.

After some time, the woods ended and we reached a hilltop,

from which we gained our first sight of Pembroke Hall in the distance. I heard Alethea gasp, and found myself staring in amazement, my preconceived notions falling away. The scene before me was far grander than any thing I could have imagined. We gazed upon a wide, delightful valley, scattered with trees, through which wound a wide stream, which was crossed by a gracefully arching stone bridge. Far beyond stood an immense Palladian edifice of gleaming white stone, with an extensive wing branching out on one side. Behind the house and all along its length, rose a steeply wooded hillside.

"Good God! That is the largest house I have ever seen!" cried Alethea.

"Indeed. It is a most remarkable piece of architecture and landscape," said the squire in amazement.

"I have never, in all my life," said I, "seen a place where natural beauty has so perfectly coincided with an exquisite taste."

Mr. Morton's observations, which I shall not repeat, were somewhat more lengthy and redundant.

Upon descending the hill, we crossed the bridge and drove to the front entrance, where we applied to see the house. We were admitted into the front hall and, after a short wait, the housekeeper appeared. She was a grey-haired, respectable-looking woman, neat in appearance, who greeted us with great civility and not an ounce of pretension.

"Please be so good as to follow me," said she.

The very thought that I stood inside Mr. Ashford's house, and that it was such a great house indeed, sent my spirits into a flutter, in which both pain and confusion bore an equal share. As we proceeded through the north corridor into a very large and ornate hall, I caught my breath in wonder. The floor was intricately laid in marble mosaic, and the high, upper walls and ceiling were painted with exquisite murals. A long marble staircase, carpeted in red and framed by gilded banisters, led up to the living quarters above.

All at once an idea struck me, and I stood frozen to the spot, lost in thought, only hazily aware that the housekeeper had begun her discourse. *This house,* I thought with sudden excitement, *this was the sort of residence Mr. Darcy should live in!* I was thinking, of course, of *First Impressions,* in which I had alluded to Darcy's estate at Eastham Park, Kent, several times; he had invited Elizabeth there while she was visiting her aunt and uncle Gardiner. I had described a pleasing edifice, worthy of its owner's pride, or so I had thought at the time of its creation. Now I saw that I was wrong.

Mr. Darcy should never live in the county of Kent at all, I thought, all at once extremely pleased that I had come. *He must reside in Derbyshire. And his grand estate should never be called any thing so prosaic and pedestrian as Eastham Park. I should call it—I should call it—*I glanced up at the Ashford coat of arms, which was emblazoned in gold and marble above an arched doorway, with the inscription: Pembroke Hall, 1626. I smiled.

I should call it Pemberley.[31]

"Sir Reginald Ashford built the great house in 1626." The housekeeper's voice broke into my thoughts. My heart still pounding with excitement at this new-found inspiration, I hurried to join my companions and our guide as she led us up the stairs, my eyes feasting on every sight, determined to memorize every detail, so that I might record it thereafter.

"He found the project so delightful," continued the

---

[31] A similar scene in *Pride and Prejudice* suggests that Jane Austen was, indeed, inspired by this personal experience, which she used to great advantage in her eventual revision of *First Impressions.*

housekeeper, "that he kept building for another five-and-thirty years until the day he died. Each succeeding generation made alterations and improvements, until it is the fine house you see to-day. When my mistress Georgiana Ashford was alive, the house was filled with friends and relations day and night, for she and my master loved to entertain, and were the best of hosts. By her wish, it has always been kept open for people to see, throughout the year."

We proceeded through a series of magnificent and stately rooms, whose lofty walls and ceilings were covered in frescoes or intricately carved wood. There was an enormous library filled with books from floor to ceiling, a beautiful marble chapel, a great dining-room, a lovely music-room and a succession of appealing bed-rooms. The furnishings in each apartment were suitable to the fortune of their proprietor, yet neither overly gaudy nor uselessly fine. They reflected, I thought, a highly refined taste.

"My master, Sir Thomas Ashford," explained the housekeeper, "engaged a very great architect to build the long North Wing, and he has dedicated his life to collecting objects of every kind to embellish the house. He purchased two complete libraries, many paintings and sculptures, and a great deal more besides." She stopped before a row of high windows looking out on the expansive gardens below, adding: "The late Lady Ashford so loved the sound of rushing water, that my master also built the fountains, the cascade and the long canal which you see there, for her pleasure."

"Such beauty! Such grandeur! Such spectacle!" cried Mr. Morton. "I imagine that all these endeavours must have cost an enormous fortune."

"Sir Thomas spared no expense where the wants of his wife were concerned, for he loved her truly." With a sad shake of her head, the housekeeper said, "indeed, her passing was a great blow to him. He has not been the same man since."

As amazed as I was by the splendour which I beheld, at the same I was seized by a new-found certainty of mind. Mr. Ashford would, one day, inherit all of this. I now understood that any conception of a future between that gentleman and myself had only existed in my imagination. No matter if he did, perhaps, admire me, for a time; it was clear why he had chosen Isabella as his intended bride. His family's wealth and position would compel him to marry a woman within his class, certainly not a clergyman's daughter with no money or connections to recommend her. This realisation did not, in any way, excuse Mr. Ashford's behaviour towards me; he should have made his engagement known, I reflected crossly. However, I could no longer feel slighted by his choice.

The housekeeper led us next into the gallery in the North Wing, where a succession of portrayals of wealthy persons in fine, old-fashioned clothing, dating well back into the seventeenth century, stared back at us from the walls. I walked on, seeking the only face which would be recognisable to me. At last I found it—a large canvas, prominently displayed, which bore a striking resemblance to Mr. Ashford. When I beheld the lively, intelligent eyes and sincere smile in that familiar countenance, I felt a pang of sadness and perturbation, mingled with (against my will) unbidden affection, for I remembered having sometimes seen a similar smile when I found him looking at me.

"And here is my master, Sir Thomas Ashford, and his family," said the housekeeper, proudly indicating the nearby portrait of a handsome, white-haired gentleman who resembled Mr. Ashford, but was no doubt some five-and-twenty years his senior. The painting beside it featured a raven-haired beauty of great sophistication; next to her was a pretty young lady in beautiful dress, with a modest expression. "That is his wife Georgiana, God rest her soul. Here is their daughter Sophia, such a delightful, amiable creature, she is! And here is the son and heir, a very fine man indeed, Mr. Frederick Ashford."

Alethea joined me in my earnest study of Mr. Ashford's portrait. "What a handsome man," said she.

"And a good man, too," added the housekeeper. "Not like all the other wild young men you see these days, who think only of themselves."

"There is nothing to be so highly valued as a good and devoted son," said Squire Bigg-Wither, with a small sigh. I guessed that he was thinking of his own son, Harris, who was a good man in his own way, but with whom the squire had never had the easiest of relationships.

"Mr. Ashford is the very picture of his father," said the housekeeper, "in looks and temperament and understanding. And Sir Thomas, why, if I was to travel across the globe, I could not hope to meet with a better master. Ask any of his tenants, they would all give Sir Thomas a good name, for he is the best and kindest landlord, and very affable to the poor. The son will surely follow in his footsteps, for he was always a good-natured, intelligent boy, the delight of his family, and he has grown into a most thoughtful, generous-hearted man. Why, only last winter, he bought a new pianoforte for his sister, for she does so love to play and sing, and with his own money, he had the music-room entirely redone, all for her own pleasure."

This fine account of Mr. Ashford was consistent, I realised, with the man that I had met, the man I *believed* I knew. It must be accurate, for what praise could be more true and valuable than that of a devoted servant? But at the same time, I felt a renewed sense of indignation. How could a man so highly thought of, so beloved by his servants and family, have treated me with such cavalier disregard? In those few weeks in which Mr. Ashford deliberately sought my company, shared his opinions and enthusiasms, and made me grow to love him, while at the same time withholding a most crucial piece of information about himself, did he have no regard for *my* feelings? Did he not realise how much pain he was to cause me? Or did he not care?

"Do the family spend much time here, in the country?" I heard Mr. Morton enquire.

"Perhaps half the year," answered the housekeeper. "The rest of the time they are in London. Although it is possible that Mr. Ashford will spend more time at Pembroke Hall in future, after he is married."

My heart began to pound with alarm at this discourse. I longed to enquire more about the marriage, but I did not have the nerve. Fortunately, Mr. Morton managed the task for me.

"Who is the lucky lady, if I may be so bold as to ask?" said he.

"Why, it is Miss Isabella Churchill of Larchmont Park."

"Ah, yes! Larchmont Park," repeated Mr. Morton solemnly. "I know its reputation, though I have not had the pleasure of seeing it, as I do not have a coach of my own. From all accounts, it is a very fine estate."

"It is fine, to be sure, but it cannot hold a candle to Pembroke Hall. But then, what property can? In all the county, nay all the kingdom, give me any Duke or Earl or Baron you like, I say there is nothing like *our* house and grounds. The family is very attached to it, and rightly so. I expect the wedding will be held here, right in our own chapel, and the reception in the great hall, or out on the west lawn, depending on the time of year."

"Is the date of the happy event not fixed, then?" asked Alethea.

"Not as yet, but I have heard that it is to take place some time next year. I do hope and pray that Mr. Ashford will be happy in his marriage, although if you ask me," said she, lowering her voice, "I probably should not say this, but she is not *half* good enough for him, for all her beauty and her wealth." She sighed. "But it will be a grand wedding, to be sure, the uniting of two great families. The Ashfords are already so very rich, and with the size of the dowry that Miss Isabella brings to the union—"

Tears blurred my eyes, and I knew I could hear no more. Picking up my skirts, I hurried down the hall, returning from whence we had come.

"Jane!" It was Alethea's voice, but I paid no heed. I ran on, through a connecting vestibule and down the steps of a long oak staircase. I heard the pounding of heavy feet behind me and Mr. Morton calling out my name, but I did not stop. As I reached the lower floor and hurried down a corridor towards what I hoped would be an exit, Mr. Morton caught up to me.

"Miss Austen!" cried he, his eyes bulging with alarm as he kept pace beside me, inhaling great noisy gulps of air, "are you unwell?"

"No, sir, I just felt the sudden need for some fresh air."

"It is all this walking," said he in between ferocious gasps. "It is too much for a lady as delicate as yourself."

"I appreciate your concern, Mr. Morton, but I assure you, I am not all that delicate, and I enjoy walking."

"Perhaps a turn about the gardens, then. To see the waterworks."

Turning a corner, to my relief, I found myself in the front hall, where we had first entered. "Another time, I think. If you will excuse me, sir, I would prefer to spend a few minutes alone."

No sooner had I pulled open the great oak front door and rushed through it, than I saw two carriages draw up immediately before me in the gravel drive. The first, an elegant chaise and four with handsomely liveried postilions, was unknown to me, but the coach behind it, similar in equipage, I instantly recognised. The Ashford crest was emblazoned in gold upon its gleaming black exterior. It was, indeed, the very same vehicle in which I had ridden to the Southampton quay some seven or eight weeks earlier, on our way to Netley Abbey.

Chapter Eighteen

⚬⚭ ⚭⚬

I froze in surprise, as the housekeeper and half a dozen servants scurried out past me in short order to the attend the arrivals. The doors of both coaches were opened; the stairs folded down; and as I stood gaping, from the first chaise, Isabella Churchill emerged and was handed down by the footman, followed by Maria Churchill. At the same time, from the second vehicle, stepped the very persons whose countenances I had just beheld in the gallery up stairs, Sophia Ashford and her father, Sir Thomas Ashford.

Their arrival and descent from the carriages took place in a matter of a minute, as I stood, incapable of movement, in the shadow of the doorway; the party had not yet perceived my presence, and I might have turned and fled back inside the building, to procure an exit through another door, had not Mr. Morton blocked my progress.

"Good gracious!" cried he, nearly overcome with excitement, "It is the Ashford family themselves! Returned from

London! We stand in their very presence!" He babbled on in a lowered tone, into my ear, "I do not know the party with them, but from all appearances, they are very great people indeed. Our timing could not have been more impeccable! Oh! How fortune has smiled upon us!"

At that moment, Mr. Ashford himself descended from the second coach, not twenty yards away. Our eyes met. He started in complete and utter astonishment, and for a moment seemed incapable of movement. I saw a blush overspread his cheeks, just as I felt the colour drain from my own face. The very circumstance which I would have been most anxious to avoid had now befallen me. The man who had won my heart most thoroughly and undeservedly, was standing before me, and at precisely the same moment, only a few yards away, stood the very woman to whom he was promised—the woman who, unwittingly, embodied the destruction of all my former hopes.

I was overpowered by mortification and vexation. I had determined to maintain as great a distance as possible between myself and Mr. Ashford, to preserve what little remaining dignity I had in that affair. I imagined that he had made the same resolution himself, after his escape from Southampton. Oh, folly of follies! Why, I thought in silent chastisement, had I allowed myself to be convinced to come there that day? It was the most regrettable, ill-judged thing in the world! What would Mr. Ashford think to find me at his *home,* of all places, and so far from my own? I had returned his letter, unopened. If he *had* admitted to his engagement in that missive, he could have no idea that I knew of it. It might appear as if I had purposely thrown myself in his way again, when in fact, nothing could be further from the truth.

Before I could think of what to do or say, Alethea and

Squire Bigg-Wither appeared at my elbow, and Mr. Morton rushed forward towards the Ashford party, both arms outstretched in greeting.

"Please forgive us our intrusion, Sir Thomas Ashford, Mr. Ashford, Miss Ashford," cried he with gushing formality and a bow to each. "I am your servant, the Reverend Lucian Morton of Hartsford Rectory, Brimington. My esteemed guests, whom you see there just behind me, are visiting from Hampshire; they are my distant cousin, the Squire Lovelace Bigg-Wither of Manydown Park, Wooton St. Lawrence; his daughter, Miss Alethea Bigg, and her friend, Miss Jane Austen. I insisted that to tour your magnificent home, while they were in the vicinity, was an honour and a privilege not to be missed."

I secretly blessed Mr. Morton, for in all his loquacious pomposity, he had actually managed to relay the explanation for my unexpected presence here to Mr. Ashford in as succinct a manner as was humanly possible. Mr. Ashford still stood rooted to the spot where he had first caught sight of me, the same thunder-struck expression on his face.

"Indeed, sir?" replied Sir Thomas, as we all approached. He shook hands heartily with Mr. Morton and the squire, then bowed to Alethea and myself. "It is a pleasure to meet you all."

"The pleasure is entirely mine," said Mr. Morton, looking as if he might faint.

"I do hope our home met with your expectations," said Sophia, with a warm smile for each of us. She looked to be no more than three-and-twenty, and her voice was soft and sweet.

"Oh! It quite exceeded them, in every way, Miss Ashford," replied Alethea.

"Words cannot express my esteem and admiration for its magnificence," cried Mr. Morton.

"Worth every mile of my journey," said the squire.

I manufactured a smile but said nothing, as my throat had, of a sudden, entirely closed, and it was all I could do to breathe.

"May I introduce our dear friends," said Sir Thomas, as at that moment Mr. Churchill descended from the first coach, and his party came forward. "Mr. and Mrs. Churchill, and Miss Isabella Churchill, of Larchmont Park. Despite the fact that the ladies have spent nearly every day together in London for more than a fortnight, they could not bear to part. And so they are to stay with us a little longer."

Mr. Morton eagerly thrust out his hand again and appeared ready to repeat his introductions, when he was interrupted by a sudden cry of wonder from Mr. Churchill.

"Miss Austen? Good God! Is it really you? Here, in Derbyshire?"

"It is," I replied, scarcely recognizing the squeak which served as my voice.

"But, how amazing! We met Miss Austen at Lyme the summer before last, and again, some months past, at Southampton," Mr. Churchill explained to Sir Thomas and Sophia.

"It is very nice to see you all," said I politely, at last recovering the power of speech. From the corner of my gaze, I detected Mr. Ashford making his approach. To the other side, I felt Alethea and the squire's looks of silent surprise, and the heat of Mr. Morton's stare of profound amazement at my being known to these people.

"I declare, Miss Austen," said Isabella, joining the party with a puzzled frown. (To my dismay, she was even prettier and younger-looking than I had remembered; I was forced to remind myself that she was, indeed, already seventeen years old.) "You look familiar to me. Have *we* not met?"

"We have." I reminded her that the occasion had been a musical party some weeks past at Southampton, and later, at the home of Mrs. Jenkins.

"Oh! Yes, I remember it now," cried she. "We were having such a nice conversation that afternoon, about London and what not, and I do not recall what else, my engagement, I think, and then you ran off in such a hurry, my aunt Jenkins and I were very much concerned for your health."

Mr. Ashford was now but a yard or two away, and he stopped. I could not look at him; my stomach was all in a flutter, and I could barely think. Fighting to maintain my composure, I replied, "I was not feeling well that day, but I have quite recovered."

"Who would have thought we would encounter each other again, in such distant locations?" said Isabella wonderingly.

"Indeed. Who would have thought?" I replied, adding, "I assure you, we had no idea of your returning home to-day, or we should not have come. Mr. Morton was certain that you were all in London. The housekeeper never said a word."

"We had a very early start," said Sir Thomas. "She did not expect us before dinner."

"How delightful that you are all acquainted," said Sophia. "Please do stay and join us for tea. You do not mind my asking, do you, papa?"

"Of course not," said Sir Thomas.

Mr. Ashford seemed to be strangled by his tongue. His eyes darted up to mine, and I could see in them a mixture of confusion, mortification and apology. I could not say which one of us was the more uncomfortable.

"Surely this is no time for visitors," I said quickly. "You have just returned from a long journey. You must be tired. I would not dream of intruding on such short notice." The Ashford and Churchill carriages pulled away, just as the squire's coach drew up to take their place. "Oh! Look! Here is our carriage. It has been a pleasure."

"So very nice to meet you," said Sir Thomas warmly, with a parting bow.

"I do hope we shall have the opportunity to meet again," said Sophia, as she smiled and curtsied, then took her father's arm and led him into the house.

I boarded our carriage without a backwards glance, my heart pounding, rejoicing at my escape. The rest of the party followed, and we were soon underway.

"You astonish me, Miss Austen!" said Mr. Morton, from his seat opposite me in the coach. "Why did you not tell us that you knew the Churchills?"

"I had no idea of our meeting them here," I replied.

"It is quite extraordinary," said Alethea, "that you knew the young lady Mr. Ashford is to marry."

"When the housekeeper mentioned the upcoming nuptials," persisted Mr. Morton, "surely you could have said something then."

"It did not seem important," said I.

"Not important!" cried Mr. Morton. "Such a prestigious acquaintance! Why it is the most important thing in the world!"

"He *is* rather handsome, do not you think?" said Alethea.

"Who?" I asked.

"Why, Mr. Ashford, of course. What a fine figure of a man."

"I did not notice," I lied.

"Although he did seem rather reserved," said Alethea. "I do not think I heard him speak a single word."

"A very fine quality in a man," declared Mr. Morton. "I admire a reserved and quiet person. I always say that verbosity is a great sin, as it can prove most tiresome to those who are prevailed upon to listen, particularly if the speaker is not an educated person, like myself, with an agility of mind and tongue, and an extensive knowledge of the world, which can provide a great variety of interesting topics from which to chuse. In the absence of such facility, I believe one should only speak when one has something of great importance to say, and even then, one should chuse one's words very carefully."

When Mr. Morton suggested a visit to another manor home the next day, I claimed a headache and said I preferred to stay behind. I looked forward to a few hours of quiet and solitude, in which I could pour out my feelings in a letter to my sister.

Hartsford, Wednesday 3 May 1809

My dearest Cassandra,

Thank you for your most welcome letter, which I received the day after our arrival. Your account of the incident with Mary and my mother and the dirty bath water was so hilarious, I must have laughed for a quarter of an hour. You are truly the comic writer of the age, and from this moment forward, I acquit all honours on that front.—However it grieves me to hear that you and my mother have been so miserable in general, and have been obliged to remove to Alton until my return, but perhaps we should not have expected more. Your decision to quit the Inn and move to Mrs. F. Austen's cottage is, I think, a good one, particularly since my mother is still not feeling well. Perhaps the exchanging of one Mary for another will do her good.[32]—Please tell my mother that I think of her every day. She ought to consider writing to Martha, who I believe knows of a new remedy for the headache.—By now you should have received my first letter from this location, in which (in a most indiscreet manner, I confess) I described all things Mr. Morton, both his personage and his parsonage. In the two days since, Mr. M. has proved himself even more odious and supercilious, if that is possible to imagine. There was a time when I considered the squire to be a rather garrulous individual, but Mr. Morton has quite surpassed him in that department; he can pontificate on a subject in a manner so lengthy and so obtuse, it can scarcely be described.—But I must quit this subject at once, or I shall soon be pronounced guilty of the same fault. Now, I cannot put off another moment, the most important news of this missive. My previous correspondence can in no way have prepared you for the intelligence which I am about to impart.—Do you recall my original perturbation at the very idea of travelling into Derbyshire? Well, my darkest worries on that score came to pass yesterday afternoon. Mr. Morton insisted that, of all the great sights in Derbyshire, we must go to Pembroke Hall! All the party wished to

---

[32] Frank Austen had recently settled his wife Mary (who was pregnant again) and their daughter Mary Jane in a cottage at Alton for the two years that he was to be at sea, so they could be close to his mother and sisters when they moved to Chawton Cottage.

go, and as Mr. Morton insisted that the family were
away in town, I felt quite safe in complying. (And I
must admit to having an avid curiosity to see the
place.) You will scarcely believe me when I tell you
what came to pass!—

I was deeply engrossed in writing when I heard a carriage
arrive outside. It was not yet half past one, causing me to wonder if something had gone wrong, for I had not expected Mr.
Morton and the Bigg-Withers to return so soon.

"Pardon me, miss," said the maid, entering with a curtsy.
"There is a young lady to see you."

"To see me?" I enquired in surprise.

"Yes, Miss. A Miss Isabella Churchill, as was."

I started, nearly speechless. "Please shew her in."

I laid down my quill and stood, greatly puzzled. What
could Isabella's business be, in coming to see *me*, all the way
from Pembroke Hall? Nothing came to mind—unless, I
thought with growing alarm, by some chance, she had learnt
of my friendship with Mr. Ashford, and felt (quite unreason-
ably) that I might pose a threat on that account. I wondered
anxiously what I might say to ease her fears, if this were indeed the case.

In seconds, the maid returned; the young lady glided in. She
wore a very pretty gown of spotted yellow muslin with a pale
blue sash, and carried a matching parasol; from the same arm,
dangled an embroidered satchel of moderate size.

"Miss Austen," said Isabella, holding out a gloved hand to
me to shake. "I pray I am not disturbing you?"

"Not at all," said I, taking her hand and searching her face
for any sign of malice. Finding none, I added, "Please, sit
down. May I offer you some refreshment?"

"Thank you, that would be very kind, my throat is parched." Setting down her satchel and parasol, Isabella arranged herself upon the sofa. I took the nearest chair and nodded to the maid, who departed, I hoped, in search of something that might unparch a throat.

"I am afraid Mr. Morton and the others are out sightseeing," said I. "They are not expected back until late this afternoon."

"All the better, for it is *you* in particular that I came to see, Miss Austen." Her condescending tone and beneficent smile left no doubt as to the honour she felt she was bestowing.

"Oh! Indeed," said I, searching for a proper response. "It is always a pleasure to receive a visitor."

"I know you must be surprised to see me. After all, we are barely acquainted. But then, true friendships have been known to start with even the most unlikely of persons, are they not? It is only through the most extraordinary circumstances that you are even known to my brother and his wife, and Mr. Ashford. Why, imagine my astonishment when Charles informed me, only last evening, that you all took a water-party to some ruined abbey or other while they were in Southampton!"

My stomach was all in a flutter, as I could not yet detect, from her expression, whether or not she harboured resentment towards me on that score. "It is true, we did make such an excursion."

"Charles said you had a picnic and a marvelous time. I cannot tell you how envious I was to hear it. I would have been among the company myself, had I not been ill, and forced to stay at home. I told Ashford I was quite put out. After all, I barely saw him while we were in London, he was always so frightfully busy. I told him that I wanted a water-party of my own, just like the one you had in Southampton! 'You simply *must* take me to the lakes,' said I. Ashford replied, 'We could go, but it would not be the same without Miss Austen.' I asked him why ever not. I must say, his response took me quite by surprise. It is the reason I am here."

"Is it?" My heart pounded. I took a deep breath, trying to prepare myself for whatever might be coming. "What did he say?"

"He told me that you are—" Isabella leaned forward, lowering her voice. "I hope you will believe, I do not mean to be impertinent?"

"I am certain you do not mean to be."

"He said that you are—" she paused, her eyes gleaming with excitement, "the most *wonderful* story-teller."

It was the last thing I expected. "Indeed?"

"Charles and Maria agreed. They said you told them the most *entertaining* tale that day, and it was a wonder it was not published. Well, I thought, any one *that* accomplished, *must* be a great reader, and a good judge of literature, and perhaps even writes her own stories down. But Ashford left the room, and no one else seemed to know. So I thought I would come here straight away, to enquire into the matter."

"I am afraid I do not follow you, Miss Isabella. What, precisely, is the nature of your enquiry?"

"A very simple one. I read an *entire* novel last year, all the way through! It took me a great while to finish, but I was glad I did. So inspired was I, that I recently took up the occupation of writing, myself! I have so *longed* for a friend with whom I could share my thoughts, some one who could guide me in my endeavour." From her satchel, Isabella produced a notebook, which she thrust at me. "Here is my first effort: a story, unfinished as yet. I wondered if you would be so kind as to read it and honour me with your opinion?"

I stared at her, astounded. I was prevented from making any reply, however, for at that very moment the door was thrown open again. The maid reappeared, carrying a tray with some sort of beverage, and made the following announcement:

"Excuse me, Miss Austen, there's a gentleman to see you."

I had not even an instant to process that remark, when Mr. Ashford immediately strode into the room.

Chapter Nineteen

———————— ❧ ❧ ————————

"iss Austen," said Mr. Ashford, bowing, an urgency to his tone.

I rose to my feet in silent astonishment. Mr. Ashford opened his mouth to speak again, when he caught sight of Isabella and froze in consternation. A brief, awkward silence followed. The maid vanished. If I had thought the events of the previous afternoon to be uncomfortable, they were nothing compared to the moment before me now. I was trapped in the same room with the two people I least wished to see or speak to in the world, without the relief of another person.

"Ashford!" cried Isabella at last, with a laugh. "Well, this is a surprise."

Mr. Ashford bowed stiffly. "Miss Churchill."

"Had I known you were coming here to-day, Ashford, we could have shared a carriage."

"I imagine so," said Mr. Ashford. He glanced at me with a frustrated and embarrassed look.

I was filled with anxiety, but determined not to shew it. Why, I decided suddenly, should *I* feel uncomfortable in front of this man? I had done nothing wrong. He had wronged *me*. Let him feel his own shame and discomfort, if he may. "Do sit down, Mr. Ashford," I entreated with a smile.

"Thank you." He perched on the edge of a chair. "I cannot stay long."

"But how odd," said Isabella, as she sipped her glass of punch. "Why have you come all this way, Ashford, if you are to arrive and depart in the same breath?"

"I came to—" He was clearly at a loss for words, and I discerned in his gaze a range of emotions which seemed to be at war within his heart—mortification, aggravation and something else which appeared to be directed solely at me—was it apology? At last he said, "I came to issue an invitation."

All those affectionate feelings which I had buried, with one earnest look from him, were attempting to retake possession of my heart. I struggled to ignore them, determined to cling to fury and indignation, but resolved to be polite. "An invitation?"

"To you and your friends. To join us at Pembroke Hall. I understand—I believe my housekeeper said—you did not see the gardens or the waterworks yesterday?"

"It is true, we did not have that pleasure. Although we did have a very extensive tour of the house itself, which I thought extremely beautiful."

"Thank you. I am glad that you—I am pleased that you had the opportunity to see it. I do hope that you will do me the honour of returning on Friday as our guests, and of course stay to dinner."

"How kind of you to offer. I am sure my friends will be delighted by the invitation. I shall be sure to tell them when they return."

"What a wonderful idea," said Isabella. "I had intended to go home tomorrow, but now I will surely stay. What is another day or two? It could not be more perfectly arranged."

The look on Mr. Ashford's handsome countenance—his furrowed brow, pursed lips and flared nostrils—all conveyed his irritation and annoyance, which he struggled to contain behind a terse smile. I could only hope that my own tortured feelings were not so readily discernible as his.

"It will give you time, Miss Austen, to read my little story," continued Isabella, "and you may share your comments when next you see me." At Mr. Ashford's incredulous look, she laughed. "You are right to be surprised, Ashford, for you do not know all. Remember the story I told you I was writing? Well! Wait until you hear! Miss Austen has agreed to read it and give me her advice."

He glanced at me. "That is most gracious of you."

"How could I refuse?" I replied.

"Indeed. How could you?" With a tense frown, Mr. Ashford stood. "If you will excuse me, Miss Austen. I shall look forward to your reply with regard to Friday. And now, I beg to take your leave."

"I must be on my way, as well," said Isabella, rising and retrieving her parasol. "Words cannot express my gratitude, Miss Austen, for your assistance in this little matter."

"It is my pleasure," I said.

Oh! The satisfaction that a pen and ink and paper can afford when one has events of such astonishing calibre to relate, and the knowledge that they will be delivered to such a vitally interested recipient! You may imagine with what an outpouring of emotion and anxiety I related every word and nuance of the above incident when I was, at last, able to finish my letter to

Cassandra. So engrossed was I in my writing, that I was unaware that another carriage had arrived in the drive, until Alethea entered the parlour.

"Well, Jane, we have had such a day!" Alethea drew off her gloves and flung herself into a chair with a tired sigh. "After seeing so many villages and castles and manor homes, they all begin to look alike. All excepting Pembroke Hall, of course. Yesterday's outing was *indeed* a bright spot in our week. How are you, dearest? Is your headache better?"

"It is. Thank you."

"Is that yet *another* letter you write?"

"Yes. To my sister."

"Did you not write to Cassandra not two days past?"

"I did."

"I have written only *one* letter to *one* sister in all the time we have been gone, and here you write to *yours* nearly every other day, it seems. You make me feel positively guilty. I was going to ask you something. Whatever was it? Mr. Morton and papa rode on to see some pigs that Mr. Morton is thinking of buying, about which he *would* seek papa's opinion. I begged them to drop me home first; the idea of being forced to listen to those two men debate the merits and demerits of a swine for the better part of an hour left me entirely exhausted. Oh! I remember what I was going to ask." She sat up of a sudden, her eyes alive with interest. "The maid said you had two visitors while we were gone. Two! Is it true? Who can you be acquainted with in these parts? Who came to see you?"

"Miss Isabella Churchill, for one."

"Miss Churchill? I am all astonishment. But wait, that is right, you *have* met before. Whatever was her purpose in coming?"

"She came to ask my advice. She has taken up a new occupation, it seems."

"What occupation is that?"

"Having failed at music and art," I replied, "she has decided to write."

I read Isabella's story, which was a brief tale of a girl's adventure, rather childish, and quite unfinished—similar in tone to my own very early juvenilia—except that she did not possess the mastery of the language which I believed sufficient for the task. I would never dream of telling her so, of course, I thought miserably.

While Alethea took to our room for a nap, I ventured out alone into the parsonage garden for a walk, my mind full of the distressing events of the past two days. Oh, how I wished I had never come on this holiday, or at the very least, had heeded my alarms and refused to visit Pembroke Hall.

When Alethea had pressed me to reveal the identity of my second visitor, I had told her, with as much calm as I could muster, about Mr. Ashford's kind invitation to make a return visit to his family estate. She had been surprised but pleased, and wondered what could have induced him to extend such a courtesy, since I was (or so she thought) not acquainted with him, but only with the Churchills. I did nothing to illuminate her on the subject, preferring to wait until we were actually in that gentleman's company again (some two days hence, should the visit in fact take place), when it would become absolutely necessary to do so. We had laughed in anticipation of Mr. Morton's response to the invitation, which we predicted would be enthusiastic, indeed.

My laughter had rung hollow, however. I could not think of the event without the greatest frustration and mortification.

Being forced into the presence of Mr. Ashford twice in two days had been discomfiting enough, and now I was faced with yet another meeting. Surely Mr. Ashford had not come today with the intention of issuing any such invitation. It had been clear, by his manner, his tone, his very words, that he had arrived with a very different aim in mind, and had been forced to invent another excuse, owing to the unexpected presence of Isabella.

The original purpose of his visit, I surmised, had been to at last reveal all, to unburden his heart of guilt. Over the past several hours of rumination, my imagination had supplied the words that he might have said, had he been allowed to speak freely. He might have explained that when we met at Lyme, he had been quite taken with me. Upon his return to Derbyshire, however, he had become embroiled in affairs of his family estate, and he had been reminded (perhaps by his father) that he was reaching that age where a man must and should marry. It had seemed only natural and right to chuse a young woman who was so beloved by the family. He had known Isabella all his life, he might have said, and had always regarded her with affection. Some one or two years past, when she had matured into the full bloom of womanhood, her beauty and attractions had bewitched him.

It had all been settled, he was to marry Isabella, and had thought himself content. And then we met again at Southampton. He was not prepared for the attraction he was to feel. The similarity of our minds, the charms of my person and intellect (or some other such nonsense) drew me to him. He knew he should have told me of his engagement; he reproached himself daily for this omission; but had he told me his true circumstances, he feared I might desist in seeing him (which would surely have been the case.) However, since he had regarded me, from the beginning, only as a friend, and had assumed that I felt the same, he had seen no real harm in continuing our association.

He would then have turned his eyes to me, (I imagined) with a look of deepest sincerity (one of his many talents), and said, "That you learned of my engagement from another source, will always be a matter of the greatest embarrassment to me. I hope that you will forgive me, and that we may remain friends, for I will always hold you in the highest esteem, &etc &etc."

This imagined discourse, which brought an unpleasant turn to my stomach, was interrupted by a distant shout and the calling of my name. I looked up across the expanse of lawn to see Mr. Morton exiting the parsonage and waving to me.

Oh no, I thought. What now? Alethea must have told Mr. Morton about our invitation to dine at Pembroke Hall, and he cannot wait to share his delight with me. The clergyman lumbered towards me as fast as his long, thick legs and heavy torso would allow; I quickened my step along the gravel path in his direction and met him at the border of the rose garden.

"Miss Austen," cried he, catching up to me and panting for breath, "may I solicit the honour of a walk with you in private?"

"It is your garden, Mr. Morton. And there does not seem to be any one else about."

He snorted out something resembling a laugh. "Your sense of humour, Miss Austen, is only one of your many qualities which I find so endearing."

"You are too kind, Mr. Morton."

"I speak only the truth. You are a woman of great charm and many surprises." He fell into step beside me, and, as expected, said with great excitement: "Why, who could have imagined, when you first arrived—a woman from a respectable family, to be sure, but one of no great consequence, who has resided in county Hampshire most of your life—that you would know the Churchills! And by that connexion, be the means of an introduction to the Ashford family! It is too thrilling! I have only just heard the news of Mr. Ashford's most gracious invitation and words cannot express with what extreme pleasure I anticipate the affair."

"No words are necessary, Mr. Morton. I can imagine your sentiments very well."

"I believe you can, Miss Austen. For you strike me as a woman of great imagination, another feature which I admire. To be able to see more than merely that which is before you, to be able to project one's innermost thoughts and ideas into a future prospect, and then to realise that prospect—from an endeavour as simple as the installation of a set of shelves in a bed-room closet, for example, to one as complex as the design and planting of a bed of roses—these activities all require a vivid sense of imagination, and a passionate devotion to their execution. Qualities which, I flatter myself, I am most fortunate to possess, and which I always observe in others with the highest regard."

I strove to devise a sensible reply, but the idea of Mr. Morton designing and fitting closet shelves with any thing resembling passion so amused me, that it required all my attention to keep from laughing. We approached a wooden bench in the shade of a great elm, and he said, "Please do me the honour of sitting with me for a moment, Miss Austen."

I sat. He heaved his great body onto the seat beside me, breathing in the scents of the garden. "Is not this a delightful spot?"

"It is indeed, sir. It is very lovely. You have much to be proud of."

"You would not find it disagreeable, then, to spend more time in this place?"

"Why no. I enjoy the out of doors; I would be happy to pass an hour or two each morning of our stay engaged in strolling about your garden."

"Would you be as happy if you were to extend your stay?"

"Extend my stay?" I replied, puzzled. "That would be pleasant, I am sure, but my friends and I are obliged to return home a few days hence."

"Are you indeed obliged, Miss Austen?"

"Indeed I am. My mother and sister await my return. We shall be moving, soon, to a new house."

"I see." Mr. Morton turned in his seat to face me, his countenance more animated now than I had yet seen it. "I shall waste your time or mine no longer with idle chatter, Miss Austen, but come right to the point. I believe I mentioned, shortly after your arrival, that until recently, I did not have the means to support a wife; but my circumstances have changed substantially. I am now able and inclined to marry, and I have chosen you, Miss Austen, to fill that role, as the future companion of my life."

I was so taken aback, I could only manage "Mr. Morton" before his flood of words intervened.

"I recognise your surprise and concern, but pray, do not distress yourself. I am aware that such a proposal does not present itself to a woman of your position every day; but the fact that you are no longer in the bloom of youth, and have no fortune, is of no consequence to me. Your value, I believe, lies in other things. From the moment I first laid eyes upon you, I recognised all the features of an active, intelligent, useful sort of person, not brought up too high, who could make a small income go a good way; in short, the ideal woman to serve as a parson's wife."

"Mr. Morton, I beg you—" I began, but he went on:

"I flatter myself that I have much to offer a woman: a comfortable home and living, and as you have yourself seen, a very beautiful garden, situated only two miles from the estate of the esteemed Lady Delacroix, who I feel certain will approve most readily of my choice; not to mention the society which we shall surely enjoy based on your acquaintance with the two great Derbyshire families of whom we have spoken. Nothing now remains but for me to assure you of the violence of my affection. May I say how ardently I love and admire you! Will you say yes, Miss Austen, and make me the happiest of men?"

Chapter Twenty

his was—at last—the conclusion of his speech?" enquired Cassandra, struggling to stifle a laugh from her
garden seat outside Frank and Mary's cottage at Alton.
"Will you make me the happiest of men?"

I had returned only half an hour before, after an expedi-
tious homeward journey from Derbyshire. Upon reassuring
myself that my mother was not, in fact, at death's door (but
was at that moment sitting up and enjoying a hearty meal), I
had stolen my sister away at the first opportunity, to regale
her in private with the illustrious tale of my proposal.

"Those were his very words," said I.

"What was your reply?"

"I said, 'Sir, although I am sensible of the honour of your
offer, I am convinced that I am the last woman on earth who
could make you happy.'"

"How did he receive your refusal?"

"My words, unfortunately, did nothing to dissuade him. He insisted that I was being coy."

"No!"

"*Yes*. He claimed he had heard it said that many women, on a first proposal, refuse the very man they mean to accept in an effort to appear more desirable."

"I have never heard of any woman doing such a thing."

"Nor have I. Where he obtains his information on the habits and attitudes of marriageable women is a subject we cannot hope to comprehend. In any case, I told him, in the most certain terms, that I was perfectly serious in my refusal; and that I would not, and could not, marry him."

"I trust that in the end, he accepted your declination gracefully?"

"On the contrary. He grew upset, and assured me that he did not require my presence to continue a relationship with the Ashford and Churchill families. He then stomped off towards the parsonage and did not speak a word to me the rest of the day."

"Oh, Jane! How mortifying!"

"When I related the events to Alethea and the squire, and it became apparent that I was no longer welcome in that house, the squire quickly made excuses for our immediate return to Hampshire. He wrote a letter to Mr. Ashford, apologizing for our removal, and for our inability to accept his gracious invitation to dine at Pembroke Hall, which only incensed Mr. Morton all the more. To my relief, we departed early the next morning."

"Well, I am sorry that you were treated so uncivilly, but to receive a proposal cannot be a bad thing in itself, even if you do not admire the man in question. That he thought so well of you can only serve to flatter. And any thing which brings you back to me so expeditiously can only be viewed with a most grateful eye."

I smiled at Cassandra with affection. "I declare, you *will* find a silver lining in every cloud. No matter how abominably a person acts, you always find something kind to say about him. I suppose you will find something good to say about Mr. Ashford next, that I should think well of him and be grateful for what little time we had together, knowing that a gentleman of his wealth and standing could never be expected to marry a woman as lowly as myself."

Cassandra looked troubled now, and said, "I confess, I do not know what to make of that affair. I cannot help but think that there is more to Mr. Ashford's engagement to Isabella than has been revealed at present. If only he had had a chance to explain; it is most unfortunate that, each time he has, apparently, attempted to speak to you on that subject, he has been prevented."

"He had ample opportunity to speak of it every day for three long weeks in Southampton."

"True. He did behave badly there, it seems; but I still think him a good man. I cannot believe we were both so completely wrong in our perception of him."

"You may believe what you like," said I, "but as far as I am concerned, that subject is closed. I think myself lucky to have escaped from Derbyshire unscathed."

A few days later, Alethea unexpectedly came to visit us with the most astonishing news, in the form of a letter that the squire had received.

"Papa shared this with me only moments after it arrived,"

announced Alethea, as she thrust the missive into my hands. "I knew I must come in person at once, no matter what the distance, to shew it to you." The letter, I saw, was from Mr. Morton.

"What can Mr. Morton have to say to your father?" I enquired. "Does he write to thank him for his visit, or to reprimand him for bringing a guest who exhibited such poor behaviour?"

"Read it," said Alethea with a laugh, "and see for yourself."

Hartsford, Derbyshire—Friday 5 May 1809

DEAR SIR,

I trust you and your daughter are well, and that you enjoyed a safe return journey from my humble home. I would be inclined, were it at all within my power, to entrust these words to you in person, but the speed of your sudden departure made that event impossible, and I am obliged to commit my entreaty to paper. I flatter myself that you will not be entirely surprised by the contents of this missive; however, pray allow me to begin with a brief but, I think, necessary preface. You are no doubt aware of a certain offer which, based on a great error of judgment, was recently made to your daughter's friend, who shall remain nameless. Please believe that my true feelings in the matter were, I see in retrospect, blinded by the prospects which that friend seemed to possess; namely, that of a connexion with the Churchill family, and through them, with the Ashfords themselves. But of these matters I will speak no further, they are in the past, they are forgotten. Time and economy require that I address the purpose of this letter without delay. I recall most vividly the intelligence you provided me of the dire circumstances which will befall your unmarried daughters in the event of your death (a melancholy event which, I trust, will not take place for several years). The thought that Miss Alethea, however well provided for, will be forced to leave your home at Manydown on that occasion to make way for your son and heir to take residence with his family is most distressing indeed. This concern has occupied all my thoughts since your departure, and made me cognizant of a regard which I have, upon reflection, felt ever since the first moment of my acquaintance with your daughter. In short, dear sir, it is your very own Miss Alethea who has captured my heart. I write to request your blessing and your permission to address my most sincere affections to your daughter, and to make an offer of marriage, an offer which I trust will be as acceptable to you as it will be to the lady herself. I remain, dear sir, with respectful compliments to your family, your wellwisher and friend,

LUCIAN MORTON

"I am, I confess, entirely amazed," said I as I folded up the letter and returned it to Alethea.

"Can you imagine it? He wrote this letter the very day after our departure! It is astonishing to me that any man could change his matrimonial allegiance so swiftly and decidedly, and with so little provocation."

"Please do not allow *my* refusal to cloud your thinking. If you would accept him, *do*. He has a very pleasant rose garden, and a set of shelves in a bed-room closet which, I understand, are of the highest quality."

Alethea laughed. "I would rather live alone and penniless the rest of my days in the smallest attic garret than to spend another five minutes under the roof of that man."[33]

"Your father will be severely disappointed, I fear."

"He is, for he continues to remind me that my sister made a highly satisfactory match with an older clergyman. But I am not Catherine."

"Nor am I," I replied.

We passed the remainder of May and June at Godmersham while waiting for improvements to be completed on our future home at Chawton. Unlike my previous visits, every day that I spent immersed in the elegant style of life at my brother's grand estate in Kent was now a painful reminder of an even more imposing edifice and park in Derbyshire, and of the gentleman who resided there. Each time a memory of Mr. Ashford came to me, I scolded myself to put such thoughts for ever from my mind. In time, I believe I actually persuaded myself that I had succeeded.

Edward, still grieving from the loss of his wife the autumn before, was glad of our company, although much away from home overseeing the work at Chawton Cottage. It was lovely to be with my many nieces and nephews for a time, but of course there was no opportunity to write; and as always, I felt I did not quite fit in there. When the hairdresser came to do the

---

[33] Alethea Bigg (1777–1847) never did marry. When the squire died in 1813, she and her sister Elizabeth left Manydown to make way for Harris and his family, and took a house together in Winchester, where they lived comfortably for many years.

girls' hair, he charged my mother, my sister and me a reduced rate for the same effort, an acknowledgement of our reduced circumstances for which we were grateful, but at the same time, acutely embarrassed.

It was with relief and excited anticipation that, on the 7th of July, 1809, my mother and I said good-bye to Godmersham. Cassandra had decided to remain another few days, and Martha would soon be joining us, but mamma and I were anxious to make ready the home which we could, at last, call our own.

During our stay at Alton, earlier, my mother had not felt well enough to endure a tour of the cottage while it was undergoing renovations and filled with workmen; as such, we had only had an opportunity to briefly view its exterior in passing.

"My, my, it *is* very close to the road," said my mother now, clicking her tongue with dismay, as we alighted from my brother's carriage and beheld Chawton Cottage in the hot July sun. "This small, fenced space is all that protects the house from the danger of collision with any runaway vehicle."

"The passing traffic will be an interesting diversion," said I, raising my voice as a coach and six suddenly thundered past not four yards behind us, causing the ground to rumble beneath our feet.

"Interesting, indeed," replied my mother, coughing and waving away the rising dust.

Chawton was (and is, and I trust will remain so, long after I no longer live here) in the midst of very pretty wooded country, its green valleys and meadows filled with beech trees. Edward's property was extensive. It included the manor house, which stood on the nearby slope of a hill above the church, a park and farms, as well as a village of some thirty cottages, most of whose tenants were labourers on Edward's farms and woodlands.

The bailiff's cottage, built at least a century ago, was not a cottage in the usual sense. A two-storied, sturdy-looking building of red Hampshire brick, with sash windows and a high-pitched roof with two attic dormers, it began life as a posting-inn, and looked plenty large for our purpose. The house stood in the centre of Chawton village, directly on the corner where the road from Gosport intersected the Winchester Road, the busy artery which connected Portsmouth to London.

"Well, we are in Edward's debt, and fortunate to have any place at all," declared my mother, studying the austere brick façade, its asymmetrical appearance a tribute to its history of alterations. "Although I *shall* miss the society and shops and diversions of Southampton."

"I, for one, am thrilled at the prospect of living in the country again," said I, as the coachman unloaded our trunks and we headed for the door. "As for shops and society, Alton is an easy walk in fine weather, and large enough to merit a branch of Henry's London bank. And the Great House, church and rectory are only ten minutes' walk away."

The interior of the house, which was snug and bright and smelled of fresh paint, proved far more promising, and even mother's spirits began to rise. The front door opened onto a good-sized entrance; to the left was a pleasant, low-ceiling drawing-room with a fire-place and moulded mantelpiece, and roughly finished, white-washed walls. What little furniture we possessed had been sent ahead, and was placed at random about the room, awaiting our decisive eye.

We admired the results of the improvements Edward had ordered; the large drawing-room window (which, in accordance with its prior use as an inn, had faced directly onto the main road), Edward had blocked up because of noise, and turned into a book-case instead. To give the ground-floor a more cheerful aspect, he had cut a beautiful, new Gothic-styled window into the wall overlooking the garden.

"Oh! Isn't that lovely!" cried my mother. "Edward always did have good taste. The view from this room is very pleasant, and the light is good. You ought to put your new pianoforte here, Jane, when it arrives."

My mother, sister, and Martha had determined many months ago to pool their resources and procure a pianoforte for me. This act of generosity—particularly in view of the fact that none of them professed the same need for, or appreciation of music, as I did—brought me close to tears every time I thought of it. I had not owned an instrument since we left Steventon nine years before. I was determined to learn country dances, that we might have some amusement for our nephews and nieces, when we had the pleasure of their company.

"We were fortunate to locate so fine an instrument for thirty guineas," said I. "It *will* go perfectly in this corner, and here, beside the fire-place, I can place my writing desk."

The vestibule connected the drawing-room with an ample dining-parlour, which looked out on the road, and a narrow stairway led to six cozy bed-chambers up stairs.

"These bed-rooms are very small, to be sure," said my mother, "but we are lucky to have six, seeing as how they are all already spoken for." It had been decided that Cassandra and I would share one room, as always; Martha and my mother should each have their own; one would be for guests; and the others would be for the servants my mother had yet to hire: a cook and a maid, and a man for the heavy work.

"It looks as if Edward has done a fine job in fitting up the place," said my mother, "although would it have been asking too much, do you think, to have added a water-closet?"

"One cannot expect the luxury of piped water in a country cottage, mamma. But Edward said he made improvements to the pump at back, and has dug a better cesspit for the privy."

At the rear of the ground-floor was the kitchen, and in back, across the yard, was a stable, a granary and a bake-house, with a bread oven and copper-lined wash-tub. "Martha will be in seventh heaven when she sees this!" cried my mother. "She can help the cook try out all those new receipts[34] of hers. I cannot imagine what we shall do with a stable, however, since we cannot afford to keep a carriage."

"Perhaps, if we maintain strict economies, we might be able to quarter a donkey and a cart one day," I suggested.

"It will be a fine day that sees *me* riding about in a donkey carriage," sniffed my mother. She was, however, delighted with the size of the garden, which contained a thickly planted shrubbery, a fragrant syringa, numerous beds of flowers blooming with straggling sweet williams and columbines, a good deal of long grass, and a fruit orchard. Around the garden ran a pleasant gravel walk and a high hornbeam hedge, which screened it from the noisy road and helped maintain privacy and quiet within.

"This is all that I could ever wish for in a garden!" cried my mother in satisfaction. "That grass will require regular mowing, but we shall have a man to see to it. And those beds of flowers want some loving care, and a good weeding, but it is nothing I cannot handle. With so much space, I can plant a nice kitchen garden with plenty of vegetables and potatoes.

---

[34] Recipes.

Why, I have half a mind to give up housekeeping to you girls from now on and spend my days working in the garden."

Three days after we moved in, I helped attend the birth of Frank and Mary's second child, a boy named Francis. His was a much speedier and less difficult delivery than Mary's first confinement, and my joy on the occasion prompted me to write a poem to my brother.

Chawton, July 26, 1809

> My dearest Frank, I wish you Joy
> Of Mary's safety with a boy,
> Whose birth has given little pain
> Compared with that of Mary Jane.—
> May he a growing Blessing prove,
> And well deserve his Parents' Love!
> Endow'd with Art's & Nature's Good,
> Thy name possessing with thy Blood;
> In him, in all his ways, may we
> Another Francis William see!—

(I continued thus for several more stanzas, expressing the many ways in which I hoped the child would, if fortune smiled upon him, become exactly like his excellent father. Near the end of the verse, I added:)

> As for ourselves, we're very well,
> As unaffected prose will tell.
> Cassandra's pen will give our state
> The many comforts that await
> Our Chawton home—how much we find

Already in it to our mind,
And how convinced that when complete,
It will all other Houses beat,
That ever have been made or mended,
With rooms concise or rooms distended.

The poem perfectly summed up my exhuberant feelings on the subject. Our house was a little odd, with some rooms too small, and others scarred by alterations, but it was *ours,* and as such, the very best house in the world. The happy business of unpacking and settling in took up our time for many weeks.

"Where shall I place this candelabra, mamma?" asked Cassandra one morning as she unwrapped the item, not long after she and Martha arrived.

"On the mantelpiece. No, no, on the sideboard," replied my mother with sudden excitement, "beside the silver plate. Set it in the middle, with the teaspoons to one side, and the tea-ladle, tablespoon and dessert-spoon on the other. Yes, just so, I declare, that looks magnificent."

"There goes the morning coach from Winchester," cried Martha, the stillness broken by the sudden roar of a carriage and horses dashing past, just outside our windows.

"You could set your watch by it." My mother nodded contentedly, for she had come to share my view, that the constant stream of coaches and wagons was a welcome reminder of the larger world that pulsed not far beyond our door.

To see my family in such high spirits was infectious, and better than any tonic. I smiled and turned my attention back to the crate that I was unpacking, when I heard a knock at the front door. I answered; it was the postman.

"Welcome to the neighbourhood, Miss," said he, handing me several letters.

I thanked him. He tipped his hat and turned to go, but upon seeing the direction on the first epistle, I quickly called him back. "Please return this one to sender," said I softly, handing him the letter, which was written in Mr. Ashford's hand.

"But it is the correct name and address, Miss, is it not? Are you not Miss Jane Austen?"

"I am," said I quietly, wondering how on earth Mr. Ashford had found me. A glance at my mother and sister revealed that they were, thankfully, still occupied with their activities in the dining-room.

"Yet you refuse the letter?" asked the postman in puzzlement.

"I do," said I emphatically, "and I would be most appreciative, sir, if you would return any future correspondence from this particular person addressed to me, should it happen to arrive."

His eyebrows lifted as he nodded in silent comprehension. "Very good, Miss. I will see it done. Good day to you, Miss."

"Who was that?" called my mother from the next room, after I had thanked the postman and shut the door. "Is it the post, Jane?"

"It is, mamma," I replied. "But do not excite yourself. It is only bills."

Chapter Twenty-one

———————— ❧ ❧ ————————

Unlike the years at Steventon, our social life at Chawton was small. There were no balls and few dinner invitations. We found and hired the requisite help; my pianoforte arrived, along with a few other pieces of needed furniture; and we fell into a new routine.

My mother gladly gave herself over to the garden, where she spent most of her days putting in potatoes, planting and weeding the flower borders and vegetable beds, and appearing each afternoon in happy spirits, wearing a green round frock like any day-labourer's, her boots and garments muddied from her toils.

Cassandra and Martha took charge of the arrangements for most of the day's meals and helped in the kitchen as needed. Our new cook was a dear, capable woman, who earned every penny of her £8 a year; but as she also handled our washing every fortnight, there was often more to do than two hands could manage. Cassandra also took up her hobby of water-colour sketching. She cornered me one afternoon and absolutely forced me to sit for an informal portrait, the likeness of which (every one agreed, to my sister's mortification) was rather unflattering. No one has ever attempted to draw my portrait since.[35]

My only designated responsibilities were the keeping of the key to the wine cupboard, and the preparation of a simple breakfast—undemanding duties, for the women in my household were determined that I should devote my time to that pursuit which was so dear to me—the writing of my book.

I had been eager to return to work. In every quiet moment in months past, whether on a long walk, a carriage ride, or lying in my bed at night attempting sleep, my thoughts had often turned to *Sense and Sensibility* and *First Impressions,* books which slumbered in imperfect states. New ideas had struck me at odd moments, but I had rarely had a chance even to jot them down. *At last,* I thought, *the time has come.*

My recent trip to Derbyshire—the image of Pembroke Hall still so vivid in my mind—made me impatient to work on *First Impressions* again, which needed to be altered, lopped, and cropped; but at the same time, my thoughts were full of Elinor and Marianne, and of Edward and Willoughby. The flood of creativity which had been unleashed during those few weeks at Southampton still simmered deep within me, clamouring for attention. The revisions were barely begun, but it was a start, and I knew it would require my undivided attention for quite some time if it were ever to reach completion. With what joy I

---

[35] Although several professional renderings of all the Austen sons exist, Cassandra's simple water-colour sketch (which her affectionate niece Anna called "so hideously unlike") is the only known "portrait" of Jane Austen in existence. In an attempt to refine it, a miniature reproduction was made in 1869, followed by a steel, engraved version which was used in James Edward Austen-Leigh's "Memoir of Jane Austen" in 1870.

looked forward to picking up my pen, that I might make those worthy characters come alive again!

The quiet of the countryside (notwithstanding the intermittent parade of traffic beyond our door), the solitude and my new-found contentment in the establishment of a daily schedule, made the ideal setting for the writer's life. I took to it with energy and relish.

I rose early, donned my white cap and went downstairs before any one else was about. On cold mornings, the maid laid the fire in the dining-room hearth, and sometimes I began writing immediately, my mind filled with new ideas in the early light of dawn. Other mornings, I played my pianoforte first. Situated as it was in the drawing-room at the end of the house, my practise did not disturb the others' sleep. At nine o'clock I made tea and toast for my family, and after a good chat, I removed myself again to the drawing-room fire (or at times, to my bed-chamber), where I wrote in happy seclusion for the rest of the morning.

The work did not always come easily. I must have been possessed, I decided, during that flurry of productivity at Southampton. Some mornings I laboured over a single paragraph for three hours, slashing out nearly every line and devising it afresh in a vain attempt at perfection. On other days I might compose half a chapter in a heated flourish, only to decide, upon later review, that it was gibberish and toss the whole, in frustration, into the fire.

There were good days as well, brilliant days in which the words flowed as quickly as rain slides down an eave, my pen barely able to maintain pace with my thoughts, days in which my characters seemed to act and speak through my very fingers—a simple transference from mind to pen, and pen to page, with little apparent thought or effort.

My characters continued to converse with each other in my mind, even when I was not at work. It seemed to matter not where I was—at the dinner-table or sitting in the drawing-room, darning a pair of socks or sewing a garment for the poor—a piece of dialogue or witty turn of phrase might jump into my mind, and with a laugh, I would throw down my fork or needle and run to my desk to record my newest gem before the fleeting thought could vanish.

Whenever one of our servants entered the room where I was working, or on those rare occasions when some one outside the immediate family party came to call, I quickly put away my pages, or covered them with a piece of blotting paper, and picked up my needlework, careful that my occupation should not be discovered. There was a swing door, located between the front door and the offices,[36] which creaked when it was opened; I welcomed this little inconvenience and refused to allow it to be remedied, because it gave me notice when any one was entering.

The seasons passed. Summer disappeared, Michaelmas came and went, and autumn arrived, with its driving rains, chill winds and flurries of crisp, brown leaves. Soon, a gentle snow fell outside our windows. I am told that our first Christmas at Chawton was merry and bright, and that the winter of 1810 was very cold and dry, but I cannot say for certain, so distracted was I by my writing.

Henry stopped by in his carriage from time to time when bank business called him to Alton, and once or twice he took me or Cassandra on an outing. Edward visited that autumn, bringing his eldest daughter, Fanny, with him. Now sixteen,

---

[36] The offices were the kitchen, stables, and other parts of a large house where the household work was done, as opposed to the bedrooms, dining and drawing rooms, which were lived in by the family.

Fanny was an affectionate, charming girl, and had become one of the delights of my life. Since the death of her mother, she had been a devoted, highly valued companion to her father, and we always enjoyed their company.

In the afternoons, I often walked to Alton with Martha or Cassandra to shop, or ambled to one of our many ponds or through the meadow across the road to the running stream. I have a vague memory of calling several times on Edward's tenants at the Great House, the Middletons, who were excellent people, and whose name I borrowed for characters in my book.[37] But for the most part, we were four women living in seclusion, our family party seldom enlarged by friends or neighbours, and I was happily engrossed in my work.

That work, by virtue of its very subject matter, often brought with it memories of a certain gentleman: memories which I endeavoured, time and again, to brush from my mind.

When I turned the calendar from February to March, I realised that ten months had passed since I had last seen Mr. Ashford. He might be married now, I thought, my stomach churning at the very thought. The housekeeper at Pembroke Hall had said the wedding was to be next year, but *when* next year? In what month? The image of his being attached for life to the childish, simpering Isabella, brought a fresh stab of pain and anger to my breast. *I hope she plagues his heart out,* I thought, rather ungenerously. And then, *What becomes of them is of no consequence to me. I will not think about it.*

I had my work, my home, my family. I had never been happier in my life. It was all I could ever need.

---

[37] She refers to the characters Sir John and Lady Middleton in *Sense and Sensibility*.

As I completed the final revisions on my novel, I began reading it aloud to the women in the house.

"It is a wonderful book," cried Martha enthusiastically one evening, when we had read through the first half. "The women in this story seem to live and breathe. Elinor is the very best sort of person, and I *adore* Marianne. But I cannot help but think that the *men* are very bad."

"They are very bad, indeed," agreed my mother, shaking her head as she continued with her embroidery. "Colonel Brandon seems a good sort. But Edward and Willoughby, the two men who have captured your ladies' hearts, they are *both* engaged to other women! They are cads, the lot of them!"

"You have not heard all, mother," said Cassandra, with a quick, sympathetic look at me. "Perhaps there is a reason behind their actions, an explanation which will resolve every thing, and a good outcome."

"I cannot see how," replied my mother. "Particularly in Willoughby's case. And I did *so* like him at first."

"So did I," admitted Martha with a sigh.

"He *was* quite wonderful," agreed Cassandra.

"It was my design that you should like him. I did all I could to make him charming, literate, intelligent, handsome, devoted—every thing that Marianne, with her romantic sensibilities, could ever want in a man—so that you might understand and respect her for being smitten by him."

"And then he leaves her without a word!" snapped my mother, "and goes off to marry another. Horrible, horrible man! Whatever possessed you to write such a thing?"

Cassandra glanced at me again with concern, and said, "Jane has a vivid imagination, mamma."

I quickly looked away, hoping the others would not notice even the barest trace of anguish in my eyes, should it exist.

My mother and Martha knew nothing of Mr. Ashford, and I was determined that they never should.

"Well, she has used it to write a very somber story, if you ask me," cried my mother. "*Very* somber. As if Willoughby's other faults were not bad enough, *now* you give him past transgressions that can never be excused or redeemed! And that letter he wrote to Marianne, casting her aside as if she were nothing. Why, it was the most cruel, unfeeling thing I have ever heard. My heart quite went out to her, Jane. When she cried, *I* was moved to tears, real tears, I tell you."

"I am pleased to hear it, mamma," said I with feeling. "That is, indeed, the highest praise you could give my work."

"How can you call it praise," cried my mother, "when I am telling you I hate the man?"

"He *is* a rascal, Jane," said Cassandra.

"The blackest villain!" agreed Martha. "Cannot you soften him, even just a little?"

"I cannot, and I will not," I insisted. "Willoughby is what he is. The world is full of rascals and villains. Better that Marianne should be apprised of it at seventeen, and learn from her mistakes."

"I think you are very heartless to poor Marianne," said my mother.

I did not agree. But as we made our way through the rest of the book, I wondered if my anger at my own situation had clouded my judgment. Even *I* found Willoughby so contemptible, that I decided I must attempt to redeem him after all, if only in a small way. At the eleventh hour, much to the gratification of the women of my household, I inserted a scene in which Willoughby returns to apologize.

"Thank you, Jane," said Cassandra, relieved, when I read the newly written scene aloud. "I feel much better now."

"As do I," declared Martha, wiping away a tear. "For although Willoughby behaved very badly, it helps to know that he truly did love Marianne and deeply regretted his actions."

"I still say, it would be a better book all around if he never married the other woman in the first place!" cried my mother passionately. "I declare, I do not understand where you are going with this, Jane. We all want a happy ending, you know. What happy ending can there be for poor Marianne now, even if she does *not* die of a broken heart?"

"Have you forgotten Colonel Brandon?" interjected Cassandra calmly. "He has loved her from the start."

"Oh! That he has," replied my mother. She sat in contemplation for a moment. "I see. I see. Well, there's a good thought. Colonel Brandon is indeed a treasure."

"I would marry him myself, if he walked through that door," agreed Martha, laughing.

"Jane has always promised that her books would end with at least one wedding," said Cassandra, "or two, if possible."

"But what of Elinor?" cried my mother in sudden distress, her hand flying to her throat.

"Yes, what of dear, dear Elinor?" asked Martha.

"How do you plan to solve *that* one, Jane?" My mother sighed, waving her hands hopelessly. "Her Edward is as good as married to Lucy Steele by now."

A pang of sadness took hold of my heart, but I forced a smile. "Do not fret. You will have your happy ending, I promise."

I finished the book in early spring, happy endings intact. My family of critics seemed very pleased with it, and encouraged me to take it to Henry in London, to see if he could secure its publication.

My heart pounded with trepidation at the thought. I had devoted my entire heart, soul and mind to this work, and two or three years of my life to its inception. What if it did not sell? What if all my efforts had, as in the past, been in vain?

"I am not sure it is ready," I protested. "It requires more attention."

"Jane," said Cassandra sternly, "you cannot work on the same book for ever. You must make a copy and take it to London."

I sighed. "Then you must come with me."

Chapter Twenty-two

⁓⧫⧫⁓

It was a delight to visit Henry and his wife Eliza at their house on Sloane Street, a long, smart avenue on the outskirts of London. In addition to their sparkling company, and the advantages of all the attractions of town being near at hand, they also employed two French maids and a superb French chef.

My dear cousin Eliza (the daughter of my father's sister), had been raised in France and had led a life which seemed to me both exotic and thrilling, yet tinged with tragedy; her first husband, Count Jean Capotte de Feullide, had died by guillotine in 1794, and her only son had died young. Henry, although ten years younger than Eliza, had fallen in love with her at sixteen, and finally convinced her to marry him a decade later. I adored Eliza, and always had. She was sophisticated, musical and very pretty, with an energetic manner, large, bright eyes and an elfin face surrounded by curls. Her capacity for extravagant shopping was notorious, and her dress always the richest in the room.

Henry's financial situation had often been precarious (even long before marrying his extravagant wife), but his banking concern at the time was flourishing, and he maintained well-situated offices in town as well as a grand style of life.[38]

"I believe it is your best work yet, Jane," pronounced Henry with enthusiasm, as we dined on a delectable *Cordon Bleu* one late-July evening. It had taken me several months to make a new copy of *Sense and Sensibility,* which I had carried in a satchel on my lap in Henry's carriage all the way to London, afraid to allow the precious manuscript out of my sight for more than an instant. Henry had read all three volumes with avid attention in the first week after Cassandra and I arrived, and Eliza was now perusing them.

"I love this novel," cried Eliza. "I am so engrossed, I cannot wait to return to it."

"You are being kind," I replied. "The book has many flaws, I am not at all satisfied with it."

"She will never be satisfied, I fear"—Cassandra sighed— "even though she began writing it at two-and-twenty, and has spent nearly every day of the past year perfecting it."

"Perhaps this is not the best book to submit to a publisher," said I anxiously. "I could not bear to have it purchased and ignored, like *Susan.* Perhaps I ought to go back and revise *First Impressions* first."

"I do not understand you," said Henry. "This book is

---

[38] Henry's bank, which was doing extremely well at the time, collapsed five years later, a result of the difficult post-war economic conditions. He quickly rebounded, reprised his boyhood intention of taking Holy Orders, and was appointed to the curacy of Chawton in 1816.

excellent, and already finished. How long have you dreamt of being an author? After all your efforts, surely you wish to see the work published, do you not?"

"Of course I do," I admitted, "but—"

"There are no buts," said Henry. "We must act quickly, Jane. We must release it to the world while the debate between head and heart is still of interest to society. One day, I fear, that subject, which is at the very centre of your story, may be forgotten."

As Henry began his quest to find a publisher, Cassandra and I busied ourselves walking into town and calling on several old acquaintances, including the Smiths and the Cookes, and a Miss Beckford and Miss Middleton, very pleasant little parties where we enjoyed good conversation with intelligent people and drank a great deal of tea. The weather was invariably fine and hot. Eliza joined us on several shopping expeditions where we marvelled at her stamina, her ability to spend, and her judicious eye for colour and style (she purchased more hats in one afternoon than any one I have ever witnessed, before or since.) Cassandra and I made do with more mundane purchases of darning cotton, silk stockings and gloves, although I did find ten yards of a pretty-coloured checked muslin at the Linen draper's shop, for which I was obliged to pay seven shillings a yard.

One particularly memorable night, Henry took us to a play at the Lyceum. Eliza, who had a cold, chose to stay home. I cannot recall the name of the play that night, or who were the principal actors in it. The memory remains vivid for me owing to the people whom I chanced to meet at the interval that night.

It was a warm summer evening, and the theatre had become

hotter than we liked. As Henry chatted with a friend after the first act curtain, Cassandra and I adjourned to the lobby, which, although filled with people, with the doors thrown open, was comparatively cool. We had not been in the outer room half a minute when a familiar voice called out shrilly, "Yoo hoo! Miss Austen! Miss Jane Austen!" and we spied Mrs. Jenkins bustling through the crowd, a formidable spectacle in satin and pearls, with her niece Isabella in tow.

My heart leapt with surprise and alarm, particularly at the sight of Isabella, who looked young and ravishing in a gown of pale pink silk, with a matching band in her dark hair embellished by a spray of flowers.

"Ladies! Ladies!" cried Mrs. Jenkins, as the two women reached our side in a rustle of skirts. "How delightful! It has been *ages,* simply *ages*! Isabella, do you remember Jane and Cassandra Austen? They are my dear friends from Southampton, who have sadly moved away."

"How nice to see you again," said Isabella, holding out her hand and smiling coolly in our direction.

I recalled, from our first meeting, that Mrs. Jenkins had promised to continue her excursions to London with her niece, even after she was married. Had the wedding yet taken place? I wondered. Isabella's long, white gloves made it impossible to tell if she wore a ring. "It is wonderful to see you," I said, smiling, although my heart pounded so loudly I could scarcely think. "You are both looking well."

"Oh! Thank you," replied the older woman. "I cannot complain. So long as I can rise each morning with a smile on my face, and manage to keep up with my niece all day long, that is all that matters to me." She enquired after our mother, and asked how we were enjoying our new home.

When satisfied with our replies, she added, "What brings you to London?"

"We are visiting my brother Henry," said I diffidently.

"How long have you ladies been in town?" enquired Cassandra.

"Since just after the season began," replied Mrs. Jenkins.

"It has all been *heavenly*," said Isabella. "First it was the annual exhibition at the Royal Academy, then a round of the most wonderful balls and parties, the Derby, and of course the Ascot; why, my head spins just to think of it. But now," she added, frowning petulantly, "it is nearly over. All the ladies think about is which country houses they are going to, and whom they are to meet. And all the men talk about is grouse, grouse, grouse."[39]

"Surely you will look forward to returning to the country after all this time, Miss Churchill," said I, my stomach clenched tighter than any sailor's knot. "Or should I say—is it Mrs. Ashford now?"

Isabella frowned. "You cannot think me married *yet*, Miss Jane, or I would surely never have been allowed to remain here so long and so delightfully with my aunt."

"But she *will* be married, soon," said Mrs. Jenkins happily. "The wedding is to be the last week in December. She is to be a Christmas bride."

"How lovely," said I, and quickly added, "How is your writing coming, Miss Churchill?"

---

[39] The height of the London season was a three-month whirlwind of parties, balls and sporting events, which typically began after Easter and continued until August 12, which signalled the end of Parliament and the opening of grouse season. At this point, the fashionable deserted London and returned to the country, where the remainder of the year was devoted to the hunting and hounding of small animals, in particular the grouse, partridge, pheasant and fox. Parliament did not begin again until the end of the year, when shooting and hunting ceased, and foxes began to breed.

Isabella stared at me blankly. "My what?"

"Your writing." Turning to Mrs. Jenkins, I explained, "Miss Churchill and I had the pleasure of meeting in Derbyshire last year, where I had the opportunity to peruse a tale of her own composition."

The young lady's eyes brightened, and she let out a small laugh. "Oh *that!* Why, that was *ever* so long ago, I had forgotten all about it! I meant to send you a note, Miss Jane, to thank you for the kind words you wrote, but I never could finish that story. Writing is such a tiresome enterprise, and it takes up so much time. It gives me a headache just to think of it."

"You should see the needlepoint pillow she is working on," said Mrs. Jenkins. "A thistle, all her own design."

"I am sure it is exquisite," I replied.

Hoping to end this conversation, I was about to make some excuse to return to my seat, when a handsome young gentleman in a dark navy full-dress coat appeared, of a sudden, at Isabella's side. "Good evening Mrs. Jenkins, ladies," said he with a formal bow. "Miss Churchill, what an unexpected pleasure to find you here. I hope I am not interrupting?"

Isabella turned to him with a curtsy and a demure smile. "Indeed you are not, sir."

Mrs. Jenkins's countenance grew tight and pinched. I wondered who the gentleman could be, but before any one else could speak, he said, "It is a stifling evening, is it not?"

"It *is* quite warm," replied Isabella.

"If you feel the need for some air, Miss Churchill," said he, "we have a few minutes yet before curtain. I would be pleased to escort you to the front of the foyer, where I found a trace of a breeze by an open doorway."

"How very thoughtful of you to offer," answered Isabella.

"I am sorry, sir," snapped Mrs. Jenkins, "but she cannot accept."

"Auntie dear, pray, do not be so old-fashioned. There is no harm in my taking the air with a friend, and as you see, we have a room full of chaperones." Isabella turned to the gentleman and, taking his arm, added, "I would be most grateful, sir, if you would lead the way."

Mrs. Jenkins batted her fan in ferocious disapproval, casting her eyes nervously about the room as the two young people moved off together. "Oh dear! I shall never live this down. Our Isabella is much too bold."

"Who is the gentleman?" I enquired.

"His name is Wellington. He is apparently from a very good family in Shropshire, and will one day inherit an estate from his uncle. He has been at nearly every event this season, and seems quite smitten with Isabella, although I have made him fully aware that she is betrothed to another, and for all that she insists they are just good friends. I have warned her that it is not at all seemly for a woman in her position to be seen so often in the company of another man, but she maintains that I am worrying over nothing."

"Their interchange *does* appear rather innocent," said Cassandra, glancing across the lobby to the front doorway, where Isabella was now engaged in smiling conversation with Mr. Wellington.

"Perhaps you are right," replied Mrs. Jenkins, "but I cannot be too careful. Dear me, it *is* hot in here. Miss Austen, would you be so kind as to accompany me closer to the door, where I might have a better view of my niece and that young rake?"

"I should be glad to, Mrs. Jenkins," said Cassandra. To me,

she added apologetically, "I shall return in but a moment, Jane."

As I watched Mrs. Jenkins and Cassandra cross the room towards Isabella and her friend, I heard a man's voice with a deep Scottish lilt behind me:

"There is nothing like a good-looking man in a navy blue dress coat for captivating the ladies."

I turned to find a well-dressed gentleman with an agreeable face, who appeared to be about nine-and-thirty; he was gazing at Isabella with an animated, intelligent eye and an amused smile.

"A well-tailored coat and a handsome face may turn a girl's head, sir," I replied, "but it is the mind behind that face that captivates a lady."

The gentleman's eyebrows lifted and he turned his stare to me. "Spoken like a true poet of modern romance, Miss—?"

"Austen. Miss Jane Austen." I held out my gloved hand, and he took it, bowing.

"A pleasure to meet you, Miss Austen. I am Mr. Walter Scott."

I nearly gasped aloud, and could not hide my stunned surprise and awe. I had never imagined that I would meet a writer of such notoriety and acclaim, whose poetry I had read many times over—yet there he was, standing before me in a London theatre. "Mr. Scott!" I cried, when I found my voice, "It is an honour and a pleasure to meet *you,* sir. Indeed, *you* are the poet, sir."

"Thank you," said he modestly, his small smile and muted tone implying a sense of dissatisfaction, "but you would be better off, I fear, reading Wordsworth."

"I beg to differ. I enjoy his work as well, of course, but I greatly admire the lively description and honest pathos of your ballads. May I enquire as to what you are working on at present?"

"Another little metrical romance."

"What is this one about?"

"An Englishman called Waverly, who travels to the Scottish Highlands during the second Jacobite Rebellion." Mr. Scott waved his hand with a bored air. "In truth I am growing weary of ballads, particularly my own. I am well aware that I shall never be more than a minor poet."

"Perhaps it is time," said I boldly (without thinking), "to leave poetry behind and move in a new direction." No sooner had the words left my mouth than I felt myself blush. Whatever had possessed me? Who was *I* to give advice to this celebrated writer?

Mr. Scott met my embarrassed gaze with a wide smile. "What new direction would you suggest, Miss Austen?"

The call was sounded for the second act; the crowd began to remove towards the theatre; but Mr. Scott stood waiting for my reply. "Prose," said I.

"Prose?" repeated he, in surprise.

"Indeed, sir. It has become quite the thing of late. Perhaps you should write your Waverly as a novel."

"A novel?" Mr. Scott laughed out loud. "Now there is a *novel* idea. Do you truly think the public would find interest and enjoyment in a *novel* about imaginary historical figures?"

"Why not?"

"Why, because it has never been done."

"There is a first time for every thing, Mr. Scott. And if any one could write a powerful novel of history and romance, it is you, sir."

He laughed again. "I daresay, if I attempted such a work, I would never put my name on it."

"Nor would I, sir," I agreed, with a laugh of my own. "But I do believe it would be popular."

Mr. Scott nodded, an introspective look crossing his countenance as he thanked me again for my kind words, and moved off with a distracted bow, muttering to himself, "Now there is an idea. A *novel*."[40]

My own literary aspirations, unlike my hopes for Mr. Scott, seemed destined for a disastrous end. Despite Henry's earnest attempts over the course of several weeks, he had been unable to interest a publisher in my book.

"It is a first novel, by an unknown author," explained Henry in some frustration, glancing at my title page which read, *Sense and Sensibility. A Novel in Three Volumes. By a Lady.* "Not only unknown, but *unnamed!* With the limitations you have placed upon me, Jane, I find it difficult to persuade any one even to read it. If you would at least permit me to admit that the work was written by my sister, I might be able to gain a sympathetic ear."

"No," I replied emphatically. "It is enough to say that you

---

[40] Sir Walter Scott (who became a baronet in 1820, and was known thereafter as *Sir*), was a popular but minor poet in his early years. The turning point of his literary career came in 1814, with the publication of his first novel, *Waverly,* which was published anonymously, as were all its many successors down to 1827. He is often considered the inventor of the historical novel. He later became a great admirer of Jane Austen's work, declaring that she had an "exquisite touch" and "a talent for describing the involvements and feelings and characters of ordinary life which is to me the most wonderful I ever met with."

represent the author. I am convinced that a publisher will think more highly of the work if they do *not* suspect it was the effort of one of your relations."

"I believe she is right in that, Henry dear," said Eliza. "It may speak better for the novel if it appears that you hold a more disinterested view."

"Perhaps," said Henry with a shrug. "Is this your only concern, Jane? Should I be so fortunate as to secure a publisher, will you *then* put your name to it?"

"No. I wish to remain anonymous."

"Why?" cried Henry, exasperated.

"I do not know precisely. It is difficult to explain." I had dearly wished to be published, it is true; yet at the same time, the idea of fame or notoriety mortified me. "It is one thing to write for one's family and most intimate friends. But if this book were to have a more wide-spread audience, it would be a most uncomfortable sensation to think that strangers knew my name and were making uninformed judgments about me."

"I understand how Jane feels," said Cassandra, squeezing my hand sympathetically.

"I think you are both being quite ridiculous," admonished Henry.

"Have you not read how the world treats lady novelists?" I replied heatedly. "They are pointed at, noticed and commented on, suspected of literary airs, and shunned by the more unpretending of my sex. I could not bear the scrutiny. I would sooner exhibit as a rope-dancer."

"A rope-dancer might have more success in becoming published," said Henry.

"Jane, dear," said Eliza gently. "You are a wonderful writer.

I am certain your readers will only look up to you. You should be proud of what you have accomplished. There is no need to hide behind anonymity."

"She will be mired in anonymity for ever if I cannot succeed in selling her book," observed Henry glumly.

"There must be other places you can take it, Henry," said Cassandra.

"I have tried everyone I know."

"Then you must try the people you do *not* know, darling," said Eliza.

"What are you suggesting, my dear?"

"I think," replied Eliza, "it is time that we gave a little party."

Eliza's notion of a *little* party was a *soirée* of some five-and-twenty couples, to take place before the end of the week. There was some urgency in planning the affair, since she felt it must be accomplished before the twelfth of August, the end of the season, when all the best families in London would remove to the country for the sport.

At Eliza's urging, Henry invited his wealthiest clients and friends, and acquaintances who he believed might have a connection to some one in the publishing world, hoping to secure an introduction of some import. I was overwhelmed with gratitude for the efforts they undertook on my behalf, and though I protested that I could never repay them, Eliza insisted that she enjoyed throwing parties, had been meaning to host one all summer, and this had seemed an excellent excuse.

I worried about what to wear, as my best gown, a pretty white muslin with short-capped sleeves, was looking a bit tired. Cassandra's gown was a lovely shade of pale lemon, but not much newer. Eliza helped us dress them up with new sashes and frills of delicate lace, and engaged her hairdresser to do our hair.

As is the way with such events, there were many solicitudes, alarms, and vexations in the week beforehand, but at last, when the guests began to arrive at eight on the evening of the party, everything was quite right. The house was beautifully dressed up with flowers, the sideboard was laden with an attractive and delicious array of consumables, and the guests, all elegantly attired and gathered in the front drawing-room, seemed to be enjoying themselves.

Cassandra and I were engaged in pleasant conversation in a far corner with our friends the Cookes, when Eliza (dressed in *haute couture*, of course—a simply divine white silk gown, the bodice and hem embellished with lace, pearls, and pink satin rosettes), took me by the arm and propelled me across the room, where she said in a lowered tone, behind her fan, "Do you see that stout gentleman, by the punch bowl? He is the solicitor for a publishing house. And that bearded gentleman in the purple coat, Henry said he has a friend who is acquainted with the brother of a publisher. Apparently, there are at least half a dozen men here who might have useful connections. Henry is determined to speak to all of them before the night is through."

"I am indebted to you both," I said.

My face must have shewn my trepidation, because Eliza smiled and added, "Have no fear, Jane, he is merely working as your representative, as you have so firmly insisted. Your secret is perfectly safe."

"Thank you," I replied in relief.

As Eliza excused herself and glided off to greet a guest,

Henry appeared, of a sudden, at my elbow. "There you are, sister dear! You will *never* guess who appeared in my office this morning, out of the blue, looking for you."

I turned. To my complete astonishment, I encountered Mr. Ashford.

Chapter Twenty-three

───────── ◦❧ ❧◦ ─────────

A surge of anger and dismay flooded through me as I stared at Mr. Ashford. I felt my cheeks grow warm and my heart begin to pound. What on earth, I wondered, was *he* doing here? And *why*, I thought helplessly, could I never encounter this man without a response of such overwhelming and obvious physical emotion?

"You may not remember Mr. Ashford," said Henry, smiling gaily and oblivious to my distress, "but we met several years past, on our little excursion to Lyme."

Mr. Ashford's countenance, although as handsome as ever, was white with agitation; his eyes, as they met mine, looked as if fearful of his reception, and conscious that he merited no kind one. "Of course I remember Mr. Ashford," I replied, infuriated by the tremor in my voice. I lowered my gaze, focusing on his bright blue coat and exquisitely embroidered vest.

"I was delighted to see him again, as you can well imagine," said Henry, "and the timing could not have been more perfect. I told him about our party tonight, and nothing would do but he must come and have a word with you, Jane." Bowing to Mr. Ashford, he added; "It was wonderful chatting with you, my good man. Now, if you will both excuse me, I must go play the host."

"I am much obliged," replied Mr. Ashford, bowing in return, as Henry disappeared. An awkward silence ensued as Mr. Ashford turned to me. "I only just learned that you were in town, from—" He stopped himself, his face colouring. He gathered his composure, and said, "You are looking well, Miss Austen."

"As are you, Mr. Ashford," I answered tersely, praying that my own agitation was not as visible as *his*, and that the wild beating of my heart could not be detected through the thin muslin of my gown.

He winced at the coldness of my reply, but went on: "Your brother tells me that you finished your book. I am so pleased for you. I wish you much success with it."

"Thank you."

For a brief interval, neither of us spoke. I tried desperately to gather my thoughts. Should I take advantage of this rare opportunity to tell him, in no uncertain terms, what I thought of him and his behaviour towards me in the past? Or should I take the high road, smile graciously, and congratulate him on his impending nuptials? I had tentatively decided on the latter, when at last he said,

"Miss Austen. It has been many long months that I have wanted, needed to speak with you—"

"I see no reason for us to speak, Mr. Ashford," I snapped, the words tumbling out before I could stop them.

"I do not blame you for being angry with me. Nor do I

blame you for returning my letters. But please believe me when I say that I never wished to cause you pain. And I—"

"Do not presume to know of my pain, Mr. Ashford." To my mortification, unexpected tears stung my eyes. Unable to bear this tortuous conversation a moment longer, I said, "Forgive me. It was good of you to come. But should you not be spending the evening with your fiancée?"

I moved away abruptly through the crowd, relieved to have made my escape. I had no sooner reached the sanctuary of the back drawing-room, which was yet devoid of guests, when, to my dismay, I heard footsteps quick upon my heels and Mr. Ashford's cry:

"Miss Austen! Wait, please!"

I fled across the empty room, towards the card-tables at the back. "I would greatly appreciate it, sir, if you would leave at once."

"I cannot go. Please, Miss Austen! Listen to me."

"There is nothing you can say, sir, that I wish to hear."

"I have waited too long, I can endure it no longer, you must hear me out! The day Isabella was born, our *fathers* decided we would marry." His anguished words and tone stopped me half way across the room.

"It was a solemn pact made between two old friends," he went on, "the marriage to take place sometime after Isabella's eighteenth birthday. I was *seventeen* years old on the day of her birth, and she was this, this newborn *infant*. I protested, I begged my father to reconsider, all to no avail. No thought was given to my needs or happiness, or hers. Their only thought was to unite two great families."

I slowly turned to face him. He stood but a yard away, and spoke with rising agitation. His tormented aspect, and the agony in his expression, sent a wave of pain and sympathy through me that tore at my heart.

"I was much away at school while she was growing up, always aware that this little girl, this *child,* was to one day be my wife. My father made it clear that *this* was my duty," Mr. Ashford spat out in a deep voice filled with anger. "I met other women over the years, of course, but I never allowed myself to feel any thing more than friendship for them. I could not, for I had no choice. I grew to esteem Isabella as a sister, and hoped that would be enough. And then," his voice finally softening, "then, I met *you.*"

His eyes rose to meet mine, his gaze so filled with affection, it nearly stopped my heart.

"I knew at once, when we met at Lyme, that we shared a deep and rarely felt connection, something most people only dream of. I knew, as well, that I should tell you of my obligation to Isabella, but every thing was so perfect that first day; you were so vibrant, and our conversation so invigorating, I did not wish to say any thing to break the spell. I promised myself I would explain my situation the next day, on our picnic, but the next day never materialized. I returned home with a heavy heart, believing I would never see you again, and I resigned myself to my fate. But every moment that I was forced to endure Isabella's company only served to remind me of how unsuited we were to one another. I did not love her, and never could, and it was clear that she did not love me. Again, I pleaded with my father to release me from my engagement, but he became incensed, and insisted that honour forbade it. I was miserable. A day did not go by that I did not think of you and wonder what might have been. The next March, I came to Southampton, Miss Austen, specifically to find *you.*"

"To find me?" My voice was so thin and reedy that I barely recognised it, while his was filled with growing urgency.

"I could bear it no longer. I had to discover if you were real, if what I *felt* was real, or some fanciful creation of my own mind. I hoped that somehow, even then, I might be able one day to convince my father to free me from my obligation, or that, at the very least, we might become friends. I intended to tell you about Isabella at once, but I could not bring myself to say the words. The time we shared at Southampton was the happiest of my life. As each day went by, and my attachment to you grew stronger, the subject became even harder to broach; I was afraid that you would send me away."

"So I would have," I whispered, wiping away a tear which had come unbidden. I would have said more, had not emotion closed my throat.

"Jane!" cried he softly, moving closer. "All these long months that we have been apart, even believing it to be impossible, it is of you alone that I have thought and planned. You are my heart; you pierce my soul. My behavior at Southampton was wrong, unjust and weak, and for that, I shall always feel regret. But it was out of fear of losing you, and the knowledge that, bound as I was by my father's vow and Isabella's expectations, I had no right to speak—until now."

"Until now?"

"There has been a recent change, most unexpected, which—" He drew in a long breath, struggling to compose himself. "I was told in the strictest of confidence, but I cannot keep it from you. Isabella, since she came to London, has apparently been much in company with a gentleman she met, a Mr. Wellington."

My pulse quickened. "I have seen him."

"Last night, she came to me, to reveal a great secret. She said that Mr. Wellington had asked her to marry him."

"To *marry* him?"

"She explained, politely, that she had always intended to honour the long-standing promise of our fathers, but that her affections were now placed elsewhere. And she deeply regretted any unhappiness this might cause me."

I turned away, my mind all in a whirl, afraid to hope or feel. "What says her father to that?" I managed.

"She will tell him next month, when he returns from the West Indies. We agreed to say nothing to any one until she has revealed all to her father, and received his blessing. Needless to say, I released her from our engagement without an ounce of regret or crimination, for which she was eternally grateful."

I was overcome with a flood of such deep emotion that I wished to run from the room, but as there was nowhere to go in a house full of people where I might avoid detection, I could only cover my face with my hands, whereupon I burst into tears of joy, which I thought at first would never cease.

"Forgive me," I heard Mr. Ashford's anguished voice, "I think only of myself. Please, Miss Austen, please, do not cry."

My tears flowed at such a rate that I was incapable of speech. Mr. Ashford, his brow furrowed with distress, offered me his handkerchief, which I accepted gratefully. As I struggled to compose myself, he said, in a concerned tone,

"My circumstances have changed in such a substantial way, that I—but perhaps too much time has passed, since—"

He waited tensely while I dried my eyes and noisily blew my nose, actions which did nothing to increase the romantic aspect of the moment. At last, he continued with resolve, "Miss Austen. You have allowed me to speak, and I have made my feelings clear. I realise I have no right to ask any thing of you. If you do not share my feelings, please tell me so at once and I shall leave, and never trouble you again."

"I cannot tell you that," said I, raising my eyes to his with a joyous smile.

"Then," said he, with new-found anticipation in his earnest gaze, "do you mean to give me hope?"

"If my deepest affection and admiration give you hope, then yes."

He quickly bridged the gap between us, took my gloved hand in his, and, bringing it to his lips, he kissed it, his eyes never leaving my face. "Then at last, I am free to speak the words that I have so longed to say. I love you, Jane, my dearest Jane. It is you alone that I wish to marry. Will you have me, Jane? Will you be my wife?"

My heart was so filled with happiness, I thought I must be dreaming. "Yes," I said, breathless. "I will."

He gave me a look of pure joy, then bent his head, and—*dare I say it?*—he brought his lips to mine, and kissed me.

This thrilling moment was very rudely interrupted when, of a sudden, Cassandra burst through the open door, a perplexed look on her face, calling my name. Catching sight of us across the room, Cassandra froze in shocked embarrassment and gasped, her hand going to her mouth.

"Oh! Forgive me!" cried Cassandra, her face turning scarlet. "I am so sorry."

Mr. Ashford released me and took two steps back.

"Cassandra," I began, but she had already turned and fled.

Mr. Ashford's eyes met mine, and we burst out laughing; then he took me in his arms and kissed me again and again and again.

Chapter Twenty-four

There are some who might complain that August in London is akin to a month in Hades; that the hot, stifling, humid air coming off the Thames is unhealthful and clots one's lungs; that the streets are reminiscent, in sight and smell, of a stable-yard; and that the glaring sun reflecting off the buildings and pavements is injurious to the complexion. But to these naysayers, I say *pshaw*. London is a wondrous place at any time of year, and that blissful August of 1810, I was unmindful of any such objections. *Au contraire,* I floated through the remainder of the month, and all of the one following, as if wrapped in the perfection of a dream.

I told no one of my secret engagement except my sister, and made *her* promise not to breathe a word of it to any one. Mr. Ashford was frustrated by the necessity of waiting. He wanted to proclaim his love for me to the world, he said, and set a wedding date at once. But Isabella had begged him not to speak of her involvement with Mr. Wellington until the matter had first been made known to her father, who was not expected back from the West Indies for at least a month. Mr. Ashford's father was currently in Derbyshire, but intended to return to London in October. It would be best, we agreed, to present the news to Sir Thomas in person when he came to town, *after* Isabella was formally and publicly engaged to Mr. Wellington.

In the meantime, it was Mr. Ashford's goal that I should enjoy all the sights in London that could possibly be of interest, and that he should be my guide. We first climbed the 378 steps to the Stone Gallery at the top of St. Paul's, where we were afforded a marvelous view of the compact city, which spread along the river, from Billingsgate to Westminster. Its borders were clearly defined by the fields and groves to the north and south, with the west end beginning at Hyde Park Corner. We could see the village of Paddington in the distance, and a series of pastures called Belgravia.

We admired what had once been the royal city of Westminster in the West End, where sat the palaces of St. James and Whitehall, as well as breathtaking Westminster Abbey and the Houses of Parliament, and we paid to cross the old London Bridge, just west of the Tower, at the entrance of the city, where we watched a great numbers of small ships and boats sail by.

With most of the fashionable elite now removed to their country houses, the town was comparatively quiet, although we were still compelled to raise our voices over the unceasing clatter of carriage-wheels and horses' hooves, the resounding cries of street pedlars, the garish songs of itinerant musicians, and the clang of the muffin-man's bell—sounds which, in their confluence, had been known to give me the headache, but which I had come to regard with a new-found affection.

Twice, that summer, Mrs. Jenkins came to call, and my sister and I returned the favour.

"Oh dear!" cried that good lady in some distress, at our second meeting. "I declare, I do not know what our Isabella is about. She has been writing letters day in and day out, and several missives have arrived for her, but she will not disclose with whom she is corresponding. I have been unsuccessful in every attempt to intercede."

Bound as I was by my promise not to mention, as yet, her affair with Mr. Wellington, or the dissolution of her engagement to Mr. Ashford, I could say nothing to elucidate the matter; but I attempted to lessen her distress by making such supportive comments regarding Isabella's strength of character, as I thought appropriate.

We dined at more cafés in those six weeks of summer, I believe, than I had frequented in the entire preceding four-and-thirty years of my existence, retreating, several times, to take our meals at the imposing Ashford family residence on Park Lane, which overlooked the immense greensward of Hyde Park on the west border of Mayfair. The magnificent rooms of that house, unused in the absence of his father and sister, were maintained by a faithful but unassuming staff, who seemed predisposed to cater to Mr. Ashford's every wish.

We attended concerts and the theatre, visited the Liverpool Museum and the British Gallery, and the fashionable shops on Bond Street, where I could not dare to look at the prices, and refused to allow Mr. Ashford to purchase me a single item.

On several of these excursions, we were accompanied by Cassandra (who had considered returning to Chawton, but was convinced by an enthusiastic Eliza to stay through the summer), and on other occasions, by Eliza and Henry as well; but as, at our ages, a chaperone was no longer requisite, more often than not, we preferred to spend our time in the exclusive company of each other. One of our favourite activities was a stroll through Kensington Gardens, which was in full, glorious bloom. We found a particular bench there, overlooking a lovely pond, to which we returned again and again, simply to sit and talk, share confidences, and bask in the delight of each other's presence.

One afternoon in mid-September, as we sat on our favourite bench in the gardens, Mr. Ashford announced that he had finished reading my book.

"Oh?" I replied, my heart leaping in sudden alarm. Henry's efforts to find a publisher, despite all the connections he had made at the party, had so far been in vain. At Mr. Ashford's urging, I had, despite my misgivings, agreed to give him the manuscript to read. I had awaited his reaction with dread, afraid that he could not fail to recognise certain situations in the novel, which had clearly been inspired by my encounters with him.

"It is clever and beautifully written, every thing that I had hoped and expected," said he. "You should be very proud."

"I am pleased you liked it," I replied in relief. Perhaps, I thought, he had not noticed his own connection to the story, after all. "At present, the manuscript is extremely useful as an aid in propping open the kitchen door."

He laughed. "It should, it *must* be published."

"I am afraid my foray into the publishing world has been a very humbling experience."

"Perhaps I might be of some help. I have one or two connections of my own. If you would permit me, I would be glad to make some efforts on your behalf."

"I would be most obliged. But you must promise me not to blame yourself if nothing comes of it. In truth, I have become convinced that my little book would be a poor bargain for a publisher. I cannot imagine it would ever sell in sufficient quantities to earn back its cost."

"I disagree. It may not be perfect, but I believe it is a work of art, good enough to sell any number of copies, and make a handsome profit."

"What? Not perfect?" I cried in mock indignation. "In what way, pray tell, is my book—this work of art which no one will publish—imperfect?"

"I cannot recall exactly," said he, "but it was some small thing about the ending. I remember feeling that something was missing, or not quite right."

"I see. If you ever retrieve your thoughts on the subject, I hope you will share them with me."

"I will." He smiled, and added, with a sidelong glance at me, "There was something else, I must confess—in no way a sign of any imperfection, but there were some aspects of the novel that I found, how shall I put it—*familiar*."

A hot flush spread over my cheeks. "Did you, indeed?"

"For example: your Elinor feels a deep attachment to this Edward character, a rather dull but amiable fellow, only to discover, after he has left without a word of commitment, that he has long been engaged to another. And she is later confronted, at precisely the same moment, by both Edward and Lucy." The knowing but discomfited twinkle in his eyes, and the raising of his brows, communicated his perfect understanding of his own part in the conception of those scenes.

"They were very dramatic situations," I replied, inwardly cursing my tendency to blush.

"And clearly, ones that you could write with insight. I must admit, when I read your book, there were times that the hair on the back of my neck stood up on end. That moment in the drawing-room at Mr. Morton's parsonage, when I walked in on you and Isabella, will be for ever branded in my memory as one of the most mortifying of my life."

"For me as well," I replied, mortified myself at the thought of how much discomfort that scene must have inflicted. "You see, now, why I was so reluctant to let you read my book."

"I am glad I read it." He turned on the bench to face me. "Tell me, Jane, am I taking this too personally, or was some of your anger towards me incorporated into your depiction of Willoughby?"

His expression was so serious, and so forlorn, it tugged at my heart, yet for some unaccountable reason, I could not help but laugh. "Perhaps it was," I admitted. "Willoughby is quite appalling, is he not?"

"He is the epitome of the self-centred cad. At the other end of the spectrum, of course, are Colonel Brandon, and Edward—who, despite his offences, is redeemed as a saint."

"Edward is no saint!" I retorted hotly, my sharp tone provoking a flock of birds to burst, of a sudden, from a nearby tree.

"Indeed he is. His sense of honour and morality is so high, that he remains committed to his vulgar, grasping fiancée to the bitter end, in spite of being given every reason to abandon her."

"Did not you do the same?" I enquired quietly.

He went silent for a moment, focusing his attention on the ducks splashing in the pond. "I suppose I did," said he at last, a hint of bitterness creeping into his voice. "But in my case, my duty was to honour the wishes of my *father,* a gentleman who has devoted his life to work, property and family, and as such deserves my respect. But had it been up to me—" He broke off with a sigh, and glanced at me with a tight smile. "It is a sobering experience to read of one's transgressions on the page, and the effects of those transgressions, particularly when they are expressed in such a heartfelt manner." He took my hand and held it, looking at me with affection. "I am so sorry, Jane, for all the pain I have caused you in the past. I promise you, I mean to make up for it."

"I will hold you to that promise, Mr. Ashford," said I teasingly.

"I hope you will," said he. "But do not you think it is time you started calling me Frederick?"

The next day, determined to escape the noise and heat of the city, Mr. Ashford (despite his protestations against such formality, he was, and would continue to be, my dearest *Mr. Ashford,* until we were formally engaged) invited me on a drive out to the countryside. We passed a very pretty afternoon picnicking on a high eminence in the dappled shade of an elm grove, with the view of a magnificent valley spread out before us. On our return journey, having decided to take a different road, we came unexpectedly upon a country fair, which we both expressed an inclination to stop and see.

Leaving the curricle and horses with the stable-boy, we ventured out onto the grounds. It was a grand, loud and colourful event, with acre upon acre of market stalls, bazaars, travelling musicians and performers, and a lively crowd of country gentlemen, women, and farmers, who had come to shop, flirt, dine, and be entertained.

As we strolled through the market-place, we passed several red-faced women in faded dresses purchasing bread and cheese, and two gentlemen haggling over the price of a brown mare; but most of the morning's business seemed to have been completed. The crowds were mainly gathered around the cockfights, the wrestling matches, the traveling shows and the rope-dancers.

We stood watching a magician for some moments, amused more by the great *oooohs* and *aaaahs* emanating from the audience, than from the entertainment itself, when all at once Mr. Ashford let out his own brief exclamation.

"Look, there!" cried he, pointing out a gipsy tent with a sign which read, *Palmistry.*

"What? Do you mean the gipsy? Do not tell me you wish to have your fortune told?"

"No, I wish to have *your* fortune told," said he, smiling; and, taking me by the hand, he began pulling me in that direction.

"Absolutely not!" I cried, laughing. "I would not waste a farthing on such nonsense!"

"It will be *my* farthing," replied he, "or pence. Come on, Jane. You do wish to know what will become of your beloved novel, do you not?"

"Nothing will come of it," I insisted, "and I do not need an old gipsy woman to crush my hopes, or raise them falsely." But he was determined that I should go, and seeing no harm in it, I curbed my laughter and allowed him to lead me to the gipsy's tent.

We entered through the open flap and found ourselves in a dim chamber, lit by several candles. I immediately discovered, to my surprise, that the gipsy was not the elderly, dark-skinned, wrinkled woman I had expected. Indeed, she had brown skin and dark eyes, but she could not have been more than five-and-twenty, and was extremely beautiful. She sat behind a small round table covered with a ragged blue cloth; several brightly coloured shawls were wrapped around her shoulders, and her voluminous black, curly hair flowed freely down her back, drawn off her face by a violet scarf.

"Come in," she uttered in a voice of indeterminate accent, as sweet and musical in tone as the flow of river water. She indicated two chairs opposite her with a bejewelled hand. "Please, sit. Have you the coin?"

Mr. Ashford paid her fee, explained that I was to be the subject, and we sat down.

"Give me your hand," said the gipsy, stretching her own towards me across the table. I removed my gloves and complied, sitting in silent, repressed amusement as she bent her head and studied my palm intently.

"There will be one true love in your life," declared the gipsy.

"Only one?" I said lightly, with a glance at Mr. Ashford, who returned my smile.

"Just one." She fell silent for a long moment, drawing her long, dark fingers along the lines of my palm, then said, "You have a good and clever mind. You think and feel deeply. May I see your other hand?"

I turned over my other hand and gave it to her. The gipsy stroked it.

"There is great energy in these fingers. I sense a heat, a magic in them." She frowned of a sudden. "Your health line, I do not like the look of it, I do not like it at all. It is too short, and most uneven. But—how odd. Your life line is *very* long. It is the longest I have ever seen." All at once, a look of awe crossed the gipsy's face. She gasped aloud and gripped my hand so tightly as to cause me pain, staring at me in genuine wonder, as if I were the second coming. "You have a gift, my lady! A special gift!"

"I beg your pardon?" I replied, startled, as I struggled in vain to remove my hand from her rigid grasp.

"Madam," said Mr. Ashford, concerned. "I believe you are hurting the lady."

"You are not like others, I tell you!" cried she, her eyes wild. "You shall live for ever! You shall be *immortal!*"

"I see. Thank you. That is most interesting." I yanked my hand back, my composure rattled.

"Go work your magic, my lady!" cried the gipsy, staring fiercely into my eyes. "*Go!* Share it with the world!"

The gipsy's prediction was the subject of much scrutiny and discussion over the next few days. Mr. Ashford was most appreciative of the notion that I should have one true love in my life. Cassandra was concerned for my well-being, but Henry reassured her that he had read about such matters, and that a long life line always took precedence over a health line. Eliza thought it absolutely marvelous that I was to be immortal, and likened me to the Goddesses Diana and Aphrodite. For my part, I deduced that the gipsy woman was entirely mad, or had indulged in one too many nips of gin behind the tent that afternoon.

Mr. Ashford and I returned to the countryside later that week, where we rented a row-boat and floated lazily down the Thames, past thatched cottages, verdant meadows bright with wildflowers, and towering elms.

I sat in the seat across from Mr. Ashford, who had removed his coat and cravat on account of the heat. His sleeves were rolled up above the elbow, and his white linen shirt lay open at the neck, a sight which had brought a flush to my cheeks upon first viewing that had naught to do with the warmth of the summer sun.

"I have a confession to make," said Mr. Ashford, as he propped up the dripping oars, allowing the little vessel to meander with the current at will.

"A confession?" I enquired languidly, my straw bonnet discarded, my face tilted up to the delicious heat of the cloudless blue sky.

"I have brought you out here to-day, in an effort to provide the very best setting imaginable while I impart some news."

"Indeed?" From his veiled tone, I could not tell if I should expect to be thrilled or alarmed. "What news?"

"I received a letter this morning from Isabella. Her father returned from his voyage two days past. She has, at last, revealed her wishes to marry Mr. Wellington, and has introduced her father to that gentleman."

I sat up straight, all attention. "And? What is the result?"

"The result is—these were not precisely her own words, but I think it best to paraphrase—that her father, although apparently gravely disappointed that she would dare to go against his choice, and uncomfortable breaking a vow of such long standing, found Mr. Wellington to be most agreeable. Swayed by their youthful protestations of love, he has given his approval to the match."

A laugh of pure happiness bubbled up from my throat. "I cannot recall a time when I have ever been so delighted in the announcement of an engagement, particularly between two people that I know so little."

Mr. Ashford laughed in return, and then grew serious, shaking his head with a sigh. "I cannot tell you how relieved I am to be free, at last, of this burden which has been hanging over me for my entire adult life."

"This whole affair only serves to emphasize how ridiculous and old-fashioned is the practice of the arranged marriage.

How any one can have the nerve and audacity to think they know which two people are right for each other, or worse yet, to pair off a couple without their consent, is beyond my comprehension."[41]

"I could not agree more. I can only hope my father will be as sanguine as Mr. Churchill when I tell him about us. I count the days until he arrives."

"When do you expect him?"

"Early next week, according to his last letter." He touched my cheek with his hand and regarded me very tenderly. "When I see him, my dearest Jane, do you know what I shall say?"

"How was your journey, father?" I replied lightly.

"I shall tell him that I am in love with the most wonderful woman in the world, and it is she that I intend to marry."

I felt a gentle jolt run through my entire body, and thought it must be my heart, about to burst with joy; then I realised that our little vessel had nudged up against the shore, and had become lodged there, beneath the shade and cover of a weeping willow. Mr. Ashford shifted from his seat, and in an instant was sitting close beside me. With a slow smile, he whispered, "Jane. I just realised what I felt was missing from your book."

"My book?" My book was the very last thing on my mind. The proximity of his thigh and shoulder to mine, the very nearness of his countenance, had caused my heart to beat too fast, and my thoughts to scatter to the wind.

"It is the ending. There is no kiss."

"No kiss?"

"No." His tone was deeply serious, but there was a teasing,

---

[41] Perhaps Jane Austen's disdain for matchmaking was born at this moment, and inspired her to later write *Emma*.

affectionate look in his eyes. "Elinor gets her Edward. Marianne is consoled with good Colonel Brandon. But there are no verbal manifestations between these lovers, no physical demonstrations of any kind, and *no kiss*. It is a rather drastic omission in a book about love and courtship, is it not?"

"I prefer to write only about that which I have experienced," said I. "And my familiarity with that subject, at the time of writing, was rather limited."

"That is a situation we must remedy," said he, and there, in the privacy of the leafy green bower, he brought his lips to mine.

It was quite some time before we spoke.

"In your next book, then," said he at length, in a husky tone, "can we expect to see an increase in passion, and an expression of physical affection, between your hero and heroine?"

"I think not."

"Why is that?"

"Some things," I replied softly, "are best left to the imagination."

Chapter Twenty-five

⟶ ⟵

On the first of October, as I sat down to a lovely dinner in Henry's dining-room with Mr. Ashford, Henry and my sisters, a very expensive-looking bottle of wine was produced, and Henry's butler began pouring glasses all around.

"I brought a bottle of my finest red," said Mr. Ashford, "as we have a toast to make."

"A toast?" I said in surprise and alarm, wondering if Mr. Ashford had, after all, decided to reveal the secret of our engagement, even before his father's return.

"Indeed. We have a momentous event to celebrate," said Henry, darting a conspiratorial smile in Mr. Ashford's direction.

"An *extremely* momentous event," concurred Mr. Ashford.

"One which, I believe, will be of great interest to all assembled," said Henry.

"It is a moment worthy of French champagne," said Mr.

Ashford, "but try as I might, a bottle could not be had for love or money."[42]

"Oh! Look at them!" cried Eliza in irritation. "They are like two smug little boys, just bursting to tell a secret. Out with it, you men! What is going on? What have you been up to all afternoon?"

"What have we been up to?" rejoined Henry. "Why, we have been *up to* Whitehall."

"What were you doing in Whitehall?" I enquired.

"Paying a visit to the offices of the Military Library," said Mr. Ashford.

"Oh, dear," said Eliza, with a bored roll of her eyes. "*Please* do not tell me that all this fuss is over some new client you have acquired from the army or the navy or Parliament for your banking establishment, Henry."

"Hardly, my dear," said Henry, eyes twinkling. "Go on, Ashford. This is your doing. You tell it."

"Thomas Egerton of the Military Library is an old friend of my family." Mr. Ashford glanced in my direction. "I brought him your book a fortnight ago, Jane."

"My book? But why? What would a library want with an unpublished manuscript? Particularly a *military* library?"

"Because they are, as it happens, a publishing house—" Mr. Ashford began.

"A publishing house!" interjected Eliza, her eyes lighting up with new-found interest.

"They are known to have a keen eye," continued Mr. Ashford, "and a predilection for a wide variety of subjects."

---

[42] Due to the continuing Napoleonic war, and the resulting blockade and embargo, French products such as champagne were impossible to come by, except on the black market.

My heart began to hammer in my ears. "But surely you do not mean—a military library would never be interested in—"

"They love your novel," said Mr. Ashford, "and have offered to publish it."

I stared at him in silent astonishment, simply stared.

"Are you quite serious?" cried Eliza. "Henry, is this true?"

"Every word, my dear."

"Jane!" cried Cassandra, reaching for my hand. "How wonderful!"

"What? Have you nothing to say, sister dear?" enquired Henry, smiling. "No witty remark? No droll observation? Has the proverbial cat got your tongue?"

I could not speak. As I bathed in the warmth of the gazes that were turned upon me, every face filled with love and pride, a wave of heat flooded my body, and tears sprang into my eyes. I realised, of a sudden, that I had dreamt of this moment for nearly the entire length of my life. I had desired it, not knowing if it would ever be truly attainable, with a longing far deeper and more fierce than even I had ever imagined; as such, the true meaning of the event could not be grasped in such a brief space of time.

"Congratulations, Miss Jane Austen," said Mr. Ashford, raising his glass to me, as the others followed suit. "You are to be a published novelist."

"Do you realise what this means?" I said later, when Mr. Ashford and I found ourselves alone for a few moments in the back drawing-room, and I had thanked him profusely for his efforts in securing a publisher for my book.

"That hundreds, perhaps thousands of people will at last enjoy your work in print?" replied Mr. Ashford with a warm smile, as he sat beside me on the sofa, his arm resting cozily behind me.

"It is more than that." I felt nearly faint with ecstasy, whether it was from the thrilling news of my impending publication, or from his nearness, I could not say. "It means, for the first time in my life, I shall earn money of my own. I shall be able to contribute to the income of my household, to buy gifts, to travel a bit without guilt, and I shall have more to give to charity. And perhaps, one day, if I am fortunate enough to sell other books, I may be able to support myself if the need arises."[43]

"The need will never arise, my darling," said Mr. Ashford, as he took me in his arms and kissed me.

At that moment, the drawing-room door flew open. We drew apart just as Marie, the French serving-woman, burst in, her face white with anxiety. "Monsieur Ashford, I beg your pardon, sir, but there is a gentleman at the door asking for you, and he will not come in. He seems in quite a state."

Mr. Ashford and I hurried through the connecting passage, and found his man-servant, John, waiting outside the front door.

"Mr. Ashford, sir," cried John, bowing and somewhat out of his breath. His hat was askew, his cheeks flushed and his hair wind-blown, as if he had been riding hard; I glimpsed his horse tethered just beyond.

"John! What is it?" asked Mr. Ashford.

"I beg your pardon, sir. I am sorry to be disturbing you, sir. But I was sent most urgently to find you, sir, by your father."

---

[43] According to a cash account Jane Austen kept in 1807, she had started the year with slightly more than £50 (the bulk of the sum was a legacy she received early that year from a family friend); her modest expenditures included approximately £14 on clothes, £9 on laundry, £4 on postage, £6 on presents, £3 on charity, and less than £1 on theatre and entertainment. Her personal luxury that year was £2.13S.6D. for "Hire Piano Forte."

"My father?" repeated Mr. Ashford in surprise.

"Yes, sir. He is arrived in town, sir, this afternoon. And he requests your presence at the house at once, sir."

"Thank you, John. I shall be there directly."

"Very good, sir."

John returned to his horse and trotted off down the street. Mr. Ashford turned to me in excitement. "Forgive me, Jane. My father—"

"Yes, yes! You must go to him at once."

"I must." He took my hands in his. "I shall speak to him this very evening. And when I return tomorrow, we shall, at last, be able to announce our engagement." Drawing me to him, he kissed me once more. "I love you, Jane." And then he was gone.

The next morning, the legal documents arrived, containing the details of the proposed publishing agreement between myself and Thomas Egerton of the Military Library, a gentleman I had yet to meet.

As I sat perusing the agreement with Henry after breakfast, he said, "Mr. Ashford seems a most admirable man. And from an excellent family."

"Indeed, he is."

"You have been spending a considerable amount of time together."

"Yes, we have." I saw, from Henry's expression, that he hoped for further confidence from me, and I was sorry to be obliged to disappoint him; but as I knew the disappointment would only be of short duration, I replied, with a modest smile, "We are *friends*, Henry. I can say nothing more at present."

"Friends," he nodded, with a knowing look. "Of course."

I turned my attention back to the document, and to a

paragraph I found puzzling. "Henry, what does this mean? *To be published on commission for the author at an estimated cost of two hundred pounds?*"

"It means that Mr. Egerton, although willing to publish your book, is not enthusiastic enough to take any financial risk. In consequence, he requires the author to cover all expenses for printing, plus something towards advertising and distribution. In return, you are allowed to keep the copyright."

I gasped in dismay. "Why has no one told me this? I cannot pay this sum! Two hundred pounds! Why, it is impossible!"

"There is no need to worry, Jane. The matter is taken care of."

I stared at him in comprehension, then shook my head. "Henry. That is a great deal of money. I cannot allow you to finance the publication of my book."

"I did *not* finance it," said Henry, "although I was quite willing to do so. *That* help came from another quarter."

"From whom?" I enquired, stunned, although I knew the answer before he spoke.

"Your *friend*," said Henry pointedly. "Mr. Ashford."

"What if the book is not a success?" I fretted that afternoon, as I sat with needle and thread, repairing a rent in one of my gowns.

"It *will* be a success, dearest," replied Cassandra.

"But what if it is not? Two hundred pounds! The book will have to sell a great many copies to return such a sum. I shall scrimp and save every penny of my pocket money for the next two years. If it does not earn a profit, I *will* repay him."

"I am certain he does not expect that. And as you are soon to be married, I cannot see what difference it will make."

"Even so, I am determined. I wonder why I have not heard

from him? He promised to call this morning, this afternoon at the latest."

"It is early yet."

Eliza's maid entered. "A visitor has come to see you, *mademoiselles*. A Mrs. Jenkins."

"Please shew her in," said I. It had been nearly a se'en night since we had seen Mrs. Jenkins, shortly after Isabella had made her astonishing announcement to her father about her broken engagement, and received his blessing to marry Mr. Wellington. Mrs. Jenkins had been quite distressed by the news, almost beside herself, in fact. What on earth, she had cried at the time, could have induced that ungrateful creature to go behind her back to see that gentleman, when she was promised to another? And how could she shew such poor judgment, as to give up such a man as Mr. Ashford? Even if he was, as Isabella had so often pointed out, twice her age? The girl, she felt certain, must have lost her mind.

Cassandra and I had calmed her down at the time; we convinced her that the ways of the heart could not be explained, and that a match based on love was certainly of higher merit and destined to enjoy a greater success than one that had been arranged years earlier, without the parties' consent.

I wondered what could have brought Mrs. Jenkins to our door now. Had Mr. Ashford's news of our secret engagement somehow reached *her,* before he had had a chance to return and share in the joy of the announcement with me?

Before I could ponder the question more, Mrs. Jenkins burst in.

"Thank goodness you are home," cried the great lady, in an even more agitated state than I had ever seen her. "I have just had the most appalling news, I cannot sit, I am all in a frenzy."

"What is wrong, Mrs. Jenkins?" asked Cassandra.

"My darling Isabella, you know that she has fallen in love with that Mr. Wellington, of whom we have spoken so often, and that her father, against my advice, deemed to approve the marriage. Well! If I said it once, I said it a thousand times, I said: George, that Mr. Wellington is no gentleman, and he is no good for Isabella! But would he listen? No, he would not! And now I have been proven right!'

"What has happened?" I asked in alarm, with a growing sense of dread.

"It seems that Isabella's father, wanting to know more about his daughter's prospective husband, conducted some investigation into his background. What he learned came as a great shock. Mr. Wellington, it seems, has been living in high style for some years, well beyond his means, and has incurred a great many debts, both gambling and otherwise. His uncle, on whom he was financially dependent, and from whom he was to inherit, has long since written him off completely, a fact which the scoundrel never disclosed. Mr. Wellington, it turns out, is a ruined man, in desperate circumstances, and was only after Isabella's fifty thousand pounds!"

"So he did not love her?" said I, stunned.

"Not enough to stand by her," rejoined Mrs. Jenkins. "When Isabella's father told Mr. Wellington he could have her, but she would be cut off without a cent, the rascal retracted his proposal and scampered off into the night, without so much as a backwards glance!"

"Poor Isabella!" said Cassandra.

"*Lucky* Isabella, if you ask me!" cried Mrs. Jenkins. "Saved by the bell! Can you imagine the disastrous consequences that would have ensued, had she gone ahead with her foolish inclination to marry that villain? But thank the good Lord, all is not lost. Her prior engagement has been reinstated."

"Reinstated?" I gasped, my heart in my throat.

"Yes! And thank goodness. Her father insisted, if some one was going to marry Isabella for her money, it might as well be Mr. Ashford."

My mind was in such a state of agitation and confusion, I thought I must have heard incorrectly. "What do you mean, Mrs. Jenkins? Surely Mr. Ashford would never marry Isabella for her money. He is extremely wealthy himself."

"So we all thought." Mrs. Jenkins shook her head sadly. "And so the family always has been, for generations. I am certain Mr. Ashford had no idea of the extent of their troubles, not until his father broke the terrible news last night. Sir Thomas, it seems, has greatly mismanaged his finances over the years. He spent so much money on that estate of his, and made so many poor investments, that he was dependent on a spectacular investment of some kind to recover. As such, he poured what remained of his fortune into a shipping fleet. He has only just learned that the fleet, on a return voyage from Spain without protection of a naval convoy, was attacked and sunk by the French. Much of the crew was saved, but not all, and the vessels themselves and all their cargo was lost. It is a very great tragedy, not only in human lives, but for the investors as well. Sir Thomas is ruined, and his family nearly bankrupt."

I found it difficult to breathe. "Bankrupt?"

"Such a terrible thing! Sir Thomas is close to apoplexy, I hear. I tell you, my heart goes out to him and that whole family. The man has never been the same since his poor wife died, spending like a young man gone wild, hiding his investments from his only son and heir, who is the far smarter man, if you ask me. Now, they are in danger of losing Pembroke Hall and all their holdings. Of course with the property tied up in entail,[44] he cannot sell or mortgage any part of it. His only chance to save the estate is for Mr. Ashford to marry our Isabella, as planned, but they will not wait for Christmas, now. The wedding is to take place in a fortnight. Jane, is any thing the matter?"

"No—" I attempted to reply, but no sound actually escaped my lips.

"She is distressed," said Cassandra quickly, leaping up from her chair and standing behind me, her hands upon my shoulders. "For Isabella's sake."

"I have just spent the last half-hour with that poor girl," said Mrs. Jenkins, tears starting in her eyes. "She is beside herself with grief. But she is young, she will recover. Mr. Ashford is a good man and an excellent catch, even with all of this, and there is the title to consider. Isabella will one day be Lady Ashford, and mistress of Pembroke Hall, a very, very fine place. If her money can save it from the creditors, then I say it is all for the best; they each bring something to the marriage, and the rest will work itself out. It always does."

---

[44] Most great landed families in nineteenth-century England maintained their wealth, status and power through the generations by transmitting their enormous estates intact to their descendants, via two ironclad practices, provided for in their wills or deeds of settlement. The first, *primogeniture,* left all the land to the eldest son, instead of dividing it among all the children. *Entail* placed restrictions on what the heir could do to the estate, to ensure that when he died, his eldest son in turn would inherit the property intact, and not mortgaged, split up, or sold. A girl must not inherit, to their way of thinking, because if she remained single, the line could die out, and if she married, the estate would belong to her husband—someone outside the family. The practice was so engrained that until 1925, by law the land of someone dying without a will went to the eldest son, and efforts to change the law were consistently defeated by the old families.

"I am sure you are right," said my sister, without conviction; then, apparently realising that Mrs. Jenkins had never once sat down since entering the room, Cassandra invited her to take a seat and offered her some refreshment. To my relief, Mrs. Jenkins declined, insisting that she must be on her way, she had only stopped to share the news.

As I stood and curtsied, Mrs. Jenkins cried, "No, no, do not trouble yourself. You really do look as if you should lie down, Miss Jane. I shall see myself out."

No sooner had the lady left, than my legs buckled under me, and I sank back into my chair. Cassandra knelt beside me; as tears sprang into her eyes, she took me in her arms. "Jane. Oh, Jane. I wish there were words."

There were no words. I was too stunned to cry.

Chapter Twenty-six

───────────── ✦✦ ─────────────

A note arrived from Mr. Ashford the next morning.

Park Lane, Mayfair—3 October, 1810

My dearest Jane,

I am so very sorry that I have been unable to come to you to-day. I have just been apprised of news of the most distressing nature, concerning my family's affairs; my father and sister are in such a state that I fear to leave them. Worse yet, I fear that you may learn of our circumstances before I have the opportunity to speak with you myself. Please, please, my darling Jane, do not be distressed or leap to conclusions, based on any thing you might hear from others. I love you, and I always will. I shall come as soon I can.

Yours most affectionately,
Frederick

I knew not what to make of such a missive. Was there yet hope? Had he some solution to this catastrophic situation, of which I could not guess?

My heart was filled with pain at the many difficulties that Mr. Ashford was facing, of a sudden: the potential loss of his ancestral home; the displacement of his family; a distraught, and possibly ill, father and sister; and yet, here he was writing to *me*, begging *me* to not be distressed.

I could not go to him, nor could I sit at home and wait, not knowing when I might hear from him again. Restless, I begged Henry to lend me his barouche, and one look at my agitated face apparently convinced him to comply. I instructed the driver to take me into town, where we rode aimlessly for the better part of an hour, until I knew, at last, precisely where I wished to go.

I soon found myself sitting on that familiar bench in Kensington Gardens, which Mr. Ashford and I had so often frequented. Most of the flowers were dead and gone, and there was an early-autumn chill in the air. I pulled my shawl closer about me, barely cognizant of the few people strolling by. Tears stung my eyes. Despite the optimistic tone at the end of Mr. Ashford's letter, I held out no hope. How, I wondered, could I have ever been so foolish as to imagine that things could work out between us?

I know not how long I had been sitting there, when I became aware of footsteps behind me, and I heard Mr. Ashford's voice:

"Jane."

I turned. He crossed to me in three great strides. "Your sister told me you had driven into town. I took a chance, hoping I would know where to find you." He sat down beside me on the bench and took my hand in his, his eyes filled with emotion.

"I am so sorry that you heard about all this the way you did, Jane. I am quite ashamed."

"You have nothing to be ashamed of," said I.

"I do. I should have been more informed of my father's financial activities. Years ago, at the time of my majority, he gave me specific responsibilities dealing with our property and tenants, and these became my complete focus. The rest, he insisted, was *his* territory. He was very adept at hiding things from me. His many improvements at Pembroke Hall seemed excessive to me. I suspected that something was amiss several years ago, and suggested that we retrench. He refused to take me into his confidence, apprising me of only the narrowest of circumstances, and maintaining that his investments would see us through. If only I had known! I would have strongly advised against putting any money into that shipping fleet, it posed too great a risk. Now, it is too late. All is lost."

"All is not lost. Isabella's fortune can save you."

"I do not love Isabella. I will not marry her. My heart belongs to you."

"And mine is *yours*," said I, my voice breaking, "but there is no room for love in marriage." With a heavy heart, I understood his intentions now. He had no miraculous solution to his family's dire situation. His plan was to throw every thing away, and be true to me. "The sad truth is, marriage is business, and nothing more."

"I will not believe that! Jane, I will not allow this—this terrible *mistake* on my father's part to destroy *my* life. I have been bound to him, to his whims, and to his promises on my behalf, for too many years. I will no longer have any part of it! I am no longer honour-bound to Isabella; her own actions have put an end to that. *You* are the woman I love, Jane. I want to spend my life with you."

"But how can that be? Will you not lose Pembroke Hall?"

"I believe we shall. It breaks my heart to lose our family estate; but it is my father's doing, not mine. We will survive it somehow. I have wasted too much time dreaming of some one like you, and then, upon finding you, wishing for a miracle that would allow us to be together. I am *through* with dreaming and wishing, Jane. I choose *you,* over any piece of land or any amount of money. But I must know how you feel, with things as they now stand. Were I only the man you see before you, without a penny in my pocket, would you still love me? Would you still have me?"

"You know I would," said I, trembling.

"Then let me come for you in the morning, my darling. I will obtain a license. We can meet the parson at my church. By this time tomorrow we can be married."

My resistance began to crumble. "I cannot help but think that it would be wrong—"

"No! It would be wrong, it would be a sin against nature to give up a love such as ours!" From his pocket, Mr. Ashford removed a lovely gold-and-ruby ring. "My father once gave this ring to my mother to wear until her wedding band was made. Will you wear it now, Jane, as a symbol of my love and promise?"

"I could not possibly—" I began, but he gently took my hand in his, removed my glove and slid the ring onto my finger. The bright red stone sparkled in the sun's light like a perfect beating heart. "I know not what to say," I whispered.

"Say yes, Jane. Tell me again, that you will marry me."

"Yes," said I softly, "I will."

I told Henry and my sisters every thing that evening, as we sat before the drawing-room fire.

"I think it the most romantic thing I have ever heard," cried Eliza, clasping her hands to her bosom with a beatific sigh, after she had admired my ruby ring with great enthusiasm.

"To know that a man's love is so deep and so strong that he would give up every thing for you, *that* is true love," said Cassandra. "I envy you, Jane. Mr. Ashford is the best of men, and your perfect match. I know you will be very happy."

"Would *you* give up everything for love of me, dearest?" enquired Eliza, patting her husband's thigh affectionately.

"I believe I already have, my dear," replied Henry, to which my sisters laughed.

"But seriously, darling," persisted Eliza. "Do not you think it the most romantic and wonderful thing in the world? To say *adieu* to property and fortune, to follow one's heart, to rest one's happiness in life solely on *l'amour*?"

"I think it depends on the size of the property and the fortune," answered Henry, a twinkle in his eyes.

"Oh! Men!" cried Eliza, indignant. "You are insufferable."

But Henry's words stayed with me, echoing a worry that had been eating away at my own conviction, even as I had said the words *I will*.

I spent a sleepless night, tossing and turning, alternately burning up as if with fever, or suffused with an icy chill, just as I had the night following Harris Bigg-Wither's proposal. On that occasion, I had suffered under the weight of the evils that would befall a marriage based solely on the acquisition of material comforts, without benefit of love. Now, I was tormented by visions of a union founded on precisely the reverse.

At last I rose, shivering as my bare feet touched the cold wooden floor; drawing a shawl about me, I crossed to the window-seat and drew back the curtain, gazing out at the nearby rooftops and inky sky. I heard Cassandra stir in the next bed; in a moment she joined me at the window-seat, lovingly draping a blanket around both our shoulders.

"You are having second thoughts?" asked she gently.

I nodded.

"But why? You love Mr. Ashford, and he loves you."

"If he marries me, Pembroke Hall and all its lands will be lost to creditors."

"I understand. But if that is his choice—" began Cassandra.

"You did not see Pembroke Hall," I interjected. "It is the most immense, magnificent estate I have ever seen, like something out of a fairy tale, each room more impressive than the last. And the woods and grounds—" My voice broke as I shook my head. "It is not something to be given up lightly."

We were packed by morning. I sent a lengthy letter by early post to Mr. Ashford, explaining why I must go without delay. The ink, I admit, was stained by tears in several locations, but the intent, I hoped, was ascertainable.

As Henry's coachman readied his carriage for our removal to Chawton, I paced alone in the shrubbery of the small back-garden, dabbing my eyes with my handkerchief; I had been weeping all morning, and the flow of tears refused to cease.

I heard the back gate open, and knew it must be he. As I heard his footsteps cross the lawn, I took a deep breath to steady myself and attempted to dry my eyes. With great effort, I turned to face him. He stood but a yard away, gripping a letter in his hand, which I took to be the one I had just sent him. His face was ashen, his voice diffused with emotion.

"You cannot mean what you have written here."

"I am sorry," said I brokenly, willing away the tears which threatened.

"Jane, do not do this. Come away with me, now."

"Come away where?"

"Any where you choose."

"And live how?"

"One day at a time."

"How will we support ourselves?"

"I will find work. I could take orders."

"It has never been your ambition to join the clergy."

"A man can change his ambition. I might be well suited to such a profession." There was doubt in his eyes, which he could not hide; he knew I saw it. In frustration, he crumpled the letter in his hand and threw it to the ground. "I could go into a trade."

"What trade? What have you trained for, other than to own and manage a great estate?"

"That training can be of use. I could work as a bailiff.[45]

"And manage another man's property?"

"Why not?" said he, but his face coloured at the prospect. I knew that such work could only be humiliating to a man with his upbringing.

"And where would we live, my dearest?" I asked quietly. "In a rented house, with rented furniture?"

"I do not need a palace to be happy," said he.

"That is true for me. But for you—once born to privilege, it is not easy to go without."

"I can learn. If it means that we can be together—"

"Pembroke Hall has been in your family for nearly two

---

[45] The term "bailiff" had two meanings at the time. One was a sheriff's officer, who carried out court orders, in particular, seizing goods or people for debt. Based on Jane's response, Mr. Ashford refers to the other type of bailiff, who was a hired overseer or steward of an estate, whose duties included managing a large farm for its owners, collecting rents, responding to complaints from tenant farmers, etc.

hundred years. It is part of who you are. It is your children's and your grandchildren's birthright, and your duty to preserve it for those future generations. You know it to be true. If you gave it up, in time you would grow to regret it, and to resent me."

"No. Jane—"

"You *would*. And even if *you* did not, think of your family. Of the disgrace. How could Sir Thomas ever hold up his head in society again? And what of your sister? You have told me how dearly Sophia loves her home. Now she will suffer not only that great loss, but she will have no dowry, no income. What will become of them? Where will they go?"

Mr. Ashford did not immediately reply. I could ascertain from his agonized expression that that very question had been tormenting him. "Sophia might still marry, even without a dowry," said he at last, "and if not, I will provide for them, somehow."

"That is easier said than done, my love. I know what it is to lose your home, to be penniless. It is too high a price to pay. I cannot let you do it."

"Jane—"

"Isabella's fortune can save you all. There is no other recourse. You know that I am right. I must be strong for the both of us. You must—you *must* marry Isabella in a fortnight."

A look of intense melancholy and defeat settled on his countenance, and tears started in his eyes. His voice was suffused with anger and intense regret as he said softly, "And be miserable all the rest of my days."

We stood in wretched silence for a long moment, each of us wiping away tears. I silently removed the ruby ring from my finger and held it out to him. He shook his head, waving his hand emphatically. "Keep it."

"I could not."

"I want you to have it. It was my promise. I will not take a promise back."

I replaced the ring upon my hand.

He sighed deeply, and said, "I saw the carriage being made ready for your journey. Where do you go, in such haste? Home to Chawton?"

"Yes."

"Where you will immerse yourself in your writing, I suppose."

I shook my head. "I will never write again."

"Promise me you do not mean that."

"I would find no pleasure in writing of love and courtship now. Surely the readers of the world do not need yet another droll tale of a man and woman who meet and fall in love at first sight."

"Then give them the opposite. Give them a man and woman who loathe each other at first sight."

"Loathe each other?"

"They meet and despise each other. Then, over time, as their true natures emerge, they grow to admire each other—"

"—as they overcome their pride—"

"—and prejudice." He took my hands in his; his eyes met mine, with a knowing look. "It is already written, is it not? In that trunk of yours? *First Impressions*, I think you said you called it?"

"I did compose such a story, many years past, but it needs alteration and contraction, and—I have not the heart for it."

"Why not?"

"Because I now know how it must end."

"Do not accept that end. Play God. Give us another witty, romantic novel by Jane Austen, with the ending *you* choose."

"Jane!" Cassandra called to us from the back door, apology in her tone. "The coachman is ready. It is late, we must start."

"I shall be there directly."

Cassandra vanished into the house. I turned back to Mr. Ashford. We looked deeply into each other's eyes; then, at the same instant, rushed into each other's arms.

"Are we never to see each other again?" said he.

I felt his tears wet against my cheek. "I shall see you in my mind. And in my dreams."

"I shall carry you in my heart, Jane. Every day, every hour, for the rest of my life." He turned his face to mine and kissed me intensely.

I never wanted the kiss to end. "Good-bye, my love," said I.

"Good-bye," he whispered.

I turned and ran, my heart so filled with pain I wondered how it could possibly continue beating.

_____ ❧ ❧ _____

Chapter Twenty-seven

I never saw Mr. Ashford again. I never returned to Derbyshire, or visited his neighbourhood in Mayfair when I went to town. I know only that he married. I assume that his family's financial ruin was averted by that marriage, as news of that threat never became widely known.

Henry, Cassandra and Eliza, the only family members privy to my relationship with Mr. Ashford, shared my view that it was best not to discuss that history with any one, but rather, to behave as if it had never occurred. Any mention of my involvement with him, we realised—particularly the reason for the termination of that involvement—could only serve to bring to light the circumstances regarding the Ashfords' financial difficulties, which might cause embarrassment to him and his family.

As for myself, I knew I should abhor the pitying looks and comments that would be certain to arise if the details of that affair were ever to be made public. A cursory telling might put one lover or the other in an unsavory light, and could never begin to reveal the emotional truth behind it. Better, I decided, to be thought a spinster with no history of love than a tragic, foolish figure who had dared to love above her station, and lost.

Henry accepted the credit for securing the publishing house for *Sense and Sensibility,* and for financing its initial printing. Alethea, who knew only that I had been briefly acquainted with the Churchill family, enquired about them once a few years later, but the topic was soon forgotten.

I received a brief note from Mr. Ashford upon the publication of *Pride and Prejudice*; his warm congratulations brought tears to my eyes and an ache to my heart. I burnt the letter, though now I wish I had not. All I have left of him now are memories, and my ruby ring.

And so the history of Mr. Ashford—*my* Mr. Ashford— was made to disappear. It was for the best, I thought, both for the preservation of the character and reputation of all parties involved, and for the sake of the story itself, for what value is there in a tale of heartbreak? A love story, to be told, must end happily, must it not?

That is how I felt at the time, and for some years since.

But I feel differently now—now that I have watched my nieces and nephews grow up around me, through all the vicissitudes of life, into fine young women and men, many of them married; now that I have lost my own true love, yet found it in my work; now that I have seen four books, my dearest children, go forth into the world, and enjoyed a greater success than I had ever dreamt of; now, though there are days when I am not well enough to walk, yet I am still always well enough to hold a pen; now, I believe there is a kind of happiness to be found in every thing in life, in all that is good and pleasing, as well as in that which is sad or poignant.

I no longer dread the revelation of failings in myself or others. I have come to believe, in the end, that there is no shame in truth, only freedom; and that, in time, every tale has a right to be told.

Finis

January 2, 1817

Editor's Afterword

Sense and Sensibility appeared in print in October 1811, and was very well received by critics and the public. By July 1813, every copy of the first edition had been sold, not only covering its original expenses, but earning a profit of about £140 for its author, and it went into a second printing. Encouraged by her success, in 1812 Jane Austen offered her newly revised *First Impressions,* now famously re-titled *Pride and Prejudice,* for publication. Egerton, no doubt recognizing a potential best seller, paid £110 for it, and secured the copyright for himself.

All four of Jane Austen's novels which were published during her lifetime, the other two being *Mansfield Park* and *Emma,* were published anonymously.

Jane Austen became unwell in the first months of 1816 from an unspecified illness, which seemed to come and go over the next year and a half. In early June of that year, Jane and Cassandra tried the waters at the spa town of Cheltenham, hoping for a cure, but the effects, if any, were not lasting. On the eighteenth of July, 1816, she finished writing *Persuasion* (which she apparently intended to call *The Elliots*). She spent three weeks rewriting the ending, and then set it aside. She did not write again, as far as was previously known, until January, 1817, when she began her final, unfinished work, the brilliant fragment *Sanditon*.

In spite of her declining health, for a writer as energetic and productive as Jane Austen (who, after moving to Chawton, wrote or rewrote six books in seven years), the silence of the last five months of 1816 has been mysterious. Why didn't she submit *Persuasion* for publication? What, if anything, was she working on?

We now have the answer. From the final date inscribed herein, we may conclude that Jane was finishing this Memoir during that time, a work she had probably devoted much of her free time to in the previous couple of years. The fact that Jane Austen was reminiscing about her own unknown love affair while writing *Persuasion* helps to explain certain facets of that novel, for it is considered by most critics to be her most passionately rendered story. Perhaps this is why she kept *Persuasion* to herself. There is an overlying sense of romanticism in the character of Anne Elliot in *Persuasion*, which Austen had thoroughly rebuked in *Sense and Sensibility*, her first published novel. The final chapters of *Persuasion* are extremely emotional, tense and moving. When Captain Wentworth reveals his love for Anne, some of his phraseology is an eerie echo of Mr. Ashford's romantic confession to Jane herself on that fateful night in Henry's drawing-room on Sloane Street.

Jane Austen's illness progressed. She suffered from debilitating weakness, fever, discolouration of the skin, and pain in her back so severe that she agreed to be taken to Winchester in May, 1817, to be cared for by the surgeons connected to a hospital there, who were considered as good as any in London. Cassandra nursed her devotedly, but less than two months later, Jane Austen passed away.

Based on Jane's description of her symptoms in her letters, current medical opinion has theorized that she may have suffered from Addison's Disease, a loss of function of the adrenal glands; the condition can be controlled by medication today, but it eventually proves fatal.

In her last letter, when speaking of her illness, Jane Austen remarks, "On this subject I will only say further that my dearest sister, my tender, watchful, indefatigable nurse has not been made ill by her exertions. As to what I owe to her, and to the anxious affection of all my beloved family on this occasion, I can only cry over it, and pray to God to bless them more and more."[46]

We are told by her brother Henry that "she supported, during two months, all the varying pain, irksomeness, and tedium," attendant on her decline "with more than resignation, with a truly elastic cheerfulness . . . She retained her faculties, her memory, her fancy, her temper, and her affections, warm, clear, and unimpaired, to the last . . . She expired on Friday, the eighteenth of July, 1817 in the arms of her sister."[47] She was forty-one years old.

On the twenty-fourth of that month, Jane Austen was buried in Winchester Cathedral in the north aisle of the nave. She was the third and last person to be buried in the cathedral that year. Henry must have arranged it, since he knew the

---

[46] Le Faye, Deidre, *Jane Austen's Letters;* Letter #161; 29 May 1817.

[47] Austen, Henry, *Biographical Notice of The Author,* 1818 (accompanied the joint publication of *Persuasion* and *Northanger Abbey.*)

bishop from his recent examination for ordination. The long, pious inscription on her fine black marble gravestone (probably written by her brothers, who also wrote memorial poems in her honour) names her father, Reverend George Austen, as the former Rector of Steventon, and refers to her patience in dealing with her illness, but gives no mention of her greatest claim to fame, merely saying,

> *"The benevolence of her heart,*
> *the sweetness of her temper, and*
> *the extraordinary endowments of her mind*
> *obtained the regard of all who knew her and*
> *the warmest love of her intimate connections."*

The loss of this sparkling talent has been keenly felt by the world. As new generations have discovered her books, they have lamented that, as had been previously thought, only six completed manuscripts had been left behind. The discovery of Jane Austen's Memoirs should prove of great value to historians, in providing answers to many of the questions about her life and her work, which have been the centre of so much debate.

There is one curious note, which I must add. Jane Austen clearly wrote this Memoir several years after the events depicted therein took place. Therefore, any small inconsistencies, if any, can be attributed to an imperfect memory on the part of the author. It will be gratifying to the reader to learn that, after a careful review, it has been established that nearly every detail covered here, as to date, time, person and place, is historically accurate, and corresponds with what is known of Jane Austen's life and whereabouts at the time. There is, however, one notable exception. There is no record of a Mr.

Frederick Ashford or a Sir Thomas Ashford residing in Derbyshire at the time of writing, and no record of an estate called Pembroke Hall in that county.

Which raises several questions.

Who, in fact, *was* Mr. Ashford? The most obvious theory, based on Jane Austen's discreet nature, is that she deliberately changed the name of her lover and the name of his estate, to protect his privacy. Only in this way could she fulfill her burning need to tell the tale, while at the same time, preserve her lover's dignity. She knew it was safe to keep the ruby ring he'd given her, which was later found in the chest with her memoirs, as it had not been inscribed with his name.

But another theory, which cannot be ignored, can best be summed up in the words of her young nephew James-Edward, who so solemnly asked his aunt Jane, on that golden morning at Steventon, "Do you mean to say, that if I believe in your story as you have told it, then it is as good as if it were true?"

A⁺

AUTHOR INSIGHTS, EXTRAS, & MORE...

FROM

SYRIE JAMES

AND

AVON A

Author's Note

Despite all efforts to convince you otherwise, this book is a work of fiction. However, the elements of fiction in the novel are all firmly embedded in the known facts of Jane Austen's life. All the dates in the story, Jane's whereabouts at the time, and the details about her books, her habits, her personal life, family members, close friends, and places of residence, are all accurately presented.

Some of the more specific facts in this novel include:

Jane Austen and her family did indeed reluctantly leave her beloved Steventon upon her father's retirement and move to Bath, where he died in 1805, leaving the women in his family in the distressing financial situation as pictured. (A heart-wrenching account of his death in Jane's own hand is included in her personal correspondence.) Jane disliked Bath and left with "happy feelings of escape" when she, her mother, her sister, and her friend Martha moved to Southampton to live at Castle Square with her brother Frank and his family.

Mrs. Austen was a bit of a hypochondriac, which Jane often mentioned in her letters and parodied in her fiction. She was extremely close to her sister Cassandra, who was her best friend and confidante to the end of her life.

After writing the first drafts of *First Impressions*, *Sense and Sensibility* and *Susan* from 1796 to 1799, Jane's pen (with the exception of a few minor, unfinished works) went silent (as far as we know for ten years. We know that she began revising *Sense and Sensibility* in 1809, after she moved to Chawton Cottage, and submitted it for publication in the fall of 1810. The poetry is all Jane

Austen's (or Mrs. Austen's), as is the letter she wrote to Crosby on April 5, 1809; that is his actual reply.

The Harris Bigg-Wither proposal (including Jane's acceptance and subsequent refusal, and her hurried and mortified departure from Manydown Park) is well-known to biographers and is based entirely on fact. Harris had a pronounced stammer, and he actually served an undrinkable wine punch to a group of guests, with that same startling announcement. Jane really did post those three fictitious marriage banns in her father's parish register. Jane traveled to Lyme Regis several times with her family and was very fond of it. She mentioned in her correspondence several visits to the ruins at Netley Abbey, which is still open to the public today.

Frank Austen was, in fact, an expert knotter of both sailor's knots and curtain fringe. The Marchioness of Landsdowne did indeed keep an outlandish equipage of eight little ponies of varying sizes and shades to draw her carriage. A chaplain (who happened to be the Prince Regent's librarian, both of whom were great admirers of her work) really did write to Jane Austen, asking her to write his life story, as Mr. Morton does here; she politely declined by post.

The information in the Editor's Notes, Foreword and Afterword is all true, with the exception of the discovery of that trunk in the attic.

Which brings us to the fiction:

Mrs. Jenkins, Mr. Morton, and Charles, Maria and Isabella Churchill are invented, and inspired by various characters in Jane Austen's novels. We cannot be certain that Jane ever visited Derbyshire, with or without Alethea Bigg and the Squire Bigg-Wither, or if she ever had her palm read.

Although a few lines here and there are taken from Jane's letters or novels, all of her inner thoughts, feelings and emotions are, of course, invented, as is her relationship with Mr. Ashford.

As far as we know, Jane Austen never actually met Sir Walter Scott; however, they were each fans of the others' work.

There are no early drafts of *Sense and Sensibility* or *Pride and*

Prejudice, so there is no way to know how much was rewritten, or when.

It has always been surmised that Jane's brother Henry secured the publisher for *Sense and Sensibility,* but no one really knows. She apparently paid for the first publication herself, with money borrowed from Henry.

Mary I. Jesse, PhD, Oxford University, does not exist, nor is there a Jane Austen Literary Foundation. Mary I. Jesse is an anagram of my name.

Jane Austen's Works

NOVELS

Sense and Sensibility (published 1811)
Pride and Prejudice (1813)
Mansfield Park (1814)
Emma (1816)
Persuasion (1818)
Northanger Abbey (1818)

SHORTER WORKS

Lady Susan (novella)
The Watsons (incomplete novel)
Sanditon (incomplete novel)

JUVENILIA

Jane Austen wrote throughout her teens for the entertainment of her family. Her early works, which she recorded in three note-books, are youthful and unrestrained (and often unfinished), and poke fun at established literary and social conventions.

Volume the First:
(Written between 1787 and 1790; most are brief tales or plays)
Frederic and Elfrida
Jack and Alice
Edgar and Emma

Henry and Eliza
The Adventures of Mr. Harley, Sir William Montague, and Mr. Clifford
The Beautifull Cassandra
Amelia Webster
The Visit: a comedy in two acts
The Mystery: An Unfinished Play
The Three Sisters
Ode to Pity

Volume the Second:

(Written between 1790 and 1792; most are epistolary tales—brief novelettes in letters)
Love and Freindship (sic; the misspelling of "friendship" in the title is famous)
Lesley Castle: An Unfinished Novel in Letters
The History of England (a parody of the history books Jane read as a child)
A Collection of Letters
Scraps (letters and tales dedicated to her niece Fanny)

Volume the Third:

(Two novelettes written between 1792 and 1793)
Evelyn
   Catharine, or the Bower

Chronology of Jane Austen's Life

1775   Dec. 16: Jane Austen born at Steventon.

1783   Jane's brother, Edward Austen, adopted by Mr. and Mrs. Thomas Knight II.

1785–1786   Jane and her sister Cassandra go to school at Reading and Southampton.

1787   Jane starts writing her juvenilia.

1792   Winter: Cassandra probably engaged to the Rev. Tom Fowle.

By 1793   Jane finishes and copies out *Volume The First, Volume The Second* and *Volume The Third* of her juvenilia.

1794   Mr. Thomas Knight II dies, leaving his estate to his adopted son and heir, Edward Austen.

1795   Jane writes *Elinor and Marianne*.

1796   January 9: The first of Jane's surviving letters begin.
January 10: Tom Fowle, Cassandra's fiancé, sails for the West Indies.
October: Jane starts writing *First Impressions*.

1797   February: Tom Fowle dies of fever at St. Domingo and is buried at sea.

August: Jane finishes writing *First Impressions.*

November: Jane's father, George Austen, submits *First Impressions* to a publisher in London, but it is "Declined by Return of Post," unread.

Jane begins rewriting *Elinor and Marianne* as *Sense and Sensibility.*

Edward Austen Knight and his family move to his estate at Godmersham Park.

December 31: Marriage of Jane's brother Henry Austen and Eliza de Feuillide.

1798–99 Jane probably starts writing *Susan* (later retitled *Northanger Abbey).*

1800 December: Mr. George Austen decides to retire.

1801 May: Mr. and Mrs. Austen, with Jane and Cassandra, leave Steventon and move to Bath.

1802 December 2: Harris Bigg-Wither proposes to Jane at Manydown; she accepts but then refuses him the next morning.

1803 Jane sells *Susan* to Crosby & Co. of London for £10. It remains unpublished.

1804 Jane makes a copy of *Lady Susan.*
Jane begins writing, but later abandons, *The Watsons.*
Jane and the Austens visit Lyme. (They made several earlier visits to Lyme as well.)

1805 January 21: Mr. George Austen dies at Bath.

1806 Jane, Mrs. Austen, and Cassandra leave Bath and begin an itinerant life, residing with various friends and relations.

1807   March: Jane, Mrs. Austen, Cassandra, and Martha Lloyd move to Castle Square, Southampton, with Frank Austen and his family.

1809   July 7: Jane, Mrs. Austen, Cassandra, and Martha Lloyd move to Chawton Cottage.
Jane revises *Sense and Sensibility.*

1810   Fall/Winter: *Sense and Sensibility* accepted for publication by Thomas Egerton of Whitehall, at the author's expense.

1811   Jane probably revising *First Impressions* as *Pride and Prejudice.*
October: *Sense and Sensibility* is published, "By A Lady."

1812   Autumn: Jane sells *Pride and Prejudice* to Thomas Egerton for £110.
Jane writes *Mansfield Park.*

1813   January 28: *Pride and Prejudice* published (also anonymously, as were all her books during her lifetime.)
Fall/Winter: *Mansfield Park* probably accepted for publication.

1814   January: Jane begins writing *Emma.*
May 9: *Mansfield Park* published.

1815   Jane completes *Emma* and begins writing *Persuasion.*
Jane is invited to dedicate her next novel to the Prince Regent, a fan of her work.
December: *Emma* is published and dedicated to the Prince Regent.

1816   Spring: Early signs of Jane's illness.

Henry Austen buys back the rights to *Susan,* which Jane revises.

August: Jane finishes writing *Persuasion.*

Jane's health begins to fail.

1817   January–March: Jane begins writing *Sanditon.*

April 27: Jane writes her will

May 24: Jane and Cassandra move to lodgings in Winchester to seek medical attention.

July 18: Jane Austen dies.

July 24: Jane Austen buried in Winchester Cathedral.

Late December: *Northanger Abbey* and *Persuasion* published together in one volume, dated 1818, with a "Biographical Notice" by Henry.

Q &A with Syrie James
Author of *The Lost Memoirs of*
Jane Austen

What inspired you to write this book?

I have long been a Jane Austen fan. One of my all-time favorite books is *Pride and Prejudice;* I've probably read it a dozen times. There are few books which can match it for pure brilliance of plot, characterization, and dialogue. *Persuasion* and *Emma* are also great. I adored the 1995 films *Sense and Sensibility* starring Emma Thompson and A&E's *Pride and Prejudice* starring Colin Firth and Jennifer Ehle. Then the movie *Shakespeare in Love* came out and won the Academy Award, and I thought: what about a love story for Jane Austen? Why hasn't anyone done that?

I began researching Jane Austen's life and reading her letters. Although there is no evidence that she ever had a love affair, and her biographers portray her basically as a spinster with a great imagination, I wasn't sure I believed that. We know that she had a brief flirtation for a few weeks with an Irishman named Tom Lefroy when she was twenty, but it went nowhere; his family rapidly sent him away because she had no money. Then there was Cassandra's story of an unspecified seaside romance. Who was that man? What happened to him?

On rereading Jane Austen's letters, I noticed a two-year gap from January 1809 through April 1811, where personal letters were either nonexistent or missing. Those two years immediately preceded the publication of her first novel, *Sense and Sensibility*— when Jane was in her early thirties and had already written the first drafts of three complete novels, but was stalled in her writing career. I couldn't help but wonder: what happened during those missing years?

It is well-known that Jane's sister Cassandra, shortly before she died, went through Jane's letters, burning most of them and cutting out portions of others. Clearly Cassandra did not want to share anything she felt might be too personal, or might reflect badly on Jane. It struck me that it was entirely possible that Jane had a secret love affair during those two years—a relationship so passionate, and so intense, that it allowed her to write about emotions that she had, allegedly, never felt—a relationship which Cassandra, for good reason, also conspired to keep secret.

I was immediately taken by the idea. I decided to invent a grand romance for our beloved Jane, with a legitimate but ultimately heartbreaking reason as to why they did not marry, and why the world never knew about him. Similar to *Shakespeare in Love,* I decided to interweave the story with the writing of one of Austen's most famous works, to showcase her inspiration and struggle, both because of and in spite of her romantic relationship.

Pride and Prejudice is, arguably, Jane Austen's masterpiece. Although you included a few elements of that story line in your book, you made Sense and Sensibility the main focus. Why?

I chose not to use *Pride and Prejudice* as the main plot device because it's believed that Jane Austen had written a fairly complete first draft of that story (under the title *First Impressions*) in her early twenties, then set it aside. Also, I was not interested in pursuing that story line—where the hero and heroine dislike each other and are at odds with each other throughout most of the book. *Sense and Sensibility* seemed the ideal book to focus on, both because it was Jane Austen's first sale after the "missing years" (and I wanted to write about her emergence as a writer), and because the story is full of the type of conflict I particularly enjoy in a romance: men and women who meet and fall in love at first sight, but are separated by circumstance and the demands of family and society, with plenty of suspense, heartache, and deep dark secrets thrown in for good measure.

Mr. Ashford is a wonderful character. Did you model him on any of the characters in Jane Austen's books, or on anyone in real life?

No. My goal was to create a love interest who was truly Jane's equal in intellect and temperament, and worthy of Jane Austen's admiration and passion; a man who could influence her life and her return to writing, but at the same time, would not take away from her own fiercely independent spirit or seem to be the only reason for her many accomplishments. I patterned some of the action on elements in *Sense and Sensibility* and *Pride and Prejudice,* to imply that her personal experiences inspired those moments in the books; as such, Mr. Ashford hides a secret that is similar (although not identical) to Edward Ferrars's, and he is heir to an estate similar to Mr. Darcy's Pemberley. However, I tried to make Mr. Ashford different from either of those heroes, who, although very good and decent men who prove themselves most worthy at the end, are both shy and awkward. (Darcy is famously introverted and aloof throughout the first half of *Pride and Prejudice.*) I wanted a hero who would be drawn to Jane at first sight, be ready and able to converse with her at length, and could openly express his feelings. If Mr. Ashford resembles anyone in Miss Austen's novels, I would say it's Mr. Knightley in *Emma,* a man who is, at the outset, the heroine's friend and confidant, and not afraid to offer her advice and criticism. (Jane Austen did once say that of all the heroes she created, Mr. Knightley was her favorite.)

You blend fact and fiction so seamlessly in the novel. How did you do your research?

I felt a great responsibility to remain true to Jane Austen's known history, and to represent her real-life friends and family members as accurately as possible. It was a challenge to interweave my love story with the dates, times, and facts of Jane Austen's life, and her whereabouts at the time. When I was finished, I hoped it would be difficult for even the most discerning Jane Austen scholar to determine where fact ended and fiction began.

I researched Jane Austen's life and her era extensively. I read countless biographies and scholarly works, reread Jane Austen's six novels and unfinished works, read every one of her surviving letters, and much of her juvenilia. I obsessively watched all her movies, not only the films but also the A&E and BBC versions from the seventies, eighties, and nineties, to familiarize myself with the customs, daily practices, and lifestyle of Jane's England. I had previously traveled throughout England, where I toured many fine English country manor homes, including the magnificent Chatsworth House, thought by many to be the model for Jane Austen's Pemberley. There was also a wealth of information on the Internet.

After I sold the novel, I treated myself to another trip to England, where I walked in Jane Austen's footsteps, both to verify and fact-check what I'd written, and to research my next book. I visited Jane Austen's house at Chawton, walked the Cobb at Lyme Regis, had dinner and stayed the night at the Royal Lion Inn (where Jane dined with Mr. Ashford), spent two glorious days in Bath, and was even granted a rare opportunity to visit Godmersham Park, which is now privately owned and not open to the public. It was an unforgettable experience.

Jane Austen is considered by many to be one of the greatest writers who ever lived. Yet you chose not only to write *about* her, but to write *as her,* in her own voice. Were you at all intimidated about taking on such a challenge?

You bet I was! I had the idea brewing in my mind for a long time before I actually had the nerve to sit down and write it. For many long months I did nothing but research and write—I rarely emerged from my house—and it was the most fun I've ever had. During the book's composition, I only read books by Jane Austen or about Jane Austen, to keep her voice in my head. My family was forced to listen to me rhapsodize nonstop about the most trivial details of Jane Austen's life, and to hear me utter phrases like, "Surely, my good sir, you do not intend to present yourself at the soirée attired in a garment of such unsightly proportions?" My husband was incredibly supportive and encouraging throughout it all. He joined me at English Regency Country Dance lessons, dressed up in costume, and escorted me to a Jane Austen ball; he also enthusiastically watched all the movies with me. But after the second viewing of *Pride and Prejudice, Persuasion,* and *Sense and Sensibility,* he finally said, "Can't we just watch a good war movie?"

What about the kiss? Jane Austen's lovers never kiss in any of her novels, yet you have included several very romantic scenes. Since the *Lost Memoirs* are ostensibly written by Jane Austen herself, how did you justify that choice?

I adore Jane Austen's writing. Her biting social commentary and masterful use of irony and free indirect speech have made her one of the most influential and revered novelists in history. But as you point out, her romantic endings are generally brief and written in the third-person narrative, which always left me unsatisfied. I wanted my lovers to express their feelings and their physical affection. Scholars have suggested that Jane was scrupulous about writing only what she knew, and perhaps she didn't include love scenes in her novels because she didn't feel qualified to invent them. I disagree. I believe Jane avoided writing those scenes because in that era, an expression of passionate feeling on the page might imply that she'd had that personal experience herself, an implication which would not be appropriate for a single woman. Luckily for us, she did write a rather romantic ending to *Persuasion,* her last book. Perhaps, as she grew older, she finally felt the freedom to express emotions she'd kept bottled up all her life.

Jane Austen Quotations

Jane Austen was a master of irony and nuance, and an astute observer of human nature. Some of her most famous witticisms can be found in her letters; others are voiced by her characters—not all of whom were expressing her personal sentiments.

The starred (*) quotes appear almost verbatim in the text of the novel.

LOVE & MARRIAGE

A woman of seven and twenty can never hope to inspire affection again.

—*Sense and Sensibility*

A lady's imagination is very rapid; it jumps from admiration to love, from love to matrimony in a moment.

—*Pride and Prejudice*

I pay very little regard to what any young person says on the subject of marriage. If they profess a disinclination for it, I only set it down that they have not yet seen the right person.

—*Mansfield Park*

I consider everybody as having a right to marry *once* in their lives for love, if they can.

—*Letter to Cassandra, 1808* *

Do anything rather than marry without affection.

—Pride and Prejudice

To be so bent on marriage—to pursue a man merely for the sake of situation—is a sort of thing that shocks me; I cannot understand it. Poverty is a great evil, but to a woman of education and feeling it ought not, it cannot be the greatest. I would rather be a teacher at a school (and I can think of nothing worse) than marry a man I did not like.

—The Watsons

She had been forced into prudence in her youth, she learned romance as she grew older.

—Persuasion

. . . that expression of 'violently in love' is so hackneyed, so doubtful, so indefinite . . . It is as often applied to feelings which arise from an half-hour's acquaintance, as to a real, strong attachment.

—Pride and Prejudice

. . . when a young lady is to be a heroine, the perverseness of forty surrounding families cannot prevent her. Something must and will happen to throw a hero in her way.

—Northanger Abbey

OPPORTUNITY

. . . why did we wait for any thing? Why not seize the pleasure at once? How often is happiness destroyed by preparation, foolish preparation!

—Emma

DANCING

To be fond of dancing was a certain step towards falling in love.

—Pride and Prejudice

I consider a country-dance as an emblem of marriage. Fidelity and complaisance are the principal duties of both . . . You will allow that in both, man has the advantage of choice, woman only the power of refusal . . . that when once entered into, they belong exclusively to each other till the moment of its dissollution . . . that it is their duty, each to endeavour to give the other no cause for wishing that he or she had bestowed themselves elsewhere.

—Northanger Abbey

TRUTH

Modesty . . . is very well in its way, but really a little common honesty is sometimes quite as becoming.

—Northanger Abbey

Facts are such horrid things!

—Lady Susan

READING & WRITING

It is only a novel . . . or, in short, some work in which the greatest powers of the mind are displayed, in which the most thorough knowledge of human nature, the happiest delineation of its varieties, the liveliest effusions of wit and humour are conveyed to the world in the best chosen language.

—Northanger Abbey *

You are now collecting your people delightfully, getting them exactly into such a spot as is the delight of my life. Three or four families in a country village is the very thing to work on.

—Letter to her niece Anna (who was writing a book of her own), 1814

The person, be it gentleman or lady, who has not pleasure in a good novel, must be intolerably stupid.

*—Northanger Abbey ***

At length, quite exhausted by the attempt to be amused with her own book, which she had only chosen because it was the second volume of his, she gave a great yawn and said, "How pleasant it is to spend an evening in this way! I declare after all there is no enjoyment like reading! How much sooner one tires of anything than of a book!"

—Pride and Prejudice

. . . but for my own part, if a book is well written, I always find it too short.

—The Juvenilia of Jane Austen

Of course they had fallen in love over poetry.

—Persuasion

He and I should not in the least agree, of course, in our ideas of novels and heroines;—pictures of perfection, as you know, make me sick and wicked.

—Letter to her niece Fanny, 1817

I begin already to weigh my words & sentences more than I did, & am looking about for a sentiment, an illustration, or a metaphor in every corner of the room. Could my ideas flow as fast as the rain in the storecloset, it would be charming.

—Letter to Cassandra, 1809

I could no more write a [historical] romance than an epic poem. I could not sit seriously down to write a serious romance under any other motive than to save my life; and if it were indispensable for me to keep it up and never relax into laughing at myself or other people, I am sure I should be hung before I had finished the first chapter.

—Letter to James Stanier Clarke,
The Prince Regent's Librarian, 1816

CORRESPONDENCE

Oh! The blessing of a female correspondent, when one is really interested in the absent!

—Emma

Expect a most agreeable letter, for not being overburdened with subject (having nothing at all to say), I shall have no check to my genius from beginning to end.

Letter to Cassandra, 1801

MONEY

Single women have a dreadful propensity for being poor—which is one very strong argument in favour of matrimony.

—Letter to her niece Fanny, 1817

People always live forever when there is an annuity to be paid them.

—Sense and Sensibility

A single woman with a narrow income must be a ridiculous, disagreeable old maid, the proper sport of boys and girls; but a single woman of good fortune is always respectable, and may be as sensible and pleasant as anybody else.

—Emma

Nothing amuses me more than the easy manner with which everybody settles the abundance of those who have a great deal less than themselves.

—Mansfield Park

It is very difficult for the prosperous to be humble.

—Emma

HAPPINESS

A large income is the best recipe for happiness I ever heard of.

—Mansfield Park

There will be little rubs and disappointments everywhere, and we are all apt to expect too much; but then, if one scheme of happiness fails, human nature turns to another; if the first calculation is wrong, we make a second better: we find comfort somewhere.

—Mansfield Park

RIDICULE

For what do we live, but to make sport of our neighbours, and laugh at them in our turn?

—Pride and Prejudice

. . . I meant to be uncommonly clever in taking so decided a dislike to him, without any reason. It is such a spur to one's genius, such an opening for wit, to have a dislike of that kind. One may be continually abusive without saying anything just; but one cannot be always laughing at a man without now and then stumbling on something witty.

—Pride and Prejudice

BEAUTY

To look almost pretty is an acquisition of higher delight to a girl who has been looking plain for the first fifteen years of her life than a beauty from her cradle can ever receive.

—Northanger Abbey

Varnish and gilding hide many stains.

—Mansfield Park

FASHION

A woman can never be too fine while she is all in white.

—Mansfield Park

I bought some Japan ink . . . & next week shall begin my operations on my hat, on which you know my principal hopes of happiness depend.

—Letter to Cassandra, 1798

Now nothing can satisfy me but I must have a straw hat, of the riding hat shape, like Mrs. Tilson's . . . I am really very shocking; but it will not be dear at a Guinea.

—Letter to Cassandra, 1811

My cloak came on Tuesday, & tho' I expected a good deal, the beauty of the lace astonished me. It is too handsome to be worn, almost too handsome to be looked at.

—Letter to Cassandra, 1800

It would be mortifying to the feelings of many ladies, could they be made to understand how little the heart of man is affected by what is costly or new in their attire.

—*Northanger Abbey*

Your sentiments so nobly expressed on the different excellencies of Indian & English muslins, & the judicious preference you give the former, have excited in me an admiration of which I can alone give an adequate idea, by assuring you that it is nearly equal to what I feel for myself.

—*The Juvenilia of Jane Austen (Frederic and Elfrida)*

NATURE

To sit in the shade on a fine day, and look upon verdure is the most perfect refreshment.

—*Mansfield Park*

KNOWLEDGE

A woman, especially if she have the misfortune of knowing anything, should conceal it as well as she can.

—*Northanger Abbey*

EDUCATION

I was therefore entered at Oxford and have been properly idle ever since.

—*Sense and Sensibility*

EFFICIENCY

The power of doing anything with quickness is always much prized by the possessor, and often without any attention to the imperfection of the performance.

—Pride and Prejudice

SILLINESS

Silly things do cease to be silly if they are done by sensible people in an impudent way.

—Emma

MEN AND WOMEN

In every power, of which taste is the foundation, excellence is pretty fairly divided between the sexes.

—Northanger Abbey

If there is any thing disagreeable going on, men are always sure to get out of it.

—Persuasion

One half of the world cannot understand the pleasures of the other.

—Emma

BEST FIRST LINE EVER WRITTEN

It is a truth universally acknowledged, that a single man in possession of a good fortune, must be in want of a wife.

—Pride and Prejudice

SELF

We have all a better guide in ourselves, if we would attend to it, than any other person can be.

—Mansfield Park

What wild imaginations one forms, where dear self is concerned!

—Persuasion

Those who tell their own story, you know, must be listened to with caution.

—Sanditon

Book Club/Reading Group Study Guide

The Lost Memoirs of Jane Austen

DISCUSSION POINTS

1. Why did the author choose to write the story in the first person, as Jane Austen's Memoirs? Do you think the novel would have been as effective if written in the third person narrative? Did you find yourself connecting with Jane Austen because it was written from her perspective?

2. Consider the scene in the parlor in chapter two, and the exchange between Jane and Mrs. Austen which follows. How many key characters and plot elements are set up in that short space of time? How do the dialogue and action serve to introduce each character? How do these two scenes set the tone of the novel and lay a foundation for the rest of the story?

3. Which character archetypes do we see in *The Lost Memoirs* that are reflections of the archetypes in Jane Austen's novels?

4. When Jane meets Mr. Ashford, she feels she has written nothing new of value in nearly ten years and has vowed to lay down her pen forever. Discuss the ways in which Mr. Ashford is influential in rekindling Jane's interest in writing, and how the ups and downs of Jane's relationship with him are interwoven into the plot of her revised version of *Sense and Sensibilty*.

5. Why do you think Jane falls in love with Mr. Ashford? Name the qualities that make Mr. Ashford the ideal counterpart for Jane Austen, and worthy of her admiration and passion. Is his influence and encouragement the only reason she returns to writing? Or do you think he is merely the spark that ignites an already smoldering flame?

6. Compare and contrast the three offers of marriage Jane receives over the course of the book, and the men making the offers. Do you agree or disagree with Jane's decisions in each case? Discuss her reasons for initially accepting Harris Bigg-Wither, then refusing him. How different would her life have been if she had married him? Do you think she would have ever written again? Was she selfish for having refused a life of comfort for her mother and sister in a time when there were not many options open to women?

7. Money, and the abundance or lack of it, was a prevailing theme in Jane Austen's work. In her unfinished novel, *The Watsons,* her heroine says: "Poverty is a great evil, but to a woman of education and feeling it ought not, it cannot be the greatest. I would rather be a teacher at a school (and I can think of nothing worse) than marry a man I did not like." Do you think this statement reveals Jane Austen's personal feelings? How is this theme expessed in *The Lost Memoirs*? Discuss the irony in Jane's final decision, where she refuses to marry a man she loves deeply, knowing that he will suffer the same fate that she has herself renounced.

8. Discuss other ways in which money affects the characters in *The Lost Memoirs*. How and why did the death of Mr. Austen change the financial status of Jane and her mother and sister? Mrs. Austen considered themselves poor with only £450 a year, yet they kept three servants. How does that reflect on the gentry class of that time? How do you think the very poor of

the time lived? Discuss why servants were considered such a necessity in that era before modern conveniences, and what functions they were required to perform.

9. Jane decides to publish her novel anonymously partly because of her society's attitude towards the novel. Do you agree or disagree with her choice? How does their view of the novel compare to contemporary attitudes regarding popular entertainment, such as playing video games or watching television?

10. Discuss the pros and cons of *primogeniture,* which left all the land to the eldest son, and *entail,* which prevented the heir from dividing up the estate or selling any part of it. How did this enable the great landed families in nineteenth-century England to maintain their wealth, status, and power through the generations? In what way is Mr. Ashford an example of the sacrifices that were required along the way? Do you think the sacrifices were worth it?

11. Discuss the romantic moments in *The Lost Memoirs.* How does the author create and sustain sexual tension between the hero and heroine? How do the plot elements keep the story moving forward at a rapid pace?

12. Cassandra, shortly before she died, went through Jane's letters, burning most of them and cutting out portions of others, before sharing them with her family. These were personal letters in which Jane gave free vent to her feelings and observations of other people. Why do you think Cassandra did this? What do you think Cassandra might have been trying to hide?

13. Were you surprised when you learned Mr. Ashford's secret? Discuss what might have happened if he'd been honest with Jane

from the start. What does Jane's returning all of his letters unopened say about her? Do you consider it justifiable, or a character flaw?

14. Consider the introduction of Isabella Churchill. How does the author establish her character traits and personality? How does Jane feel about Isabella, both before and after she learns the truth about her? In what ways does the Isabella story line enhance the plot of *The Lost Memoirs*?

15. While reading *The Lost Memoirs,* did you learn anything new or surprising about Jane Austen's life, and/or the customs or social conventions during Jane Austen's era?

16. Jane's younger brother Edward was adopted at age sixteen by Mr. Thomas Knight II, from whom he inherited a fortune and three large estates. How do you feel about Mr. and Mrs. Austen's decision to allow their son's adoption? How did Edward's status as a wealthy landowner affect Jane's life and contribute to her emergence as a novelist?

17. What was your perception of Jane Austen and her work before you read *The Lost Memoirs*? Do you feel the same or differently after reading the novel?

18. What are some of your favorite moments in the book?

19. How did your experience reading *The Lost Memoirs* compare to Jane Austen novels you have read? In what ways was it similar or different? If you are not familiar with Jane Austen's work, did *The Lost Memoirs* inspire you to read her novels? Why or why not?

A+ AUTHOR INSIGHTS, EXTRAS, & MORE . . .

William James

SYRIE JAMES is a Jane Austen scholar and a long-time admirer of Miss Austen's work. A member of the Writer's Guild of America, Syrie is a screenwriter and playwright; this is her first work of historical fiction. She, her husband, and their two sons live in Los Angeles. Syrie welcomes visitors and messages at her website at *www.syriejames.com*.

Syrie James